The
Summer
Goddess

Joanne Hall

www.kristell-ink.com

Paperback ISBN 978-0-9935766-3-8
Hardback ISBN 978-1-911497-02-8
Epub ISBN 978-0-9935766-4-5

Cover art by Jason Deem
Cover design by Ken Dawson
Typesetting by Book Polishers

Kristell Ink

An Imprint of Grimbold Books

4 Woodhall Drive
Banbury
Oxon
OX16 9TY
United Kingdom

www.kristell-ink.com

For Aiden.

ONE

WHITE SAILS CAME with the sunset.

Asta saw them first, as she was making her way down from the high peak where her mother lived. At first she thought they were birds; the great white gliding sea hawks, bigger than eagles, which floated above the turbulent eastern sea. But they were too low, and moved with too much purpose, crossing back and forth ahead of the opposing wind.

It took her a long moment, staring into the darkening sea with her back to the fading sun, to realised what they were. Her father had told her about ships, but her own people didn't sail. And there was nothing beyond this eastern ocean, no lands that Asta had heard legend of, so how could there be ships?

She quickened her stride, stones turning under her bare feet as she hastened down the narrow, twisting track towards the bush where she had tethered the strawberry roan, her favoured ride. From here she couldn't see the ships any more, could barely see the ocean due to the rise and fall of the land. By the time she'd cantered to the top of the cliffs and reined in, the sky had darkened to violet and the sails had vanished. Candle light flickered in the windows of the village, strung out along the top of the cliff, and in the lower windows of the tower.

She left her mare in the corral with the rest of the horses. The

cliff path was crumbling in places, and she had told her people it wasn't safe to ride at night. She wasn't about to disobey her own protocol. She took a torch from the stash in the barn, and lit it with her candlestones. It wasn't full dark yet; the twilight was long in this part of the world, but the light made her feel more secure.

She peered out to sea once more, but the light that cast a halo around her left the ocean dark, sighing against the rocks. No sails, and no ship could put in to shore here. That was why her father had chosen this place, built western-style walls for their tribe to hide behind, here at the furthest end of the world. No enemy could reach them here.

Still, Asta felt exposed as she made her way down the zigzagging path hewn from the side of the cliff. She trailed one hand along the sea-smoothed rock walls, feeling for the markers she had carved to warn others, in the dark, of the patches where the path was wearing away. The cold salt spray brushed her face, throwing her damp hair across her cheek, and she shivered. Even on the hottest days it was chilly in the shadows. And the height of summer was still a good four moons away.

She traversed the last switchback, sticking close to the wall. She didn't need the torch any more; the lights of the tower were bright enough to guide her home. The tower was circular, and it seemed to grow out of the living rock, its base resting on a basalt column rising from the edge of the sea, the topmost floor level with the village. It was hard to tell where nature ended and human work began. The door stood open, spilling light like a beacon across the sea, and Asta knew that meant her brother was waiting for her. Which meant he was worried. She quickened her stride, boots crunching across a light layer of gravel.

"Asta!" Finn started forward out of the doorway. "There were sails . . . I was worried about you! Where have you been?"

"With Mother." She handed him the torch and shucked off her leathered cloak, letting it fall in a brown puddle on the floor. "You saw them too?"

Finn scooped up the cloak with a shake of his head. He was

as fair in skin and hair as she was dark. He took his looks from their father, while hers came from their mother. At least, the looks her mother had once had.

"I saw them through the spyglass. How was Mother?"

"You'd know if you went to see her yourself," Asta retorted. "She deserves to see her grandson."

Finn's face darkened. "You know I won't take him up there."

"Please yourself." Asta smothered a yawn. It was an old quarrel, and she was too tired, and too hungry, to want to discuss their mother in any depth. "Where did the ships go?"

"I lost them as the dark came down. I think they were heading south."

Asta shrugged. "They might be from the Kingdom." Her father's people. It didn't seem likely, but the sea stretched to the end of the world, vast and empty.

"Might be?"

"Who else would they be? Who else is out here, on land or sea? You can relax." She clapped her younger brother on his upper arm as they walked up the stairs to the floor of chambers. "There's no one in this part of the world but the Tribe. This land is ours. Father gave it to us."

Finn groaned. "Don't I know it! I must have told Rhodan the story a thousand times, but he still asks to hear it again."

"That's what children do, Finn. They drive you insane, slowly and deliberately."

He chuckled. "I thought that was what parents did?"

Asta laughed. "Your turn will come, brother! You can drive Rhodan as crazed as Mother makes us!"

"I'm looking forward to it." They paused outside the entrance to Finn's rooms, and a high voice was raised in excitement within. Rhodan must have heard his father's laugh. The door clattered open, and Finn was almost knocked off balance as the small boy raced out and crashed into his legs with the enthusiasm only a six year old can muster.

"Da! Did you tell Tante Asta about the boats?"

"Of course." Finn winked at her over Rhodan's head as he hugged his son. "Tante Asta says it's nothing to worry about."

"Did Granda come here on a boat?"

"You know he didn't. He came here on his special grey mare. I've told you so many times."

Rhodan pouted. "Will you tell me again? Can Tante Asta tell me?"

Asta backed off. She loved her nephew, but the way he asked the same questions and demanded the same stories over and over again stretched her patience to its limit.

"Tante Asta needs her sleep." Finn rescued her from Rhodan's shrill demands. "I'll tell you a story, if you like." He guided his son back into the chamber, and nodded at Asta over his shoulder. "Sleep well, sister."

"You too." The door closed behind him with a soft click, and Rhodan's questions were cut off. Asta allowed herself a wry smile as she headed for her own chambers, thanking the ancestors she had never made that mistake.

She paused at the foot of the stair that led up to the solar. The moons were dark tonight. Was there any point in looking through the glass, just once, to settle her mind? It would be like trying to see through a blanket. Even on a clear night there would be nothing to see. Whoever the sails belonged to, they were long gone. And there was spring planting to attend to tomorrow. No use lying awake half the night worrying, when there was nothing she could do until morning.

She turned away from the stairs, and headed for bed.

Sunrise bled through the shutters of Asta's chamber, dragging long fingers across her face. She tried to push them away, to burrow under the blankets and catch the dream that trotted away when she stirred, but it was no use. She was awake, and there was work to do in the fields. Rhodan was already hammering on her door,

calling, "Tante Asta! Breakfast!" She groaned as she rolled out of bed and dragged on her clothes.

The household ate together on the lower floor, with the doors open so that anyone passing up or down the cliff could join them if they chose. Finn loved to cook, and this morning he served warm floured biscuits soaked in a savoury sauce, with mugs of hot, spiced fruit juice, slightly fermented and fizzing. His wife, Lefalli, brought the dishes to the table and constantly hushed Rhodan as he chattered.

"What will we do today, Tante Asta? Will the boats come back? Are you going to see Grandmother?" And then, inevitably, "Will you tell me a story?"

"Later," Asta promised. "Tonight, when you're in bed." She privately hoped he would forget.

"Story time is for when you're sleepy," Lefalli added, tousling his brown hair, then teasing it tidy again. "Are you going to help with the planting?"

"Will Connjur be there?" Connjur was Rhodan's best friend. The two boys were inseparable, close as twins, but Rhodan sounded anxious.

"Of course he will," Finn told him. "Everyone will be."

Rhodan scowled, and kicked his feet against the leg of the table. "I don't want to go."

"Why not?" Lefalli asked. "Everyone has to work."

His frown deepened, and his voice dropped to a mutter. "I don't want to go if he's going to be there."

"Connjur?" Lefalli shrugged. "I thought you two were friends."

Rhodan twisted in his seat. "He's mean. He said mean things, so I hit him with a stick."

Finn snorted with laughter, then bit his lip and made himself scarce as Lefalli glared at him.

"What did he say?" she asked. "It's good you hit him, if it was to defend your honour. But only then."

Asta swallowed a sigh. Why did men, even the youngest ones,

always have to solve their disputes by fighting? "Did he insult your honour?" she asked her nephew.

Rhodan nodded, but he looked uncertain. "I – I think so . . ."

"Well, what did he say?"

The boy wiped his nose with the back of his hand. "He said I was a halfbreed, and Grandmother," he sniffed hard, eyes welling, "that Grandmother was a freak. So I hit him."

Asta pushed her plate away, her appetite lost. "Halfbreed? Where did he learn a word like that?"

Rhodan rubbed his eyes. "Is it true?" he asked, bottom lip trembling.

Lefalli slipped from her chair and swept him into a hug. "Little one, you're not a halfbreed!"

"But Grandda was—"

"Your grandfather," Asta swallowed hard, "was a leader amongst his own tribe, and a mighty warrior in ours. You have his blood; leader's blood, warrior's blood. And Grandmother . . ." She trailed off. He was too young to understand her mother's blood. She wasn't sure she understood it herself.

"Do you want a story?" Lefalli hauled Rhodan on to her lap. He was almost too big for such embraces, arms and legs spilling out awkwardly. "Grandmother was a warrior too. She rode over the mountains to strange lands when your Da was still a dream in her belly. Tante Asta was there too . . ."

Rhodan rested his head against his mother's shoulder and closed his eyes, losing himself in the story. Asta, who had been there, and had heard it recounted too many times, excused herself from the table and laid her plate in the washing bucket. Finn had already left for the planting. If she walked fast, she could catch up with him.

He waited for her outside the corral, mounted on his own bay, holding the reins of her mount loosely in the crook of his arm. His face was grim.

"Did you hear what Rhodan said, back there?" she asked him.

"I heard enough of it," he said.

"Halfbreed? Where would a child get such a word from?"

"I'll tell you where." Finn nudged his gelding into a trot. "From the adults around him."

"No one in the Tribe would—" Asta shook her head, hastening to catch up with him, matching him stride for stride.

"Someone did. Old hatreds cut deep, Asta. However much in harmony we appear, there are always some who can't forget that Father was a short-haired western dog." He chuckled, flicking his own warrior's braids over his shoulder. "I just look like one."

"Hardly." But it was true. Finn had the lightest skin of the tribe, the fairest hair, and he was slight, like a westerner. In dress and manner he was of the Tribe, but there was no disguising his roots. "I'm not having that in my tribe."

"You can't make laws to govern the way people feel, Asta."

"No," she conceded, "but I can keep an eye on them. If someone is spreading hatred, I want to know who it is. We're not a tribe if we all pull in different directions."

The planting grounds were sheltered from the wind that charged in off the sea by the neat row of stone-built houses, conical, like the nests of ground bees. The houses had given Asta's people their new name, when they had finally come to rest at the end of the world. When they had embraced their new way of life.

Asta slid from the back of her roan, letting the mare roam free. She wouldn't go far, cropping the tough cliff-grass with the rest of the mounts. Not unless something put the wind under their tails, and that seemed unlikely. The distant threat of passing ships seemed far away under the spring sunshine. The planting land was divided into neat squares, marked out with white pebbles from the beach. A square for each crop. They had learned quickly that the crops needed to be swapped around to keep their yield up, and to keep the soil healthy. Ground nuts, roots, low bushes with sweet berries, trained along thin strings of horsehair. It had taken a long time, and a few lean years, to work out what would grow and what wouldn't, but they had time. The tribe wasn't going anywhere, not any more.

Most of the older women of the village, the children and the nursing mothers, were hard at work by the time Finn and Asta arrived. The young men and women had taken some of the older children off to hunt goats, and their youngest siblings rolled in the dirt or chased each other with sticks. The old men with their bad backs and twisted legs worked alongside the women, grumbling about the wind, the cold, the chances of getting a good crop that wouldn't be ruined by rats or mould. Asta had heard it all before. She ignored them. If the old men didn't grumble, they would have nothing to talk about.

The fruit bushes had grown unruly with the air of spring. They needed tying back, teasing along the strings and fastening, the dead wood cut away above the green buds. It was tough work. The hard wood resisted Asta's knife and the thorns on the bushes clawed her exposed skin, raising bloody spots. She was grateful when Rhodan tugged her sleeve. He held up a cup of fresh water from the spring.

"Da said I could be a water carrier today!" he said, beaming with pride.

The water was so cold it numbed Asta's lips. She mumbled her thanks.

"Am I doing a good job?"

"Excellent!" She twisted his ear affectionately.

"Shall I get some for the brass man too?"

"What?" Asta wiped her mouth. "What are you talking about, Rhodan?"

"The brass man." He stared at her, as if she should know what he was talking about.

"Who is the brass man?" Rhodan knew the name of every man in the tribe.

"Back there." He waved his arm vaguely towards the stream, which gurgled its course between high banks thick with bushes before plunging headlong off the cliff. "He was standing in the shade, but I saw him. He saw me, he went like *this*." He raised his finger to his lips, and winked. "Do you think he was thirsty?"

Asta felt a chill, crawling all over her body, tickling with the feet of insects. In the distance, a dog barked.

"Rhodan, go back to the tower."

His lower lip thrust forward. "I don't want—"

"Just go!"

Asta rarely shouted, and Rhodan backed off at once, eyes filling with defiant tears. "Why don't you talk to him? He's over there!" He pointed behind her, then turned on his heels and fled.

The chill had seeped into Asta's limbs. It was hard to turn around, but she forced herself to look, hoping it was nothing. Just another childish fantasy of Rhodan's. Her eyes met the stranger's, locked for a long instant, taking in his strange dress, his short hair, skin the colour of brass. In his left hand he held an axe, and it dripped crimson on the grass.

Then she heard the first screams.

The piercing sound broke her out of her trance. She ran, through the maze of horsehair strands and straggling fruit vines, hooked barbs snatching at her skin. The trailing branches wrapped around her ankles, treacherous, trying to drag her down. Any moment the axe would smash down into the back of her skull, and she wouldn't even know it had hit her.

She stumbled out of the fruit canes, into a plume of smoke blowing across the cliff top. The Beehive village was in flames, smoke and fire bursting from doors and windows. Asta tried to shout, but her mouth was full of smoke and she could only utter a long wheeze and a spluttering cough. She tried again.

"Finn! Lefalli!"

"Help me!" A woman of the tribe, she couldn't see who through the haze of smoke. One of the bronzed warriors dragged her towards the cliff, her braids tangled in his clenched fist.

Her shout struck Asta like a kick in the gut, but it spurred her into action. Her confusion had already cost precious seconds. She drew the stout blade she wore on her hip and lunged at the warrior. He backed off, a startled look on his face, as if he had not expected her to fight. The woman he clutched kicked out, a numbing blow to his shin. She wrenched free, leaving dark strands of hair between his fingers. Spinning around, she pushed him away, as Asta's blade punctured his gut. The man's eyes rolled back in his head, and he grunted a few indecipherable words, sinking to his knees as she slid the knife free.

"Asta!" The woman clutched her arm. Asta recognised her as Borteth. She had a daughter the same age as Rhodan. "Asta, what's happening? What can we do?"

"Find the children. Get everyone you can and send them down to the tower. We'll be safe there until the hunters get back. Can you do that for me?"

Borteth was trembling, and she looked sick, but she nodded as she drew her own blade and wiped the blood from her scalp. "Have you seen Terthine?"

Asta shook her head. She hoped Rhodan had the sense to obey her, that the strangers would leave the children alone. "We have to find them. Come on."

The two women ran side by side, knives held ready, through swirling smoke as thick as sea-mist. A figure lunged at them through the gloom. Borteth screamed, and Asta lashed out, barely catching the movement at the Atrathene yell of protest.

"Hey! Who's there? Asta?"

"It's me." She put up her knife. "I thought you were one of them, Tehakken."

"What the shit is going on, Asta?" The old man moved with a lurching gait, his right leg twisted and stunted. He couldn't ride. If you couldn't ride in the tribe you were as good as dead, but Asta's father had taken pity on him, and when Tehakken had asked for his life, he had been spared.

"I don't know."

"Where are the children, the women?"

"I don't know!" She was off and running again, his anxious question haunting her. She yelled for Finn, for Lefalli, but there was no reply. She moved through a dream, through quicksand, her limbs heavy and slow to respond, her voice muffled by smoke. Where were they?

"Asta!" The voice was high, trembling on the verge of tears, and Asta was knocked off balance by the impact of the dirty little figure colliding with her. She swung her blade out of the way just in time, and dropped to her knees to embrace the little girl.

"Samana? It is Samana, isn't it?"

The girl nodded, wiping the blood from her nose with the back of her hand. Her sleeve was ripped open, and her arm bled from an ugly cut. Her skin and clothes were smeared with dirt, and her hair was tangled.

"What happened?"

"The brass men—" she waved her arm, wincing. "They came so quick. Mama told me to run and hide. I didn't want to go but the man knocked her down." Her eyes were wide, startling white in the darkness of her face, and her lips quivered. "I hid under the bushes. She'll be all right, won't she? Tante Asta?"

The clutch of her hand, the term of endearment, only served to fuel Asta's rage. She gave the girl a push, harder than she intended. "Go with Tehakken. He'll take you to the tower, and I'll come and find you there."

Samana sniffed. "Will you bring Mama with you?"

"I'll meet you at the tower," Asta repeated, with a warning glance at Tehakken, hoping he would take the hint and not say anything about Samana's mother. "Borteth, come with me."

The women moved more cautiously as they neared the fields, Borteth letting out the occasional soft whimper as they stumbled across the bodies of their tribe. From ahead, cutting through the unnatural quiet, Asta could hear the grating speech of the strangers. They sounded like they were arguing amongst themselves.

"Where are they?" Borteth whispered. "I don't see them . . ."

"In the cove," Asta muttered back, through tightly clenched teeth. Her head thumped with the effort of holding in her tears, her fear. There would be time to mourn, to panic, later. When she had found her brother.

"And where are the hunters?" Borteth's voice was rising, and Asta hastily hushed her. The men, and the fighting women who had gone with them, could be miles away, might not be back for days if the hunting was poor. Might not have anything to return home to.

The smoke was thinner at the edge of the cliff, blowing inland, and they had come out from under the worst of the concealing cloud. The raider's voices were louder now, and Asta could hear children crying, women protesting, cut off by the dull thump of a fist hitting flesh, and a loud splash. The strangers, and their captives, were on the beach.

Asta dropped flat, wormed through the sharp, salt-withered grass to the sandy edge of the bluff, and looked down. There was a ship in the cove. Not a ship, she mentally corrected herself, a *boat*. Wide and flat bottomed, like an upturned beetle shell, and crewed by rowers. Some of the children were huddled in the bottom of the boat, at the feet of the muscular raiders. The rest stood close together on the narrow crescent of sand at the base of the cliff, surrounded by a ring of steel. The women of the Beehive Tribe made a last stand to protect their children, and the brass-skinned strangers couldn't get near them.

Next to her, Asta heard Borteth's hissing intake of breath as the younger woman reached for the bow slung across her back. "My baby's in that boat, Asta!"

Asta wished she had her own bow. She wished she could see the cliff path to the tower, hidden by the curve of the headland. She wished Finn was here. "Do you see Rhodan?"

"No – yes." Borteth pointed with her arrow. The children were crushed so tight together Asta could hardly make him out, until the boat bobbed on the waves and the movement revealed her nephew's unruly brown hair, a shade lighter than the dark heads that surrounded him.

Asta had to prevent herself from starting forward, from sliding down the sheer cliff in a flurry of sand and rubble. Metal clashed as the women were driven back into the darkness below the cliff, their ring of steel wavering, coming apart. Her hand closed on a rock.

The missile found its mark, smacking into a raider's

unprotected knee. He stumbled, uttering a curse that was cut off as Borteth's arrow tore through his throat in a bright red plume. Confused, the strangers backed towards the sea, flinging up their round shields to protect them from assault from above, leaving their bellies exposed.

"Come on!" Asta sprang to her feet, Borteth a heartbeat behind, and raced for the path that led down to the beach. It was marked with blood. Asta saw the abandoned bodies of the village's defenders cast aside, but she couldn't stop to see if any still lived. Rhodan was in the boat. She had to get him back before the raiders put to sea with him.

The curve of the path meant she lost sight of the beach, in fragments, dipping in and out of her field of vision. The shouts, the screams, the grate of steel on metal and flesh, grew louder as she ran. She heard thunder in the distance, rhythmic, approaching fast. She thought for a moment it was her own racing heartbeat, and then Borteth yelled, and pointed back down the beach.

"The hunters! The hunters are coming back!"

Asta saw them now, black shapes racing across the rocky sand, hooves pounding dull against the earth. They must have known what was happening, to come so fast, deadly and sharp as an arrow in flight. But the bronze strangers were climbing into the boat, dragging or pushing the surviving women before them. The warriors would not reach them in time.

"Rhodan!" Asta rounded the last corner with a desperate burst of speed, the cove opening out before her. She drew her blade as she ran towards the boat. The raider in front of her was a big man, but he had his back to her, half-turning as the blade sliced through his leather armour, his kidney, across his spine.

He fell twitching across the stern of the boat, mouth open in a soundless scream, and rolled into the shallows. Asta braced herself against the movement of the boat, the strength of the rowers, feeling her soles drag across sand and shingle as she was jerked from her feet. The thunder in her skull was deafening, but she couldn't turn to see where the horses were, couldn't yell for

Finn as the surf slapped against her mouth and over her head. Bare toes stubbed against the rocks of the sea floor as she hung all her weight off the side of the heavy rowing boat, trying to tip it, to stop it leaving. An oar jabbed her in the stomach, knocking the wind out of her, and her right hand slipped, losing its grip, splashing to keep her afloat with no air in her lungs.

"Asta!" In the bows of the boat, Lefalli stretched to try and catch her hand, but Asta couldn't reach her. Her feet lost contact with the sea bed and she was swimming, barely able to keep her head above water as blows rained down on her face and arms. Her vision blurred, and as the flat paddle of an oar smashed against her jaw, she felt the wooden side of the boat slip away from her desperate fingers. She was sinking, seaweed entangling her limbs, dragging her down into water clouded with blood.

Asta kicked out, reeling head breaking the surface. She couldn't see the boat, couldn't even see land, just a grey expanse of shifting ocean. Her lungs were full of salty water and she vomited, wiping her mouth and ducking her chin to clean her face. It sounded like her skull was full of bells.

She splashed around, trying to get her bearings. The beach was behind her, the rowing boat pulling out to sea with smooth strokes. She tried to swim towards it, but her limbs were made of lead and the waves threw their mockery in her face. Her legs were cramped, and boat and beach both seemed so far away. It was easier just to drift, to watch Rhodan pass before her eyes. That was why she had to swim . . .

Strong arms grabbed her beneath her armpits, and she kicked out, spluttering water. "Let me go! Go after them!" Her throat was raw, her words no more than a squeak.

"I've got you, don't fight!" Her rescuer, the man who would prevent her from saving her nephew, dragged her slowly but relentlessly back towards the shore, and she fought him with every morsel of her fading strength. All she could see was sky, blurred with salt water. The sea chuckled in her ears, whispering her defeat.

He dropped her in the shallows. The surge of the tide sucked over her prone body, trying to drag her back into the depths. Someone held a water skin to her lips, and she drank and vomited and drank again. She shivered in her soaked clothes, and someone – someone else? she wasn't sure – draped a horse-blanket over her shoulders. Beyond the ringing in her skull, it was quiet on the beach. Too quiet. The quiet of graves and plague houses.

"Asta?" A woman's voice, and a man's, hushing her. But Asta wore the leader's robes, and she had to lead.

She staggered to her feet, pulling the blanket tight around her shoulders as if it gave her the authority of a cloak. She spat, salt and blood frothing on the sand, and rubbed the dirt from her eyes. She looked around, taking stock. Looking for her brother.

"Where's Finn?"

The boat was gone. Long gone, and the hazy, smoke-shrouded sun gleamed off white sails in the distance. She rubbed her aching head. It had all happened so fast. Why would anyone want to take the children of the Beehive Tribe?

"Finn?"

The beach was a sacrificial altar, running with blood. The dead lay where they had fallen, and the survivors moved listlessly among them, some of them glancing at her as if they expected her to fix things. Bring their fallen back to life, bring their children back from the sea. From the shadow of the cliff, she could hear a man's broken sobs.

Asta tried to shake the sense back into her head. Nothing would be done without her authority. Standing like a rock while the tide lapped around her ankles wouldn't bring Rhodan back, or his mother. The tide . . .

She hadn't thought about the tide. It was coming in fast. This beach was underwater at high tide, and the route back up the cliff was cut off, the water rising to twice the height of a man. The wounded needed to be moved. Where, in all the grasslands, was Finn?

"Asta? What do we do?"

She recognised his voice now, the man who had pulled her from the grip of the sea. Connjur's father, wide eyed, bottom lip swollen from a blow. Had his son been on the boat? She had to make a decision, had to drag herself out of the water. Do what she could for the living, and try to work out a way to get the children back, if she could.

"Meyloy, get the wounded off the beach. The sea can take the dead. We don't have time to move them all." So many dead. She tried to avoid looking at their faces.

"And the children? Connjur, Rhodan . . . what about them?"

"We'll get them back." She spoke with a confidence she did not feel. "Where's Nur? And have you seen my brother?"

"I haven't seen Finn, but the shaman has taken the Spirit Trail." Meyloy waved his hand at the cliff. It was hard to tell one slumped figure from the rest. "We have no shaman. If you give the dead to the sea, it will require a sacrifice—"

"Haven't we sacrificed enough today?" Asta snapped. "If we don't move the wounded, now, we'll be sacrificing them too! The Spirit Realm has taken enough from the people of the Beehive today. I won't lose any more – I can't . . ." She dashed the water from her eyes. "Help me?"

"You wear the leader's robes." Meyloy shrugged.

"Take them to the tower. Those that can walk must carry those that can't. I'll take care of the dying. My father showed me how."

Meyloy looked as if he wanted to say more, but he merely turned and began to shepherd the walking wounded up the cliff path. The water was already ankle-deep on the lowest stretch of the road. Asta would have to work fast.

She drew the blade her father had left her, and weighed it in her hands. Light steel, thin and pointed as a needle, but it felt as heavy as rock. A western mercy-blade, quick and clean, and used only to end mortal suffering. She had asked her father once how many times he had used it, but he had pressed his lips tight and looked away. Now Asta was beginning to understand why. She moved among the dead and barely living, releasing the lives of those who would never ride again, feeling sick and helpless as the blade punctured life veins and the dead bled out into her hands.

The women of the Beehive had fought hard, and it wasn't their blood alone that stained the rocks and sand of the cove. Asta moved among the dead, separating the brass raiders and her own people where they lay tangled in death. She only gave mercy to her own people. Not the raiders. They could find their own mercy. It was hard enough to free those she had loved.

She acted numbly. It was too much to take in, to cope with all at once. When she reached the sanctuary of the tower she would mourn. Until then, she had a duty to perform. But her eyes flicked over the fallen, searching constantly. She knew now she would find Finn here, on the beach.

He lay face down, and his head and outstretched arms were lifted and dropped, lifted and dropped by the rhythmic surge of the tide. His warrior's braids were undone, and his hair fanned around his head like strands of pale seaweed. Asta waded knee deep in the water to lift her brother, using all her strength to drag him up on to the sand, out of the grasp of the incoming sea. She rolled him over and pushed the hair back from his face, willing him to stir under her hands.

Any of his wounds could have killed him: the deep slash across his chest, the severed stump of his right arm, the caved-in mess of his temple, washed clean by salt water. Asta sank to her knees beside him, holding him tight to her chest, half-expecting him to cough, to wriggle away as he had done when they were children. But there was nothing.

"Finn? Finn, I have to leave you here . . ." The sea pulled at her, insistent. The cove was full of floating bodies. If she didn't leave now she would be trapped, dashed against the rocks and drowned. The longer she stayed the harder it was to leave.

"Rhodan, Lefalli . . . They're alive. The raiders wanted them for a reason. I'll get them back. I know you were fighting for them. I won't let you down, little brother."

She let him fall back onto the sand, and closed his eyes, the way their father had taught her. The water swirled around them both, up to her ankles, and then her knees, gently lifting Finn and spinning him away from her. The white foam of the breakers crashed over his face, and she couldn't watch any more. Nor could she say goodbye. Her throat felt tight and hot, and tears scalded her eyes. She had to go. The cliff path was already underwater.

Asta pushed through the floating bodies, trying not to see them. She waded waist deep, soaked to the skin, without feeling the cold or the slap of water against her face. The sea tried to throw her against the cliff wall, and it was hard to keep her footing on the slippery rocks. She clung on to the rope, strung through iron loops hammered into the cliff for this purpose, and dragged herself along, hand over hand. The sucking sound of the sea was in her ears, but she didn't hear it, didn't taste the salt in her mouth. Numb from head to foot, Asta hauled herself away from the deadly embrace of the tide that would carry her brother to the Spirit Realm.

As she reached the top of the cliff, she realised she was trembling all over, and her legs wouldn't support her any more. She sank to the turf, water streaming from her clothes and hair, and from her eyes. How could she lead without Finn? He had always been at her side, backing her up, telling her when she was wrong, or when she was being stubborn. And she had lost his wife and son to barbarians from beyond the sea. She had failed her people, and her family, and all she could do was weep.

In the distance, white sails flashed against the sun.

TWO

I T WAS A long, lonely walk to the tower. Asta shivered in her soaking clothes, twisting the water out of her braids and tying them in a heavy knot at the nape of her neck, one that matched the knot at the pit of her stomach. Every eye would be on her, accusing. She deserved their accusation. She had let everyone down, and she didn't know how to make things right.

Tehakken waited for her at the last turn of the path, leaning against the rocks to rest his twisted leg. He looked as if he had been there a while. He extended his arms and she walked blindly into them, seeking comfort in the embrace.

"Didn't want to give you a hug in front of everyone," he confided. "How are you bearing up?"

"Fine," Asta lied.

"Your brother . . . ?"

She managed to shake her head. She felt the older man's lips tremble against her hair.

"Have you told your mother?"

"I can't . . . She wouldn't understand."

"She might." Tehakken gripped her by the shoulders. His rheumy eyes were swimming. "Will you go to her, Asta? For me? I knew her before Finn was even born . . ."

Asta looked beyond him to the tower, blazing with lantern light from every room. Lit up like a beacon, a pyre.

"I'll go," she said, "if you support me with the tribe. They'll be looking to me, and I don't know what to do. I don't want to let go of their reins."

"You won't, as long as you remain your father's daughter." Tehakken kissed her once more, and straightened. "Want me to keep them quiet while you get your leaders robes on?"

"Please." Her head ached. All she wanted was to lie down, to burrow under the blankets and not have to face her tribe without Finn at her side. But it was too late for that.

"And you'll go and see your mother?" Silence. "Asta?"

"I'll see her. Tomorrow. I promise."

Asta slipped into the tower through a side passage used only by her family, and hurried up the winding stair that led to the second floor. She could hear muffled voices from the room below, some raised in anger, others wailing their despair. She let herself into her chamber and barred the door behind her against the sound, leaning against it as the strength leached from her legs. Slithering to the floor, she clutched her gnawing gut, a wordless cry of despair strangled in her throat. She crawled to the bed, dragging the blankets off and huddling beneath them, creating her own dark world where she could cry and show weakness, and mourn her brother. Where she didn't have to be a leader, just for a little while.

She didn't know how long she lay there, but the effort of trying to get up was too draining. She felt made of lead, welded to the floor, eyes gritty and heart and stomach aching with grief. Even when the hammering came at the door, and the latch rattled, it was too hard to move. Even raising her head was a colossal effort.

"Asta!" Tehakken's voice. "Asta, I'm sorry. We need you downstairs. I can't hold them off any longer . . . Are you in there?"

"I'm here." Her voice sounded thick, not her own. She swallowed, and coughed. "Tehakken?"

"Come down." It wasn't a request.

She listened to his feet retreating down the stairs before she pushed away the blankets. The chill bit into her skin through clothes still damp from the sea. She peeled them off, slowly, and let them fall to the floor. It was time.

Her leader's robes lay at the bottom of a steel-bound chest at the foot of her bed. A calf-length shift, heavy with beads and gems, a light chain mesh to lay over her hair, and the cloak. She lifted it to her face and breathed in deeply. It still smelled of horse. There were a few spots of dried blood on the velvet patchcat fur, and some loose threads around the hood, but it had served her father for many years, and now it was hers. When she was a baby, he had carried her in the folds of this cloak. It held stories in every stitch.

She swung it around her shoulders, remembering how she used to hide under it with Finn, how it had been a tent, a cave, a fortress. Now it was just a cloak, but it was a leader's cloak, and as it settled about her shoulders Asta felt the mantle of responsibility fall on her. She straightened under the burden, wiped her eyes on her sleeve, and steadied herself to face her tribe.

The downstairs hall was crowded and noisy, everyone bickering, wanting their say. The dead hadn't yet drifted from the bay and already the recriminations had started. She hesitated outside the door to listen.

"Where is she then?" Meyloy's voice, ragged with anger and grief. "You say our leader wants what's best for us? Why isn't she here? Why hasn't she come up with a plan to get our women and children back?"

Someone must have remonstrated in a lower voice. Asta didn't catch the words, but she heard Meyloy's response.

"I'm sorry she lost her brother, but everyone in this room has lost someone they care about. We can't trust a woman to lead us if she can't set aside her feelings in a crisis."

She heard the rumbles, of agreement, of protest. It was time to step in. Asta drew herself up to her full height and pushed both doors open, hesitating on the threshold to make sure everyone saw her and grasped the significance of her attire. She fixed Meyloy with an iron gaze.

"If you ask me not to show compassion, I will fail. But I can set aside my feelings for the good of the tribe, Meyloy. Can you?"

He sank cross-legged to the floor under her gaze, and inclined his head. "I couldn't do what you do, Asta."

She took that as acquiescence to her rule, and looked around the room for further signs of dissent, shaming those still standing into taking their places on the floor. She tightened her fists under the cloak so none of the tribe could see her hands shaking.

"I lost my family today, as you all lost people you love. But we're still here. The tribe is not broken. Our story goes on."

"What about our children?" a woman on the far side of the room protested. "What did the raiders want with them? How do we get them back?"

Asta nodded to acknowledge her. "We can take hope that the raiders, whoever they were, wanted our children alive. They could have cut every throat on the beach . . ." She tried not to falter, thinking of the horrors in the cove. "They didn't take men, only women and children. Maybe they would have taken our hunters, if they'd been here, but they didn't take the old ones. They came here to steal."

"They took our crops," Meyloy said. "Everything they couldn't steal, they destroyed. How will we eat? How will we honour our dead properly, without a shaman? They've ripped the heart from our tribe, Asta. What are you going to do about it? And what if they come back?"

"How do we rescue our children?" the woman repeated, louder, springing to her feet. She thrust forward her bandaged arms so Asta could see them. "I had two little girls. What will happen to them?"

Asta closed her eyes. Her jaw ached where the oar had struck it. She would be a mass of bruises tomorrow, and she still felt she hadn't fought hard enough. "Kulisa, I understand . . ."

"No you don't!" Kulisa clenched her fists in her braids. "You don't have children. How could you understand?"

"Asta lost her brother, and her nephew," Tehakken reminded her. "Sit down, Kulisa. We'll get your girls back."

"How?" she demanded. Every eye in the room was on Asta, and she gripped her cloak tighter.

"We need a shaman," she said.

Meyloy snorted. "To honour our dead, yes, but a shaman won't be able to fight, or sail. What good would he be?"

"He will be able to tell us where they went, if our families are still alive. We need to trade with other tribes, for food, and for knowledge."

"What kind of knowledge would be any use to us?" Kulisa asked, letting her hands fall, to hang empty at her sides.

"We need to learn how to build boats."

There was a ripple of consternation at this.

"Why do we need boats?" Meyloy demanded. "We have horses. We don't need the sea."

"The sea took our children from us, and we must go to the sea to get them back." Silence followed Asta's words, but she saw she had planted a new seed. It would take time to grow, and in that time she could send for knowledge, and skills. It was rumoured that the tribes to the south used boats for fishing. They would be able to help her, if she could find anything to trade.

"Did they take our horses?" she asked.

"Not one," Tehakken said. "But we can't ride over water, Asta!"

"We can trade horses for boats, and learn how to sail them."

"And how long will that take?" Meyloy groaned. "Asta, the strangers have our women and children! What they could be doing to them—"

"Ride into the sea then, and get them back!" He recoiled from her sudden fury. "I would if I could, Meyloy! But I can't, and nor can you. So what will you do? Sit here and beat down my suggestions, or try and help?"

His eyes were cast downwards. "You lead the tribe," he

muttered. "I only want to help you."

"What will you do to help?"

"I can ride, for the shaman and the boat-people. I will take horses to trade for food. Women too, if they're willing to go—"

"No women." Asta cut him off. "We need our women. Are you sure you want to do this?"

He shrugged. "There's nothing for me here now." He looked up, and caught her eye. *Nothing for you either,* his expression said. Asta merely nodded, and turned away.

The meeting dragged on late into the night, although all the decisions had been made. The people of the Beehive, the tribe her father had forged, clung together in the face of adversity. They drew their strength, their protection, from the tower. From Asta and her blood. It was exhausting to have every eye on her, expecting her to know what to do and to act decisively, when all she wanted to do was mourn her loss in solitude. It was long after midnight before she was able to escape to her chamber. As she fumbled with the latch a lithe figure stepped out of the darkness and laid a hand on her wrist. She startled, and cursed.

"I'm sorry. I didn't mean to make you jump."

She pulled away. "I didn't see you downstairs, Nochai. I looked for you . . ."

He raised her wrist to his lips. "I stayed out of the way. I heard what was said, that we hunters should have been there to protect the village. I heard the abuse. I couldn't deny it. I heard . . . about Finn. I'm so sorry."

Nochai caught her as she slumped against his chest, strong arms holding her up, guiding her to the bed. Her hands closed against his jerkin, and, finally, she sobbed in his arms while he stroked her back and loosed the warrior's braids from her hair.

"I should have been here. I should have been here." He kept repeating the words, over and over, as if saying them could erase the horrors of the day.

Asta swung her feet up on the bed and curled up with her head in his lap, comforted by the feel of his fingers running across her scalp, soothing the bruises on her face and shoulders. She winced as his rough skin caught a tender spot.

"Does it hurt?" he asked.

"Aches." Asta worked her lower jaw from side to side, feeling the swelling. "I don't think anything is broken. There's some cream in the cupboard."

Her head felt heavy as she lifted it so Nochai could slip out from beneath her and collect the pot of salve. He massaged it into her skin, the cool mint smell stinging her eyes and making them water. Nochai wiped them with his little finger.

"Have you told your mother about Finn?"

Hot and miserable, Asta sighed, and pushed his hand away. "I'll do it tomorrow."

"Do you want me to go with you? I will, if you need me . . . ?"

"No." She shook her head, and felt him relax. Nochai was no coward, just a boy of nineteen, seven years her junior. She knew he took other women, and sometimes men, when he was away on the hunt. She did the same thing herself. But he was a comfort to her, and she needed comforting tonight. Her arms tightened around him, and her bruised mouth sought his, sought to blot out, for a short time, her aching sense of loss.

Nochai's arm around her waist was overly warm, and heavy. Asta threw it off without waking him, dressed, and left the tower with the first light of dawn still blushing over the eastern ocean. The spring morning was so calm and still, it was hard to believe the events of the day before had been any more than a hideous dream. Only the taint of smoke on the breeze belied the quiet of the morning, at least until she reached the top of the cliff.

Up here, on the exposed headland, the stink of fire and death cloyed in her throat. She tried not to breathe in too deeply. The tide had gone out, smoothing the sands of the cove, scouring them clean of blood and gore. But the retreating water couldn't wash away the loss, or cleanse the ash from the line of huts that had been reduced to smouldering foundations. The ground was stained and boggy, and Asta skirted a wide circle around it. There would be bodies in the remains of the village, and they must be dealt with before they spread disease, but she wasn't ready yet. First she had to break the news to her mother, and hope she could make her understand.

She caught a horse from the corral. They were restive, the scents of smoke and blood disturbing them, and she had to coax her tall roan to the gate with soft crooning. She mounted, bareback, burying her fists in the mare's mane, and nudged her towards the hills. She wished she could keep going, over the pass and down into the tribal heartland of Atrath, back the way her parents had come. Put distance between herself and the sea that had so callously betrayed her tribe. But her destiny lay along a different trail.

She abandoned her ride when the hill path became too craggy for horses, dissolving into a mess of boulders and scree. The horse would be content to wander the grassy uplands until her return.

Asta picked out the path, following a dried up stream bed that marked a meandering line of smoothed grey pebbles down the hillside. The path was steep; in places she had to climb with hands as well as feet. She didn't have the breath to curse her mother for making her home so inaccessible, not this time. Her mind raced with the fear of how she would take the news, and she periodically touched the blade at her belt for reassurance.

The cave stood at the back of a small plateau looking down on the dead stream, and the air around it was rich with the copper tang of fresh blood. A goat, its throat and belly ripped out, was wedged into a crevice between two rocks, and sticky crimson flowed down the stone, over older stains that had faded to brown. Asta forced herself to relax. If her mother had fed, she would be sleepy and passive. Hopefully she would still be alert enough to understand.

She picked up a stone and flung it into the darkness of the cave, to announce her approach. There was no reaction, and Asta took that as a good sign. Either her mother was out, or she was drowsing. She took a few steps closer, hand resting on the hilt of her blade, and heard a shuffle from the cave, saw faint movement beyond the sunlight.

Drowsing, then.

"Mother? Mother it's me, Asta . . ."

A low rumble. Not a warning, but not a welcome.

"Can I come in?"

The rumble pitched higher. Asta moved slowly, from sunlight to grey dimness, letting her eyes adjust. She made no sudden movements, and she never turned her back on her mother.

"I'm going to sit down now. I need to talk to you."

Amber eyes flared like twin lanterns in the darkness at the back of the cave. Asta twisted her hands in her lap. The sweat on the back of her neck made her shiver. She stared down at her nails, at the blood still crusting around the edges, and swallowed. Her head felt too heavy for her body. "Mother . . ."

"I know." Nasira's voice was distorted, unfamiliar words pushed out of a throat that was the wrong shape, hoarse with disuse. She padded forward and laid her great shaggy head in Asta's lap, and Asta's hands tightened in her fur as she began to cry.

"How did you know?"

Nasira's jaw twisted with the effort of speaking, consonants dragging over each over like pebbles sliding down a hillside. "I smelled his blood on the breeze. I know my own son. You wouldn't be here again so soon if he lived."

Asta buried her face against the softness of her mother's shoulder. "Tell me what to do?"

"Be your mother again?" Nasira's heavy paw was soft on her arm. "It's too late for that."

Asta wiped her eyes. "I could stay up here, with you . . ."

"Follow." Nasira padded to the mouth of the cave, long tail swishing. When she was a girl, Asta sometimes slept with her mother's tail wrapped around her like a fur stole. That was when Nasira had been human, most of the time.

The sunlight was harsh after the darkness of the cave, the smell of fresh blood stronger. Nasira sprang up onto a nearby rock, coiled muscles bunching, and sat upright. She wrapped her tail around her massive front paws, like a domestic cat drawn huge and terrible. Asta climbed up and sat at her feet, staring out over the ruined village and the bay of death. White sails. She shivered. She wished her mother would cry, or show some emotion, but the patchcat was too deeply embedded in her spirit, and the patchcat did not mourn.

She leaned against Nasira's foreleg, wishing she could be a child again, snuggled in her mother's fur and free of responsibility. "Why can't I stay with you?"

"Your duty lies with your people, Asta."

"Then come with me. Please?" Nasira remained silent. "I need your support, mother. I don't want to be on my own."

Nasira's claws tightened against the stone. "They would not have me back. The tribe loved your father too much. They could never forgive me for killing him. Finn . . . never forgave me."

"I couldn't, in my heart," Asta confessed. "Not until I drew Father's mercy blade on the beach. Then I understood. We can make the tribe understand!"

"Mercy is a western concept. No," she shook her head, an almost human gesture of regret, "I can't come back. And you can't live here. Tell me, did you honour Finn in the custom of his father's people, or mine?"

Asta stared at the stone beneath her hands, eyes misting. "I let the sea take him."

"Why?" Nasira's claws were sharp.

"We have no shaman. The tide was coming in, and I couldn't carry the dead. What was I supposed to do?"

"Leave him to a better fate than that!" Nasira's jaws snapped, an inch from Asta's shoulder. She felt her mother's breath lash her face as she slithered down from the rock, clutching for her blade. Nasira crouched, eyes glowing, tail lashing.

"Go back to your people, Asta. Lead them. Hope that your brother can find peace. Don't come here again."

"But, mother—?"

"I said go!"

Her words ended in a snarl, ears flat to her head, lips drawn back to expose long canines. She lashed out with a front paw, narrowly missing Asta's face. "I can't hold it, Asta! Go!"

Asta ran, stumbling on the loose rocks, knowing she couldn't outpace her mother. She expected any moment to feel Nasira's paws bearing down on her shoulders, or around her legs, dragging her to the ground. She had seen her mother's teeth close on too many animal throats to believe that she could escape once she was brought down.

Nasira pulled up, swiping the back of Asta's calves, shredding her breeches and scoring shallow lines in her flesh, just below the patch of pale skin on the back of her knee. Nothing more than a love pat, but it stung. It hastened her on her way, her mother's coughing roar echoing around the rocks and gulleys. Asta cursed. A patchcat roar carried for miles, and her horse would be spooked, likely to bolt. She wondered if Nasira had done it on purpose to punish her. By the time she reached the bottom of the path, limping, her tattered breeches flapping at the backs of her legs, her ride was nowhere in sight.

"Fucking hells!" One of her father's favourite curses, though she wasn't quite sure what it meant, or even the language she spoke, only that it was a western tongue. She ripped off the torn bottoms of her breeches and tied them tightly around her bleeding calves, hoping to staunch the flow. Her mother had given her no comfort, and now she had to walk home. As if the spirits themselves were determined to mock her, it began to rain.

"Asta! Asta!"

She looked around as her name was called. A rider trotted

towards her, leading her lost mount on a loose rein. He held up an arm to hail her, and she recognised Meyloy.

"Got your ride back!" he said, as he drew alongside her. "Did you see your mother?"

Asta nodded.

"How did she take it?"

She indicted her bleeding calves. "Could have been worse."

"She doesn't want to come back, does she?" Asta shook her head, and Meyloy blew out his cheeks in relief. "I don't want to give offence, Asta, but I'm not sorry. You can't turn your back on a patchcat."

"I know," she said, ruefully, swinging one leg over the narrow back of the mare. "I thought you'd left already."

Meyloy flicked his braids. "I wanted to see you safely home first."

"You *followed* me?" Asta was torn between amusement and irritation. "I'm not a child, Meyloy. I can ride to see my mother without your supervision."

"I didn't know how she would react. I was worried about you." His voice softened. "We've lost too many these last days. The tribe can't afford to lose you too."

"My mother wouldn't hurt me." The blood trickling down the back of Asta's legs reminded her she was lying. She scowled. "Now you know I'm safe. When are you leaving?"

"I wanted to ask if I could take a few fighting men with me, for safety on the trail. I know we're short on warriors . . ."

"We're short on everything now. If they come back . . ."

"If they come back, three or four extra fighters won't make a spit of difference. You might as well lock yourself in your tower and starve to death, or throw yourself onto the rocks."

Meyloy was right, but that didn't make it any easier to hear. "You can have four," she told him. "Which way will you go?"

"South, to the fishing tribes. They don't move around much this time of year. With luck, they can spare men, and a shaman."

"The boats are more important than the shaman," Asta said.

Meyloy glanced sidelong at her. "Are you sure? Or is that your father talking?"

She nudged her horse to greater speed. His questions were thorns against her skin. Meyloy paced alongside, matching her stride for stride. "Asta?"

"My father was a shaman, as well as a warrior, and a leader. Why would he say a shaman wasn't important?"

"They have no shamans in the west. The tribe need someone to talk to the spirits, to perform the ceremonies—"

"I know that!" She wheeled away from him, and he followed, hooves thundering across the turf towards the ruined village. "But if we're not careful, there won't even be a tribe! Boats first."

"Asta! Asta!" Meyloy caught her arm as she dismounted in the corral, and pulled her close. "I know you feel bad about letting your brother go without honour. I'm just trying to help . . ."

"Don't." Asta jerked her arm free. "That's exactly what I'm doing. I—" she turned away so he couldn't see the tears welling in her eyes. "I want to honour Finn by getting Rhodan back. Can't you understand that?"

Meyloy stared at the ground, and shuffled his feet. "Boats," he said. "Right. I'll get them, don't you worry."

"Thank you." She walked away, refusing to wipe her eyes with her sleeve until she was certain she was out of Meyloy's sight. A true leader didn't show weakness, not even with blood running down her legs and her heart cracking inside her chest. Her father had taught her compassion, but her mother, her wild, dangerous, infuriating mother, had taught her courage.

Three

"HERE'S A LIGHT."

"Where?" Asta rolled over in bed, not sure she had heard Nochai properly. Not wanting to believe him. "Out to sea?"

"On the headland at the far side of the bay." He stood at the window, smooth back towards her, staring out. She sat up and gathered the blankets around her.

"What kind of light?" she asked. "Fire?"

He shook his head. "Lantern light. Flashing on and off."

Signalling.

"The brass men?"

"It's stopped now." Nochai turned his back to the window. "It was probably nothing. One of the fishing tribes come north."

"A long way north." *Too far north . . .*

"Or our new shaman, communing with the sea." Nochai chuckled. "He's a strange one, isn't he?" He caught Asta round the waist as she walked to the window, and kissed her at the base of the throat. "Don't worry about it. Take off your leaders robes and come back to bed."

Asta elbowed him gently in the ribs and pushed past him to look out into the darkness. The moons were shrouded; the Child invisible, the Mother a faint white smudge. There were no stars. Her father had called the moons by different names, Western names, but to Asta they were the Mother and Child, always. And thinking of mothers and children brought her thoughts back to Rhodan and Lefalli, to all the stolen people of her tribe. Where were they tonight?

Nochai was right, there was no light on the cliff. Most likely it had been the new shaman, Cree. He had returned with Meyloy from the fishing tribes, less than a moon before, and thrown himself into his duties to the Beehive Tribe with an enthusiasm that bordered on that of a zealot. Before he had even cast off his travelling cloak he had sacrificed a young mare on the beach to appease the restless, storm-tossed dead, and swept the remaining children of the tribe under his arm for tuition. If anyone was swinging lanterns or lighting bone-fires on the cliffs, it was likely to be him.

"I'll have a word with him," she said. "We don't want to attract any more attention from the sea. I just hope he'll listen to me!"

"If he doesn't he's a fool." Nochai stretched out on his side. "Come back to bed. Stop looking for things that aren't there."

Asta took a last long look in the direction of the headland, and sighed. "You're right," she said. "Shaman business is nothing to do with me, but I'll ask him to be careful."

"Ask him in the morning." Nochai shuffled aside to let her slip into the blankets next to him, and she cuddled up against his chest. He kissed her forehead. "It's night now, Asta. By day you belong to the tribe. At night, we belong to each other."

The new village was being built on the corpse of the old one. The charred remains, the broken wood, the dead, all had been cleared away. The new houses would have a defensive wall around them, in the manner of her father's people. It had been Asta's command, grumbled at by her tribe, who did not like to be hemmed in. "Better enclosed in walls than taken by strangers, or dead," she told them.

The wall grew slowly, stone on stone, a rough ring around the village that she could still step over if she took a long stride. The houses, of wood and stone, were emerging more quickly, but not one of them had a roof yet. The tribe would be sleeping in the tower for a few more moons.

She nodded encouragement to the builders, stopping to field their questions. Yes, there would be boats built. No, she couldn't say when. Yes, she wanted the crops sown inside the wall. No, she didn't know when Samana's missing mother would come back. The little girl asked every day, and the answer was always the same. Her simple, misplaced faith in Asta made her heart ache every time.

She rose from talking to Samana to see Meyloy gesturing for her to join him outside the wall. She followed him along the cliff path to the spot above the cove, where the greasy stench of a bone-fire rose from the sand. Cree was sacrificing again, and she remembered her pledge to talk to him about his rites. They couldn't spare the animals, for a start.

"My leader, I'm worried."

Asta wasn't used to hearing such respect in Meyloy's voice, and she threw him a sideways glance to see if he was mocking her. He kept his eyes down, his face smooth and serious.

"What about?" she asked him.

"I saw lights on the cliff last night. I think someone in the tribe might be trying to signal to the raiders."

"I saw them too," Asta said. "I thought – I hoped – it was Cree. His rituals . . . I was coming to ask him."

"Do you think he'd tell you if he was?" Meyloy linked his arm through hers and drew her closer, so he could mutter in her ear. "I didn't have a chance to tell you before. I thought it was nothing."

She moved her face back from the heat of his breath. "What? What are you worried about?"

"The fisher tribes make trade with the brass men. I didn't realise until I reached them. Their links aren't close, but they are real."

She pushed him away. "Why didn't you tell me this before?"

"Because I didn't think he'd be signalling to them!" He caught her arm once more as she took a stride towards the path that led to the cove. "Where are you going?"

"To have a word with our new shaman!"

"Don't." Meyloy's grip tightened. "If you accuse him without evidence, he might leave. And then the tribe would turn against you. I've heard whispers, that you haven't done enough to get our women and children back, that you dishonoured the dead. That you're not the leader your father was . . ."

"The tribe think that?" Asta was appalled to hear her deepest fears thrown back at her so openly.

"Some of them do. Scaring off their shaman without proof would make things worse. But if you had that proof . . ." He glanced significantly at the headland.

"You think he would have been so stupid?"

"It wouldn't take much," Meyloy said. "A scrap of cloth, a few footprints . . ."

"Will you come with me?"

Meyloy glanced back at the building work going on in the village, and grinned. "I guess the tribe could spare us for a while."

Away from the edge of the cliff, the fire-smell was easier to bear, and Asta felt her throat clearing. The stiff sea breeze tugged at her braids, swirled under her father's cloak and lifted it. She licked the salt from her lips as she led Meyloy over springy turf and through patches of ground-hugging weed. The soil here was too thin for crops, but perhaps they could corral some goats to clear the weeds. They would provide more milk, and meat, if they could be caught. She could rebuild, given time. If the raiders stayed away.

A low screen of twisted trees shielded the headland from the shore. Deformed by the wind, bent-backed like old women, their arms stretched away from the sea as if they were trying to escape. Her fingers brushed their gnarled bark as she passed, and a stray branch snagged her cloak. She tugged it free, leaving a small rip in the fabric.

Beyond the trees, the wind felt even colder. Asta shivered as she stepped out onto the bare expanse of headland, Meyloy lingering behind. The cliff dropped sharply to her right, rolled away in a long slope to her left that led down to a tangle of trees and bushes that concealed hidden paths and dips. She scanned the horizon for sails, but the mist hugged the grey surface of the water and it was hard to see anything.

"Over here!" Meyloy beckoned her to the southern side of the headland. "I've found footprints."

Asta scanned the smooth, springy turf at his feet. Her own stride left no indentations in the ground. "Where?" she said. "I can't see anything."

"Right here." Meyloy dug his toe in the earth. "Can't you see them?"

As Asta looked closer, the sudden, sharp blow to her back drove her to her knees, jarring her wrists as they caught her weight. Meyloy grabbed her braids and twisted them tightly in his fist, clapping his other hand over her mouth before she could cry out. It happened so fast she barely had time to gasp.

"I've got her! Come quick!"

Asta snatched for her dagger, but Meyloy kicked it from her hand and sent it spinning across the turf. He dragged her to her feet by the hair, still covering her mouth as she tried to bite him. He swung her around, and she saw the brass men, running from the cover of the shrub on the southern side of the headland. Not just brass men; her heart sank as she recognised men of the tribe running with them. She struggled as they surrounded her, feeling sick to her guts. Whatever they wanted of her, she wouldn't go down without a fight.

Meyloy bound her hands behind her back with a strip of leather, while one of the strangers stepped forward and took hold of her chin, tipping her head back to study her face. "This is her?" His voice was a rumble.

Asta felt Meyloy's heart thumping against her back, he was so close. So nervous. "Do you have my son? We agreed the trade!"

The man who held Asta's face shrugged, and let her go. He wore heavy bronze arm-rings around his biceps, and she wondered if that was an indicator of rank among these strangers. "You said she had the marks," he said. "Show me."

Meyloy's foot twisting between her ankles pitched Asta forward once more. Without her hands to save her, she smashed her chin on the ground, jarring her teeth and biting her tongue. She cursed thickly. "Meyloy, what are you doing? Let me up!"

"I'm so sorry." His voice was low in her ear, his knee pressed into the small of her back. "I have to do this. You'd understand if—"

"Show us the marks." The man with the arm rings stood in front of Asta. She could see the salt and sand clinging to the toes of his boots.

"What marks?"

He ignored her question, but Meyloy shuffled aside, still pinning her down, and the brass-skinned man crouched. Up close, his face was beaten by time and tide, and he had an identical white scar on the outside of each chestnut eyebrow. He pressed one hand down on her shoulder. "We don't want to hurt you."

"Then let me up!" Asta struggled, but his weight was an implacable force, pinning her down. He pushed aside her cloak and lifted her riding skirt.

Asta kicked out, her boot landing a glancing blow. Meyloy yelped at the contact, and she tried to squirm away from his grip. She made it only a few inches before the brass man's hand closed on the back of her neck, pressing her face into the turf. She breathed in earth and salt, blood and sweat, kicking uselessly against the men that surrounded her.

"Hold her feet," he ordered.

Pinned down, Asta could do nothing but lay still, heart racing. She could see her blade, lying on the ground just out of reach, and she willed it towards her with every fibre of her being as the leader of the foreigners lifted her skirt once more.

A chill like the cold wash of tide flowed over Asta at his touch.

He ran probing, exploratory fingers over the matching patches of white skin at the backs of her knees, and she heard a murmur of surprise, almost respect, from the other strangers. The touch made her retch.

"I told you she had the marks!" Meyloy sounded triumphant. "Will you give him back now?"

The pressure at the back of Asta's neck eased. The brass leader rose, dragging her up with him, gripping her wrists. "Where did you get these marks?" He spoke to Asta. His voice was low, without aggression.

"I've always had them, since I was a girl." Asta never thought about the marks, paler than Finn, even paler than her father, which lay in broad brushstrokes across the backs of her knees. She only remembered them when they burned in the hot summer months, white skin flaring scarlet and painful.

There was muttering among the brass men, in their harsh tongue. Meyloy twitched. Asta couldn't bring herself to look at him. It seemed she wasn't going to be raped, but the raiders obviously had plans of some kind.

"Meyloy, tell me what's going on!"

His voice was wretched. "I made a deal. When I told you the fishing tribe made trade with the raiders, it wasn't a lie. I made a trade of my own, while I was in the South. They want you for your marks, my leader. I'm so sorry . . ."

"You *traded* me? Without my permission? You can't do that!" She tried to wrench free, but the man with the arm rings held her firm. "I'm not coming with you. Let me go!" She turned to the men of her own tribe, pleading with them. "Are you all with Meyloy on this? Why?"

The nearest man spat, shuffling his feet.

"Meyloy?"

"You're a halfbreed. Your father was a western dog. Your mother—" he shrugged. "I don't know what your mother is, but she's not human. And you're a woman. If your brother had wanted the leader's robes—"

"My brother had the same blood as me!" Her eyes stung at the mention of Finn. "Don't drag my brother into this."

"Cree said your soiled blood has brought a curse down on the tribe." Meyloy sounded increasingly unsure.

"How long have you been listening to Cree? You've known me all your life . . ."

"And . . . they promised." He turned to the brass leader. "Turgesu, you promised. Where is he?"

"In time." Turgesu turned to Asta, and inclined his head. "You will come with us now, *sumri gudienne*."

"I will not!" Asta lunged, her forehead smacking into the bridge of his nose so hard her vision erupted into stars. The shock made him let go of her arms, and she broke free, tried to run. But Meyloy was there, Meyloy with men she had thought of as her friends, her tribe, and they would not let her pass. He grabbed her arm as she tried to push free.

"What are you doing?" he demanded. "You stupid mare, you're going to ruin everything!" He raised his hand, and she steeled herself for the blow, determined not to flinch, or cry out. She would show him the courage of her blood.

Brass fists grappled Meyloy's hand away before the blow could fall. The blood gushing from Turgesu's nose was the same colour as Asta's, and he dabbed his nostrils as one of his companions laid a stone knife to her bare throat, and asked what sounded like a question.

Turgesu shook his head, his forehead creased in concern. He let go of Meyloy and pushed him away. "We need to leave this place," he said. "Do as you must, and then we will make the trade."

The raiders held her still, Asta silently seething, as Meyloy lifted her father's cloak from her shoulders and draped it around his own. It was so short on him it barely brushed his hips. Meyloy ran his hands down it. There was no satisfaction in the gesture, only resignation. "Hand me her blade," he said.

One of the raiders collected Asta's knife from the ground and passed it to Meyloy. He tested the edge with his thumb. "I'm sorry," he said, with a blunt nod to the men of the tribe.

Their hands, not rough but determined, forced Asta to her knees. She was feeling sick again, trying to hold back bile and tears of fury. Meyloy gathered her warrior's braids in his hands and slowly, one by one, he began to slice. Turgesu took a few steps back. This was the business of the tribe, and it seemed he was inclined to leave them to it.

Asta twisted to spit up into Meyloy's face as he cut through her hair, almost ripping it from her scalp with his savagery. "How *could* you?"

Her spittle dripped from his chin. He made no move to wipe it away, just carried on carving relentlessly through her braids. "The bronze men have a word," he said. "*Slave.* They own men and women the way you own a cooking pot, or a necklace. You can't be a warrior and a slave, Asta."

She said nothing, burning with frustration and humiliation as her dark hair tumbled around her as if she was an enemy he had defeated. Every cut Meyloy made took her further away from her tribe. She understood what was happening now, and if she couldn't fight it, she could endure it like a warrior, not like a frightened woman. When she raised her head it felt strangely light, and cold. She tried not to shiver in the wind blowing straight off the sea.

"Now?" Meyloy asked

"By the sea." Turgesu nodded to his companions. "I'll have them hood her."

The bag swept over Asta's head before she had the chance to struggle or cry out, strings tightening around her throat like a noose. The loose hair on her scalp itched like pox, falling in her eyes as she allowed herself a few hidden tears. She was pulled and prodded down the long slope to the sea, the ocean spray soaking through the hood and plastering it to her face. She wished she could see. Her heart leapt into her mouth every time she stumbled. Still, maybe a quick plunge from the cliff was a better prospect than whatever it was the strangers had in store for her?

A quick squeeze of her fingers, a voice in her ear. She didn't think it was Meyloy.

"Find our children, my leader!"

The man of the tribe moved away before she could respond. Someone, at least, still followed her trail. It made her feel a little less sick.

Rock gave way to sand beneath her feet. She guessed they were on the southern side of the point, shielded from the village. She didn't know why Turgesu had felt the need to have her hooded, but the brightness of the sky cleaved her skull as he pulled the wet sacking from her face.

The tide had come in and withdrawn again, smoothing the sand around the long rowing boat that looked like the one the raiders had used to snatch the women and children from the cove. They must have been waiting for her all night. The thought made her feel ill all over again, to think how Meyloy had planned this, just to take her robes. Whatever he'd traded couldn't be worth her freedom, could it?

Turgesu waved his hand towards the boat and issued what sounded like a command. There was a stout box, halfway along the boat, with a hatch opened by an iron ring. As one of the raiders threw it back, Asta heard a high, thin wail that drove her forward into the waves, heedless of her bound hands. Meyloy pushed past her, splashing into the water, and dropped to his knees with a strangled cry.

"What are you doing? That's not my son!"

The little boy, no older than five, floundered through the breakers towards them. He threw his arms around Asta's thighs, nearly knocking her from her feet. "Tante Asta!"

She would have held him close, if her hands were free. He reminded her so much of Rhodan it was hard to breathe.

"Tante Asta, the men took me on a boat and there were lots of us and then they put me in a box . . ."

"I know, Kilu. You're safe now." She gave him a nudge up the beach. "Go with Meyloy. He'll look after you."

Kilu rubbed his eyes and stared at her. "What happened to your hair? Don't you fight any more?"

"It doesn't matter!" She had to raise her voice. Meyloy and Turgesu were nose to nose. Meyloy screamed obscenities, and the brass-skinned raiders gripped his arms to keep him from striking their leader.

"You promised my son! This isn't my boy! What have you done with him?"

Turgesu stepped back with a shrug. "What's wrong with this boy? You wanted a boy, I gave you one. You should be grateful."

"Give me back my son!" Meyloy tore himself free and lunged at Turgesu, lashing fists clumsy with rage and desperation. Turgesu didn't seem to move with any speed, but somehow his axe was in his hand, and he swung it in a lazy arc. It crunched into the side of Meyloy's head, throwing up a spray of blood and brain. Asta tried to shield Kilu with her body, but she couldn't protect him from the gargling sounds Meyloy made as he slumped on the sand, twitching his last on the bloodied shore.

Turgesu stood over his body, staring down at it with his axe hanging limp in his hand. He looked up, directly at Asta. "The trading is done," he said, breaking the shocked silence. "Let go of the boy."

"Run!" Asta pushed Kilu, as best she could with her hands bound. "Run away now! All of you!" There were too many raiders, and they were too well armed, too quick to strike. Like snakes in summer.

Meyloy's men, the cowards, scattered and fled, one of them snatching up Kilu as he ran as if the boy was no more than a bag of grain under his arm. Asta was left alone, cold water sucking at her knees, salt stinging her cuts. Turgesu gestured with his axe.

"Into the boat, *sumri gudienne*. I don't want to hurt you."

The white-sailed ship was anchored a mile out into the bay, like a gull settled on the water. It looked too far to row. Asta clambered awkwardly into the boat and sat on the box where Kilu had been imprisoned, feeling splinters of wood snag the skin of her thighs. Her wet skirt clung to her legs, and she itched all over.

The brass men took up the oars, in front of her and behind. The man behind was so close she felt his breath on her neck as he grunted over the oars. Carefully, moving slowly, she crossed her ankles and rubbed her feet together to loosen the laces of her boots.

No one was watching her. The raiders were intent on their rowing, showing no interest in their cargo. She gave them time to relax, hoping Turgesu would let his guard down the nearer they got to the ship.

They were halfway across the bay. The sun was out, turning the water around the rowing boat to white and gold. Dazzling spray flared from the tips of the oars as they twisted in the sunlight, and the land falling away behind them was nothing but a dark mass. She couldn't see the tower, but she knew what direction it lay in, and that was enough.

Asta shuffled to the edge of the boat. If her hands had been free, she could have reached the green water, darkening to unfathomable depths. Her father had taught her to swim in rivers and lakes, but she had never swum so far out to sea. It would be hard, with her hands tied, but the alternative was unthinkable. She might drown, but that was better than life as a slave.

She swung her feet over the side, and kicked her legs. One boot tumbled lazily into the depths, the other stayed wedged on her foot. Too late to struggle with it now; there was a yell behind her and the awkward splash of oars as the rower's rhythm broke. Before any of the raiders could snatch at her, she pushed off the side and into the water.

The sea was cold, far colder than she had imagined. The water stabbed knives all over her body as she sank down, dragged by the weight of her remaining boot. She kicked out, lungs bursting, striking for the sunlit surface far above, a patch of blue in a rapidly darkening world.

Her head broke the surface and she gasped in a mouthful of

air, boot and heavy skirt conspiring to drag her under again. The muscles in the backs of her calves spasmed. She couldn't make them do what she wanted any more, couldn't make them kick out for shore. The shore that suddenly seemed very small, very distant. The contours of the land were strange to her, as if seen through the wrong end of a spyglass. She fancied she caught a glimpse of the tower, of home, as she went under again.

A wave crashed over her head, dragging her down. If she opened her mouth to cry out, it would all be over. So easy, to sink beneath the waves and let the sea consume her.

Asta . . .

Someone was calling her name, a familiar voice, much loved. Asta felt the cold tendrils of water clawing at her throat, and she surrendered to the chill embrace of the sea.

Four

THERE WERE BEAMS above her and wooden panels beside her head, which rested on scratchy fabric. Asta closed her eyes as quickly as she had opened them. If this was the spirit realm, it was nothing like her father's description.

"Finn?"

Her whisper sounded hoarse, even to her own ears. If her brother was here, he was not talking to her. She heard the creak of a chair, heavy footsteps and the sound of a door opening and closing, but her head was too heavy to lift.

The surface she was lying on lurched beneath her, and her stomach roiled. She clutched at the wall for support, and struggled into a sitting position.

She was in a wooden room, compact and sparsely furnished with bed, table and chair. There were no windows, but an oil lamp swung from the beams above her head, casting a pool of light. The covers on the bed and the cloth on the table were woven in the patterns of her tribe, and the blanket she lay under smelled of horses. The homesickness was like a swelling, rising in her throat as she tried the door. It was locked. A quick exploration of the room revealed no other way out and nothing she could use as a weapon. Her chest tightened, a tide of panic that closed her throat and brought urgent tears to her eyes. She kicked against the door, scrabbled at the walls, dizzy as the room spun around her, before a strong hand seized her by the back of the neck, pressed her down on to the bed and forced her head between her knees.

"Breathe. In, out. In, out." The steady voice calmed her as she followed his instruction, and the presence of a warm body beside her helped the moment pass. She felt a stray tear creeping down her face, and she hastily brushed it away before she sat up. She was her father's daughter, and she would not weep in the face of adversity.

"It will do you no good to panic, *sumri gudienne.*" Turgesu's voice, and he eased the pressure on her neck, allowing her to sit up. "No harm will come to you here. I'm glad to see you awake."

Her breath returned, sudden and painful, and she pushed away the hand that lingered on her back. "Don't touch me."

"Are you better?"

He had left the door open a crack. If her limbs had felt less like water she could have pushed past him, made a break for it. He caught her looking, and patted her hand.

"There are thirty-eight oars on this ship, and she carries a double crew. Do you think you can fight seventy-six men? Even if you could, where would you go?"

She was on the ship. That explained the lurching floor. Asta forced herself to relax, inch by inch. She had shown too much fear already. She would not let panic overwhelm her again.

"I told you not to touch me."

Turgesu moved from the bed to the chair, his eyes sweeping her appraisingly. "How do you feel?"

"Fine." She wiped her hands along her arms. They felt sticky with some sweet-smelling ointment, and she could feel the bruises spreading on her skin.

"The salve will help the bruising fade, *gudienne.*"

It felt like her skin was struggling to breathe. If he expected her to thank him for the treatment, he would have a long wait.

"Is there anything you need? Food, wine? Are you comfortable here?"

Asta's mouth was dry. "How long will I be here?"

"It's under a moon of sail to the Scattering, wind be with us."

"The Scattering? Is that where you're from?" She didn't want to ask him questions, give this stranger the satisfaction of knowing he had her at a disadvantage, but they were tripping off her tongue. Maybe she would learn something useful. "Are you the leader of this tribe?"

"Me? No." Turgesu chuckled, a warm, rich sound. "I am the speaker of many tongues, that's all. I am to teach you."

"Teach me? Teach me what?"

"How to make our words. You will need them, my *sumri gudienne.*"

"You keep calling me that. What does it mean?"

"What is your name?"

Asta scowled, lips set in a hard line. Her tribe only gave up their names to those they trusted. She trusted Turgesu about as far as she could throw a horse.

"Tell me, and I'll tell you what it means." He rose. "I'll bring you some food later, and then we can make a start."

Asta had nothing to do but wait in her floating cell, fretful hands picking at the loose threads on the blankets, trying to work out how much time had passed. Prowling the room did nothing to relieve her mounting anxiety, and it felt like the wood-panelled walls of the cabin were pressing in on her, smothering her with their weight. If she could just see the sky, or the sea, feel rocks beneath her feet, she would feel a little better. But there was no sky, just this wooden box, six paces across and ten long, with a ceiling she could brush with her fingertips. It was like being wrapped in a shroud and buried in the earth.

It was almost a relief when Turgesu returned, carrying a covered dish. He set it down on the table and regarded Asta cynically.

"No knives," he said. "You eat with your hands."

Under the dish was a slice of hard, dry biscuit, slathered with a grey paste that reeked of fish. She was already feeling nauseous, and the smell lodged in Asta's throat, making her gag. She replaced the dish quickly. "I'm not eating that."

"That's all there is. You'll eat it when you're hungry. When we get to the Scattering the food will be better." He smiled. "Let us begin."

Asta's father had spoken three tongues fluently, and he had taught her a little of each language, mostly curse words when her mother was out of earshot. She had inherited his ear for language, and her lessons with Turgesu quickly became the highlight of her days. They discussed food, the weather, parts of a ship, and he taught her to curse, for his own amusement. But when it came to greetings and he asked her name, she merely closed her mouth and shook her head.

"I'll tell you," she said, "if you let me out of this room. I've been in here for days. I need to feel the breeze on my face. I feel sick. I feel like I'm suffocating in here."

"I can't." Turgesu's face fell. "If we lost you to the sea . . ."

"Why would it matter? I'm no-one." Asta ruffled her cropped hair in disgust. "Just a slave. What's one more slave here or there?"

"You think you are a slave?" Turgesu's eyes widened. "In this cabin?"

"You had my braids cut." The humiliation was still an open wound, rubbed with salt.

"Why does that matter so much? I don't understand."

How to explain to this stranger, with his short hair, fair as her brother's had been? "Long hair, it shows that you're an adult, a fighter. By cutting it, you made me a child to my people, and a slave to yours. Meyloy said so."

"A slave . . ." Turgesu was on his feet, pacing back and forth, as if the suggestion unsettled him. "That was not our intent."

"Then what was your intent, in taking me from my home?" Asta demanded. "Why did you take the women and children of my tribe? What do you want with us?"

"You're not a slave."

"What am I then? A prize?" She had been so sure she was a slave. Turgesu had tilted the ground beneath her with his words. It felt like the initial lurch of the ship, and she fought the panic down once more.

He tightened his fists. "I don't know how much I can tell you. I have to ask . . ."

"Ask what? Ask who?"

He hesitated with his hand on the door. "Tomorrow. Maybe I'll tell you more tomorrow, if I can."

"Why can't you tell me now?" But he merely pressed his lips together and shook his head, departing without another word.

Asta didn't expect Turgesu to tell her anything the following day. It was hard enough persuading him to answer questions even on topics he wasn't so obviously anxious about. He would shut his lips like a clam, smile enigmatically, or ask her name once more. But when he arrived at her cell he carried a sacking hood in one hand, and a short length of rope dangled over his shoulder. He held them out to her.

"You don't need to hood and tie me," Asta told him. "Where do you think I'd run to?"

"This is not to prevent your escape." Turgesu pulled her hands behind her back and bound them securely.

"Just for your pleasure, is it?"

He didn't rise to her barb. "My job is to keep you safe, both from yourself and from curious eyes. There are those on this ship whose passions might rise at the thought of seeing the *sumri gudienne* before the appointed hour. I am forbidden to show your face."

"At least tell me where you're taking me," Asta protested, before he could plunge her into darkness.

Turgesu said nothing, and the hood came down, the rough cloth scratching her face, making it hard to breathe. His heavy hands on her upper arms steered her out of the door, into a space that felt less enclosed. There was even a hint of fresh air on her skin.

"Along here, and down." Turgesu guided her through the ship, blind and mute, shielded from prying eyes. Sometimes he exchanged words with men she couldn't see, and she caught snatches of greetings, of questions, and that name repeated over and over. The *sumri gudienne,* a charm that seemed to command respect. If they respected her, why lead her hooded and chained like a mare that needed taming?

Down they went, and down again, deep into the bowels of the ship. The fresh air vanished, replaced by a cloying sensation at the back of Asta's throat, like a furry coating on her tongue. It smelled of death, of blood and shit and misery. Turgesu stopped her walking with a hand against her chest. "I'm sorry about this." He lifted her hood.

It was dark in the hold, but not so dark that Asta couldn't see the hunched figures, crammed together in the shadows, wedged between hides and wooden crates as if they were just another cargo. She heard the rattle of chains as one of the figures, a woman by her size, or a child, stretched against her shackles before slumping in greater dejection, but no one spoke. A child cried out, swiftly hushed by an adult, and the words of disgust died in Asta's throat. There was nothing she could say. She was not a slave.

"You see?" Turgesu read her mind. "You're the lucky one. Your marks have saved you from a dark fate."

"My . . . marks?"

"They are identical, the marks on the back of each knee that you carry. Symmetry is perfection. The *sumri gudienne* must be perfect. You . . . must be perfect."

Nothing he said made any sense. Asta found her voice. "These people—" she couldn't look down into the hold, couldn't tear her eyes away, "they're slaves. This is a slave ship?"

Turgesu sounded deeply offended. "This is a *trading* ship, out of the port of Mikligard in The Scattering. We trade in wood, cloth, hides, precious metals—"

"Slaves."

He shrugged.

"Are any of my tribe down there in that festering hole? My nephew? Rhodan!"

Her cry fell away into darkness, as if the blackness of the hold swallowed it up. There was no reply.

"Your people are not here, *gudienne*. They have already been taken to Mikligard. These are people from the southern tribes, the fishers, the wall-builders. We only came back to your village for you."

"Why?"

"We met your man Meyloy in the south," Turgesu explained. "We told him what we were looking for, and he told us of the marks on your legs. I had to see them for myself. I had to know that you really were fit to be the *sumri gudienne*. Otherwise, yes, we would have taken you for a slave. Meyloy bargained you away to get his son back, the fool."

"And you cut him down. An unarmed man. A father. What sort of people are you?"

"We are traders." Turgesu spoke without rancour, as if such trades and betrayals happened every day. Asta turned her back on the hold, sickened to her core. But for a happenstance of anatomy, she would be down there with the enslaved. Suddenly her bare, close cabin seemed a luxury.

"What does it mean?"

"What does what mean?" Turgesu sounded nonplussed.

"*Sumri gudienne*." All at once it was vital for Asta to know what had saved her from a slave's fate. What made her so special? What was this *gudienne*, that made the men of the ship mutter their respect, that kept her out of the hold? "Tell me what it means! I need to know."

"Tell me your name."

Asta bit her lip. "You know my name."

"I want to hear it from your lips. I want to know you trust me."

"Trust you? A slaver, a murderer? Why should I trust you?

He shrugged. "Then don't tell me. Live in mystery, if you can."

It felt like there were weights on her mouth, making it move more slowly than she wanted. Asta would never give up her name to a stranger. It went against every tradition of her people. Turgesu moved to pull the hood back down over her head. "We've seen enough here . . ."

"Wait!" She writhed in indecision, listening to groaning in the hold below her feet. "My name . . . My name is Asta, daughter of Rhodri of the West."

Turgesu bowed. She couldn't tell if he was mocking her defeat, or offering respect. "Thank you for trusting me."

"I don't trust you. Tell me what it means."

"*Sumri gudienne*. It is you. It is the highest honour a woman can hold in Mikligard. You, Asta of the horse tribes, you are our Summer Goddess."

Five

The Summer Goddess? What did it mean? Turgesu refused to be drawn. He kept his lips clamped as he led her back to her cabin. She still thought of it as a cell, but a cell was preferable to what she had seen below decks. She shuddered all over as she thought of it. Had Rhodan and Lefalli been transported that way, in chains? How could her nephew be a slave? He was only six, and it sickened her to think what manner of man would buy a six year old boy.

"Did you sell Rhodan and Lefalli?" she demanded, as Turgesu released her from the hood.

"I don't work in the slave markets. What happens to slaves has nothing to do with me."

"What would happen to them? Who might buy them?"

He avoided her eye. "Your people were sold in the slave markets of Mikligard. That will not be your fate."

"Who were they sold to? Who buys women and children as if they were horses to be traded without their consent?"

He stared down at his nails. "That is not your concern."

"It is! I—"

"You do not lead them any more, Asta. You are our *sumri gudienne* now. You sail on a different tide."

She said nothing. He could tell her that until he grew blue from lack of breath. Asta would not give up on her people, on the children of her tribe. She would not give up on Finn's wife and son.

"You asked what would happen to you. You will be taken to . . . a place of safety. You will not be hurt."

"For how long?" Asta demanded. Rising, Turgesu shook his head.

"It's not my place to tell you. Your duties will be explained to you, but not by me. Once I have delivered you to Mikligard, we will part."

"You're not going to stay with me?" Asta was annoyed at the feeling of sudden loss. Turgesu was her chief captor, her chief tormentor, but he had showed her kindness, and patience. She didn't know if she would get that from the people he handed her over to.

He smiled. "Would that I could, sweet *gudienne*. Try to rest now. I have seen the seagulls flying, and that means Mikligard is only a few days away."

Only a few days, he'd said, but it could have been a lifetime to Asta. Trapped in her windowless cabin, the only way she had to measure time was by the periodic arrival of her meals. More biscuit, more fish-paste, the occasional withered fruit. She missed the air on her face and the blue skies above her, and she was haunted by the crumpled, defeated figures in the hold. She had worn her fingers bloody trying to get out, and the door was scuffed from kicking and beating, but the wood refused to yield. If she could free herself, she could free everyone, take the ship, sail it back to the village. Somehow . . .

Her hair had grown a little, but it was a shaggy mess, and she couldn't twist it into braids no matter how she tried. She was toying with it when a series of long shudders ran through the ship. It was as if it had hit something and bounced off several times before coming to rest. Maybe they had struck rocks. Perhaps this was her chance to escape.

She dropped into a fighting crouch beside the door, listening for the sounds of running feet, of panic. She could hear distant excitement, and she clenched her fists, ready to lash out and run the moment Turgesu opened the door.

She heard his tread in the corridor, slow and measured. It didn't sound like he was in any hurry to save her from drowning. Perhaps the ship wasn't as badly damaged as she'd hoped.

The door opened. Asta leapt, punching out, fist smacking into flesh. Turgesu reeled, and she was past him and into the corridor before he could recover, running towards a short flight of stairs as the ship lurched once more. She stumbled, smacking her knee on the step so hard it sent a numbing jolt down her shin, but she pressed on. She could see the top of the hatch, a square of brilliant blue, for an instant before it was blotted out by shadow and darkness.

Turgesu shouted behind her, and the stairs were blocked. Asta tried to duck around the wiry man in her path, and he caught her hard around the waist and flung her back into Turgesu's arms. His face was bleeding, warm blood sticking in her hair as he dragged her back by the armpits and flung her into her cabin. She landed on her bruised knee, and barely managed to swallow a cry of pain.

He stood over her, face gleaming with sweat, blood marking trails down his face and over his shirt and arms. "What do you think you're doing?" he yelled. "I told you to stay here! Do you want to get hurt? Do you want people to die because of you?"

Asta dragged herself to her feet. Her knee was swelling, and it wouldn't take her weight. She tried to lean subtly on the edge of the table, hoping Turgesu wouldn't notice her weakness. He sighed, and swept a hand across his face, staring at it as if noticing the blood for the first time.

"Why would people die because of me?"

"No one can see the Summer Goddess before the proper time." He wiped his hand down his leg. "Do you think I locked you away in here to punish you? Now Leif will have to die. It's a bad omen, the worst."

"Worse for him." She limped over to the bed and sank down, feeling hollow. "You say I'm some kind of Goddess. Don't I have the power to spare him? In my tribe . . ."

"You are no longer in your tribe." The reminder again, fierce, implacable. Asta's hand strayed to her hair, reminded her she was no longer a warrior. But she was still her father's daughter. They could cut her hair, beat her, lock her up. It wouldn't change her blood.

Turgesu noticed the gesture, and a frown flitted across his bronzed features. "I came," he said, "before your little escape, to tell you we had docked. The ship will be cleared, and you will be carried into Mikligard."

"I don't need to be carried. I can ride."

He snorted at that.

"What? Are horses not allowed to see your precious Goddess either?"

He walked over to her and raised his hand. Asta braced herself, expecting a slap, but he merely cradled her cheek with his palm, still tacky with blood, and chuckled softly.

"Silly *gudienne*. This is The Scattering. There are no horses here."

A life without sky was bearable. A life without horses . . . What did they eat, on The Scattering? How did they make their tents, their clothes? How did they get about? She couldn't imagine such a land, and the thought both terrified and slightly thrilled her. She limped around her wooden cell, impatient, listening to the bumps and scrapes around her as the ship was cleared. She thought of the sorry cargo in the hold, and her fists tightened against the hem of her skirt. What would happen to them now? Had Rhodan and his mother followed the same path? She could find them; she would get away from Turgesu as soon as she could. He said there were no horses, but that must be a lie. There were always horses, and when she found Rhodan she would ride the broad curve of the world with him until she brought him home.

There was a rustle outside, the lock clicking, and the door opened. It was Turgesu, his cut cheek stitched with black thread, like an insect crawling across his face. It made her shudder to see it. She thought she hadn't hit him that hard, but the broken skin on her knuckles, and the bruising around the cut, told a different story. When he turned, she saw an identical mark crawling up his other cheek. She hadn't hit him there.

"What happened to your face?" she demanded.

"The ship is clear," he said, no hint of evasion in his generous features.

"And Leif?"

"He has been punished."

Asta swallowed her nausea. "The people in the hold . . . ?"

"Come." Turgesu extended his hand, all smiles, as if the fight had never happened. Only the twin scars to show for it, and he was giving nothing away. "Would you like to see the Scattering before we disembark?"

What Asta wanted to see were the cliffs and coves of her homeland, gentle smoke rising from the Beehive village, the round tower set into the cliff. But knowledge of this place she had been brought to would do her no harm.

"Am I allowed? No one will get killed for it?"

"No one will see you," Turgesu promised. He held out a light gauze, lilac-hued and perfumed. "Wrap this round your head. You'll still be able to see."

She hesitated, soft cloth held in her hands. "The men on the beach, back home. Were they killed too?"

"Cover your face, my goddess."

"Why are you allowed to see me? Are you going to die when we land?"

"I have special privilege. Some do."

"Is that something to do with the extra cut on your face?"

His smile dimmed. "You ask too many questions, Asta. You don't have to see anything. Your litter is waiting for you. I have offered you a kindness." He turned away.

"Wait! I'll see it."

Turgesu looked pointedly at the cloth. It was cold and smooth against her skin, and the scent caught in her throat as the fabric covered her mouth. On her lips, it tasted alcoholic, and too sweet. She could see out, the world blurred and blue-tinged, and Turgesu fussed with the cloth, pinning it to her hair, making sure it wouldn't slip.

"Follow." He took her arm and steered her out into the passage, back towards the hatch where Leif had caught his fatal glimpse of her face. There had been blue sky up there. She yearned towards it, like a filly pulling against the reins. Turgesu held her back.

"Your knee is hurt," he warned. "Careful on the steps."

She would suffer any discomfort to feel the sunlight on her face again, and she waited, shifting her weight on her bruised leg as Turgesu lifted the hatch and thrust it aside, spilling light into the gloom of the hold. He clambered up, heels flashing close to her face, and stretched down to haul her out on deck for the first time since she had been carried aboard, a lifetime ago.

Even with the veil, the sudden light hurt her eyes. The sky was deeper blue than it should be, the sun hazy, and she screwed up her face and unthinkingly lifted her hand to the cloth. Turgesu snatched at her wrist and pinned it down at her side with a hiss of warning.

"Not here! Not yet!"

"Where then?" She could hear the sounds of the town beyond, but she could see nothing over the high sides of the boat. The deck was neat, rope snaked in coils around cylinders that stuck up from the wooden planks, and she saw housings that she assumed led to more entrances to the hold. Pulleys for moving cargo, and sails, were folded neatly where they lay. There was no human in sight, and the abandoned ship felt eerie. It had been a living thing, bouncing across the waves. Asta had felt it tremble under her hand like a horse after a good run, but now it was so many tonnes of dead wood, bound head and tail by ropes that stretched beyond her sight.

"Can you climb?"

Her knee felt stiff, unbending. "Of course I can climb."

Turgesu pointed. "Up there. I'll go behind you in case you miss a step."

She followed the line of his finger, up into the dazzling sky. It was impossible to see what he was pointing at, but there was a long pole with branches, a strangely symmetrical tree, growing from the deck of the ship, and it had staples hammered into it to form a ladder. She hoped they held firm. If she slipped, it was a long fall back to the deck.

She nodded, slapped her palms together, and took hold of the ladder. The rungs were cold and damp, and Turgesu's heavy breathing at her heels was no comfort. If she kicked out she could take him in the chin, send him hurtling through space. But who would catch her then? Turgesu wouldn't let his precious *sumri gudienne* fall.

She climbed ever upwards, gripping the bars until her knuckles stood up like tight knots. She didn't look around, concentrating on the snagged wood in front of her, the bars, the places were some enterprising sailor had carved something that could be his name, or an obscenity. The sun beat down on the back of her neck, and her hands were sweaty. Empty air yawned beneath her, and she struggled not to look down.

"Not far, not far, not far . . . ." Turgesu repeated it like a chant, whispered on laboured breaths. Asta wondered which one of them he was trying to convince.

There was a platform above her head, and the ladder disappeared through a hole in it. They had passed other platforms, but this one was wider, and beyond it there were no more rungs. Asta scrambled sideways to avoid Turgesu as his head emerged through the gap. She looked around, and the world lurched beneath her feet. She uttered a short scream, and grabbed for the pole behind her as the world dropped away.

"It's all right." Turgesu extended a hand towards her. "You're quite safe."

"Safe? You call this safe?" One of her father's curses was all she could muster in the situation. "*Fuck* am I safe! Why have you brought me here?"

His brow furrowed. "You said you wanted to see."

Asta could see, once her head stopped spinning at the distance unveiled before her. Below, impossibly tiny, was the deck of the boat that had stolen her and brought her here, white sails like discarded cloths. Behind her was the sea, vast, endless, brilliant blue and hazy through the scarf that shrouded her eyes. In front of her lay Mikligard, and the Scattering.

Mikligard was a grey and brown city of square houses, few more than two stories high, hugging the curves of the island. The ship stood against a grey wharf, and there were others in the harbour, loading and unloading. Unloading timber, fabric, cast metal, mysterious crates. Loading hides, live goats, driven bleating up the ramps and into the belly of the black-and-gold ship beside them that dwarfed Turgesu's vessel. Loading slaves.

She could tell they were slaves, even from that height. They shuffled along together, linked by a long chain that ran from one neck to the next. There were children there too, and she would have started forward if she hadn't been balanced so high, on such a small platform. She could only stare helpless as they vanished into the hold of the ship, just behind the goats.

"You can't do anything about it." Turgesu spoke close to her ear. "What do you think of the Scattering, my goddess?"

She tore her eyes from the ship and stared out over the city, wind whipping at the scarf across her face and dragging it loose on one side. The city was square, the roads laid out in geometric lines that made her eyes hurt. There were no straight lines where she came from. Beyond the distant city walls, the island rose, craggy and bare. Not one island, she noticed, but dozens, maybe hundreds. A land held together by bridges, and by the will of Turgesu's people to stamp order on the wild places of the world. It made her feel sick.

"Isn't it beautiful?"

"It looks like shit," she snapped. "I want to go home."

But she didn't want to go home at all. She wanted to go wherever the black-hulled ship was taking its brutalised human cargo. She wanted to go where Rhodan was.

Six

B Y THE TIME her feet hit the deck again, Asta was trembling all over. She didn't have the strength in her arms to push Turgesu's hand away as he drew the scarf back over her face. He looked hurt, almost bewildered, as if he couldn't understand why she would loathe the Scattering for all it stood for, all it had taken from her. He kept shaking his head, and muttering, "But this is your place!"

As if that made a spit of difference. As if some myth about her being a Goddess because of the light patches on her legs would make her love this unnatural, barren place, this cluster of islands with their barbaric ways. She wanted to punch and kick her way out of it, grab the boat, press a knife to Turgesu's throat and force him to sail away. How many men did it take to sail a boat this size? She guessed it was more than one.

He gripped her arm. "This way. We've wasted enough time."

There was a hinged door in the railing that surrounded the deck, up near the pointed end of the ship. A narrow ramp led down to the quayside, to a large tent perched right on the edge of the water. Her first step onto the Scattering would be into that tent. Was she forbidden from even walking on their land? Had the men been cleared from the wharf ahead of her passage? Certainly there was no one in sight, but she could feel eyes watching her from nearby buildings, and she sensed a stir in the air.

"Not the right time," Turgesu muttered, as he lifted the flap of the tent and ushered her under his arm into an enclosed room, canvas hot to the touch. Her legs were wobbly beneath her, and she almost fell, reeling like a drunkard until Turgesu took her arm to steady her.

"Careful," he said. "It takes a while to get used to being on land again. Take it slowly."

She shook him off. "I can walk by myself." She could, she found, if she concentrated on every step.

Her transport waited for her inside the huge tent. She had hoped for horses, longed for horses, but what stood before her was a litter, like one that would carry a wounded man, but high-sided and shrouded with curtains. Turgesu nodded towards it. "Get in and close the drapes. Tightly. Don't look out, if you value other men's lives."

"I don't give a shit about Scattering lives," she lied. "Where are you taking me?"

"Asta, you try my patience with your questions. Isn't it enough that you're here? Why must you always ask things I can't tell you?"

"Why must you always evade me?" she countered.

Turgesu grinned. "I'll miss sparring with you, *gudienne*. Get on the litter. It won't be long now."

When she arrived at wherever she was going, she could try and work out her escape. Running across the wharf leaving a trail of doomed men behind her seemed pointless. What could she do? Jump in the sea? Throw herself on the black ship and demand to know where they were going? Seek her stolen people in the markets Turgesu had spoken of? Her father had said, when she demanded stories of heroism from him, that sometimes it was more heroic to act quietly and calmly than to throw your blades in the air and make a scene. He was lying, she had thought then. Trying to get her to behave herself.

"What should I do?" she wondered aloud, as Turgesu gestured impatiently at the litter.

Go along with it. The voice seemed to come from directly

behind her left ear. Asta started, looking for someone who wasn't there. There was no one here but Turgesu.

"Goddess, I don't want to pick you up and throw you in, but I will . . ."

"I'm going." The litter was even hotter than the tent outside. Three layers of suffocation, with the gauze over her face. Could she take it off now? She raised her hand to it, and Turgesu shook his head as he shut the curtains, trapping her in soft, airless luxury.

"Fuck you." She ripped the gauze free and crumpled it in her fist. This was ridiculous. She would have laughed, if she hadn't been so hot and uncomfortable and frustrated that she felt like crying.

The litter swayed, rising from the ground, and she grabbed hold to steady herself. Turgesu's hand snaked through the curtains to grip her arm, and she wondered whether he meant the gesture as comfort or restraint. She was strangely grateful for it, and for the drift of air it allowed into the closed litter. She wished she could see out, as they swayed through the streets of Mikligard. Could people see her passing? Did they know their summer goddess had landed? Did they even care?

It wasn't a long journey, but she was sweating by the time the litter was set down. Turgesu held her firm, and she heard him exchanging low words with another man. She wondered if she could ask for a drink.

"Come." He pushed the curtains back. All Asta could see beyond him was white canvas, fluttering in the light breeze. More bloody tents, more hiding from the city. The canvas formed a tunnel between the litter and a small door. She couldn't see how big the building was she was being steered into. Couldn't see anything but white. The light made her head hurt.

The door swung open, and Turgesu led her into a stone hall with wooden beams supporting the roof. Asta had expected somewhere bigger, more impressive. She was still trying to clear her vision as a stranger's hands fell on her and a long, pinched face stared into hers.

"Is this her?" The new man was as bronzed as Turgesu, straight hair falling down around his ears, grey-streaked and limp. "You didn't give us much time . . ."

"You should have been ready," Turgesu replied. "It's your duty, after all."

"Are you sure it's her?"

Turgesu shrugged. "She has the marks. If you don't think it's her, sell her and I'll keep looking. I get paid either way."

Asta shook free of the lank-haired man's grip, spluttering in her own tongue. "You're *selling* me? You said I wasn't a slave!"

The stranger looked enquiringly at Turgesu, who translated. He laughed.

"What's funny?" she demanded.

"You're not a slave," Turgesu explained patiently. "I was hired to find the Summer Goddess. I found you. Olafur will decide if you are the *sumri gudienne* we have been praying for."

"I thought you decided that?" Asta felt sick. "What if I'm not?"

"Not for me to say. We must part now, my goddess."

Asta felt a wrench. She had not expected him to leave so soon, so suddenly. He had been her one constant since she had been taken from her tribe. She resented him, but how would she manage without him?

He smiled, as if he read her mind. "You will do well without me. If not—" He shrugged. "I can always resume the search." He raised her hand to his lips, and she recoiled from the touch. "But I believe you are the one we've been looking for."

"Come." Olafur caught her shoulder in a pincer grip.

She shook him off. "I can walk by myself."

"Walk by yourself, then." He sounded hurt. They were quick to take offence, these men of the Scattering. They acted like she should be grateful for this honour she had never wanted.

Olafur led her up a wide, carpeted flight of stairs, onto an opulent landing. He hustled her along, but she caught a glimpse of pictures, murals, the gleam of gold and gems. He ushered her through a door at the end of the landing, and two women, sitting sewing in cushioned armchairs, sprang to their feet at his entrance.

"*Mestari!*" the younger one cried. "We were not expecting you so soon!"

"That much is obvious," Olafur sneered.

The older woman folded her sewing neatly and tucked it into a bag at her feet. "Is it her?" She regarded Asta with bright, curious eyes.

"It has yet to be established. I thought that's why you were here, Gerhild?"

The older woman rubbed her hands, all business. "Does she speak our words?"

"I speak them well enough." Asta tried not to stumble, hoping her accent would pass muster. She wouldn't let these strangers belittle her, or dismiss her as an ignorant foreigner.

"Turgesu said she had some marks. Check them." Olafur took a seat in a high-backed chair beside the door, stretching his legs out in front of him. "Let's see what she's made of."

Gerhild nodded at her younger companion. "Leanti?"

Leanti picked up a long pair of cloth scissors, wicked sharp in her hand. "I'm ready."

Asta looked from the scissors to Leanti's open, smiling face, and dived for the door. She was fast, but Olafur was faster, catching her round the wrist and dragging her back into the room. He flung her to the carpet and stood over her, chest heaving.

"Why are you trying to run? We're not going to hurt you!"

The sunlight gleaming on silver blades made a lie of his words.

"Gerhild, we're going to need help here. Bring in Syven. No," his foot pressed against her throat as Asta tried to rise, "the less you struggle the quicker this will be over. For good or ill, we'll find out who you are."

"I know who I am! I'm not your fucking goddess!" She choked as he pressed harder against her windpipe.

"I'll judge that, daughter of the Western Land. Do you want to be bound? No? Then lie still." Olafur nodded to Leanti, who knelt at Asta's side. The cold metal brushed her cheek, and she flinched at the touch, remembering how her hair had tumbled down around her.

Leanti moved the scissors down, snagging against the neck of Asta's shirt, lifting it. The fabric parted, and Asta held her breath.

"Don't mark her skin." Olafur sounded bored, as if this happened every day.

"Skirt too?" Leanti asked.

"Everything. We need to see every inch of her, to be sure."

Asta's skirt fell away with three sharp slices of the scissors. She cringed away from the blades, fighting the urge to scream. Some tribes cut women between their legs, to make them more obedient. Did the Scattering do that? She would never obey, no matter what they did to her.

"Where are these marks?" Olafur demanded. He lifted his foot. "Roll over."

Asta swallowed hard. "Die, you piece of shit."

"Listen!" He dropped to his knees beside her, face close to hers. "I could decide you're not the one we're looking for. What do you think will happen to you then? It only takes one slip of the scissors and you're useless to me. Do as I say if you want to live." He gave her a shove, and she rolled, slowly. Letting him know he hadn't beaten her yet.

Leanti sat back on her heels and her breath hissed. "*Mestari,* look!"

"Do they match?" Olafur snapped a folding ruler from his belt. "Let me see!"

Asta felt him measuring the white patches on her legs, breath hot and excited. It made the back of her neck crawl. Her fingernails scratched against the wooden floorboards. She would not lose control, she wouldn't cry, or scream. No matter what they did to her.

"They match!" Olafur breathed the words, a long sigh. "She is perfect in every other way, too." He ran cold hands over her thighs, her back, his touch repellent to her skin. "No scars, no moles. Just these . . ." His mouth brushed the skin at the back of her knee and Asta kicked out, one foot catching the scissors and spinning them from Leanti's hand. She muttered a curse, sucking the cut on her palm.

Olafur's hand snaked out, grabbing Asta's ear, pulling her head back until her eyes watered at the pain. She struggled and tried to kick, but Leanti leaned heavily on her legs, and when Olafur let go her head thumped on the floor.

"Roll her over again," he said. "Better find out if she's pure. Even if she isn't, I'll argue in Council for her." He stroked the nape of Asta's neck, and his voice was reverent. "To find you, after so long . . . I had almost given up hope of it happening in my lifetime, but here you are!"

"I'm not who you think I am—" but he rolled her on to her back while she was still protesting. She was dizzy from the blow to her head, tired of fighting. Every limb ached with tension. If she gave them what they wanted, they might leave her alone. But she would bring shame on her tribe, her family, her father's name . . .

Leanti forced her hands between Asta's tightly-clamped thighs, pushing them apart. Where had the scissors gone? She felt the scream welling inside her, and she arched her back and lashed out, fist catching Olafur on the jaw, legs thrashing against empty air.

"Hold her down! Syven, get in here!"

The room was blurred with the tears that sprang to Asta's eyes. The door crashed open, and suddenly there were hands everywhere, pinning her down, cradling her head, forcing her legs apart. She felt the violation of Leanti's fingers, and she choked on a scream as a heavy hand clamped across her mouth.

"Well, Leanti?" Olafur demanded.

"I'd say she's not a virgin, but these horse tribes learn to ride before they can walk. It's possible she was broken by a horse, rather than a man."

"I'll tell the Council she's pure, then. That will sway them." He snatched his hand away as Asta tried to sink her teeth into the ball of his thumb. "I've no doubt she's our *sumri gudienne*.

This is a special moment, for all our people."

There was a respectful silence in the room. Asta's stifled sobs sounded loud to her own ears. Leanti wiped her fingers on a scrap of silk and tossed it behind her. She looked at Gerhild, and the stranger kneeling next to her with his weight pressing on Asta's calf, and she raised her eyebrows.

Gerhild voiced the unspoken question. "*Mestari?* What if she isn't? You'll tell them she has the marks, but what if she's just a horse-girl with blotchy skin?"

Olafur shook his head. "You don't understand, any of you. She's the Summer Goddess if I can convince the Council she is. We've waited so long for the right girl. We will *make* her our Goddess. We haven't got time to look for another one. You all know that." He cradled Asta's cheek, his thumb stroking her lips. "Do not weep, *gudienne*. You will save us all."

Asta pushed his hand away. "I'm not your goddess. I will never be your goddess." She felt heavy and defeated, knowing her words fell on stone. "The only people I care about saving are the women and children of my tribe. The ones you stole."

"You need to leave your tribe behind." Olafur stroked her hair as he got to his feet. "This needs to go. All of it. You horse-people set too much value on your hair. Leanti, get rid of it."

As the scissors scraped the back of her neck, Asta broke. "Please . . . You've taken everything else from me. Let me keep my hair . . ." The hot tears rolled down her cheeks, but Leanti was relentless, snipping her hair right back to her scalp. Asta huddled, knees drawn up to conceal her nakedness, more exposed than she had ever felt in her life as her hair fell around her. Her last shield, her final sense of self, sliced away. She was no warrior of her tribe, without her hair. Instead she was their Summer Goddess. That was all she was, all she was allowed to be, and she was too exhausted to fight any more, not today. Today she would be whatever they wanted her to be, but her heart and gut were sick at the prospect.

She was aware of a hand brushing the shorn hair from her

shoulders, her face, but the room was a messy wet blur. Her head ached, and her throat and chest were tight with weeping.

"Syven, make sure she doesn't kill herself, or you'll be explaining why to the Council," Olafur said. "Gerhild, Leanti, come with me. Her robes will need to be readied. There's much we still have to do." His hand landed on Asta's bowed head, a gesture that dislodged the cut hair around her ears. "So much responsibility, on the shoulders of one so young . . ." he murmured. "I leave her to your care, Syven."

Olafur swept out, ushering Gerhild and Leanti before him. Asta barely saw him leave, through eyes swimming with tears. She slumped, and strong arms caught her, held her while she cried herself out. She clung to the stranger, his skin more copper than brass, the only comfort she could find in this alien world, and as her head fell against his shoulder she felt herself lifted and carried. She was sure she should have mumbled a protest, but she was too tired to even form the words, much less make herself understood.

SEVEN

ASTA WOKE UP in bed, hot under the sheets, cold around her skull. She couldn't remember getting there. Her eyes stung, and she felt soiled from the day before. At the tower she had dived into the sea from her chamber window on sunny mornings, plunging down into the cool depths to free herself from the shackles of sleep. It seemed the most natural thing in the world. She wanted to feel that again. But everything about the Scattering was unnatural, twisted. There would be no diving here, she was sure. Just robes and Councils and hard-faced women with scissors.

Her head was too light as she lifted it, and there was movement by the window. She sat up, clutching the blankets to her chest, though he had seen everything of her last night. She burned at the humiliation.

"What are you doing in my room?"

"Waiting for you to wake up, my Goddess."

She held up a hand. "Don't . . . call me that. Why?"

Syven moved in front of the window. She couldn't see his face, just a blurred impression of metallic skin and bulk. He was tall and broad, a hulking barbarian in her room. She didn't want him anywhere near her.

"I am the guardian of your body. My one duty is to protect you, to see to your needs. Where else would I be?"

"I don't need anyone to guard me. I'm . . ."

"Not who you were last time the moons changed?" His teeth flashed. "I'll pour you a bath. Olafur will want you clean for the ceremony."

"What ceremony?"

"You are the Goddess. There has to be a ceremony."

"Get out!"

He let the door bang shut behind him, and the pillow she threw fell short of its target. Asta sank back, feeling quivery and lost. Now there was to be a ceremony? Did Olafur intend to parade her before his Council, shorn and humiliated? What did he expect her to do?

She ran her hands over her scalp, feeling the stubble. The pillow was covered in cut hair, which clung to her face and shoulders and prickled her skin. A bath would help that, but a bath meant dealing with Syven, and she doubted she could bear his presence. She scanned the room, trying to gather her jumbled thoughts.

The room only had high windows, like the slits for arrows her father had built in the tower. Too thin to escape from. There was only one door, the one Syven had left through. The furniture was bulky, crafted from solid wood. She saw nothing she could use as a weapon, even if she could have made a dent in the solid copper head of her bodyguard.

Clutching the blankets around her, she dragged an oaken chest across to one of the windows, and climbed up to look out. She was high up, far above the sloping roofs of Mikligard. They rolled over the low hills of the city, a blanket of dull colours. No green, no trees or fields. She saw the rocks rising high beyond the town, and sea birds wheeling in the sky. She wished she could see the ocean from her window, but the room faced inland. She could smell the sea, and the stink of the city, but saw nothing but houses, more houses than she had ever seen in her life. She knew there were many people in the world; her father had told her about the great western cities of Northpoint and Cape Carey, but she had never been able to imagine so many people living so close together, until now.

"Enjoying the view?" Syven lounged in the doorway. Asta swallowed the urge to curse. She hadn't heard him come in, and he had startled her. "Your bath is ready, my Goddess."

She had no weapon but her mind. She had to learn about this place, about the Summer Goddess, to be able to escape. The more she knew, the more chance she had to turn the situation to her advantage. If she was a Goddess, surely she had some power, some influence? "How many people live in the city, Syven?"

"As many as there are nests on the cliffs, Goddess."

Fuck you, then. Clearly he had been taking lessons in evasion from Turgesu. Did no one on the Scattering have a straight answer to a straight question?

"I'm a Goddess, Syven. You're supposed to answer my questions."

He merely smiled and bowed, holding the door open for her. She wasn't sure if he was mocking her. She noticed, as she passed, that his left ear was clipped, a neat triangle of skin taken out of the lobe in the spot where her people wore ear-jewellery.

The adjoining room was large and light, with floor-to-ceiling windows like a series of arches running the entire length of one wall. They looked out onto the sea. She caught a splash of blue, and the reflections rippled against the whitewashed wall opposite. She didn't have time to look for more than a moment, as Syven swept her through a curtained arch into the bathing room.

No windows in here, she noticed at once, dismissing it as a potential way out. The bath was a circular pool sunk into the floor, filled with gently steaming water, tiled with pale green mosaic. Four steps led down into the water, and there were towels heaped at the side of the pool.

Asta glared at Syven. "I suppose you want to watch?"

"I'll wait outside."

"So I don't try and throw myself out of one of the big windows?" He said nothing. "I wouldn't give you the satisfaction."

"I'm charged with making sure no harm comes to you, Goddess. By your hand, or anyone else's. I'll be outside when you're done."

He pulled the curtain tight behind him, and Asta wondered if he could see through it, if he was standing there staring at her, waiting for her to drop the blanket. The hair on her skin itched like insect stings, and the water looked so inviting . . .

"Ah, to the hells with it!" She let the blanket fall and stepped into the pool, gasping at the heat of the water as it lapped around her ankles, then her knees. When she sat on the bottom of the pool, the water reached her chin, and she ducked her head under the surface and scrubbed the last of the hair away from her neck and her ears.

She leaned back, head resting on the side, letting the water cradle her. She had not expected such luxury, after the violence and humiliation of the day before. And she valued the privacy. It gave her time to think.

Maybe she could command Olafur to bring the stolen people of her tribe to her? What was the point in being a Goddess, if only in name, if she couldn't make people do what she said? If she could find them, she could work out a way to get them home. She would not leave the Scattering without Rhodan, however long it took. She owed that much to her brother.

What happens at the end of summer?

Asta spluttered as she slipped under the water, and surfaced with a muffled curse. She had been dozing. The steam was off the water and her fingertips were wrinkled as dried fruit. She looked around for Syven, but she was alone in the room. And the voice hadn't been Syven's. It had spoken in the tongue of her tribe, so beloved, so familiar, that it brought homesick tears to her eyes. She ducked under the water one last time to cleanse her face, and climbed out of the pool, wrapping towels around her body and her head.

Syven stood on the far side of the big room, well away from the curtain. She had half-expected him to be standing smartly to attention beside the arch, but he stood with his back to her, staring out of the window. It crossed her mind that she could run and push him, send him toppling to his death. Instead she cleared her throat.

"I'm done."

"The *mestari* left robes for you. You're to wear them for the ceremony." He nodded towards a long, low table, where two bundles of turmeric-yellow cloth gleamed in the reflection from the window, bright as the sun. "Would you like me to help you into them?"

"When is the ceremony?" She could be evasive too, play the game as well as he could.

"Sunset."

"What does it involve?" Not turmeric-yellow, but poison-bright.

"Olafur will take you out on the balcony and introduce you to the people. They are already gathering to honour you."

He was being unusually forthcoming, and it made her skin prickle. "That's it?"

"Just that, for today."

"And . . . after today?" *What happens at the end of summer?*

"Olafur will tell you what you need to know, when you need to know it."

"Why can't you tell me?"

Syven inclined his head. "Even if I knew, it's not my place. Olafur speaks for the Council. Do you need my help?"

"I've been dressing myself since I was four years old. I don't need you."

"Then I'll empty your bath." He had an air of amusement about him, as if he laughed secretly at a joke she couldn't understand. He vanished behind the curtain, and she unfolded the robes and shook them out.

Belts and buckles, under-tunics and swathes of cloth. Random rectangles of fabric, and clips that seemed to have nothing to join on to. It was a world away from the simple shift she had arrived in, or the plain shirts and breeches the tribes wore. Was this one a head-dress, or a skirt? She picked it up and held it against her, turned it upside down and laid it down again, baffled. Maybe there was a way out of the window? She walked to the glass and laid her hand on the pillars on either side, staring out.

Below was a square surrounded by buildings, all built of whitewashed stone and dark red wood. People milled around, looking up in anticipation at her window, at the sky. Their faces were pinched and their clothes looked tired, and there was a weary air about them, as if they worked too hard and slept too little. Maybe they had stayed up all night waiting for the ceremony? She locked eyes with a tall, cadaverous man with wispy grey hair at the edge of the crowd, and drew back against the pillar.

"They can't see you." Syven's voice from behind her. He had a light tread for a big man. "The glass has been treated. You can see out, but they can't see in. They know you're up here, though. Olafur has made sure of that." He stirred the discarded pile of clothes with his foot. "Having trouble?"

"I'm fine!" Asta snapped, feeling small and stupid.

"Been dressing yourself since you were four, I know." He tossed her a loose shift. "Put this on first. I'll help you with the rest."

"I don't need your help."

He shrugged. "Do it yourself, then. I'll watch."

She glared at him, and he returned the look with a thin raised eyebrow, sitting down in an armchair facing the window and studying his nails as if she bored him utterly. She swore, wriggled her head and shoulders into the shift, and let the white towel drop at her feet.

"Dressed enough for you, my guardian?"

"Hardly."

She kicked the abandoned fabric. "What next?"

"The dress. Then that robe goes over the top. They clip together. The headscarf . . ."

"I'm not covering my head."

"Want everyone to see your warrior's braids, do you?" He said it mildly, without sneering, but the words cut her deep.

"My people don't . . ."

"This isn't the tribal lands, Asta!" He leapt up, seizing her by the shoulders. "It's easier for me to keep you safe if you go along with what Olafur wants. Not everyone out there" – he waved towards the window – "accepts or welcomes the Summer Goddess yet. Don't fight our ways, and they could come to love you."

"I don't *want* them to love me! I want my family back, and I want to go home . . ." She wiped her angry tears on the rippling fabric. "If I do as you say, will that happen?"

"Get dressed, my Goddess, and things will go better for you. Here." He held out the heavy dress so she could step into it. It had a wide swathe of blue around the cuffs and the hem, which brushed the floor. It covered up the patches at the backs of her knees, and she was glad she wouldn't have to show them off. She had barely thought about them before, accepting them as part of her skin, but these people seemed obsessed.

She stretched around to fasten the laces.

"Let me." Syven's fingers were calloused against her wrist as he pushed her hand aside. He pulled the bonds tight, drawing in her waist until it was hard to take a full breath in. His hand lingered on the back of her neck, brushing away the last of the stray hair. She could hear water trickling in the distance, the murmur of the crowd in the square below, but the air was suddenly very still.

"My Goddess . . . ."

"Is she ready?" The door thumped open. Syven let his hand drop and stepped aside so smartly Asta wondered if she had imagined the touch. Olafur stood on the threshold, dressed in a robe of high sky-blue. Eagle's wings drooped from his shoulders, and a hook-beaked mask hung from one hand. "I thought you'd have her ready by now!"

"I fell asleep in the bath." Asta had no reason to defend Syven, but she disliked the injustice almost as much as she disliked being talked about as if she wasn't there.

"Do I have to do everything myself?" A vein on Olafur's temple throbbed, and his hands shook as he draped the outer robe over her shoulders. "Nothing can go wrong today, do you understand me? The Council took considerable persuasion . . . You must do as I say, *gudienne,* or we are all lost."

Asta pushed him away as he tried to wrap the cloth around her head. "Why? You can't stop me saying what I like in the ceremony. How about I go out there and scream to your people that you kidnapped me, you murdered my tribe? That I spit on your Goddess and everything she stands for! How would your Council feel about that, Olafur?"

He let the cloth fall. "You wouldn't do that."

"Why not? It's the truth."

"Please, Goddess," he twisted the headdress in his hands. "Please do this thing. So many people are relying on you . . ."

"You are, you mean? You don't want me to make you look bad in front of your council, is that it?"

"You don't understand!"

"I don't *want* to understand!" But she heard the weakness in his cry. Olafur badly wanted something from her, and that was her leverage. It wasn't much, but it was all she had.

"Listen," she snatched the cloth from his hands. "I'll play your puppet, your Goddess, but I want something from you in return."

"You are not in a position to negotiate, Asta."

"Oh really?" The cloth tore between her fingers, and Olafur twitched. "I'm sorry, I've completely forgotten what you wanted me to say. I could say anything that comes into my head out there. How could you stop me, without gagging me? How would that look, a mute prisoner Goddess? Very powerful . . ."

She ripped the headscarf another inch, and Olafur lunged for it. "What do you want?"

"I want my nephew back." He looked blank. "My brother's son. Your people killed my brother, and you took Rhodan from the beach, with his mother. I want my people, all my people, brought back to me."

"Women and children? You would defy me over a bunch of slaves?"

"They may be slaves to you, but my tribe is my family, and I swore to protect them. And for them, I would defy you to the ends of the earth. So, do we have a deal?"

His lips thinned. "I'll see what I can do. I can't promise anything. If you behave well . . . anything is possible."

Asta had to be content with that. She sensed she had pressed her luck as far as it would go today. She nodded, and let him wrap the cloth around her skull, binding it so tight her head ached with the pressure. "What would you have me do?" she asked.

"Just do as I tell you. Agree to everything. Be demure and well-behaved, and it will go better for both of us." He glanced at Syven. "For all of us. I'll do what I can about your people."

"Thank you." She allowed him to lead her towards the end of the room, to a door she had previously mistaken for part of the wood panelling, so cleverly was it disguised. It had no visible catch, but it clicked open as he leaned his weight against it. Another potential escape route?

He must have seen her looking. "I wouldn't try it," he said. "Wait here until I call you."

He vanished through the door, to reappear a moment later on the balcony on the far side of the glass. She could hear his muffled voice, the expectant hum of the crowd rising in pitch. She felt Syven's steadying hand on her elbow, and realised she was trembling.

"You'll be fine," he said in a low voice. "Go on, he's calling you."

The tint on the windows must keep out the worst glare. As Asta stepped out onto the balcony the low sun was dazzling, forcing her to screw up her eyes. She was hit by a wall of sound, a roar that almost swept her from her feet. She stumbled, and Olafur caught her outstretched hand and drew her towards him. His lips were moving, but she couldn't make out his words over the sound of cheering.

"Look at them!" he barked, directly into her ear. "Acknowledge them! They're your people, they need you."

Asta waved awkwardly, and a collective sigh rose from the gathered throats. Olafur pushed her forward. "Talk to them. They need to hear your voice."

"What do I say?" she asked.

"Tell them you've come to save them."

Asta stepped forward, clenching her hands against the stone balustrade, and looked out over the crowd that filled every inch of the square. As she opened her mouth a hush fell, broken only by a child crying softly in the throng. The cry was a soft pull against her heart. Everything she did, she did for Rhodan, and for her people, for the chance of getting them back.

"People of the Scattering! I am the Summer Goddess! I'm here to save you!"

A ripple ran through the crowd, people falling to their knees, on to their faces, dragging their neighbours down with them. One man stood alone. He held something in his hands, but she couldn't see it clearly.

Asta! Look out!

At the silent command, she ducked instinctively. She heard a crack, right beside her ear, saw a puff of dust and stone shear free from the wall. A heavy weight against her back threw her to the floor. Olafur yelled, but she couldn't understand his words, and the square was full of screams and panic. There was blood on her face, staining the yellow robes, and the ringing in her ears made everything a jumble.

"Syven!"

At Olafur's shout Syven was there, lifting Asta in his arms, cradling her bleeding head against his chest. Four long strides and he was back to the door, behind the glass, into the safety of her rooms. The roars outside were muted, but they had a different tone now, celebration giving way to panic, to anger.

Syven dumped her on the couch. Asta tried to sit up, but his heavy hand against her chest held her still. The cloth in his other hand was cold as he pressed it to her scalp. Everything had happened so quickly it was hard to make sense of it.

"Did you shout?" she asked.

Syven shook his head. "Shout what? Maybe someone in the crowd . . ."

"It doesn't matter." She turned on Olafur. He was pacing a tight line before the high windows that shone blood-red with the sunset. "What happened? You said your people wanted to worship me, not kill me!"

The cloth of his ceremonial robe was bunched in his tightly-clenched fists. "That was . . . unfortunate."

"Unfortunate? He nearly took my head off! What the shit is going on?"

"That was not supposed to happen!" He paced from the window to the table, back to the window, his face bathed in the fading light. He took in a deep breath and clasped his hands, but he couldn't disguise the tremble in his fingers. "There are . . . certain factions of our society who don't believe in the Summer Goddess. Don't believe she can save us. Some are violently opposed to the idea. And some think you would be better off away from the protection of the Council . . . You are perhaps not what they would have expected. A Goddess from our own people would be more acceptable. But it's too late now. You are who you are, for good or ill."

Asta sat up, and pushed away Syven's hand that held the cloth. "You haven't told me," she said, "what it is you expect me to save you *from*. Or how."

"Always defiant, Asta. Haven't I given you enough today?"

"You nearly got me killed! You've given me nothing!"

He glared at her for a long, obstinate moment, meeting her gaze with equal stubbornness. "If I can find you some information about your boy, will you stop asking questions?"

If you bring me Rhodan, I will be the best Goddess your stinking isles ever had. "That would do for a start, yes."

"I'll see what I can do. Syven, a word?" Olafur beckoned

her big guardian out of the room with him. As the door closed behind them Asta collapsed back on the sofa. Her head ached and her limbs trembled from the shock of the assault, but there was a tiny flame of elation burning in her heart. The voice that had warned her she was in danger, the voice she heard on the ship . . . She had finally recognised it. Not only recognised it but knew, in the vaguest way, how to reach it. She had been stolen, stripped, shorn, shamed, but she had something Olafur and his Council knew nothing about, and that was a source of power.

When Syven returned he carried a tray of food, a dish of the lumpy fish porridge that appeared at every meal, and some pitifully thin strips of roast meat and roots. He smiled, as if he carried a secret. "I've got something for you."

From behind his back he drew a smooth-skinned yellow fruit. It was the first fresh fruit Asta had seen since she left the village, and she almost snatched it from his hands, sinking her teeth into the soft flesh. "Where did you get this?" she mumbled, dribbling juice down the crumpled, bloodstained ceremonial robe.

"I stole it from a dish downstairs. For a Goddess, they don't feed you well. The Council take more than their share. Don't tell Olafur!" He winked, as if drawing her into a conspiracy against Olafur and his cronies on the Council.

"How's your head?" he asked, as she spat the pips into her hand. "I'll take them, we always need seeds." He wrapped them in a cloth and stashed them carefully in his pocket.

"It's only a scratch."

"Let me see." He brushed supple fingers over her scalp, and she slapped his hand away.

"Don't touch my head, Syven. It feels too strange."

"I'm sorry, my Goddess. Does it hurt?"

It stung. "I'm fine. What was it?"

"A catapult. An inch lower and you would have been dead."

"No Goddess for you then?" She tried to make light of it, but she felt a growing sickness in the pit of her stomach.

"We would all have been doomed, not just you."

"Why? What am I going to do that's so special? How can I do anything if you won't tell me what you want me to do? What happens at the end of summer, Syven?"

"I can't—" He was interrupted by a knock at the door. Asta started up, but he shook his head at her. "I'll get it."

Leanti was at the door, with a note. She and Syven had a muttered exchange, but Asta was too tired to strain her ears to catch it. She heard Syven say "I'll give it to her," as he closed the door, and she straightened in the chair.

"What's that? What do you have for me?"

"A note from Olafur."

"Give it to me! What does it say?"

"That your boy is unharmed, and safe." He turned the paper over, as if expecting something more on the back. "That's it."

"That's it? That tells me nothing!" She whipped the paper from his hand, stabbing at the pictures. "What does this mean?"

"What I said. No more."

"That can't be all, Olafur promised . . ." Her face burned, and she crumpled the paper in her hand and flung it towards the window. "He tricked me!"

"He said he'd see what he could do." Syven shrugged. "Maybe he could do no more than that?"

"Why not? Doesn't he have the power to buy and sell people?"

"He does . . ." Syven's hand brushed his clipped ear. "Maybe your boy has already been sold on. Maybe his buyer doesn't want to part with him. Olafur's power is not limitless. There are . . ." He clamped his lips shut.

"There are what? People on the island more powerful than Olafur?" Asta sat up straighter. "I want to see them, if that's the case."

"We can't allow that, my Goddess."

She sank back in her seat. "Fuck him then," she said. "And fuck you too. I'll find him myself." She slumped in the chair, trying not to cry. Rhodan might be safe, if Olafur wasn't lying about that too, but that didn't mean he was in Mikligard, or even on the Scattering.

"I'm sorry you're upset." Syven's thumb wiped away the tear that crept down her cheek. "I wish there was something I could do."

His open sympathy, his touch, ignited the adrenaline that still coursed through Asta's limbs after the attack. She was so alone, so far from home, and Syven was the one man who seemed to care. Who saw her as more than just a puppet Goddess to be turned to his purpose.

She caught his wrist and bought the palm of his hand to her lips. He stiffened, but didn't pull away.

"My Goddess – Asta – you shouldn't be doing that."

"Why not?" She wanted his hands on her. She craved the sensation of touch, fingers against her skin. "Does Olafur forbid it? Are you scared of his anger?"

"Olafur doesn't scare me." Syven helped her to her feet. His fingers brushed the shimmering cloth of her ceremonial dress in a way that made her quiver. "It's you that scares me."

"Me?" He was standing so close she felt his breath on her face, but he was taking great care not to touch her. "Why do I scare you? I have no power here."

"Because if anything happens to you, Olafur will have me flayed alive. You're so wild, Asta! I know your tribal ways, and they scare me. You'd think nothing of leaping from the balcony to escape. And you have power over me. I am the guardian of your body. I am yours to command, within these walls, as long as that command wouldn't harm you, or my people."

Asta shrugged. "What good is a Goddess with no power? What good is a leader who can't defend her own family?" The tears were threatening again, and she blinked them back. "Help me out of these stupid robes, Syven."

She turned her back on him so he could free her from the laces. His fingers brushed her throat, her shoulders, the hollow at the small of her back, as he let the fabric fall around her hips. He muttered something that sounded like "flat arse."

Asta turned around. "What did you say?"

Syven's eyes were downcast. "I'm sorry, my Goddess."

"Never mind sorry, what did you call me?"

"We have a name for your people . . . They say you spend so much time on horseback your arses are flat . . ." He pushed the dress to the floor, one hand smoothing over her buttocks. "It's true. I like it."

"You like it?"

"It's different." He grinned, digging his fingers in to pull her closer. Asta allowed him to push the shift from her shoulders, letting him trace the outline of her nipples with his thumb. "Not flat," he observed.

"Not right now, no."

His mouth was warm, eager, and Asta responded to it. The last few days had been too much. If she could lose herself in desire, she could ease the turmoil in her head. And danger always roused her lust. The best times with Nochai had always been on the hunt, after the chase and the kill.

"*Gudienne*, are you sure?" Syven's hands stilled against her hips, lips brushing her throat.

"You said you were mine to command . . ."

"I am yours, my Goddess." He drew her down to the floor, one hand pressed into the curve of her back. "Yours to command . . . ."

Asta woke, lying on the floor in a patch of moonlight. Her limbs were tangled with Syven's, sticky-sweet with sweat. He lay on his back, one arm flung out, and there were bruises and bite marks on his chest and upper arms. Had she done that? She couldn't remember.

She pushed his legs away, and his eyelids fluttered. "Goddess?"

"I want a bath."

Syven rolled over, and groaned. "It's not dawn yet. The fires are banked for the night. The water will be cold."

"I don't care about cold water. I used to bathe in the sea." Would she ever touch the sea again, Asta wondered. She sat up, fighting a stab of homesickness. "If you won't let me near the sea, at least let me wash."

"As my Goddess commands." Syven rose, pulling on his breeches and running his hands through his close-cropped copper hair that needed no tidying.

The moment he vanished into the bathroom, Asta wriggled into her shift. If she was in the bath, she hoped she would be left alone for long enough. She had never tried this journey before, but now she had recognised the insistent voice in her mind, it was time to act.

She paced anxiously before the window, stomach growling with hunger. The moonlight streamed through the treated glass, bands of pale blue striking across the floor. She walked from light to dark, to light again. The world was monochrome. If she lit a lamp she could chase out the shadows, but her mind was turned to dark purpose, and she let them stay.

"Goddess? Your bath is filled."

Syven stood in a patch of light, his skin suffused with blue. He looked worried. Probably anxious that Olafur would find out what they had done. Well, Olafur didn't own Asta.

"Can you get some food for when I come out?" She would be exhausted on her return. Such travel was draining.

"I don't know. The kitchens—"

"Steal some then. You did that last time." The longer she kept him away the better.

"I'll see what I can do. I'll bring fresh towels, too."

"Go on then." She stood with her back to the night, watching him leave. As soon as she heard the lock drop, she headed for the bathroom, pulling her shift over her head as she walked. By the time her toes touched the water, she was naked and the dress lay in her hands, shredded into long strips. There was a metal ring embedded in the wall, and a small hand towel hung from it. She flung the towel towards the pool, and knotted the strips of fabric together to form a rope. She tied one end to the ring, the other around her left wrist, tugging to make sure it was secure.

Her father had told her how it was done. When he was alive she had harboured ambitions to become a shaman, and he encouraged them, teaching her about ancient ceremonies, healing herbs and journeys into the world beyond. Until her mother's claws and teeth had taken him away from her, and sent her galloping down a different path.

She wouldn't think of that now. She sat against the wall, wrist pulled awkwardly behind her by the short tether. She closed her eyes and searched through her memories, looking for a moment of peace, of harmony shared, that she could fall into, focussing on that memory with all her will.

The world inside her eyelids turned misty grey and Asta tumbled forward, head over heels into the Spirit Realm.

Eight

I T WAS HER tower, her home, but it wasn't. It looked like a painting on the cliff wall, flat and almost featureless. The sea was as smooth and dull as a blanket, and it made no sound. Even the mewling gulls were silenced. It was as if heavy gauze lay over the landscape, smothering all natural sound and movement.

No puffs of sand rose from her feet as she walked along the shore, and no pebbles clicked or shifted with her footsteps. Her tread was as silent as the heavy paws of her mother, but he must have heard or sensed her approach. He had been sitting on a low rock staring out across the ocean, but now he looked up. His face was grave.

"What are you doing here?" he asked.

Asta stopped walking. She had been so sure of her reception, but now it seemed she was an intruder. "You called me. You *kept* calling me. I thought you needed me?"

"I *need* my wife and son brought home safely!" Finn sprang to his feet and strode across to her. His slap passed through the flesh of her face as if he had dashed her skin with freezing water.

"Hey! What was that for?"

"You fucked him. Rhodan and Lefalli are missing, and all you can do is rut on the floor with the savage? How could you, Asta?"

"He's not a savage . . ." but Finn turned away in disgust. That wasn't what he wanted to hear.

"Where's Rhodan?" he demanded. His voice was hoarse. "Where's my wife? What have you done to find them?"

"Lefalli, I don't know . . . But they tell me Rhodan's safe—" Her words sounded as pathetic as Olafur's note.

"Safe? They bought your body with 'safe?' I *died,* Asta! I died to protect him, and you've done nothing to get him back!"

"I'm doing all I can!" she protested. Finn's face spoke his betrayal, but at least it wasn't the bloodied mask she had washed clean in the sea that took his body. He looked whole, unhurt. As long as she avoided his eyes. "How can I find him? They keep me locked up. I can't even walk under the sky. No one will answer my questions. So tell me, little brother, what would you do in my place?"

He stared at her for a long moment, lips working soundlessly. There was no wind, and his fair braids hung lifeless around his face.

"You can't think of anything either?" Silence. "Finn! Answer me! Tell me how I can fix this!"

He hung his head, toe digging into the flat sand. "I don't know," he muttered. He sounded broken, and as Asta stepped towards him he slumped down on the rocks once more, shoulders sagging in defeat. She felt a rush of sympathy for him, and a terrible, crushing responsibility.

"Finn, I'm sorry." She sank down beside him, the tips of her fingers sinking through his to rest on the smooth stone beneath. "I'm sorry you died. I'm sorry about Rhodan, about everyone. It was my fault . . ."

"Because you saw the sails, and dismissed them? Any man would have done the same. It doesn't make you a bad leader." He shrugged. "I don't care about being dead. Rhodan is still alive. That's all I care about. Him and Lefalli. And you." He managed a smile. "Even if you are bedding the foreigner!"

"How did you know about that anyway?" Asta asked.

"I can see your thoughts." He grinned. "You don't hide them very well. You're a dirty girl, my sister!"

"Shut up!" Her punch passed through his upper arm, and she let her hand fall. "Does that hurt?"

"No punch or kick or arrow can hurt me now." He stretched out his legs, disturbing the quicksilver surface of the sea. "But I'm tired, Asta. My mind is churning with worry, all the time. I can't make it settle, not until I know Rhodan is safe. You need to get him back for me."

"What about Lefalli? I don't know if the brass men kept them together, whether they kept them with the other people they took." Her toes stirred the water. "If I have to choose between finding them . . ."

"Find Rhodan. Lefalli would want that too." Finn's face clouded. "I don't know about her . . ."

"You don't know if she's dead?" Asta glanced around the empty beach. "Wouldn't she be here, if she was?"

"I don't know if that's how it works," Finn confessed. "I would have thought . . . on the beach, when it happened . . . There were lots of us, but I'm here alone. I don't know if she'll join me, in the end . . ." He rested his head in his hands for a moment, but when he lifted his face, his eyes were dry.

"Lefalli," he went on, "she was always strong. Stronger than me in lots of ways. She'll ride her own path, in the world of the living or in this one. But Rhodan is my own blood. I know he's alive, and he's scared. I can feel it in my gut, his blood crying out for comfort. You have to get him back."

"How? I'm on my own, Finn. I'm a prisoner on a strange island where no one will talk to me about anything real. They've fed me snippets and lies, nothing of substance. If I could get out and look for him, trust me, I would."

Finn raised his head. His fingers twitched. "You came here, didn't you?"

"That's different, Finn. A different kind of escape. It doesn't help me save Rhodan, does it?"

"But if you came here," his eyes brightened, "I could come back with you, maybe . . ."

"Come back? How?" He said nothing. "You're dead, Finn. There's no coming back."

"Yet here you are talking to me as if I still lived. The road to the Spirit Realm can be travelled both ways. Father told me—"

"He never told me . . ." The rope at her wrist twisted unexpectedly, and she snatched at it in alarm with her right hand.

"What's wrong?" Finn asked sharply.

"Someone's messing with my lead rein. I have to go back." Asta tightened her grip as the fabric uncoiled from her left wrist, rising panic in her chest. If she let go of the rope, how would she find her way back? No one in the Scattering knew the secrets of the Spirit Realm, and whoever was trying to free her could kill her with his clumsy, misguided efforts.

"Take me with you!"

"How? Finn, I—"

His cold hand slipped like water through the flesh of her wrist, and closed around the fabric. It jerked hard, nearly wrenching Asta's arm from its socket. The beach darkened, calm sea and dull sand falling away beneath her feet. For an instant she felt her brother, his arm around her waist, his hand clutching next to hers on the rope that drew them both back to the world of the living. And then her back slammed against solid marble, with a jolt that forced her eyes open to candlelight, to Syven's anxious face looming over her, and she was alone.

Not quite alone. There was an itch in the back of her mind. Something new nestling in her skull, that hadn't been there before.

Finn?

No reply. If she had brought him back, he wasn't talking to her now.

"Asta! Asta, what are you doing? Are you hurt?" Syven had a firm grip on her shoulders, shaking her slightly. Asta's lead rein was draped across his arm. "What is this, my Goddess?"

"I was—" she choked, her throat parched. Her limbs ached as if she had a winter fever, and her head pounded. Her father had said travel between this world and the Spirit Realm was hard on the body, but she had underestimated how hard.

Syven scooped some tepid water from the bath into his hands and trickled it down her throat. "Asta? What's going on?"

"Help me stand." As he pulled her to her feet her knees buckled, and she slumped against his arm. In a single, easy move, he scooped her up and carried her into the lounge, laying her on the couch with a cushion under her head. The sun was up, the sky behind the glass a dull pink, and it was several degrees warmer than in the bathroom. Syven pressed a honeyed biscuit into her hand and poured a glass of fruit juice. Asta stared at the biscuit without seeing it.

"Eat. If you're faint you need sugar in your body."

"I'm not faint." But the sweetness of the biscuit steadied the tremor in her hands, and after a second one she felt well enough to sit up.

Syven pulled up a footstool and sat beside her head, taking the glass from her unresisting fingers and setting it on the floor. "Goddess? What were you doing in the bathroom?"

Asta was silent, trying to think of an explanation he would understand, that wouldn't lead to more restriction on her movements.

"Were you trying to hang yourself?"

"No! Why do you think that?" Even in her darkest moments, suicide had never crossed her mind for more than a few moments. She had made a promise to her brother. She couldn't find Rhodan if she was dead.

"The rope . . ." It lay over the back of the sofa. "Why make a rope, if not for suicide or escape?"

Asta licked her lips. They tasted sweet from the biscuit, and the sweetness made her jaw ache.

"I was meditating," she said.

"Meditating? With a rope?"

"It's the way of my people." His doubtful expression forced her to explain more than she wanted to. "When we go into a trance, it's very deep, deeper than sleep. Nearly as deep as death.

The rope tethers us to this world, stops us falling into darkness. It's a sacred tradition of my people."

Syven raised his pale eyebrows. "I never heard of it."

"You have no interest in my people, though, do you? You herd us as goats, fit only for slavery, but you don't give a shit about our traditions, our culture. Only," her hand brushed her scalp, "only when you can find a way to use them against us."

"Asta," he reached for her, and she pushed his hand away.

"No. You've taken away everything I have; my home, my identity as a warrior, my family . . . Can't you let me have this one thing, this last connection to my tribe?"

Syven narrowed his eyes. "What do you see when you're in this trance? Can you talk to your people?"

"No," she lied, "but I can see my home, see how my tribe are surviving without me. It's very spiritual, and I don't feel comfortable talking about it with you."

"Olafur will have to be told."

"Why? It's none of his bloody business!"

"Because it might be a risk to you." His hand brushed her cheek as he rose to stand with his back to the window. "What if I had untied your rope, without realising, and we had lost you forever to your trance?"

The sun was behind him, streaming through the glass. It was hard to make out his expression. She followed him, onto her feet, trying again to make him listen. "Syven? Why are your people so scared of losing me? You've never told me what I'm here to do. If you tell me, I'll do it, and then I can go home. Can't I?"

His fingers brushed her throat. "Maybe I'm the one who's scared of losing you, Goddess."

"Why?" Her hand reached up, mirroring his gesture, found the notch clipped from Syven's right earlobe. Too regular to be an accident. "What's a big man like you got to be scared of?"

"The Council will rip the hide from my bones if anything happens to you. My one duty, above all others, is to protect you."

She shrugged. "Couldn't you just tell Olafur you don't want

that duty any more? Make them give it to someone else?" *Someone less vigilant, less conscientious . . . .*

"A slave doesn't pick and choose what orders to obey, Asta. You should know that by now."

Asta grew cold, a chill that had nothing to do with her journey between the Realms. "You're a slave?"

He caught her hand and drew it to his lips. "You touched my slave mark, on my ear. I thought you knew?"

"Slave mark?" By all the spirits, had they held Rhodan down and sliced a chunk out of his ear, branded him as no more than a possession? In the dark of her mind, Asta felt Finn's howl of rage and grief.

I'll get him out, brother. I swear it.

She swallowed her revulsion. "Were you born a slave, then?"

Syven chuckled. He seemed remarkably at home with his fate. "Not me! I fell into a debt I couldn't pay back, and this is my punishment. Maybe one day I'll win my freedom again."

"You can do that?"

"Some are born slaves and die slaves. It's easier to earn your freedom if you were born a free man."

"If I bought a slave, could I free him?" Wild plots burst like bubbles on the surface of Asta's mind.

Syven laughed. "Do you want to free me, little Goddess? What do you have to trade, besides your smile?"

"How much would I need?" Asta tried to keep her voice light, but inside she seethed. Maybe it was all a game to Syven, but she was in deadly earnest. "Don't mock me. I'm serious. How much?"

"More than you could afford, Asta of the Western Tribes. More horses, and more gold. But you don't need to worry about me." He smiled. "I can win my freedom by keeping you safe. That's all I have to do. So if you want me to be free, all you have to do is behave, just for a few months."

"Until the end of summer?"

Syven nodded.

"What happens at the end of summer?"

"The cold wind blows off the sea. Come," he extended a hand to her. "You must be tired. Would you like me to warm your bed?"

Still she hesitated. "If I do what you say, Olafur will free you?"

"That's the size of it, yes."

"What about meditating? Can I still meditate? I need peace for that. I need to be alone in the room . . ."

Syven looked doubtfully at the rope. "I don't see that it would do any harm," he admitted.

"Then I'll be your good little Goddess, until the end of summer." *At least in this realm.* Asta yawned. She was tired from travel, and the idea of her bed was appealing. "I'm going to bed. To *sleep.* You can do as you please." She stretched out before the window, feeling the sunlight on her face, drinking in the little patch of sky she could see from here and concealing her smile. She had made a crack in the walls of her prison, and soon she would prise it open.

Across the square, something fluttered, like a great black crow hovering between the pillars. She squinted against the sun. "Syven? What's that?"

"Come away from the window, my Goddess." His voice was sombre. "You don't want to see."

"Why not?" A cloud passed the face of the sun, throwing a shadow across the square. Across the humble petitioners of Mikligard, who bowed their heads at the balcony as they passed, and across the thing that looked like a crow. It wasn't a bird. It had once been a man, before the skin was torn from his back and spread out between the pillars like great bloodied wings. He was tied hand and foot, a grisly star shape against the sky, and the sun shone through the thin skin spread between the pillars, tanning it the rich red hue of autumn.

Asta didn't make it to the bathroom before she was sick, doubled up, eyes and nose streaming. Syven silently massaged her back while she heaved until there was nothing left to come up. She choked, and spat.

"What the fuck *was* that?"

"The man who tried to kill you. It's right he should be punished for his crime. An example to the others . . ." Syven trailed off.

"An example? Is that what you call it? Torture and murder!"

"It's not murder—" but she didn't want to hear his excuses.

"Yes it is! Slavery and murder and public flayings! What kind of savages are you? You're inhuman, all of you!" She pushed past him as he tried to console her, turning her back on the window, on its gruesome spectacle.

"Olafur said you'd be pleased!"

"Pleased? Shit on that! No," as he reached out to her once more, "don't touch me. I won't be your Goddess. Not yours, not Olafur's. You people make me sick."

"Asta! I—"

The bedroom door slamming behind her cut off his words. She sank down against it, head in her hands, trembling in fury and disgust. If the men of Mikligard could do that to one of their own, a free citizen, how did they treat their slaves? How could Olafur think she'd be pleased with such a grisly trophy? They lived in a different world to her, and she felt small, very homesick and incredibly alone.

Not alone. The touch was light, the briefest hug around her hunched shoulders. Finn was still with her, that burning spark of spirit swirling inside her. She didn't know how it would help her, but it was a comfort knowing he was there.

Syven hammered on the door. "Asta? Are you all right?"

"Leave me alone!" she cried. But later, when the stuffiness of the room became unbearable and she needed a warm touch on her skin, she let him back into her bed, and into her body. She could feel her brother's silent condemnation, but Finn was spirit only, and what she craved was a warm living embrace, and a beating heart next to hers.

NINE

FINN? COME OUT, talk to me. I don't have much time; he'll be back soon. Finn?"

There was silence. Communication with her brother was hard enough when he was willing to talk, but now she sensed he was sulking. Probably muttering something under what passed for his breath about her betrayal. Well, fuck him. Any man held hostage in her situation would have used his body to get a female captor on side. It shouldn't be any different for her.

"Don't make me come in there and get you."

No reply. Asta sighed, and looped the silken rope around her wrist. She didn't know where Syven had got it from. She suspected it was one of the cords Olafur used to hold his day robes together. She had been surprised and touched when he pressed it into her hand.

"Save you from ripping up the sheets," he said.

She tied the other end of the cord to the towel loop, lay down on the cushions she had dragged in from the sofa, and thought about Finn, about how she wanted to be where he was, even if he didn't want her there. The fall between the realms took a long time, and when she opened her eyes, she was still in the bathroom.

"Shit."

"What's the matter, sister? Can't find what you're looking for?"

Asta sat up sharply. He was nowhere in sight. "Finn, that's not funny! Where are you?"

"Right here." He appeared on the edge of the empty pool, legs dangling. His braids were pinned up hunting style, criss-crossing his head, and seeing them reminded her of her own loss. One hand passed over her scalp, and she saw his brow furrow. "You take their men, Asta, you take their ways."

"I had no choice and you know it." She changed the subject. "What are you doing here? This isn't the Spirit Realm."

"Isn't it?" He beamed. "Look down, Asta."

Her body slumped on the cushions, on her knees, head hanging forward. One arm twisted up behind her, caught on the cord that ran from her wrist. She looked dead.

"Am I dead?" She hadn't felt her spirit part from her body. She thought she would have been in pain. She should have felt something.

"Not really dead, no," Finn said. "But your spirit is no longer in your body. Sever the tie to this world, and you will be."

The cord was silver around her wrist, like a bangle. When she twisted her arm it slithered cold and snake-like across her skin.

"Where am I then?" she asked.

"Exactly where you were."

"But I can see you, talk to you . . . ."

"You still can't touch me." He jumped to his feet and walked towards her, across the empty air that filled the bathing pool. The effect was unnerving. It made her eyes water, and she had to look away.

"Asta." He stepped down from empty air in front of her. "Asta, look at me. I'm as real as you are."

She could see the blond roots of his hair drawn up tightly into his braids, the distinctive dusting of freckles across his nose, the pale skin that marked him as their father's son. His deep black eyes were the only hint of her mother about him, until he smiled, and flashed his sharp canines.

"Can anyone else see you?" she asked.

Finn shook his head. "They can't see you, either. We can't touch anything, but we can learn. Come on!"

He held out his hand. Asta felt a twinge of excitement at their rebellion. "Where are we going?"

"We're going to find Rhodan. I'll carry you in my head, the way you carry me. Just grab my hand."

"You said I couldn't touch you—"

Finn gestured impatiently. "Take it!"

"You know you were a lot more relaxed when you were alive?" Asta's hand slithered though Finn's, a chill tingle against her skin. She shivered, and all at once she was looking out through his eyes, at her own body kneeling on the floor, at the pale skin, the blue veins standing out on the back of his hand.

"Shit, this is weird!" Her voice wasn't her own, but his, deeper, forced over unfamiliar muscles. Her body felt heavier, stretched and compressed, distorted in myriad tiny, subtle ways. She moved with a heavier tread than she was used to, despite the fact that her body was incorporeal.

"It's weird for me too," Finn assured her. "But they say two minds are better than one!"

"Not two minds crammed into the same skull, surely? Can we touch things?"

Finn's hand reached for the towel rail and passed smoothly through it. "It would appear not," he said.

"What can we do?"

He shrugged. She shrugged, but he had control of their shared spirit-body. "I'm not entirely sure. I guess we'll find out as we go along. Are you ready?"

"I'm ready."

"Then let's find my son." Together, combined, they walked through the curtain into the lounge. It didn't even rustle at their passing, falling through and behind them in a way that made Asta shudder. She was a ghost now, her living body left behind on the bathroom floor, and she rode inside Finn's restless spirit.

Syven lay on the couch, arms behind his head, staring at the ceiling. Presumably he was waiting for Asta to call on him, taking advantage of the time to put his feet up. Asta felt herself shrink away from him, in her mind, as Finn started forward. "Can he see us? Hear us?"

"Not a chance. So this is the beast you've been rutting with?" He leaned over Syven, head tilted to one side, and Asta felt his curiosity. "You've had better, sister."

"Leave him alone, Finn."

"As if I could do him any harm!" Finn was scornful. "I can't even disturb the dust motes landing on his face, let alone knife him in the throat. Why is he crying?"

Asta hadn't noticed the tears gathered at the corners of Syven's eyes until Finn pointed them out. "I don't know," she admitted.

"Try and get it out of him. It could be useful. Is that his slave mark, on his ear?" as Syven signed and wiped his hand across his eyes, lips moving in a way that could have been prayer, or a murmured name.

"Are you sure he doesn't know we're here?"

"Of course he doesn't. Watch!" Finn snapped his fingers before Syven's open eyes, and the copper man didn't blink.

"Come away, we're wasting time. Do you want Rhodan to end up ear-clipped?"

"You know I don't." Finn straightened, and looked around. "What's the quickest way out?"

"They keep the door locked." Asta remembered belatedly that locked doors were no barrier to them now. But Finn was striding towards the windows.

"What's out here?" he asked.

"The balcony. You don't want to go out there . . ."

"Why not?" He strode through the glass as if it was no thicker than a soap bubble, out onto the balcony, and froze. "What's that?"

Asta wished he would look away.

"Is that – was that – a *man*?"

"Finn, please! Stop looking at it!"

He turned his head away in response to her plea, and she felt his disgust. "These people aren't human."

"And they have the children of our tribe. They have your wife and son. So let's not linger?" She nudged him on, over the edge of the balcony, floating down through empty air. It was like flying. It would have taken her breath away, if either of them had been breathing.

They landed in the square. It wasn't crowded, but there were still more people moving through it than there had been in the whole of the Beehive Tribe. Each one inclined their head at the balcony, and she got a good look at their faces as they passed by, and sometimes *through*, her. That was the strangest sensation; the cold water splash, and the barest glimpse of swift, jumbled thoughts before they moved on. It was like overhearing fragments of conversation in a crowded room, these blurred impressions of thought and feeling. She caught faint hope, desire, frustration, and overwhelming fear. Fear and hunger. The people of Mikligard were starving. Their pinched faces and swollen bellies were the outward signs of a hunger that ate deep into their bones. Not just the usual pangs of spring famine, but an ache that had lasted for years. They were starving, and they were terrified. She reeled away from the feel of their frightened minds, and felt Finn's calming mental touch, steadying her, holding her up.

"What's wrong with them?" he asked.

"I don't know. I haven't been allowed to talk to them. I got pushed out on the balcony and dragged back in before I could really see anyone."

"Do you think it's linked to him?" Finn jerked his head towards the flayed man hanging on the opposite side of the square, far above the crowds who were giving it a wide berth.

"It could be. He tried to kill me. Maybe there's wider dissent. These people," she gestured around at the square, "they're not happy. You can feel it in their blood."

Finn snorted his derision. "Fuck them, Asta. They stole your life. They took our people and sold them in chains. They don't deserve any happiness."

"Harsh, Finn," Asta chided. "They're not all raiders and slave dealers, I'm sure. There's good in some of them."

"In Syven, maybe?"

"We should look for Rhodan by the docks." She felt his mild scorn at her blatant attempt to change the subject. "I saw slaves being led on to a black ship when I arrived. They'll keep them nearby, those they don't sell into the city."

"Let's find the harbour, then." Finn chose a lane off the square, seemingly at random. It was a street of craftsmen, cobblers, women selling dolls twisted from tough-stemmed plants, men selling whistles hewn from bone. There was a crowd around the stall selling a thin stew made with stringy meat, and everywhere was the evidence of poverty. The stallholders and their customers were tired and ragged, with bare, dirty feet. They shovelled stew into their mouths from cracked earthen bowls, pushing and scrapping with each other for the dregs of the barrel.

There was a blare of trumpets at the far end of the road. Finn turned in surprise, and Asta saw the street clearing, women dragging children to their skirts and hustling them into doorways. The man next to her seized the opportunity caused by the distraction to punch his neighbour in the ribs and snatch his bowl from his hands, draining it before his victim could protest.

Two burly men dressed in identical clothes marched down the street, barging aside anyone not quick enough to evade them. They were followed by a litter, like the one Asta had ridden into the city, but the curtains were open to reveal a middle aged man lolling on the cushions eating fruit, looking around with a mildly curious air, as if wondering how he had got here. There were more guards around the litter, keeping pace with it, all hewn from the same rock. They carried stout iron bars with ends that curved in savage hooks. As they swept past Asta noticed that their ears were neatly clipped.

The litter swept onwards, and some of the children scampered after it, crying to each other in the hope that scraps might fall from the rich man's hand.

"Shall we follow him?" Asta asked.

She felt Finn shrug. "Might as well," he said. "We could learn something."

They hastened down the street, the darting urchins passing through their spectral body in a way that made Asta's conscious mind shudder. "Doesn't that bother you?" she asked her brother.

He didn't answer, but he increased the pace as the litter rounded the corner ahead of them. One of the slave-guards yelled, and the street children scattered. One boy held his prize, a fruit stone with yellow flesh still clinging to it, high over his head as he scampered away, his companions in fierce pursuit.

The light was dazzling, sunlight bouncing off a silver sea, hitting the whitewashed stone of the square buildings that lined the harbour. Gulls wheeled and cried over the ships that jostled for position along the wharf, the sleek, high-prowed raiding vessels, little single-masted pleasure craft painted red and gold, and a pair of fat-hulled black ships that stood alone at the end of the stone jetty that stretched out into the bay. No other vessels were berthed near them, and the end of the jetty was roped off.

Asta felt Finn's mental nudge. "They don't want people to go there," he said. "That's where we should go."

"Just a moment." A stall on the wharf had caught Asta's eye, as well as that of the fat man in the litter, who had ordered his slaves to stop so he could take a closer look. He leaned out, another fruit grasped in his hand, and the juice ran over his fingers and splashed on the stall. The stallholder frowned, lips twitching, but uttered no protest. As he spread out his wares Asta noticed he was missing the fingertip of his left index finger, but Finn had noticed something else, and he dragged her in for a closer look.

"These are fine cameos," the rich man said, as Asta passed through him. She caught his boredom, his attempt at being polite, the sensation of something recently remembered. She tasted the sweetness of fruit at the back of her throat. "What do you carve them from?"

"Coral, *mestari*." The man on the stall bobbed his head. "I fashion them myself."

The man on the litter picked up one of the corals and studied it. "This is fine work." He nodded at the stallholder's damaged hand. "How do you manage it, with your disability?"

Asta didn't hear the reply. She was staring at the heavy pendant in his hand, as Finn hissed softly. "Asta, it's you!"

The face was picked out in dark blue, raised from a lighter turquoise surround. There was no doubt it bore some resemblance to her own. "Are you sure?"

"They're all you. Look!" Finn ran his hand through the stall, and his fingers fell through the tumbled cameos, blue, jade, turquoise, white.

"It's a remarkable likeness," the rich man observed. "Did you see her on the balcony?"

The stallholder nodded. "Briefly. And I've seen etchings. The council have issued a portrait of her, and I took the image from that."

Asta had wondered why Olafur had been so insistent that she pose for sketches. She had been too tired to argue at the time, too worried about her people. Trying to play the good little Goddess. Now it seemed her fame had spread beyond the confines of her quarters, in a way she couldn't control or understand. She had been so detached, while down here in the city her image was sold in the streets without her knowledge.

"Our Summer Goddess." The man on the litter lowered his voice. "Think she'll save us?"

The seller shrugged, but spoke in the same hushed tone. "To be honest, *mestari*, I don't care. As long as I'm making good coin from her likeness . . ."

"Ah yes." The fat man cleared his throat. "How much?"

"Come on," Finn gave Asta a prod. "Let's get a look at that boat."

She wanted to linger over the stall, but the merchant was exchanging coins with the seller, and she let Finn drag her away.

The boat was empty, to Asta's frustration. It had obviously been unloaded not long before, and was waiting for the tide to turn before filling up with human cargo. The deck bobbed below the level of the wharf, on the low, greasy tide. A small boat floated alongside, crewed by two men who were using sharp curved knives to pare the molluscs from the water-raddled wood, dropping them in a bucket on the stern. Neither of them looked up as Asta and her brother, light as thistledown, leapt overhead and floated down to the deck, past the white cat sleeping on a coil of rope, through the solid wood planking and into the echoing holds beneath. The air smelled of spice and salt and sweat, and fear, but the holds were freshly washed down, if the soap bubbles and damp patches on the floors were any indication. Shackles, welded to metal plates riveted to the floor, were placed every few steps. Asta scanned the room. The hold was in darkness, but Finn had the night-sight of the dead, and she heard his furious mental calculation.

"There are more decks below this one," she reminded him.

"They must pack upward of two hundred people on a ship this size." She could taste his disgust.

"Maybe not. I saw them boarding other cargo with I arrived. It might be just this one room . . . ." She trailed off, knowing he wasn't listening.

"Cargo," he muttered. "Chained cargo. Human cargo. My wife and son are not *cargo*, Asta."

"Maybe that was the wrong word," she conceded. "Anyway, there's nobody here. Where now?"

"Will you be missed, if we look around a little more? Your *friend* won't try and bring you back?"

"I warned him not to, last time. I tried to explain—"

"Not too much, I hope. Don't sell the secrets of our tribe, sister."

Asta wished she could get away from Finn's disapproval. "Do you want to look in the warehouses on the dock? We might find some clue there."

He kicked at one of the shackles, foot passing ineffectually through the metal. "Might as well," he said. "There's nothing here. And this place smells of death. A death ship for a bloody trade. Can't you stop it?"

"Me?"

"Aren't you supposed to be a Goddess or something?" he sneered.

"Shut up, Finn." She felt his guilt, his misery. Couldn't he feel hers?

The warm, rustling air above deck was a relief after the foetid dampness of the cargo hold, and Asta shivered as Finn stretched his spectral limbs in the sunlight. She could see the warehouses through the pale skin of his arms, his jerkin hanging loose on his slender frame. There were a number of buildings fronting the wharf, uniform one storey blocks of white or grey stone, windowless, with heavy double doors banded with metal. A few stood open, and their halls were empty and echoing, the air thick with swirling motes of dust. More were closed, and she felt the drag of wood and metal on her skin as Finn pushed through them to look around, reminding her that she was not all spirit, that she might still be hurt.

They hit good grazing at the far end of the wharf, in a building that stood slightly out of true with the rest in the block, as if shrinking back from the sea. The interior of the warehouse was divided into walled pens, surrounding a central ring with seating for spectators running around it in a half-circle. The room was lit, unlike its counterparts, by large glass skylights in the sloping roof. And, unlike the other warehouses, it was crowded, noisy and hot. The sound and heat hit Asta like a wall after the ominous brooding silence of the ship, and she reeled.

"What is this place?" Finn demanded.

Asta looked around with a rising feeling of revulsion. "It's a fucking market," she said. "A market for slaves, for buying and selling people like horseflesh. Maybe they keep them somewhere else, but this is where they bring them before they load them on the ships."

"Rhodan?"

"Be quiet and listen." They swept through the crowd to the side of the ring, touching keen, interested minds. None of the spirits Asta felt seemed especially cruel, but all were bright and alert, keen to get a bargain or turn a profit. None of them were concerned at the fate of the three shambling, hobbled men being paraded in the ring. They all had the brassy skin and copper-hued hair that marked them as natives of the Scattering, their left ears clipped like Syven's. Big, well-muscled men, they had obviously been treated well, but for the clipped ears and the chains that linked them ankle-to-ankle.

"Shall we go closer?" Asta asked.

Finn was indifferent. "They're not our people."

"Maybe our people have already been sold? It's been a long time since they were taken."

Finn shook his head. "Rhodan is here. I can sense it. My little boy . . ." She felt his pleading, his desperation, but she couldn't tell if his vision was true, or that of a desperate father hunting his lost son.

"Let's look for him then," she said.

There were people from many tribes in the stone pens, separated by race and by gender. Not just men and women of the Scattering, but tribes Asta didn't recognise. Some pale, with white hair spun out like puffed cotton; some with skin like ebon wood, some that looked like they could be of her father's tribe. All the tribes of the world, gathered in a Mikligard warehouse for the same fell purpose. But who was buying?

Asta looked across the ring at a group of olive-skinned men and women in long robes of bright, clashing colours, dripping with tassels and lace. They leaned on the barrier and chatted casually amongst themselves, separate from the people of Mikligard, as if their hauteur enclosed them in a bubble. "Over there," she said. "I want to go closer."

She felt Finn hang back. "If Rhodan's here they might know about it, brother. I just want to touch their minds, that's all."

"If you must." If he wanted to fight her there wasn't much she could do about it, but they drifted across the ring, leaving no footprint on the neatly raked sand, avoiding the white cotton-haired girls being paraded. They clutched each other's hands in a quiet, defiant display of solidarity, and Asta's heart went out to them as she passed through the barrier to join the trio of strangers in their garish costume.

"This is sick," Finn muttered.

"I know."

The foreigners at the rail showed little interest in the delicate girls, putting in a few bids that seemed more for show than anything else. Asta was surprised to discover that she understood what they were saying.

"They already have plenty of those," Finn supplied.

"I heard that. How can I understand their tongue?"

He shrugged. "Another unexpected advantage of being dead, I think. I can understand it, so you can."

"You have your uses." Finn pressed closer, walking through the three to taste their thoughts. Asta could sense that they were bored, impatient, homesick, eager to please . . . *someone.* She couldn't tell who, some higher power that was desired and frightening and respected, all at the same time. A leader in their own land? And she caught a name.

Inyesta.

As Finn moved into the woman, hoping to learn more, she felt the stranger's mind recoil at the touch. The woman shivered, clutching her robes tighter around her, and waved her hand as if trying to brush a fly from her face.

Asta felt a sharp jerk in her chest as Finn pulled her away.

"She could sense us?" she asked.

"Seems that way," he said.

"How?"

"Maybe she's more in touch with the Spirit Realm. Maybe she's a shaman, or whatever they have that's the equivalent. You need to be more careful."

She forbore from pointing out that she had no control over their shared form. "Who's Inyesta? A woman?"

"No idea. Maybe your savage can tell you?" Finn sounded bored. Why should he care? "Are we done here?" He turned his attention to the ring, and Asta felt him stiffen. The pale women had vanished, sold presumably, and passed into the hands of their new owner, or set aside for collection at the end of the sale. Asta wondered how the mechanics of the sale-house worked. How did they sell people, with consideration and an understanding of their fate, as if they were horses? More to the point, how *could* they?

Finn darted forward, and Asta felt the pain welling in his breast, a constriction of his stilled heart. The barrier fell away behind them and they were running across the soft sand that was no impediment to flying, spectral feet, towards the gate that had opened in the far side of the ring.

Asta dimly heard the words of the auctioneer, announcing he was taking bids on two healthy children, fresh from the horse lands to the west. His words were hollow and booming, a senseless noise.

The little boy stumbled into the ring. For a painful, shocking instant Asta thought it was Rhodan, but this child was taller, a year or two older, his skin rendered pale with dust. His eyes were wide and dark, and his arm was wrapped around a smaller girl who huddled against his side, heedless of the tears and snot she was wiping on his shirt. In the vastness of the ring, he was tiny, and defiant, fists clenched as he glared around him.

Not one of her tribe, she saw, and her heart cracked a little inside her as her hope was shattered. For the boy, and for the people he had been taken from who may never know his fate.

This could be two children of her tribe standing there, up for sale to the highest bidder, and she had been unable to save them. She fought back tears.

"Asta?" Finn's voice was soft. "Asta, they live. They don't kill their slaves. They took our children; they didn't put them to the sword. If they live, we can find them. You could save them. If not all, then maybe some of them."

"How?"

"You're meant to be a Goddess. Don't you have some power?"

"Not much. Not enough."

"Maybe . . ." He looked over to where the gaudy trio were bidding, with slightly more enthusiasm than they had shown before. They had little competition, and the hammer swiftly fell on the Atrathene children, with a final slam that made Asta wince.

The sale was breaking up, some people drifting from the building, others moving to collect their purchases. The three they had been watching, two men and the woman who had sensed them, walked across the sale ring towards the auctioneer. They moved with purpose, and Finn pushed closer to listen to the exchange.

"We can't learn anything here, Finn. Let's go."

"Rhodan *is* here," he insisted. I'm not leaving until I find him."

"What will you do if you do find him? Answer me that, Finn!"

"Shut up." The woman was talking. She seemed to be the leader of her little tribe, and the auctioneer regarded her with deference and a barely-concealed dislike.

"Do you have more children of the horse tribes we can buy? Our . . ." she seemed to be searching for the word, ". . . our *client* values them for their strength."

The auctioneer glanced down at his hands. "I'm aware of that," he said. "We have a few, but they're troublesome. They were returned to us for laziness, or insolence. You might not want any of them."

The woman tightened her lips. "Are they strong? I want to assess them?"

"Follow me." The auctioneer climbed down from his podium and led the three towards the back of the vast warehouse, through the pens, past the money changing hands and the slaves being claimed. Finn and Asta trailed along behind them.

Against the back wall the warehouse was quieter, and there were more empty pens. "I kept them back here," the auctioneer explained. "I was going to let them stew for a few days, think about what they'd done."

"What did they do?" one of the brightly dressed men asked, toying with one of his earrings as if bored.

"They were sold together to a merchant who has a place just out of town. Seems they conspired to escape. Stole a heap of coin and did considerable damage to his stock, and got quite a long way before they were apprehended. Waste of money and time for all concerned." He sniffed disapprovingly. "Of course, no one wants to keep a troublesome slave."

The three exchanged glances. "Spirits can be broken," the woman said. "We will see them, and judge."

The auctioneer turned a corner and stopped in front of a rough pen. "Here they are," he said.

Finn cried out, pushing forward through the bodies of the three foreigners, not caring whether the woman could sense him or not. He dropped to his knees in front of his son. Asta heard him screaming. Her own mind felt torn and battered, a loose rein flapping wildly. A sob rose in her throat as Finn's arms passed through Rhodan's fragile body, useless, offering no comfort. Rhodan blinked and glared up at the newcomers.

He wasn't alone. With him were two of the precious children of the Beehive tribe. Killion, who had recently turned ten and was just beginning to grow his braids, and little Valtet, clinging to the oldest boy's hand and frowning obstinately. Killion stepped forward, nose to nose with Finn, pushing the two younger children behind him, and Asta noticed bruising around his eye.

Finn reached out and together they touched Rhodan's mind. Asta felt a jumble of fear, confusion, and an obstinate determination not to be parted from his friends, his tribe. She sensed that was all that kept him from bursting into tears.

"Finn?" They knelt on the sand, Finn twisted in despair. With her mind alone Asta could not make him get up.

She felt a tug at her wrist, and looked down to check the fragile cord was still in place, tying her to her body lying on the bathroom floor back in the mansion.

"They look strong," The woman was saying. "Maybe not the girl . . ."

"Might as well take the girl, Carmile," one of her companions urged. "They might behave better if they have to protect her."

Carmile regarded the children coldly, and turned back to the auctioneer. "How much for the three?"

"Rhodan, Rhodan, my little boy! Can you hear me? We're coming for you, we're going to get you out of here . . ." Finn's hand was air, passing across his sons face as he rocked back and forth in the agony of despair.

The tug came again, harder this time. "Come on, Finn. My rein . . ."

If he heard her, he didn't acknowledge it. He stared at Rhodan, reaching for him but unable to hold his son. Asta wanted to gather all three children to her breast, to tell them that they would be safe, that she would find them and free them, somehow. Somehow . . .

"Finn!" She made a grab for the rein around her wrist, sensing it unravelling. Someone was trying to pull her back. If they untied the rope, against her severe warning, she would never return to her living form. "Finn, I have to go back!"

"Rhodan . . ."

Carmile and the auctioneer clasped hands, sealing the deal, and one of the men reached out to grip Rhodan hard by the shoulder. He squirmed and yelled at the pressure. Finn howled, but Asta could hardly hear him over the wind rushing in her ears, the rope tightening as it pulled her back, faster than sound and thought. The streets of Mikligard blurred and darkened around her, and the breath burst from her lungs as her spirit slammed back into her body. There was smooth marble under her limbs, and a warm hand pressed down on her inner thigh. Barely conscious, she raised her hand, and without even looking at her assailant, punched him in the jaw with all her strength the instant before she blacked out.

Ten

She must have only been out for a few moments. The light seared through her skull as she flickered open her eyes to see Syven sitting back on his heels, clutching his jaw and regarding her with an air of injured innocence. "Goddess? Have I done wrong?"

Asta ripped the cord from her wrist, savage nails scratching her flesh. She wanted to fight, but there was nothing to fight against. "I didn't give you permission to touch me."

Syven blinked. "I didn't know I had to get your permission every time I—"

"In *my* tribe, you ask first."

He inclined his head as she staggered to her feet, clinging on to the wall for support. "How was your meditation? I must say," his eyes narrowed as he scanned her, "you're looking well on it . . ."

She pushed past him, trying to disguise the tremor in her limbs. "Fuck, I need a drink."

She poured a mug of the fiery, blood-dark spirit, threw it back in two large gulps, and slumped on the couch, feeling it burn down deep into her chest. It warmed her, but it didn't quell the dizziness, her head still spinning with Finn's grief and her own pain. She gestured impatiently, and Syven poured her another. He stood with his back to the windows, running a finger along his bruised jaw.

"Don't stare at me like that. I told you to leave me alone while I was meditating."

He dropped to his haunches. "What's it like?"

"What's what like?" The spirit was making her head hurt, a sharp stabbing between her brows. She needed sugar, but sugar wouldn't take the edge off what she had witnessed.

"When you meditate. What do you see?"

Her hand tightened on the arm of the sofa. "Why?"

Syven shrugged. "It seems important to you. I want to share it."

"It's private . . ." But maybe he could help her. He knew things she didn't, after all. She took a deep breath, and that helped to calm her jangling nerves as much as the alcohol did. "Sometimes I see places, hear names . . . Sometimes it's clear, other times it's more jumbled. I can see the spirits of the dead, old friends, members of my tribe who were taken from me by your people. And occasionally," she lowered her voice at the lie, "I see the future, in prophesies and visions."

He brushed a hand over her close-cropped hair. "Of course you do. You truly are a goddess."

Her eyes were itchy with exhaustion, but she had to find out before it slipped her mind. "I saw a great building, filled with men and women from many tribes. Some were slaves, like you. And I heard a word – *Inyesta*. What does that mean, do you know?"

Syven's hand froze, and he stiffened. "You heard about Inyesta? In your visions?"

"I wouldn't be asking otherwise!"

He leapt up to pace before the windows, a shadow figure, arms waving with anxiety. "We sought to protect you from Inyesta. It's nothing you need to know about, not here."

It. Not *he* or *she*. Asta pushed her fortune.

"What is Inyesta? It obviously means something to you . . ."

"You should not have heard about it." His brow furrowed. "I will have to speak to Olafur."

"Why?"

"Because you should not have heard that name, not in real life, not in a vision!" He strode over to her and caught both her hands in his, so tight her knuckles ground together. She felt him shaking and trying to control it.

"What is it about Inyesta that scares you so much?" she asked, trying to keep her voice sweet.

He pulled away from her. "I'm going to get Olafur."

"Fine." She made an effort to appear casual, though her guts ground with tension. "Can you bring some of those little sugared biscuits back with you?"

The moment he left she let her head fall back on the couch. It felt too heavy for her to continue the effort of holding it up. *Finn? Are you there?*

He twitched in the back of her mind, anxious, miserable, but clinging on to a fragile thread of hope.

I'll learn what I can for you, brother.

Asta wrapped her arms around her stomach to ease the hungry tremble in her belly, and tried to sort through everything she had learned. Rhodan was alive, and so were Killion and Valtet. That might mean that more of her people still lived, either on the Scattering or beyond its rocky shores. It was a small hope, but it was still hope, gleaming and golden, and she clung to it hard. Because if they lived, she could find them.

The slavers wouldn't have kept Rhodan alive this long only to kill him, she was sure. The people, the trio of bright, fluttering strangers who thought of Inyesta and were anxious to please – she had detected no bloody thoughts in their minds. They did not feel cruel, but they may pass her nephew and his companions on to someone else, someone with a blacker vision for them. Wherever he was taken, even if he stayed with his little tribe, he would not be free. But how could she save any of them, when she was as much a prisoner as they were? It was more urgent than ever that she get away from the watchful eyes of Syven and Olafur. Not as a spirit, but as a living woman who could affect the world around her. She could not do it alone, and Finn could do little to help her. That left only one option.

She sat up as the bolts drew back on the door, and plastered a smile to her face. She smoothed her skirt over her knees as the door swung open, and Olafur strode into the room. The veins on his forehead throbbed with tension as he hastened to her and grabbed her by the shoulders.

"What did you see?" he demanded, giving her a shake. His eyes were wide, and behind the anger there was fear.

Asta slapped his hands away and rose, stretching up to her full height until they stood nose to nose. Drawing on the memories of her mother, she drew her lips back to expose her teeth in a snarl. "How dare you lay hands on me! I am your goddess!"

"Only as long as I say you are!" But he fell back a step, regarding her with narrowed, greedy eyes.

"Really? You must have spent a lot of time and coin setting me up as your goddess . . . The Scattering isn't rich. How do you think people would react if you turned around now and said, 'Oh sorry, I made a mistake, she's not really a goddess . . .'" She jerked her head towards the window, to the bloodied, flayed corpse that dominated the view. "Do you think you might end up like that poor bastard out there?"

"Be quiet! What was your vision?"

"May I sit?" She reached for the plate of biscuits Syven had brought back with him, and ate one with deliberate slowness, enjoying Olafur's discomfort, but disliking the way he watched her mouth as she ate.

He chewed the ball of his thumb, lips smacking wetly. "You didn't tell me you were a prophet."

"You never asked."

"I should have been told!" His glare swept over her to include Syven.

"Syven didn't know either. All my people are prophets, of a sort. I didn't think it was worth mentioning." The sweetness of the biscuit was calming her nerves, and she took another. "Don't you expect your gods to be able to see the future?"

"We expect our gods to do as we bid them. As you should do as I bid you, you wilful child."

"Then you have poor gods," she said crisply, "existing only to serve the whims of you and your Council."

"And what are the gods like where you come from?" Olafur snapped, and she faltered. "That's right, you don't have gods. I suggest you are not an expert on their behaviour. I am. That is why you must tell me what you saw."

She pressed her lips and turned her head. He sighed. "You drive a cruel bargain, Goddess. Do you want me to tell you about Inyesta? Then tell me what you saw."

Asta grinned. Stories were the lifeblood of her tribe. They were how her people learned, how they made sense of the world, how they remembered the past. If there was one thing she could do, it was weave a story.

"Come here."

Olafur knelt beside her. She tried to ignore the fact that his hand rested on her thigh. If it crept too high, she would punch him, Council or no Council.

"I saw a black ship, with holds crammed with people to be carried away. I saw my own face carved in coral by a man with a crippled hand, and a warehouse by the harbour, teeming with people from strange lands. I saw a fat man in a litter ride down a starving child in the street, and," she pushed it, "a man looking for his lost child. And I heard a name, or a word, *Inyesta*, whispered by the sea over and over, as if I was meant to remember it. You must tell me what it means."

Olafur paled, and withdrew his hand. "These are things you could not know. Syven, did you tell her?"

Syven shook his head. "I haven't left the manse all day. I swear on my honour, I have told her nothing."

"A slave's honour is worth little, Syven."

How much was Rhodan's honour worth? His life? Asta clasped her hands tightly in her lap, digging her nails hard against her palms. "Syven didn't tell me anything," she confirmed. "I am your

Goddess. You must trust my visions, if you want me to save you."

Olafur shook his head, but all he said was, "Very well."

"Tell me about Inyesta," she said.

"Inyesta is the empire to the south of here. We trade with them."

"Trade what? Slaves?"

"Slaves, yes, among other cargos. Inyesta has," he pursed his lips, "an insatiable demand for slaves. In return they send us grain, rice, dried meats . . . ."

"Food," Asta said.

"Yes, food, obviously!"

"The Scattering cannot provide for its own people?"

"Enough!" Olafur barked. "You still don't understand, do you? You are here to serve us, not the other way about. Such visions are dangerous. They will have to be reported to the Council. Syven, see that she doesn't meditate again." His sharp hand gesture cut off Asta's protest, and Syven's faint rumble of dissent. He swept from the room, swirling his robes around him, and the door slammed at his heels.

Syven shook his head. "Be careful, my Goddess. He will take what you've told him straight to the Council. They may decide it's dangerous having you around, however much Olafur wants you."

"He's not having me. In any way." It was worth the risk, to learn something that might help her get her missing people back.

"Don't look like that, Asta. You're not irreplaceable."

"Where are you going to get another Goddess? Buy one from Inyesta?"

Syven looked dark. "Don't joke about it. We never buy slaves from Inyesta. It's a one-way trade."

"What happens to them?" she asked.

"Are you tired, my Goddess?" He knelt in front of her, taking one of her ankles in his hand, raising the arch of her bare foot to his lips. She tingled. His free hand slid up to stroke the patch of white skin on the back of her right knee, his hands so much less invasive than Olafur's had been.

"You're trying to distract me."

"Is it working?"

Asta tried to pretend it wasn't, but she knew she wouldn't get any more information out of Syven tonight. She had ridden her luck to the end of the trail. She *was* tired, and his massaging hands were soothing, inviting. When he climbed up onto the sofa with her, hands pressing into the small of her back, copper head resting against her breast, she wrapped her thighs around his waist and let him take her until they both fell into an exhausted sleep.

It was days, long, anxious days, before Syven left Asta on her own for any length of time again. The tension crackled between them. She kept herself fit by pacing the length of the apartment for hours on end, every muscle clenched with frustration. She would burst if she didn't get out soon. Her back and shoulders ached constantly, and all she could think of was Rhodan. His ship must have sailed by now, carrying the children of her tribe to Inyesta, to an unknown fate. Finn's spirit scratched at the back of her mind, a running sore she could not heal. She was suffocating, and her brother was dying with her, dying all over again, imprisoned by her body and the locks that held them in, and the ever-watchful guard.

Syven kept his own counsel, but he watched. His eyes followed her constantly, fingers flicking over his sewing. Often he would leave her in the middle of the night and she heard him prowling the reception room, or grunting as he exercised. Sometimes she remembered that he was as much a prisoner here as she was. But Syven had the hope of regaining his freedom, if he performed his duty to Olafur's satisfaction. For Asta, there was only uncertainty.

She was staring out of the window when the knock came. The remains of her would-be assassin had finally been taken down, but the stench lingered over the square, a permanent miasma of death and rotting. But the sun shining through the windows cast long, broad bars of light across the floor. Midsummer must have passed, by Asta's count of days. The turn of the season could not be far off. People in the square clutched their cloaks tighter around them as the wind sliced through the Scattering. They looked thinner and more pinched than ever, and the glances they cast towards her balcony were doleful and pleading. Asta had a feeling of tightening, of compression, of the city reaching a tipping point. She was about to ask Syven again what happened at the end of summer, when she was interrupted by the knocking.

It was Gerhild. She always knocked, while Olafur breezed in and out with impunity. Today she had a dour expression, and a tray of food balanced on her hip. She dumped it on the table and nodded at Syven. "Meeting," she said. "With the Council. Now."

He rose. "It's nearly time then." It wasn't a question.

"The nights are getting shorter." She managed a respectful nod for Asta. "My Goddess."

"If your council is about me, shouldn't I be there?" Asta asked.

"No," Gerhild told her firmly. Syven shook his head.

"Will you be long?"

He shrugged. "The Council like to take their time. I'll tell you what I can."

As soon as the door locked behind them Asta raced for the bathing room. Her meditation rope hung on a hook, and she wrapped it around her wrist with fingers that fumbled and snagged her skin in their haste. She tested the knots angrily, the one around her wrist, the one that tied her to the towel loop. It had been so long, too long, since she had spoken to Finn, since she'd left these halls even in spirit form. Since she'd felt alive.

The fall was quicker this time, smoother. Asta opened her eyes to see her brother standing over her, lips twisted into a scowl. He extended his hand without speaking. Their palms brushed, and he recoiled as if her touch burned.

"Shit, Asta! What the fuck have you done?"

"What are you talking about?"

Finn retreated a step, over the empty pool. His eyes were

narrowed, black and fierce. If he'd had a tail, it would have been swishing, his hackles raised in displeasure. He still looked like their mother, disturbingly so. "Finn, what's wrong?"

"There's life there."

"Where?"

"There!" He flicked his fingers disdainfully towards her. "You're pregnant, Asta."

She shook her head. He was wrong, or he was lying. "Not possible. I haven't missed a moon-bleed yet."

"Trust me." He grabbed her hand, yanking her spirit into his. She felt his disgust, and below the surface, deep down, a fragile spark of life. No, not one. Two sparks, swirling inside her like distant stars in the heavens. Life. Lives. Inside her.

He pushed her away again, out of him. She reeled, and Finn's hands brushed her skin as if he sought to steady her, but there was no affection in his touch. His eyes were the black ice of a frozen sea. "Halfbreeds, Asta. How *could* you?"

"You can't say that!" She flashed her defiance, hoping it stung. "We're halfbreeds ourselves, you and I . . ."

"Born from love, not boredom or manipulation or whatever possessed you to take the copper savage to your bed!" He turned away, but their minds were one, merged in mutual anger and fear.

"What now?" she asked.

"Now? If you're lucky the breeding will fail . . ."

"That's not what I meant." She didn't want to talk to him about it until he was calm. Didn't even want to think about it. She needed time alone to gather her thoughts, and right now, there was no time. "Where do we go? Do you want to look for Rhodan and Lefalli? The other children?"

He shook his head. "The ship has sailed. It's too far to Inyesta. We have to find another way, and you've just made things more difficult . . ."

"Bottle it, Finn. Now's not the time. They're having a meeting downstairs, a full Council. We might learn something. And I need," she stretched, faintly hearing their joints pop, "I need to get out of these fucking walls, Finn!"

His mental touch was more sympathetic. "I know. This is killing you. Let's find out what this Council knows."

Even walking like spirits, with no door barred to their wraith-like form, the corridors and rooms of the mansion were still a maze of private apartments, meeting rooms, banqueting chambers and a vast kitchen that stretched the length of the back of the house. It looked abandoned; the pantries were all but empty and most of the pans and skillets were grey with greasy dust. A single lantern burned at the far end of the room, an island of light amid the gloom and neglect. Here the pans shone with reflected flame, and the oil-stove was warm as Asta's hand passed through it. Finn sniffed, and she caught the scent of fresh-baked biscuit and fruit.

"It looks like they don't cook much," he said.

"It looks like they used to cook a lot more."

Finn twisted as the kitchen door opened. A woman in a grey woollen robe, hair pulled into a bun to reveal her clipped ear, hastened towards the oven. As she passed through them Asta felt her anxiety, her hunger, and a deep grief not so distant from what Finn lived and died with. She wrapped a cloth around her hands, bent, and retrieved a tray of biscuits from the belly of the oven. As she stepped back Asta felt her hunger quicken. She noticed her sunken cheeks and the deep circles under her eyes, the way the tray shook in her hands as she dumped it on the table and began loosening the biscuits with a spatula, piling them on to a brightly-painted plate. She looked around as if she feared she would be overlooked, and guiltily stuffed a whole biscuit into her mouth, rubbing her lips with her thumb to make sure she gathered every crumb. She swallowed, eyes watering, and rubbed her lips again. Balancing the plate on her forearm, she left the way she had come in.

By unspoken consent, Finn and Asta followed her, slipping

through the wood of the door as it closed. They pursued the woman down a corridor and up a flight of stairs, to a door decorated with a symbol of a burning sun, where she paused and knocked politely. Finn pushed through her before the door was half-open, and Asta felt his thrill of triumph. "This must be the place," he said.

It was a windowless chamber, stuffy with the heat of bodies. Ten figures sat around the circular table which bore the same image as the door, half-obscured by mugs and flagons of pale wine. Asta had expected them to be hooded, muttering incantations under candlelight, but the council were neat and alert, none of them as cadaverous and greyed as the citizens that roamed the streets, though they were all thin. She saw Olafur's eyes brightening as the plate of biscuits was placed on the table. He didn't acknowledge the grey-clad woman as she withdrew.

"Shall we break for food?" He offered the tray politely to the woman on his left, who took a biscuit, snapped it in half, and passed the plate to the man next to her, who did the same.

"I notice your man doesn't get to eat," Finn said.

She noticed Syven for the first time, standing like a statue against the wall. No seats for slaves, obviously, and no biscuits either, though as the plate passed close enough for him to reach out and grab it she saw his hands twitch. Brushing against him she felt his hunger, his misery and frustration. She wished she could comfort him.

Finn snorted. "You're getting soft, sister! Are they going to say anything useful?"

The biscuits went round again, broken into quarters this time, as if everyone was too well-bred to take a whole biscuit when there were people starving in the streets. Olafur licked the crumbs from his lips and cleared his throat. "Shall we continue?" He shuffled his papers, and made a note in the picture-writing of the Scattering. "Where were we, Erikah?"

The woman opposite smiled. She was younger than most of the council, with smooth skin and a wide, generous mouth.

Asta felt Finn's ardour stir and checked him with her mind. "Too weird!" she muttered.

"It's only what I have to live with when you rut with the ginger slave," he flashed back.

Asta hadn't thought of it that way and she retreated, embarrassed, and felt her brother chuckle.

"The slave of the Goddess was about to speak," Erikah was saying, and Asta dragged her attention back to her words.

Syven started. He had been staring at the plate. "Already?" he said.

Olafur gestured impatiently. "Come forward, Syven. Make your report."

Syven licked his lips. "First I want to know about my wife, and my girls."

His *wife?* Asta felt the heat rush to her face as Finn let out a mocking whoop. It had never occurred to her that Syven might have a family outside of the mansion, a family he was barred from seeing. Were they slaves too? Had they been sold into the belly of one of those dread black ships, to Inyesta or even further?

Olafur nodded. "Your wife is well. Your daughters too. I checked on them a few days ago, to make sure they were well fed. They look forward to your return."

"So do I." Asta was close enough to feel his longing, a faint echo of Finn's desperation. Her brother must feel it too, there was guilt in his mind, and he warmed slightly towards her lover, her captor.

"Not long now, and you will be a free man!" Olafur sounded almost affectionate. "How goes it, upstairs?"

Syven frowned. "She still bleeds with the new moon. I've done my best . . ."

"We're running out of time. Does Gerhild need to check her for abnormalities?"

"Asta, what are they talking about?" Finn asked, and she urgently hushed him.

". . . might be a good idea," Syven was saying.

"If she doesn't breed, will the ceremony still go ahead?" a weather-beaten man on the far side of the table asked, pouring a mug of wine and straining it noisily through his greying moustache.

Olafur nodded. "It has to. It's too late now to find another Goddess. Besides, she is the one, I'm sure of it. The marks on her legs . . ."

"No one doubts you, Olafur," Erikah said gently, and the rest of the council muttered their agreement. "We have one more moon. She will start twins in that time, I'm sure of it."

"I don't trust her," Finn hissed. "Let's get closer. I want to feel her mind."

"Just her mind?" Asta tried to make a joke of it, but her lower gut clenched and she rested her hand there, feeling the life stirring under her palm, each spark no bigger than her smallest fingernail. Twins. The Scattering wanted her to have twins, and now she had them. What did they want them for?

Brother and sister drifted through the table towards Erikah, while the weathered man snorted, glaring at Syven. "I know you've fathered twins. Might it have been a fluke?"

Syven shook his head, but Olafur answered on his behalf. "Syven is a twin himself, the father of twin daughters. His father's brothers were twins, and his mother's cousins. There are twins on both sides of his family stretching back generations. Of all the men on the Scattering, he was the one most likely to father twins. We looked into his heritage most carefully before we selected him, Hrulf. You know that."

"It has been an honour to serve." Syven's tone was bland, but his stance suggested it was anything but.

"And you will win your freedom by it," Olafur assured him.

Hrulf snorted again, his habitual contribution to the meeting. "Fine," he said. "But if he can't get her with twins, will the ceremony do any good?"

They were so close to Erikah now that Asta could reach out and brush her arm. The woman stiffened, and gasped.

"It might not do as much good," Olafur was saying, "but it will do something. It must, or—"

"Stop talking!" Erikah's voice was sharp, and hushed him instantly. "Something's wrong. We are overheard."

"Pull back, Asta." Finn snatched their hand away, but Erikah was alert, nostrils quivering like a hound on a scent.

"Overheard?" Olafur demanded. "How? Inyestan spies in the walls?"

One of the younger council members huddled in his seat. "Their priests can see through the eyes of crows and flies," he muttered, almost to himself.

"There are no crows in here!" Olafur snapped. "Erikah, what did you feel?"

Her eyes were glazed, her mind seeking. Asta felt it reaching out, and she withdrew before the blind, questing touch. "I think we should go," she said to Finn.

"Agreed."

"There's something here," Erikah said. "Not hostile, but curious. It touched my mind. It's still here, but I can't grip it . . ."

Asta stepped back as the sweep of Erikah's mind brushed past her. "Finn, let's go!"

He dragged her back, though the wall, into the tight space behind, too narrow to be a corridor, but wide enough for a man to stand and press his ear to the thin wood panels of the wall. Asta half-expected the tunnel to be crawling with Inyestan spies, but there was only the two of them, and Erikah's mind was still pushing in their direction. Finn pulled her through the next wall, into a smaller chamber. "How do we get outside?" he asked

The questing touch was still following them. "Keep going in a straight line," Asta urged. "Run!"

They ran, heedless of obstacles that they passed through like fleeting shadows, until they burst out of the thickest wall onto a wide strip of grass and earth at the side of the mansion. The building towered above them, and ahead lay an iron fence, twice the height of a man. Asta could no longer feel Erikah reaching for her. They rested, hands on their knees, Asta marvelling that they could run so far, so fast and not be out of breath.

"Your breath lies on the bathroom floor, Asta," Finn said. "Do you want to go back to it?"

She checked the binding at her wrist. It was secure. "Not yet," she said. "With any luck they'll be looking for Inyestan fly-spies for a good while. I want to get out of this fucking city."

"Me too." Finn sniffed the air and turned his back on the sea. "Let's head inland, see what we can discover."

His determined stride took them through roads, houses, people, with equal obliviousness. Finn looked neither left nor right, and Asta sensed his simmering anger. She wasn't sure she wanted to address it. She wished she could get out of his head and spend some time alone, coming to terms with all she had learned since she started her spirit walk today. It was too much to cope with all at once. She felt like curling up in a corner and weeping.

"You won't, will you?" Finn plucked the thought from her mind. "You're our father's daughter, after all."

"And our mother's."

He snarled. He didn't want to be reminded of that. They walked on in uncomfortable silence as the city petered out to a few straggling houses, battered by sea and salt. They were so misshapen they resembled nothing more than jumbles of stone piled haphazardly on the ground, until they got close enough to see signs of habitation: smoke curling from chimneys, bright, defiant lines of washing, skinny goats tethered to spikes. It was not so different from the Beehive Village, and the remembrance made Asta's heart sick with longing.

She felt her brother's mental hug around her shoulders, and knew he felt the same. At least there was a chance she could return to their lands. For Finn, only the Spirit Realm lay ahead.

"I'm sorry . . ."

"*I'm* sorry," he interrupted. "This hasn't been a good day for you, has it?"

"Master of the understatement!" His laugh made her feel a

little better. They sat, carefully, on a boulder not far from the path and surveyed their surroundings. Finn passed his foot back and forth through the stubby, wiry grass.

"They've used you harshly, Asta. It's not you I'm angry with, but them. And myself, for not being able to punch that bastard Olafur in the face. Fucking useless body!" He kicked against the stone, and his heel vanished into the rock. "Can't do anything, can I?"

"You can think." Asta wasn't sure she could any more. Her mind was buzzing. "Think us out of this, brother."

"I wish I could." She could hear his thoughts ticking, fingers drumming on his chin. "This land is poor. The Scattering is in thrall to Inyesta; they need the Inyestans for food, and the Inyestans, in turn, demand slaves. Why do the Inyestans need so many slaves? And why does nothing grow here? And you—" he jabbed at her sharply with his mind, "what's your part in it? They want you to breed twins, for a ceremony. What happens there and what will it achieve?"

She shrugged. "Syven and Olafur tell me nothing."

"Let's walk and think." He was restive, springing lightly to his feet. "Inyesta . . . My son is in Inyesta, and so is the answer to all this." He waved his hand, taking in the treeless landscape, the rocks, and the bridges over the dozens of little streams and rivers that carved up the terrain. It reminded Asta of the steppes, far to the west, where they had travelled before her father founded the Beehive village. There had been a few trees there, low, stumpy ones twisted by the wind, and endless seas of grass. Here there were only patches of toughened sea–grass, lichen, earth and bare rock. The path was a narrow band of white pebbles wandering from bridge to bridge, scarcely wider than a rabbit track. Occasionally skinny wild goats bounded across their path, and a few insects buzzed and chirped. A lone bird called high overhead, again and again, as if seeking an answer that didn't come.

Asta shuddered. "These isles are desolate, Finn."

"There must be other towns," he reasoned. "Every path leads somewhere."

"This isn't a path; it's a goat-track!"

"It's a path." He pointed to a carved stone that lay beside the trail. Hewn on the face of the boulder was the same sun-symbol as on the council chamber door, and the table. "That means something. Let's keep going."

The path widened, leading slowly uphill. When Asta looked behind, the city of Mikligard lay below them, hugging the ground, curling around the harbour. The ships at berth were mere dots. She strained her eyes across the ocean, looking south for Inyesta, west towards her own land, but there was nothing beyond the Scattering except wide grey ocean. The islands clung to the edge of the world.

They crossed a high stone bridge, a single arch over a chasm, far above the white water that tumbled below. Another sun-sign at the crowning stone of the bridge, picked out in glass-smooth marble this time, vibrant red and orange in a blue disc. She glanced to the opposite side of the bridge to see the image mirrored there, as she knew it would be. Symmetry.

Finn's hand brushed the image. "I thought this road would be busier," he said. "It's obviously a major path, and it's a fine day."

They had seen almost no one since they left the jumbled stone huts. Maybe the people of the Scattering had better things to do than walk in the country. Finn quickened the pace. From the bridge, the ground sloped up sharply, the path growing smoother underfoot, with occasional steps. Ahead was a high square arch across the road, and from either side of it a low, smooth wall extended, curving away east and west round the sides of the hill. It served no defensive purpose that Asta could see, it wasn't high enough to keep a goat out, and there was no gate blocking the arch.

Was it magic? She felt a tingle as they stepped through, a prickling of the hairs at the back of her neck, and the *scritch* of insects was magnified. Finn's voice sounded unnaturally loud in her head. "What *is* this place?"

Asta shook her head. "I don't know," she admitted. "I've never seen anything like it."

Up the slope was another arch, another low wall of smoothly polished stone, and beyond that a broad pavement of white marble that encircled the brow of the hill. Looking around, she saw they were at the highest point for miles around, the Scattering flung out before them like a handful of gravel tossed into the sea by a careless giant. Myriad islands, none bigger than the one they stood at the summit of, were linked by bridges too numerous to count.

Crowning the hill were flagstones of the same pristine marble, clinging to the earth like a skull-cap, banded with concentric rings of blue that grew tighter and tighter as they reached the centre. The crickets were so loud now Asta looked down to see if they had settled on her arms and legs, before she remembered that any buzzing insect would fly straight through Finn's spectral body as if it wasn't there. Finn crouched and brushed his hand over the seamless stone, and she felt his awe, and his surprise.

"Nothing I saw in Mikligard prepared me for this," he admitted. "This site must be very old. I doubt those sorry starving creatures in the city could build anything like this now."

"Nor could we," she reminded him.

"True," he straightened, "but why would we want to? What's over there?"

She looked. She couldn't help but look, as he was looking. In the very centre of the diminishing circles, the highest spot on the island, was a block of white stone, waist high and as long as a tall man lying down. The sun-symbol was carved into every side as they walked around it, and channels led down from each corner to vanish into the ground.

"Is it a table?" Asta wondered. "Do they feast out here?"

"Nothing to feast on in the Scattering," Finn remarked. He crouched, running curious fingers over a faint smudge of brown that marked the ice-white surface of the stone platform. He frowned. "This is blood. Old blood."

"From a goat?" Asta asked.

"Maybe. Probably a place of sacrifice."

Sacrifice, at least, was something Asta could understand about this strange place. Sacrifices to help the harvest, for good luck, to appease the angry Spirits. Her father, in death, daubed with the fresh blood of a stallion as befitted a warrior.

"You should ask your savage about this place," Finn said.

As if responding to the mention of Syven, Asta felt a faint tug at her wrist, tentative, but transmitting some urgency. "I think they've stopped looking for their spies," she said.

"Time to go back?" Finn spoke lightly, but she felt his bitterness. Back to being trapped, a muted voice inside her head, powerless to do more than watch as she played out the story that should, she hoped, bring Rhodan back to her arms.

"Finn, if there was another way . . ."

"There is no other way. This is the only way I can help you. I want to help you. I *need* to help you, Lefalli would want that too . . ." They were racing back down the path as he spoke, the landscape a blur of green and brown around them. The wind whistled sharper than crickets' cries, more piercing than a lone bird call. The Scattering fell away below Asta, and she had a hazy glimpse of the city below, rooftops rushing to meet her. Then sucking blackness, the jar as her limbs hit the bathroom floor, and hands closing around her skull.

The breath rushed back in her lungs and she tried to cry out, but a powerful hand was over her mouth. "Hush, my Goddess!" Syven's whisper was urgent. "Olafur waits in your chamber. If he finds you meditating . . ." He left the threat hanging, as he tipped a pitcher of warm water over her hair. "You've been bathing, my Goddess. Haven't you?"

"Bathing," she repeated numbly, as he pressed her to sit up and wrapped a towel around her scalp.

"That's right."

She caught his arm, nails digging through fine hair to the flesh beneath. "Syven, I have to tell you—"

"Later!" he urged. "It's not safe."

"But things have changed—"

"For me too. Just," he squeezed her shoulder, "do as Olafur says, for now. We'll talk when he's gone. Gerhild is with him."

To check Asta for abnormalities. What would she do? Asta caught her hand straying to her belly and stayed the gesture, but Syven wasn't looking at her. He was untying the rope from the towel loop and fastening it around his waist, pulling his shirt down to conceal it. He winked at her. *You'll be fine*, he mouthed.

She felt far from fine, but she raised her head as she left the bathroom and met Olafur's stare as a Goddess and tribal leader. Gerhild regarded her with her citrus-sucking expression, lips pursed, cheeks sucked in. "She looks normal, for a horse-girl," she said.

"That's what we're here to ascertain," Olafur said. "Take her into the bedroom and check her over."

Asta's lip curled. "You don't want to have a look yourself, Olafur? Bet you'd like that."

He shot her a dark glare, but let the comment slide. Gerhild gestured for Asta to follow her, but she stood firm. "I'm not going anywhere until you tell me what's going on."

"We want to make sure you're well," Gerhild said.

"Perfectly well, thank you for the concern. Disappointed to have my bath interrupted . . ."

"My apologies." Olafur's voice dripped with insincerity. "Go with Gerhild. It won't take long."

"Goddess, please?" Syven's voice was anxious, and it was only that which stopped her digging her heels in. They wanted her to have a child. They would do nothing to hurt any child already growing inside her.

She allowed Gerhild to take her hand and lead her into the bedroom. The old woman's palm was rough, but her touch was gentle. Still, Asta had to fight not to recoil, remembering how those hands had probed and invaded when she first arrived at the manse.

"I won't hurt you, Goddess." Gerhild closed and barred the door behind them. "Lie down on the bed."

"What's this about, Gerhild?" Asta wanted to see what lie the old lady would spin.

She smiled, showing the gaps in her teeth. "We want to see why you haven't started a baby yet, Goddess. Do you bleed as normal?"

"Perfectly normal." She felt a spark of defiance. "Maybe there's something wrong with Syven's seed? Had you considered that?"

"Syven has been tested in every way." There was a dirty gleam in Gerhild's eye. "He has not been found wanting. You were with men, before you came to us?"

"Some. And some women, when I felt like it." Asta hoped, perversely, that Gerhild would be shocked, but she merely drew her thin brows together in irritation.

"Yet you did not fetch then?"

"Fetch? Oh, I see. No. I took steps to prevent it. I like children, but I don't want one of my own."

"I see." Gerhild's mouth snapped on the last word, as if she was disgusted. How could Asta be selfish enough not to breed, her expression said. Asta ignored it. She had heard it from Lefalli, from her aunts, from everyone except her mother, who smoothed her whiskers and kept her own counsel.

"Why didn't you tell us this before? You could have damaged yourself. Lie back, I'm going to have to investigate."

Asta lay on her back. Her thighs trembled as she parted her legs, and she hoped Gerhild would put it down to cold, not fear. She stared at the cracks in the ceiling, and a tear squeezed from the corner of her eye.

Don't.

She rarely heard Finn when she walked in the realm of the living, but she heard him now, felt him shifting around in her consciousness.

Don't cry.

Don't show weakness, or don't be afraid? It was impossible to tell what he meant. Gerhild slathered a minty lotion between her legs and the sensation was cold, and slippery. The woman laid a hand, as bronzed as an ancient copper coin, on her stomach.

"Won't be long, Goddess. This shouldn't hurt."

Asta bit her lip, and Finn fidgeted again. She felt his awareness travelling down her body, drawing a veil of darkness over it like a shadow across the moon. Gerhild didn't seem to notice.

"What are you doing?" Spoken aloud, and in her head. Finn didn't reply, but Gerhild did.

"Checking you haven't ruined yourself, you selfish girl." Her fingers were invading again, but the salve made everything numb. Just a tingling and pushing between her legs, as the shadow wrapped around her womb like a blanket, gathering her babies, keeping them safe. Keeping them secret.

Gerhild managed a twisted smile as she raised her head and wiped her hands on a cloth. "Get up." She tossed the cloth to Asta. "Wipe yourself down, then come back to the lounge."

"No harm done?"

"Not that I can tell. There's no reason you haven't got a baby yet." Gerhild sucked her gums noisily as she banged out of the room, leaving Asta to cleanse herself as best she could. She wondered if she could ask Syven for another bath. She wanted to talk to her caring, clever brother.

Instead she tossed the cloth on the bed, straightened her skirt, ran her hands over her hair. Still too short to braid, and they would cut it again soon, but they couldn't cut away her spirit.

"Still a warrior," she muttered. "Still fighting."

She drew in a deep breath and steeled herself to face those she had disappointed. But when she emerged from the bedroom, Syven was alone. He slumped on the couch with his head in his hands, a posture of utter defeat.

"Have they gone?" she asked.

He nodded.

"What are you looking so miserable about? Olafur didn't find out I was meditating, did he?"

"No. I kept your secret."

"Then you're not in trouble?" Moved by his misery, she

snuggled next to him and drew his hands down from his face. "So why so sad?"

"I've failed in my duty. I won't be freed this cycle."

"What duty? The duty of making me pregnant?" Restless, she sprang to her feet to pace the well-worn carpet before the windows. "Is that the only reason you showed interest in me? So you could breed on me to fit in with Olafur's plans?"

Syven stared at his feet. "At first, yes. You should know, I have a wife—"

"And daughters. Twins, am I right?"

He leapt up, caught her wrists, dragged her to him. "How could you possibly know that?"

She wrenched away. "I told you, I know more than you think . . ."

"The bloody meditating! Olafur was right. I should never have let you do it. I thought I was doing you a kindness. I like you, Asta. What they're doing to you is disgusting, and I wish I could prevent it."

This was new. She felt Finn's surprise echoing her own. *I'll handle this, little brother*, she told him, and he receded to a state of watchfulness behind her eyes. She tried to project how grateful she was for his protection of her children, how she would do the same for him, if he took a step back and let her control the situation.

"Asta? Are you all right? Your eyes are glazed . . . ."

"I'm fine." She shook her head.

"What else do you know? What did you see?"

She debated what to tell him. "I saw a chamber, with your people sat around a table. There was a woman. I think her name was Erikah? She was a witch, or an enchantress, she could touch people's minds with her own. Maybe a visionary, like my people. You were there . . ." She had the satisfaction of seeing the colour drain from his face. "Then I travelled past stone houses, over bridges and chasms. I saw the whole of the Scattering unfurl before me like a blanket, and I saw how poor it was. No trees, little grass, only soil and bare rock. I came to a gate, rings of blue and white marble, where the insects cried too loudly, and a table with a sun carved into it, the same sun Olafur wears on his robes. That was as far as I went before you called me back."

He turned his back to her. His shoulders were shaking, though whether with fear or suppressed rage she couldn't tell. "You couldn't have. You couldn't have got there and back so fast . . ."

"I told you, it was a vision." She resumed her seat, hands folded in her lap, watching him wrestle with the revelation.

"Truly, you are the one the prophets foretold!"

"Maybe." Asta smiled. "What was that place?"

"The Temple of the Summer Goddess."

"I have my own temple? I'm honoured . . . ."

Syven said nothing. He stood at the window, one arm and his forehead resting on the glass, a shape against the late-afternoon sun.

"I saw blood on the stone, Syven. I know about sacrifices. My people—"

"Your people sacrifice horses and goats!" He spun around. His eyes were bright with tears. "I thought I could do this, for the good of the land!"

The chill ran down Asta's spine, to the pit of her stomach. "Syven? What do your people sacrifice, if not horses and goats?"

What happens at the end of summer?

Syven ran his hand across his face. He looked broken.

"Gods, Asta. At the end of summer, we sacrifice our Gods."

ELEVEN

hIS WORDS FELL away, into a silence that went on and on. Asta tried to suck in air, clutched the arms of the sofa as the room span around her. She opened her mouth, but her throat was tight, and the words choked and died before they could be born. She felt Syven sit beside her, take her hand, press it between his own. She felt his tears splash cold on her skin.

"Me?" Her tongue felt too thick for her mouth.

"You asked me, over and over, what would happen at the end of summer. How could I tell you?"

Asta swallowed. "What will happen . . . then?"

"Olafur will take you to the Temple. He will cut your throat on the White Altar, and your blood will pour on to the earth to feed the land. You will give the Scattering your life, and it will grow and prosper."

It was a shock to hear him speak so calmly, so graphically, about her death. "When?"

"Just over a month from now, when the moon is full."

"How many days is that?"

He did some mental calculation. "Thirty-six."

No time at all. Asta felt sick, and she realised she was shaking. Syven poured some wine and pressed the glass into her hand, but she could hardly hold it and the liquid slopped into her lap.

She looked at the spreading stain on her skirt, and thought of blood. "Do you find a girl like me every year, to be your Summer Goddess?"

"There hasn't been a Summer Goddess for over three centuries." He took the untasted wine from her hand, and squeezed her fingers. "We're desperate, Asta. The Scattering is dying."

It was easier to think about the problems of the Scattering than her own dark fate. "What's wrong with this land, Syven?"

"The trees were sick. Some kind of fungus – it spread like fire. And without the trees the wind and rain washed the soil into the rivers, and the crops failed. We were starving, dying. There were barely three hundred of us left when the Inyestans came. Their priests brought food, goats, wood for our fires. We thought they were sent from the gods, and at first we didn't ask the price. But when they demanded payment, the cost was a terrible one."

"Slaves?" Asta already knew the answer.

"When there were enough of us to sustain the population, the Inyestans demanded one in every ten. To be herded like goats into their black ships. *Decimation*, they called it, as if giving it a clever name could conceal what it really was. But we had ships now, and we made a foul trade. We would give them the numbers they wanted, but they wouldn't all come from the Scattering, not if we could help it."

"So the eastern sea became your hunting ground," she said. He nodded. "You need me – my blood, my death – to make the Scattering flourish, to break the hold Inyesta has over you, so you can end this trade."

"Your life, Asta. Your life to save thousands from slavery."

My life, and the lives of my children.

"What about twins?" Syven looked startled at her change in tack. "Olafur wants me to have twins . . . ?"

"Twins are sacred in our culture. Perfect symmetry." He smiled. "If you conceive twins, the sacrifice will have many times the strength. That's why . . . I was chosen." His face darkened. "I misled you. I'm sorry."

"Sorry? Fucking *sorry*?" She pushed him away as he offered a comforting embrace. "Shit, Syven, I'm going to die! My children, your children, are going to die, and the best you can offer is *sorry*?"

His touch faltered, his hand falling away. "My children?"

"You did your duty." Asta spat. "Now you're a free man, and I'm dead. Enjoy your liberty."

"Gerhild said there was no baby. Is this a trick?"

"No trick," she said. "My people know how to keep things secret we don't want revealed. The twins are safe, for now. At least until Olafur wields the knife and saves your country." She hesitated. "Will you tell him?"

Syven's hands twisted over each other. "I should . . . ."

"Will you give me a few days? I only found out this morning." It felt like an age ago. So much learned, so much to think through and deal with. Asta felt like the tide was rushing over her head, sweeping her away.

Syven nodded, reluctantly. "I need to think too. May I use your bath, my Goddess?"

She would welcome the time alone. Not just away from Syven, but from Finn, as much as she could be. Time to work out how she could save her own life, and that of her children, from a dying land thirsty for her blood.

Syven avoided her for the next few days, as much as he could in their cramped life together, penned up like slaves awaiting sale. He spent his nights twisted uncomfortably on the couch, and whenever she entered the room he muttered an excuse to get out of her sight as quickly as possible. He looked sick, though whether in heart or body Asta couldn't tell, and she didn't ask. She could wait for him to come around, but she couldn't wait forever. She sat docile, pretending to be reconciled to her fate, but inwardly she seethed. She had to get out of there, and she couldn't escape without Syven's help.

"How will Olafur kill me?" she asked, catching Syven in a doorway as he tried to evade her. "Will he cut my throat, as they do to goats in my country? In some southern lands, they cut out the hearts of sacrifices. My father told me—"

"Stop talking about it!" Syven tried to pull away, but she held his arm, making sure it brushed her belly. Just a little reminder.

"I want to know, Syven. Shouldn't I be told how I'll be killed?"

"You have an advantage. For most, death is a surprise. You have a chance to reconcile yourself with your gods."

"There are no gods where I come from," she reminded him. "Only the vengeful spirits of my ancestors. They'll be watching, you know. The retaliation from the Spirit Realm will be swift and terrible for the injustice you've served on me."

He shook his head. "I don't believe in your spirits, Asta."

"What do you believe in? Justice? Fairness? Olafur's righteous fucking . . . *right* to kill me? What makes you think it will even work?"

Syven frowned. "Olafur knows what he's doing. He is guided by a greater power."

"And if it doesn't work? How many more girls will you lock up here and send to the slab to feed your barren soil?"

"You are the last," he said. "The last Goddess. Most of our people are dead; the isles are bare. Mikligard is our last city, our lifeboat. We can feed people here, for now, but the seas are empty. The cliffs have been stripped of birds, and every month the supplies from Inyesta diminish, even as they grow more greedy for our people. We don't have enough men here to supply them with the slaves they need any more, or the crews for the hunting ships. When the trade fails, they'll cut us off, and the last men of Mikligard will starve, or sell themselves into slavery for a handful of grain."

"Can't you go somewhere else?" Asta thought of the wide, empty steppes of Atrath with a deep pang of homesickness. The steppe could swallow the Scattering a hundred times over. All that land, yet Syven's people clung to a barren rock, waiting for death or divine salvation.

"Where would we go? We've made every other nation on the eastern sea hate us. Refugees from the Scattering would not be welcomed anywhere. And Inyesta has a long reach."

She caught his hand. "Let me go, and I can go back to my people and convince them to accept you. My country is vast and empty. My father was a warrior, a great hero. My words have power there."

Syven snorted. "Olafur will never allow it. You'd go, and we would die."

"Does my word mean nothing to you? My word as a warrior, as leader of my tribe?"

"You're not a warrior here, Goddess." He smiled, but it was weak and fleeting. "I wish I could save you."

"You can, and I can save you in return. If you won't do it for me, do it for your children. How can you send your own blood to their death? Think of your daughters. What if they were going to the White Stone, instead of me?"

"Do you think I haven't thought of that?" He wrenched away from her, eyes welling in furious despair. "That's all I've been thinking about since you told me! I'd spill my own blood for my country, but the blood of my children?" He drew a deep, trembling breath. "I want to help you, Asta, but I want to save my people too. You say your father was a warrior. He fought for his country. This is my fight. But I never considered . . ." he sighed. "When the Council told me to get babies in your belly, in whatever way I could, I was sick at the thought. I'm no rapist, Asta. The idea of betraying my wife was torture, and without her blessing I couldn't have done it, no matter what threats I was under. A barbarian horse girl, a Goddess? But you made it," he grinned, a flash of his old humour, "less difficult. I never considered that any babe I got on you would be mine too. I told myself I was doing a job, for my country and to win my freedom. I never thought I'd come to care about you," his hand strayed to her stomach, resting there, strong fingers flexing, "or our half-breed children."

Asta allowed him to lead her to the bed and they sat side-by-side. His fingers brushed the nape of her neck as she talked.

"More mongrel than half breed. My father was a Kingdom soldier, my mother was of the tribes. He betrayed his people to save hers, and he suffered for it. What would they do to you if I escaped? You're a slave. Would they kill you, or your wife?"

"No," he said. "Slavery on the Scattering is different to Inyestan slavery.

"How so?"

"I'm only a slave until I work off my debt. I belong to the Council because my debt is with them, but they can't beat me, or kill me, or transfer my debt to another. While I'm indentured to them they have to protect and provide for my family, because I can't. I have rights. Slaves sold to Inyesta are no more than property. They have no more rights than a saucepan, or a goat."

She thought of Rhodan and Lefalli, of the stolen people of the Beehive tribe, with a deep stab of guilt. They had hardly crossed her mind since she learned about the twins, and the White Altar. Where were they now? No rights, no protection . . . How would she ever find her nephew? How could she even start looking, if she couldn't get off the Scattering?

"So if you helped me . . ."

"The Council couldn't kill or beat me, but they could extend my period of slavery as punishment, or lock me up. My wife wouldn't be held responsible. She would be safe no matter what happened. But you can't ask me to help you, Asta."

"Can I ask you to help your children?"

His hand stilled on her throat, below her ear, where the pulse beat in her life vein. Was that where Olafur's knife would pierce, to end her life? The spot where the mercy-blade drank?

"Yes," he said. "You can ask me that, but I don't know if I can answer. Not yet."

Two days later Syven vanished from her rooms without a wo uttered. Asta debated diving into the Spirit Realm to talk t Finn, but she didn't know when her bodyguard would be back. He could have gone to Olafur, betrayed all he knew. Maybe she was wrong to trust him. Finn muttered dire warnings in the back of her mind, and she tried hard to shut out his sceptical voice.

I'm doing this for you, brother. For Rhodan, if I can find him, and for our tribe. Let me fight my own war.

All day she was tense, startling at the slightest sound, expecting any moment that Olafur would arrive at the door with a band of heavies to drag her to a cell, or to the marble ring. He wouldn't bring the ceremony forward, surely? It was connected to the full moon, and the turn of the season. Killing a Summer Goddess before summer was over would, she sensed, not be as effective. At least to Olafur's fanatical mind. And while she lived, she had hope.

By the time the next day dawned, with no sign of Syven, she was growing frantic. She considered beating on the door and yelling, but if he had sneaked out against Olafur's wishes that would only cause trouble for both of them. She paced the room, too anxious to be bored, a deep and growing ache in the shoulders and the small of her back. By the time she heard the bolts on the door shoot back, she was drawn tighter than a bow string. What would she say if it was Olafur?

But it was Syven, nipping through the door almost before it was open and closing it firmly behind him. He pressed a finger to his lips, and she bit back a cry.

"I'm sorry, my Goddess."

"Where the fuck have you been?" she demanded.

"I brought food." From a bag over his shoulder he brought out a heavy chunk of dark bread, and Asta fell on it. With the anxiety waning she realised she was famished.

"Where did you go?" she asked, mouth full, spraying crumbs.

"At first I walked along the coast. I needed to clear my head, before I headed back into the city."

"You were walking all this time?" Asta heard the doubt in

her own voice. The bread was dry, and stuck in her throat as she swallowed.

"Hardly. I called in to see my wife, and we talked for a long time. She's smart, she knows people who know people. I told her about your . . . difficulty."

"She wasn't angry?"

"She knew since I was enslaved that my duty was to father twins with the Summer Goddess." He smiled. "She's wiser than me. She anticipated my loyalty to the Council might be tested. She doesn't want to see anyone dead."

"She'll help me?" Asta asked. "How?"

"She wouldn't tell me. She asked me to find out the route you'll take to the Summer Temple, the day you . . ." He trailed off.

"The day I go to die. You can say it, Syven. I'm not afraid of words." She thought quickly. "That's over a moon away, just about. Is there no chance it can be sooner?"

Syven laughed, the first genuine laugh she had heard from him in a long time. He pulled her into his arms, heedless of the crumbs. "My impatient, demanding Goddess! Always wanting more than I can give."

"I am a Goddess," she reminded him. "Isn't it the nature of your gods to be demanding?"

"Believe me, Asta," his lips sought hers and she did not resist, "none of them are quite as demanding as you . . ."

Three days later, and Syven beamed as he brought in the lunch tray. The food was nothing to grin about, a bowl of watery fish soup, and more of the hard, salty bread. He set the tray down with the air of a man imparting an important secret.

Asta eyed him warily. "What do you look so pleased about?"

"I've been talking to Olafur."

She glared at him over the terracotta bowl as she raised it to her lips. "And what does he have to say?"

"I persuaded him it would be wise to rehearse the ceremony. This will be the climax of his life. How terrible if he was remembered as the man in charge if things go catastrophically wrong?" His eyes sparkled as he snatched up her bread and ripped a chunk from it with his teeth. "It would be good for the morale of the city to see you going happily to your fate. Ready to lay down your life to save us."

Asta drained the last of the soup and set down the bowl. "And . . . your wife?"

His face was a studied blank. "I don't know anything about that."

A fly buzzed against the curtains, and she remembered Erikah's warning about Inyestan spies, watching through the eyes of birds and insects. Surely that power could not belong to Inyesta alone? She pressed her lips tight. "I see."

"Will you be ready at the call?"

"I've been ready a long time, Syven."

His face darkened. "It may not work, mind . . . Whatever the plans are."

"Then I go to my death a willing servant of the Scattering," she said pointedly. "You can let Olafur and his cronies know that. Shout it from the balcony, if you like. I'm ready to do . . . whatever it takes."

He dropped to one knee before her, head sweeping low. "My courageous Goddess," he murmured.

She nudged him with her foot. "Get up, you big lump. You know I'm no more Goddess than you are!"

"But you are courageous. I see why your people chose you as their leader."

"They didn't." She could not pretend she wasn't flattered. "I inherited the position from my father. My brother didn't want it, and there were only the two of us. There was always opposition to my leadership."

"Yet you led, and no doubt led well."

"Until the Scattering came, yes." She didn't want to be reminded of that hideous day. It felt so long ago, but she could remember every tiny detail; the screams, the smoke, the warm lifeblood of the dying gushing over her hands as she pulled her father's mercy-blade free. The Scattering had forced her to kill her own people, and now the Scattering meant to kill her. She may tell Syven she would go without a fight, but that was a lie. She would kick and scream and bite until the moment the blade silenced her last breath.

Twelve

SYVEN SHOOK ASTA awake before dawn on the day of the rehearsal. He rubbed her back while she heaved her guts up into a bucket, and trimmed her hair, even though it was still too short for defiant braiding. She felt hollowed out, as if she had vomited up the best part of her and all that remained was a shell, the spirit of her brother swirling around a body emptied of blood and life. If Olafur was to cut into her today, all that would pour forth was dust. The Scattering could not thrive and grow on dust.

Fuck the Scattering.

She was reassured by Finn's contempt, his phantom nudge in her ribs. No matter what happened, he was with her, and she drew strength from his presence. If Olafur killed her, she hoped Finn would rush forth and wreak terrible vengeance. Not just for her, but for all of her tribe who would never be free if she died, and for the loved ones they had left behind. She heard Olafur making a fuss about some minor detail in the outer chamber, and she directed her loathing towards him, a wave of hatred that she hoped would stab him in the gut like a spear. See how he liked it.

Syven returned, arms laden with ceremonial robes, frowning as he shut the door on Olafur's barrage of complaint and criticism. "He's fractious today," he observed. "Try not to piss him off, my

Goddess."

Asta's mind immediately calculated the best ways to piss off Olafur. She picked up a glass of wine and let a few blood-crimson drops fall on the rustling yellow silk before Syven could snatch it away.

"Asta!"

"They're going to end up bloodstained anyway," she said innocently, smiling to hear Finn's chuckle deep within her.

"Not *today.*" Syven dabbed the silk with his own sleeve, his frown deepening. "Timing is everything. Give me that wine." He clicked his fingers impatiently and she handed over the cup, which he drained with one gulp.

Asta glared. "I was drinking that."

"You were spilling it on your robes to spite Olafur. No time for games today, Asta. Get dressed."

She stripped down to her undershift, slow and insolent, feeling Syven's hungry eyes follow her every move. "Go on then." She held her arms up, like a child waiting to be dressed by her mother. "Make me pretty for Olafur and his knife."

"I don't need to make you pretty, Goddess." He took the broad swathe of silk which cinched her from bust to hips, and slid it round her back, cool and smooth against skin that burned under his scrutiny. His fingers brushed her spine, her flat buttocks, the treacherous white patches on the backs of her knees as he dressed her. Every touch was feather-light, but charged with static, his breath lifting the fine hairs on her dark skin as he swaddled her in silk the colour of summer. She leaned into him, her own breath tight as he laced ribbons and bows. He wrapped her head in a soft turban so no hair showed, his lips brushing hers as, at the last, he drew the gauzy mask down over her face.

She looked like a beam of light. But her heart was black and heavy, and the finest silks on the Scattering could not conceal her hate.

Syven brushed her cheek through the gauze, a quick swipe as if he was wiping away a tear she hadn't shed. His hand on her shoulder steered her into the reception chamber where Olafur was waiting to pounce as they emerged.

"Are you ready?"

Asta shrugged, dislodging the gauze from one side of her face. "Why so impatient, Olafur? It's just a rehearsal."

"I know." He replaced the cloth before she had a chance to raise her hand. "Nothing must go wrong, do you understand? My competence has already been called into question . . ."

"So if it falls apart today, will my care be taken from you and given to someone else?" Asta asked sweetly. "Erikah, maybe?"

"How do you— another vision?" Olafur startled. "I thought I told you—?"

"You just told me there wasn't time." She delighted in needling him, in seeing him so unsettled. She took her victories where she could these days.

"There isn't." He propelled her towards the door with a hand on her arse. "Syven, you've done well. Have a meal ready for her when we return."

Asta's heart sank. "Syven isn't coming with us?" He had been such a constant. The thought of venturing into the streets without him, in physical form so she couldn't even rely on Finn, was as if her lead rein had been cut. She looked over her shoulder at him. His figure was blurred through the gauze, as if he was already fading from her life. "I thought you'd be there with me."

"It's not my duty, Goddess." He inclined his head, keeping his eyes downcast as Olafur pushed her out of the door and shut it firmly behind her.

Now she was alone, without allies she could call on. She gritted her teeth and followed Olafur downstairs. This was the first time since she was brought to the mansion that she had walked these halls as a living form. It unnerved her to be able to touch the walls without her fingers sinking through them, and as Olafur led them to the door emblazoned with the sun emblem, she was glad the gauze concealed her smile.

"The Council Chamber," she said.

"Will you stop doing that? You make me look irresponsible!" Olafur barked, his voice high with anxiety.

"Do you sometimes wonder if you picked the wrong Goddess, Olafur?"

"Constantly. But I'm stuck with you now, so may it do us all some good. Just . . . behave, will you?"

"Of course," she demurred, as he swung the door open to allow her entry.

The chamber was full, every chair occupied by the men and women she had spied on before. There was Erikah, on the far side on the room, regarding her with keen interest. Would she recognise Asta by the touch of her mind, try and invade as she had before? She had no doubt of Erikah's power, but how far did it extend, and did the woman of Mikligard wish her well, or harm?

Don't think about it.

She felt Finn drawing a veil over her thoughts, hiding them the way he had concealed the twins from Gerhild's probing. A blanket of fog descended on her brain, like the morning after a heavy bout of drinking. It dulled her wits, her sensations. She dimly heard Olafur introduce her to the council, who muttered their respect, but it was as if more than a physical veil lay between them. She was hardly aware of what was happening as they fell into step behind her and Olafur took her arm.

"Are you feeling ill?" he hissed in her ear. "You seem a thousand miles away. Wake up!"

She nodded, dully. Erikah was still too close to lift the veil of secrecy. She had to trust Finn now.

They marched down the corridor, past the kitchen, and up a short flight of steps to the hallway she had crossed when she arrived. The front doors stood wide, letting in the sea breeze, and in the distance Asta heard a dull roar, like waves crashing and breaking against the rocks. In the walled yard stood a litter, and four big slaves waiting to carry it. Asta was repeating the journey she had made when she arrived, and, as on that day, her final destination was a terrifying mystery.

It's only a rehearsal, she reminded herself, as she stepped into the litter and reclined. Olafur fussed with the concealing curtains. She expected him to drop them, but he was tying them back.

"Do people get to look at me today?" she asked.

"From a distance."

She thought back to the incident on the balcony. "What if someone takes another shot at me?"

"Any crowds will be kept back. The rehearsal hasn't been publicly announced, and all known trouble makers have been rounded up and confined until the ceremony is over."

"That seems a little harsh," Asta observed.

"It's the only way to break up their plots against your life," Olafur told her. "Are you comfortable?"

"I was more comfortable before I was given the impression that every man in Mikligard wants me dead before my appointed time."

"A minority." He dismissed her fears.

"But why would they? Don't they believe in the strength of your precious sacrifice?"

Olafur cut her off with a sharp gesture. "You're perfectly safe," he said. "I'll be with you every step of the way." He uttered the command and the litter lurched forward. Asta clutched at the cushions to steady herself.

"Where are we going?" she asked.

"Just to the edge of the city. I anticipate any problems that need smoothing out will occur within the city walls."

"What problems?"

Olafur flashed a bland smile. "There won't be any problems."

"Fine." She slumped back among the cushions and watched the clouds scurry overhead as the cortege passed into the streets of Mikligard. It was an awkward procession, armed men in livery moving ahead of her and to either side, then the litter. Olafur walked beside her, his hand clamped tight on her forearm. His limbs shook with suppressed tension, and she wondered what would happen to him if things went wrong. Behind, in formation, the Council marched. Erikah walked at the rear, carrying an empty cushion with utmost reverence, and moving with a precise, measured tread. Behind and around her were more soldiers, hands on their blades, poised and alert.

"What's the cushion for?" Asta asked Olafur, more for something to say than out of any real interest.

"It would carry the Summer Blade, if this was a real ceremony. The Summer Blade cleaves summer from autumn, it feeds the land . . ." He trailed off.

"It kills me," Asta finished for him. She stared into the sun until black dots danced before her eyes and made them water. "I'm glad she's not carrying it today."

"You should be honoured!" Olafur hissed. They were turning into one of the main thoroughfares from the narrow, gated lanes behind the manse, and the roaring in Asta's ears increased in volume. She had to strain to hear him. "You are doing a great service for this country. Thousands of women have lived and died and never had the honour you will receive. You are the saviour of our people!"

"I'd be a lot happier," she flashed back, "if I didn't have to die in the process. If I'm going to give my life, I'd like it to be for something I give a shit about."

His nails dug into her arm as the column came to an unexpected halt. "How can you say that? Why have we stopped?" This was directed at a liveried soldier hurrying down from the front of the line. She snapped off a crisp salute.

"*Mestari,* there are bigger crowds than we thought. They want to see the Goddess. What should I do?"

Olafur thinned his lips. "Do you have enough men to hold them back?"

"I think so, *Mestari.*"

"Then we continue along the planned route. Be ready to make changes, though."

The soldier nodded, and hurried back up the column. Olafur huffed through his nose, nostrils flaring, and glared at Asta as if this was her doing. "Smile and wave, and say nothing," he snarled.

"Why do we need all these soldiers around me?"

Olafur sighed tightly. "Some want to cause you harm, some may try and snatch you, to hold you hostage, to force the Council to do their bidding. I just want you to be *safe*."

"Safe until it's time to kill me, you mean?"

He lowered his eyes before her glare.

"It must be a real itch under your saddle to know that not everyone agrees with your addle-brained plan to save them?" Asta kept her barbs mockingly sweet.

Olafur's fists clenched. "You will *be quiet* or you will be returned to the manse and locked in a cupboard for the next month. Do you understand me?"

"Yes, *Mestari*."

He didn't react to her mocking tone, contenting himself with a glower and a pinch. Asta sat forward, more interested now that the view around her wasn't confined by high grey walls, as the column turned into the wider street that passed in front of the mansion.

The sun was dazzling, the noise a barrage that pressed her back against the cushions, for all Olafur tried to steady her. A sea of people lined the street, held back by wary soldiers with hooked steel pikes. The coloured rags they waved fluttered like ripples on the tide, bright and defiant as they cheered. Cheering for her. Cheering because she would save them by laying down her own life.

There was a tight knot of misery at the back of Asta's throat that was impossible to swallow. Her face was hot, her palms itchy with uncomfortable sweat. Her cheeks hurt from the fake smile plastered to her lips, and she felt the tears welling, no matter how hard she forced them back. She was pressed down by the weight of their expectation, and the pressure grew heavier as the crowds thickened and the parade came to another grumbling halt.

Olafur rolled his eyes as the same soldier trotted back from the head of the line. "What now?" he demanded.

"A house has collapsed in the next street. It'll be hard to get the Goddess through. The crowds are thick up there, and restive. *Mestari,* I recommend a different route. The harbour road, maybe? It's wide enough for any crowds to gather . . ."

Olafur chewed his lower lip, looking up and down the road. His fingers drummed on Asta's wrist as he came to a decision. "If you think it's safe," he said at length. "You have the head of the column, soldier. Lead the way."

The soldier nodded smartly, and Asta watched the guards around the litter press back the crowds that surged against them. There was no anger in their eagerness, no malice in their desire to be near her, but if that thin black line broke she would be swarmed and trampled before she could draw breath.

She shuddered as the litter lurched onwards, heading towards a narrow alley between two buildings, so tight that she only had to lean over a little to touch the cold stone walls towering on either side of her. Olafur was forced to relinquish his grip and fall behind. Sunlight gleamed off the surface of the sea ahead, and she heard the rattle of chains and the flap of cloth against the stiff breeze over the tramp of boots in front of her. She wondered how far she could swim, how fast, if she could make a break that way.

The column swung out on to the harbour side, boots splashing though the puddles on the dock. The cold water splashed against the litter, marring the silks and brocade. There were less people here, and those roaming the street were intent on loading and unloading the ships that were lashed to the harbour walls. Smaller boats scuttled between them like darting minnows, tiny in the shadows of the full-bellied cargo vessels. The litter passed a line of shuffling slaves, linked ankle-to-ankle by a long, looped chain. Asta winced and had to look away from the whip-scores across their shoulders. A nudge in her mind, a voice that was her own, not Finn's.

Your blood could free them too.

It wouldn't. Olafur's deluded belief in his blood-hungry land would lead to nothing but her death. Inyesta would keep her fist closed, and everything would go on as it had before. She wished she could make him understand that.

"Olafur? Do you really believe—?"

It happened so quickly the question was snatched from her lips and scattered to the wind.

A group of dock workers manhandled barrels from ship to shore across the width of the road ahead, lifting them on to their backs with sturdy harnesses. She looked up at the sudden curse to see one of the barrels come free and shatter, spraying wine and splinters of wood across the street in a bloody and tangled tide. The column came to a stumbling halt, throwing her hard forward. The dockside was full of running feet, men pouring from the harbour, from a nearby alley. An abrupt command was cut off with a squeal like a horse being slaughtered.

"Olafur!" Asta twisted to grab him as the litter tumbled to the ground. He clutched at her, hands opening and closing as if in spasm. Eyes wide, mouth open, the sharp hooked point of a spear emerged from his throat.

He dropped to his knees, nails raking her skin, and Asta recoiled as arms closed around her shoulders, her waist. She kicked out, the world a whirl of sky and sea and stone, and her foot crunched against a knee that gave way before her. She felt rough, stinking cloth against her face as a bag came down, throwing her into darkness. She lashed out as she was lifted and carried, heard the clash of steel all around her. She tried to scream, but a hand tightened over her mouth, and the sacking swallowed all sound.

Thirteen

Asta was suffocating in the dark. Her face was dry and itchy, and when she breathed in the scent of onions was overwhelming. The heat, the smothering and the smell made her gag. She was surprised to discover her hands were free, and she ripped the hood and the sweaty, blood–spattered gauze from her face and threw them aside.

She had been pushed into in a small, humid room piled high with crates. She could see only one door, and a narrow slit in the wood provided a sliver of light. Fumbling, cautious in her steps, she walked over to it and tried it. It was locked, inevitably, but on a table beside the door was a stub of candle, a pair of candlestones, a cup of wine and a plate with sliced bread and fruit. Whoever had locked her in here obviously didn't intend her to starve. Was this a kidnapping, then, or a clumsy attempt at rescue?

She hated being locked in, hated the dark. It reminded her of the cabin on the ship where she had been sealed in for the journey. She needed the sky above her, not walls that closed in around her. She felt the familiar constriction in her chest, and she tried to focus on her breathing.

Not now. Please, spirits, not now . . .

What's wrong? Finn asked. She ignored him. It was her own weakness, nothing to do with him. She would fight it in her own way.

Asta?

By some miracle the pain eased, her limbs steadied. Maybe just having her brother there helped. She swallowed hard. *I'm fine. Can you see a way out of here?*

I think we're in for the duration. You might as well eat.

The motion of chewing made her head ache, but Asta forced down the fruit and stashed the bread in her robes. Who knew when she might be fed again? Fortified and calmed, she had another look around, at her makeshift prison and at herself. She was bruised and smelly, but otherwise unhurt, although her ceremonial robes were tattered. She thought how upset Olafur would be, and then she remembered Olafur was dead. Whoever came looking for her, it wouldn't be him.

Asta put her mouth to the door slit and yelled experimentally, but her cries brought no hurrying feet, no demands for silence. Most likely she was alone in the building. She rattled the lock again and kicked the door a few times, but it was old wood, solid, and it didn't budge. With a curse, she turned away in search of another escape route.

The crates around the walls were piled up higher than her head, and she studied them under the candle light. Square wooden boxes, banded with iron, marked with symbols she couldn't read. Some of them looked old, and if she set the candle down she could dig her fingers between the staves and prise the wood apart to get at the goods inside. With a grunt and a stumble one of the planks came free, a splintered bar of wood as long as her forearm. She hefted it in her hands. Not much of a weapon, should she need it, but better than her bare fists. She laid it on the table and returned to the crate, which was full of soft sacking that concealed something lumpy, and there was a strong scent of onions. With a sigh, she pulled the sack free, spilling onions on the floor, and ripped the sides to form a rough blanket. Maybe she could grill onion in the heat from the candle, if she ran out of bread. She would not starve.

She sat down, rank blanket pulled across her knees, trying not to inhale too deeply and failing to ignore the growing pressure in her bladder. There was a steel bucket under the table, and she assumed it must have been left for that purpose. Asta wasn't squeamish, but adding the smell of urine to the onion stench was something she wanted to hold off for as long as possible. She wished she could talk to Finn properly, but it was too risky. To travel with him meant leaving her body vulnerable, and in this strange place, with her unknown captors or saviours, that was a stride too far.

She peed at last, blew out the candle to save wax, and returned to the blanket on the far side of the room. There was little to do but wait, with one hand resting on the wooden plank, an ear alert for footsteps outside. She wondered what would happen to Syven now Olafur was dead. Would the Council be hunting for her? Would her captors ransom her back to them, or did they have some other fate in mind for her? Or was this the plot of Syven's wife, and the onions just – she smiled grimly to herself – just some kind of mild revenge?

She didn't know how long she sat in the blackness, feeling the knots of tension deepen in her shoulders, listening to rats scurrying in the walls. She tightened her grip on the club in case they came near. When she dropped off, uncomfortable, it was for only a few moments at a time, and her dreams were full of blood, permeated with the smell of raw onion. She woke to find her eyes streaming in the dark. How long had she been here? It could have been over a day. She could only tell the passage of time by her increasing hunger.

She ate the bread, and was debating trying to cook one of the onions when she heard brisk footsteps in the passage outside, and the lock rattled. She snatched up the plank of wood and scrambled to her feet. She would not be caught lying down.

The door opened, and the light from a swinging lantern dazzled her. From behind it, a woman's voice spoke.

"Oh good, you're awake! How are you feeling?"

"Fine," Asta lied, groping the wall behind her for support. She had dozens of questions, but she wouldn't show her ignorance before strangers until she knew what they wanted with her.

"Come into the light." The woman's voice was gentle, but Erikah had been gentle, and she carried the knife. Asta hung back.

"I'm sorry I had you shut in here. It was the best I could manage under short notice, and then Olafur died and I couldn't get back here as fast as I wanted to. But come on, you don't want to stay in this stinking room, do you? You're safe here, no one will hurt you."

She lowered the lantern, and Asta saw her face for the first time. A woman in her third decade, she guessed, with copper hair that curled around her ears, the same hue as her skin. She wore gold barrettes to keep her hair out of her face, and her cheeks were plumper than most of the Scattering women Asta had seen. When she smiled, she still had most of her teeth.

"I'm Heylan," she said, and paused, as if the name was meant to mean something to Asta. When no response was forthcoming she added, "I'm Syven's wife. He told me all about you."

"Oh." Asta lowered the plank of wood, belatedly recovering her manners. "Thank you. And . . . I'm sorry."

"Come on." Heylan extended her hand, drawing Asta into the circle of light and warmth. "Come upstairs. I've got hot food for you, and clean clothes. You look like you could use them."

The simple kindness in her words and actions moved Asta more than she would have thought possible. She felt the heat rise in her face, and her bottom lip wobbled treacherously. She wiped her eyes, and smiled. "I'll be glad to get out of the smell of these onions!"

Heylan smiled, but pressed her finger to her lips. "Follow me and keep quiet," she whispered, as she led the way out into the corridor. The windows were shrouded with sacking, and muted sunlight gleamed around the edges. The corridor was straight and narrow, built of whitewashed stone, and a sharp flight of stairs led up to an equally narrow landing and another door, which Heylan unlocked. She showed Asta into a room that was around the same size as the store room she had been locked up in, but free of boxes. It contained a long couch, a desk with papers shoved haphazardly up one end of it, two chairs, and a window covered with a white sheet. On the table was a bowl of gently steaming water, and a plate of stringy meat and rice.

"It's not much," Heylan said again, "but there are no onions in it, if that makes you feel better!"

"If I never see another onion . . ." Asta collapsed into the chair and fell on the food, scooping it up with a spoon and shovelling it into her mouth. It wasn't the hottest meal, but it filled the grumbling maw in her belly. "Thank you for your kindness," she muttered, catching grains of rice as they fell on her bloodied dress. "I'm not sure I deserve it."

"There's a clean shift for you here." Heylan looked at her doubtfully. "You're taller than me. It might be a bit short."

"I'm grateful for anything you can spare—" Asta broke off, embarrassed at being forced to rely on charity from Syven's wife, a woman who should have hated her. "Why are you doing this?"

"Why am I helping you?" Her eyes flicked downwards. "Are the babies safe?"

Asta laid her hand protectively on her stomach. "I think so," she said. Finn would tell her, surely, if that wasn't the case. He was protecting them, as she had promised to protect Rhodan. But she had failed. Now she didn't know where she was, and he was further away from her than ever. She tried to struggle to her feet.

"I'm not ungrateful, but I must . . ."

"Sit down." Heylan pressed a hand to her shoulder. "It's not safe for you on the streets. You're to stay here until things calm down."

"Calm down?" Asta didn't want to press the argument. There had been force in Heylan's hand, and she was still exhausted and dizzy. It wouldn't take much effort for Heylan to hustle her back to the onion room and leave her there, if she wanted to.

"The Council are looking for you, and the Fatalists. Luckily neither of them knows about this place, so far." She smiled. "You look confused . . ."

"A little," Asta confessed. "Who are the Fatalists?"

"Their faction doesn't believe in the Summer Goddess. They think having you here is a waste of precious resources. They think we should allow ourselves to be absorbed into the Inyestan Empire. It's going to happen anyway, so why prolong the pain?" Heylan wrinkled her nose as if a foul smell had drifted underneath it.

"I take it you don't agree?"

"If I did you'd be dead by now." Heylan pulled up the other chair to scrutinise Asta more closely. "I don't agree with the Council, either, if that's any consolation. Human sacrifice is barbaric and pointless. More of us think that way than I'll wager Olafur ever told you about, and we're growing in numbers."

Asta regarded Heylan's face, her broad cheeks and wide, honest eyes. "I think I trust you," she said at length. "But if you don't want me dead, for one side or the other, what do you want?"

Heylan blinked. "I don't want anything of you."

"No one does anything for nothing, Heylan . . ."

Heylan sighed, her gaze dropping to her hands, fingers twisting the ring she wore on her left thumb. "I want my husband back, and my children need their father. With you gone, the Council will have no need of him, and he'll be free to return to us. I could give you back to the Council, or the Fatalists, but then your blood would be on my hands. Or we could help you get home."

Home. She felt Finn twitch in the back of her mind, alert to the possibilities of freedom. "Home? On a ship?"

"A small boat, if I can arrange it with my friends. It'll be risky . . ."

"Safer than staying here." Asta tightened her arms around herself in a silent, secret embrace for her brother. A boat meant a way off the Scattering. It was a chance to search for her lost people.

Heylan rose. "I'll see what I can do," she said. "You can stay here for now, but I'll have to lock you in. Keep away from the windows. I'll bring food when I can, but it might be a few days.

Is that all right with you?"

"Yes. And . . . Thank you."

Heylan smiled, but said nothing as she closed the door behind her and Asta heard the key scrape in the lock. For a long moment she sat, chewing on what she had learned, before the itching of the fabric that enclosed her became unbearable and she ripped it free of her skin. She kicked the discarded robes away and pulled the plain grey shift down over her head. It was short, reaching only to mid-thigh, and it was more close-fitting than she liked, but she was no Goddess now, nor a tribal leader. Just a beggar forced to rely on the generosity of a stranger. She couldn't afford to be fussy.

She rummaged through the papers on the desk. She had picked up a few words of the pictorial writing of the Scattering, but not enough to be much use, and she threw the pages down with a sigh of frustration. There was nothing to help her there. She itched to look out of the covered windows, but Heylan's warning had been firm. But there was one way she could explore.

"I'm sorry, Olafur." She had had no liking for him, but his death had been brutal, and she felt a shred of guilt as she ripped the gold dress into long, wide ribbons. Soon she had a whole pile of them. She would be his Goddess no longer.

She tied her lead rein around the table leg, checked it was secure, and dropped into Finn's world.

"I see you've given up being a Goddess," he remarked tartly, from his seat on the couch. "Queen of Onions is hardly a step up, my sister."

"It's better than being a corpse, like poor old Olafur. Where are we, Finn?"

He walked over to the window and pushed his face through the curtain as if he had plunged it into a sheet of milk. "Well," he said, "we're still in bloody Mikligard."

"I assumed that much."

"I can see streets and houses, but not the harbour. Want to go exploring?"

Asta shook her head. "Too risky. Heylan seems pleasant enough, but . . ."

"I think you can trust her," Finn said.

"It's not your life on the slab if I make a mistake."

"No. I already spilled my blood for your mistakes, remember?"

She turned her face away from his expression of betrayal. "How could I forget, when you never stop reminding me?"

An awkward silence hung between them. Finn kicked his feet through the couch and cleared his throat. "The Scattering woman said something about a boat?"

"A small boat. I don't know how small."

"To take us back to Atrath?" he asked.

"I assume that's their plan. It's not mine."

Finn's lips set in a thin, hard line. "What is your plan, then?"

"We're not going back to Atrath. We're going to Inyesta, to find our people."

"How? You can't steal a boat. You don't know how to sail! And, let's face it, I'm not going to be a great deal of help in that situation, am I?"

"Are you giving up, little brother?"

He scowled. "Of course I'm not—"

"Because I made a promise to our tribe, and I intend to keep it, if I can."

His fingers closed over her shoulders, his hands chill with death, and she tried not to shiver. "If you do this, Asta, you could drown. You're taking a terrible risk."

"It might be the only chance we have to get them back. To get Rhodan back. Do you have any better ideas?"

He shook his head. "Just get us to Inyesta, if you can. Maybe I'll be more help to you there than at sea. We need to get Rhodan away from those people. They're dangerous, Asta. I can smell it on them. Something bigger—" He broke off. "Someone's coming. This is too risky. You're on your own, for now."

The landing back into her own body was easier from such a short distance, but Asta barely had time to untie her wrist, stash her rein and stand up before the door opened. Heylan again, dropping off some paperwork to add to the teetering pile on the desk. She smiled at Asta and pressed her finger to her lips, but said nothing, and left as quickly as she came.

Finn was right. It was too dangerous to slip in and out of the Spirit Realm in this unpredictable place, with such uncertain allies. She would have to ride this trail alone for the present, and see where it took them both.

They were frustrating, boring days locked in the office, with only the occasional visit from Heylan to bring food or swap over the latrine bucket to relieve the tedium. Still, it was ten times better than the onion cellar, and only a little worse than the manse, where there had at least been windows to look out of, and company, and sex. Asta caught herself missing Syven, and felt guilty for it. Heylan was risking her life in this enterprise, and it didn't feel right to be lusting after her husband.

Asta gathered by the passage of hazy light through the sheet over the window that it was late evening on the fifth day when Heylan arrived, breathless, locking the door behind her. She carried a basket, and draped over her arm were two long robes of midnight-black velvet. She shook one out and handed it to Asta.

"Shadow-cloth," she said. "Inyestan assassins wear these cloaks. They're the best thing for travelling at night when you don't want to be seen. You wouldn't believe the lengths I had to go to, to get these. Is it long enough?"

The cloth grazed Asta's ankles as Heylan swung it round her shoulders and fussed with it, making sure every inch of her limbs were concealed in the soft folds. She pulled the sweeping hood over her head, and drew across the face covering so that only Asta's eyes remained exposed. She chewed her lip thoughtfully.

"You pass well," she said. "Better than me!"

"As an Inyestan assassin?" Asta had doubts. "What if someone talks to me? I don't speak Inyestan. I know nothing of their ways, and I don't know what an Inyestan assassin would be doing on the streets of Mikligard. What do I do if someone asks me what I'm about?"

"No one will talk to you. People here like to pretend the assassin creed doesn't exist, in case they attract the wrong sort of attention. Trust me, if anyone does see you, their eyes will slide over you as if you're not there. No one in Mikligard wants to deal with assassins."

Heylan shook out and swung on her own cloak, which brushed the ground. She rummaged in the basket.

"There's a little food here," she said, "and a flask of wine. And a blade, should you need it. Herbs, in case the sea voyage makes you sick . . ." She trailed off. "I couldn't think of anything else, I'm sorry."

"You've done more than enough. How can I repay you? You've done so much for me, kept me safe . . ."

"Oh hush!" Heylan stroked her arm. "You don't deserve the hand you've been dealt, and if I can fix the deck in your favour, I will." She lifted the corner of the cloth and peered out of the window at the darkness beyond. "It's a cloudy night. We should go, and we'll have to move quickly. Are you ready?"

Asta nodded, and Heylan pulled up her own hood, eyes glittering blue over her mask. She pressed her finger to her covered lips, turned, and led the way downstairs on soft feet. The velvet muted every sound, and all Asta could hear was the bass rumble of her own heartbeat.

Syven's wife led her past the room where she had been imprisoned, along the corridor and round a sharp turn into a warehouse stacked high with crates and boxes, ceiling lost in the gloom above. There was an earthy taste to the air, of mud and grass and fresh-grown plants. It didn't smell like the Scattering to Asta.

Heylan must have heard her sniffing. "We import vegetables," she said, by way of explanation. "My husband fought with an Inyestan over prices. That's why he was enslaved."

"He told me he gambled, and lost," Asta remarked.

Heylan chuckled. "What is business, if not a gamble? Quiet now, we don't know who's about."

Asta followed her through the maze of boxes to a high, wide door made of metal, with a smaller door set into the base. She had to duck her head as she followed Heylan out on to the streets, and the moment she breathed in she knew Finn had been wrong. They were right on the harbour front, and, even in darkness, the work here never stopped. It carried on under lanterns swung from high poles to cast pools of light the length of the wharf, and it carried on more quietly, but it never ceased.

"The tide waits for no one," Heylan muttered. "We'd better hurry, or we'll miss it."

The two women darted from shadow to shadow, dodging the brilliance of the swinging lanterns, and the bustle of the harbour workers. When Heylan stepped more than a foot away Asta lost her in the dark, only able to follow her by the sound of her hard, anxious breathing. Her footfalls were as soft as a cat's, and the shadow-cloak swallowed her up, made her part of the surrounding night. Asta swathed her own velvet shroud around her and tried not to take her eyes off her rescuer.

They came to an intersection, a blaze of light and traffic. The lanterns cast a wobbling cross on the ground that illuminated the street ahead and the one that crossed it with a blaze as bright as daylight. Heylan held up her hand for Asta to stop. "Walk proud," she said. "Don't look at anyone. They are beneath you. You have a dark mission of your own."

"Heylan, how do you know—?"

"I've seen things you'd struggle to believe. I wasn't always an onion merchant, or a slave's wife. Walk with me."

Asta fell into step beside her. Heylan was half a head shorter than she was, but she walked as if she was ten feet tall, head held high, defying anyone to get in her way, so Asta did the same. It wasn't hard, she was of a proud people, and she drew on all the dignity of the tribe she had left behind.

The chatter fell away as they stepped out into the lighted crossroads, as if a great hand had stilled all motion. Heylan did not break her stride for an instant, and Asta was amazed by the way the dock workers seemed to melt before her. There was no scramble to get out of her way, but somehow, with no apparent effort on either side, their passage was clear. She could feel the dock workers trying desperately to pretend the two women weren't in their midst, while at the same time putting every effort into avoiding them. Her heart was in her throat by the time they vanished into the darkness on the far side of the crossing, and she saw Heylan shrink back into her normal posture. She blew out her cheeks, and offered Asta a grin.

"That was harder than I thought it would be!" she admitted. "My heart's pounding up and down my body like a mountain goat!"

"Mine too," Asta told her. "Is it far now? I don't think I could do that again . . . ."

"Just around this next corner," Heylan said. She glanced around, and fell back with a soft curse.

"What's up?" Asta asked.

"Council patrols. I should have known they'd be prowling."

Asta had a sick feeling in her gut. "Is it Erikah? You need to watch out for her, she has powers."

"Powers?"

"She can sense spirits. I think she can read minds, to some extent. I'm not sure how strong she is, but she's dangerous."

"Thanks for the warning." Heylan nodded, face grave. "We long suspected there was some magic at work on the Council, but we couldn't pin down who it was. That's useful to know." She risked another darting glance towards the sea. "It's not Erikah. It's an older man, with a moustache. I know his face but not his name."

"Hrulf," Asta supplied.

Heylan sighed. "I wish you could stay. You know so much about the Council. Syven told me about your visions."

Asta shook her head. "I need to be with my tribe, my family. I need to breathe free air again." *To find Rhodan, to bring him home . . . To bring them all home.*

Heylan glanced up, at where the moons would be if they weren't suffocated under a thick grey blanket of cloud. "You need to go," she fretted. "We're going to have to risk it."

Asta drew in a deep breath, honing her courage. She drew the knife from the basket on her arm and wrapped her fingers around it, the trailing velvet sleeve of her robe concealing the weapon. She felt Finn's hand on hers, and drew strength from her brother's presence in her mind.

"I'm ready," she said.

Heylan swished her cloak around her and stepped around the corner on to the harbour side, Asta only a pace behind. Barely a hundred paces away, a small boat was moored, a solitary lantern hanging from the stern. The sails were up and it was poised, ready to escape. A soldier in Council livery loomed over the man sitting by the tiller, and Asta's confidence faltered. Had they come so far only to be betrayed?

Heylan didn't hesitate, and if she was afraid, her fear was concealed under the deep folds of her hood. If anything, she increased her pace, shouting a demand in a language Asta didn't know.

Inyestan. Finn elbowed his way to the front of her mind. *She wants to know why the soldier is harassing her servant.*

Asta breathed her thanks as Heylan switched back into the language of the Scattering, thickly accented and deeper than her usual register. She kept her back to the lantern, its brightness shining from behind her like a halo, casting her face into shadow so deep only the glitter of her eyes was visible.

The soldier's hand was tight around his pike, his voice unsteady. "We're looking for a woman. She killed one of the Council. She might be trying to get off the Scattering."

"Your failure to protect your citizens is nothing to do with Inyesta. Would you stop us going about the business of our

Emperor? Do you not recognise my order?" Heylan's eyes blazed and she spat at his feet.

The soldier backed off a pace. "My lady, I would never interfere with your business, but—"

"What's going on?" The gruff voice was familiar. Asta's heart sank.

Heylan gave her a subtle prod, and said something in Inyestan.

Finn obligingly translated. *Get in the boat, my sister. I'll take care of these Scattering dogs. Never forget your vow of silence.* He snorted. *Silence? You?*

Shut your food-hole, she snapped back.

Do you want my help or not?

Asta didn't grace that question with a reply. She stepped down into the boat, the helmsman taking her arm to steady her as the deck pitched beneath her feet. She wished she could see his features, but in the darkness beyond the lantern light he was no more than a flash of teeth. She felt the mooring-rope tense against her elbow as she sat down.

On the wharf above, the argument grew heated. That blowhard Hrulf was stomping back and forth waving his arms, the soldier had faded into the background, and still Heylan stood her ground, never letting her mask slip.

"You want to set foot on Inyestan soil—?"

"It's not soil, lady, it's a boat."

"A boat that belongs to Inyesta, and is therefore sovereign property of my nation, my Emperor. You want to strip away my sister's protection, reveal her face to those who could have reason to hate her, just because you cannot catch your own fugitives? Why should a Shadow-cloak of Inyesta be put at risk over an affair of the *Scattering?*"

Asta had never heard a word uttered with such contempt. Was this what all Inyestans were like, she wondered, or just the assassin-creed?

"I just need to look at her face," Hrulf protested. "No one else need see it. Unless you have something to hide?" He stepped towards the boat, and Heylan deftly blocked his way.

"We are the Shadow-Cloaks of Inyesta. Secrecy is our protection and our strength. If you violate that, you will have to answer not just to me, but to all my kind."

Hrulf's voice was low, threatening. "You're a long way from Inyesta now, assassin-lady."

The mooring rope trembled, and Asta shook the dagger from her sleeve into her hand, gripping it securely. The outside of the rope was slick under her fingers as the blade bit into it, and the salt water stung the grazes on her palms.

"Maybe I should have a look and see who you are?" Hrulf went on, his hand reaching for Heylan's face. "You talk like an Inyestan, but that doesn't mean you are . . ."

Heylan didn't flinch. "Touch me and that touch will be your death, copper man."

"We'll see about that!" As Hrulf's hand closed on Heylan's upper arm the rope parted under Asta's knife with a soft tearing sound. The boat, freed of her fetters, leapt forward with the breeze behind her and the tide surging beneath her hull. In the flickering, bouncing light, Heylan swung her arm, and Hrulf collapsed to his knees, air exploding from his lungs in an eruption of breath and blood that Asta felt patter warm across her cheeks. He sank to his knees, then his stomach, crumpling slowly, head and arms twitching in the empty air over the surging waters of the harbour. Heylan gave him a firm shove with her foot, and lifted her arm in salute as he was swallowed by the sea with a soft splash and gurgle, like the last breath from a dying man's lungs. That was the last thing Asta saw, as the helmsman of the boat stretched over and extinguished the light, plunging ship and passengers into moonless darkness.

FOURTEEN

OR THE LONGEST time the only sound was the swish and clop of sea water sucking around the hull, and the rustle of the sail against the wind. As well as protection from prying eyes, the cloak was welcoming in its warmth. Asta wondered if she should speak to the pilot as he steered a course between the larger moored vessels that suddenly loomed up out of the night, and just as suddenly fell away behind them. Every time her breath caught in her throat. The lurching of the little boat was far more severe than she'd experienced on the cargo ship on the journey from Atrath, and she had to press her lips and swallow down the rising nausea. She kept glancing behind for signs of pursuit, but the harbour was a shifting mass of light and shadow, and it was impossible to tell if a boat had been launched to hunt them down.

All at once the wind blew colder. The lights of the harbour, and the city beyond, fell away behind them. The boat had reached open sea; Asta could taste salt spray, and the wind lifted her cropped hair by the roots. She was free of the Scattering, for now. She was no longer their Goddess, their sacrifice, but her journey still lay ahead of her. And they would come after her, she realised with a sinking heart. They had sent Turgesu and his men to scour the coasts for their *sumri gudienne*. It was too late to find another girl, and they wouldn't give her up so easily.

"So have you really taken a vow of silence?"

They were the first words the pilot had addressed to her since she boarded. Asta debated whether she should say nothing, go along with the charade while she worked out whether or not she could trust him, but decided against it. She opened her mouth to reply, then lunged for the gunwale as the sickness she had been holding back came spilling out. For a long, painful moment she couldn't have replied even if she'd wanted to.

The sailor sat back on his heels, watching impassively as she vomited, then wordlessly held out a small flask. Amusement danced in the depths of his eyes.

Asta spat. "It's not bloody funny."

"I wondered how long your vow would hold." He shook the flask at her. "Take it. It'll help you feel better."

The liquid was fiery, but after a few mouthfuls Asta's stomach settled. She handed it back, and muttered her thanks.

He tucked it back into his belt, regarding her with his head cocked to one side. "You're not really a Shadow-cloak, are you? You're not even Inyestan under that hood, I'll wager."

The lantern flared once more. Asta blinked in the sudden brightness. "Is that safe?" she asked.

"Safer than sailing blind at night with an assassin on my boat," he remarked tartly, moving to bring down the single sail. "The ocean is wide. They won't find us tonight."

"And tomorrow?"

"Tomorrow's fears are for tomorrow. Throw out the anchor, Shadow-cloak. We'll rest here tonight, and you can tell me who you are." He jerked his head towards the anchor on its long chain, and she heaved it over the side while he unscrewed the lid on a small barrel containing, by the smell, salted fish. He handed her a bowl of the cold fish, and she sat on deck under the light, finally pushing back the hood of the cloak to reveal her features.

He scanned her, lips pursed. "You're no Inyestan, as I thought, and no woman of Mikligard either. Where does your blood come from, lady?"

"Where does yours come from?" she asked in return.

His teeth flashed. "Now, I am Inyestan. That's how I know you're not, and mighty daring to be wearing the shadow-cloak when you're not of that creed! No Inyestan would take that risk . . . So where are you from? The truth, mind!"

"My blood is mixed, but I'm from the Beehive Village, on the eastern coast of Atrath." She nibbled on one of the oily fish, salted water running down her chin, while the Inyestan served up a third, smaller, bowl.

"Atrathene?" He gave her a long, appraising look. "I was going to ask your name, but I know your people don't give up your names easily. Not before you trust someone." As he spoke he made his surefooted way across the gently rocking deck to a hatch set just before the mast, and lifted the latch. "You can come out now," he said, to someone Asta couldn't see. "I've got fish for you."

There was no movement in the darkness. "Suit yourself," the Inyestan snorted, and resumed his seat. "He'll be out when it suits him. My name is Ranmiro, but I won't ask for yours, lady."

Asta kept a wary eye on the half-open hatch as she ate, wondering who, or what, might emerge. It was only as she was lapping the last of the brine off her fingers that there was a stir of movement in the mouth of the hatch, and a head emerged. A small head, bewhiskered and flat nosed, followed by a plump body. The fluffy black cat limped across the deck, giving Asta an inquisitive glance before deciding she wasn't worth bothering with. Ranmiro broke into a grin as he set the small bowl down by his feet. "Decided to come out and say hello, did you, my boy?"

He ruffled the cat between his grey-tipped ears. "This is Marcio," he said. "He crept on board when he was a kitten. His legs are a bit stiff now, but his appetite only gets bigger!" He gave the cat a prod, and he obligingly rolled over on his back to allow the Inyestan to ruffle his well-fed stomach, purring contentedly. Ranmiro looked up at Asta, and his brows knit in sudden concern. "You don't mind cats, do you?"

She smiled. "I like cats. My mother is a cat."

"You mean your mother *has* a cat?"

Asta suppressed a chuckle. "Not quite."

Ranmiro looked inquisitively at her. "There are mysteries about you, lady of Atrath, but I'm too tired to dig them out of their shells tonight. Come below and sleep. The morning brings a fresh tide."

"Below?" Asta asked. Ranmiro pointed to the hatch.

"Out of the wind and weather. Room for three below deck!" Ranmiro scooped up the cat and draped him over his shoulder like a fluffy scarf, pushed the hatch back, and vanished down the ladder. Asta hesitated only a moment before following him down the ladder into the space below the deck.

Ranmiro lit a lantern, and she looked around at the narrow galley and the triangular space in the bow that was stuffed with mattresses and piled high with sleeping furs. There was a lot less space down there than she'd imagined from the width of the deck, and her suspicions deepened at the hollow ringing under her boots. "This is a smuggler's ship, isn't it?"

Ranmiro looked evasive. "Might be. She's fast, my *Aguia*. Not the fastest ship on the ocean, but she'll get you where you want to go swift enough."

Asta wondered if it would be fast enough to outrun the slave-galleys of the Scattering. Somehow she doubted it.

"Do I sleep in here with you?" she asked.

"Unless you'd rather sleep on the floor. You needn't worry about me." He grinned. "I'm no scoundrel!"

Asta crawled into the low space, trying to avoid bumping her head, and pulled the furs around her. The mattress was soft, and surprisingly comfortable. She firmly turned her back as Ranmiro crawled in beside her, forced to shuffle over as Marcio determinedly pushed his way between them, flexed his needle claws against her back, and began to purr. The sound was a comfort. It reminded her of her childhood, of her mother, when her father and Finn had been alive and they had travelled in the wagon to start their new life, and she'd often fallen asleep with the cat warm and rumbling against her back.

Ranmiro was as good as his word, leaving her to sleep in peace until she was eventually woken by the rattle of pans in the galley and the smell of hot food cooking. Marcio was a vibrating bundle sitting on her stomach, forelegs tucked beneath his chest, eyes closed, pink tongue protruding slightly from his black lips. At her prod he rose, stretched fore and aft, and clambered off her, shaking out his stiff legs like a tribal elder trying to shake life back into ageing joints. She followed him into the galley, her nose twitching with anticipation.

"Sit," Ranmiro urged. There was a tiny folding table bracketed to the wall, and a folding chair clipped to it. Asta freed the chair, kicked it out and sat. The table was barely big enough to hold the bowl the Inyestan plonked down in front of her. Porridge, with a couple of stray cat hairs snagged on the rim. She fished them out, as discreetly as she could, and wiped her fingers on her shift.

Ranmiro leaned against the ladder that led to the deck. His eyes bored into the back of her neck as she ate, while Marcio worked a figure-eight through her ankles. She wanted to turn and study him; she hadn't had a chance the night before, but she didn't want to be rude. Instead she scraped the bowl clean.

"Bring it." He headed back up on deck, while Marcio wheezily clambered up on the table to lap up any stray drops of porridge. Asta, bowl and spoon in one hand, climbed up the ladder, leaving the black cat to his own devices.

"Washing up, in the bucket." Ranmiro jerked his head, and Asta crouched to dip her bowl into the salty water, scouring it clean with a handful of sand. She did the same with Ranmiro's bowl, and the pan, squatting on her haunches and watching him as he pulling in the anchor and adjusted the sail. He was a short man, but bulky with hard muscle, with chin-length black hair and a short, tightly-curled beard. His eyes were the solid dull green of olives, with no whites or pupil that she could see, and his skin, while not as dark as hers, was deep tan with weathered creases like a map of the world thrown across his features.

He caught her looking, and winked. "Where to, lady of Atrath?"

She startled. "What?"

"Heylan said you wanted to go back to your horse-lands, but I sense another desire in you. The ocean is mine, but the *Aguia* is yours. Tell me where you want her to take you."

Asta's fingers brushed the knife at her belt. She had never expected it to be this easy. "I want to go to Inyesta," she said.

"I see." Ranmiro made a small shift to the sail and came to sit beside her, taking the tiller in his hand. "I can take you there, on one condition."

"What's that?"

"You tell me why you want to go there."

Asta sighed, stretching her legs out before her, enjoying the play of wind through her hair that reminded her of riding hard along the cliffs of Atrath. She wondered if there were horses in Inyesta.

"My nephew is there," she said. "My village was raided by slavers. They took many women and children from my tribe, along with my brother's wife and his little boy. I want my people back."

Ranmiro's thick eyebrows meshed together. "Your brother cannot sail this tide himself?"

"My brother is dead." *Dead, but not silent, nor yet defeated.* Finn stirred in her mind, his curiosity aroused, warning her to watch her tongue around this stranger.

"A noble quest. I hope it ends well." Ranmiro stroked his thumb across his beard in thought. "There are many slaves in Inyesta. It's a big country. How will you find your horse-tribe?"

"First I need to get to Inyesta. Then I'll work out a way."

Ranmiro chuckled. "I like a woman with confidence!"

For a while they sat in silence, listening to the beat of the sail, the creak of ropes, the splash of water. Asta leaned her head over the gunwale to watch the ocean rushing past, catching fleeting glimpses of rainbow-hued fish as big as grown men falling in their frothing wake. Ranmiro trailed a line over the side, barbed along its length with a dozen hooks. "My boy likes his fish fresh," he said. "Let's see if I can satisfy him."

The salt in the air dried Asta's tongue, but the nausea of the previous night had passed and did not return. She enjoyed the ocean, wider than the grasslands of Atrath, bluer than the sky. The breeze, the freedom, sloughing off the months of imprisonment in Mikligard. It lifted her heart to be moving again.

"Tell me about Inyesta," she said.

"Facts for facts, stories for stories. You tell me about Atrath. All I see is a land of high cliffs and curving bays." He resumed his seat, glancing at the sky, pushing the tiller. "Six days fast sail to Inyesta, if the wind stays with us and the weather holds. Plenty of time for stories. You first."

Stories were in the blood of the tribe. Asta told of the long journey east, the sea of grass, her father's decision that they would no longer be nomads, that her tribe would have a new way of life, and how it had almost torn the tribe apart. "But he was the leader, the saviour of our tribe. All the tribes. So the people of the Plains Hawk followed my father into the east, and he found us a new home, and a new name."

"How did he save the tribes?" Ranmiro asked, but Asta shook her head and took a long drink from the flask he offered her.

"Your turn," she said. "What about Inyesta?"

His face grew dark. "I don't know if I should tell you . . . ."

"Unfair!" she protested. "I shared my story!"

"Not half of it, lady of Atrath, if I'm any judge. Inyesta is . . . There's a darkness there that goes beyond slavery." He looked at the sky once more, at distant clouds hovering on the horizon, and shivered. "No stories. What you need to know about Inyesta is how to survive there. The city on the bay, Abonnae . . . That's where we'll dock. It's the biggest city in the world. At least, that's what they say on this side of the ocean. And it's hot, in summer the pavements steam if you spit on them. Hot and fierce and stinking and ugly."

"You sound like you hate it," Asta remarked.

"Hate it? No! I was born in the Nidus, in the slums of Abonnae. I love every ugly inch of her, for all she drove me to drink and then to the sea. And there are spots of such beauty they will steal the breath from your mouth. The Water Gardens, the Plaza of the Dozen Stars. Even the Red Temple . . ." He fell silent for a moment, and when he resumed it was in a more practical tone. "You want to start in the slave markets on Winding Street. Your people will have been sold on there. From there . . ." he shrugged. "Do you speak Inyestan?"

"After a fashion." At least Finn would be of use in that department. "I'm good at languages. Quick to learn."

"I'll teach you." He smiled. "You can pay me in stories. I will coax out your mysteries, lady of Atrath!"

The rest of the day was spent learning a few words of Inyestan, *please, thank you, boat, sail, cat,* and *where, who* and *how.* Marcio, breathless from his clamber up the steps, stretched out in front of the hatch like a fat furry tripwire. Ranmiro fished and Asta watched the clouds race past and listened to all the things the captain was *not* telling her about Inyesta. By the time the bloated blood-red sun dipped towards the horizon and the Inyestan threw the anchor, she didn't feel she was any closer to finding her tribe. She was exhausted, and the white patches on her legs were sun-reddened and hot to the touch. The burn reminded her that although she had left the Scattering behind, she still carried part of it with her. Their tangled tale was not over yet, and that thought caused her to scan the ocean behind her anxiously, looking for white sails.

The next day dawned colder, and cloudy, the wind less predictable, and Ranmiro's mood was as contrary as the weather. Asta spent much of the time scampering back and forth, letting out and hauling in ropes until her hands were chafed and bleeding. To make things worse her sickness had returned with the choppy sea, and when she wasn't hastening to obey Ranmiro's commands she was lying with her head drooping over the ocean, empty stomach heaving painfully. Even the rainbow fish had forsaken them for calmer waters. There was just the boat, and the restless grey ocean. The cloud was so thick they could have beached on Inyesta without ever seeing it, or sailed right past and into some new sea.

"Cheer up!" Ranmiro rubbed her between her shoulder blades, and handed her some of the herbs from her basket to chew on. "We're making good time. You owe me a story."

"I can't tell stories when I'm being sick," she protested.

"The herbs will help. Stay in the middle of the deck and fix your eyes to the horizon. That might make you feel better."

The wind was cold, and Ranmiro brought a blanket up from below and draped it solicitously around her shoulders. Marcio kneaded his paws and purred in her lap, flicking his long tail to brush her chin no matter how many times she pushed it down. She scratched him between his ears. "Stupid cat."

Ranmiro sat cross-legged beside her, letting the cat bump his hand with his head. "About your mother?" he prompted.

Asta felt Finn's grumble of resentment. *Let it go*, she told him. It had been such a long time. He found it so difficult to forgive.

"You've told me much about your father, but almost nothing about your mother. Surely she has a story?"

Asta's hand brushed rhythmically down Marcio's back, long strokes, feeling his spine arch under her hand. She felt the misery rise again. She missed her mother, her *human* mother, who could have advised her in her pregnancy, held her while she gave birth, taken care of her grandchildren. She was deprived of her mother just when she needed her most, as Nasira was deprived of her grandchildren.

"My mother has the spirit of a cat inside her. Or the cat has the spirit of my mother. It's hard to tell where one ends and the other begins."

Ranmiro grunted. He did not seem surprised. "A shape-shifter?"

"No. I mean, not any more. She used to be. When I was young, I remember her as woman and patchcat . . ."

"Patchcat?"

"Like Marcio, but much bigger. A fully-grown patchcat can easily bring down a horse."

Ranmiro laughed. "If Marcio could catch a horse, he would bring it to me as a gift!" He prodded the cat's stomach. "If he wasn't so lazy."

Marcio flicked his ears at the insult.

Asta resumed her story. "After my father died, and she was driven from the village, the cat took over. I don't think she can shift back now. I think sometimes she even forgets she *was* human." She sighed at the memory of her last meeting with her mother, wondering if that would be the last time she saw her. They had parted in blood and snarling. She hoped their story would not end that way.

"Why was she driven from your village? Because of the wildness of the cat?"

Asta stared hard at Marcio's grey ears, as they blurred before her eyes. "No," she said. "It was because she killed my father." She had kept the story close for so long, unable to talk about it even with Finn, who was younger. Too young to wield a mercy-blade. Now it all came spilling out, to this stranger she couldn't even trust with her name.

"My father fell from his horse. An accident, it could happen to anyone. He'd been riding all his life, but his mare popped a foot in a rabbit-hole. She fell and broke her neck. He was thrown, and the fall shattered his spine. When my mother found him—" She broke off, remembering the heat, the buzz of flies around the dead horse, the grey pallor of her father's face as he hugged his children goodbye with arms he could barely lift through pain. She wasn't on the boat any more. She was far away on the steppe, fighting memories she had never been able to banish.

"My brother and I were allowed to say goodbye. He was younger than me, too young to fully understand. I was only a girl myself, but Finn was a child. Then my mother sent us away. They call it mercy, in my father's land. To live on as a cripple, unable to ride, or even walk . . ." She struggled with the words, her tears falling free and unheeded.

"You don't have to tell me this," Ranmiro said, in an undertone.

"When she came back to the village, she was the cat, with blood on her teeth. The people – my tribe, her tribe – drove her out for killing my father. I told them it was mercy, but they wouldn't listen. They threw stones and chased her away with burning branches. They were so angry with her, because she had taken him away from them." Her voice drifted into quivering silence. Ranmiro patted her hand.

"No more stories tonight, lady of Atrath. Some mysteries you deserve to keep for yourself."

After three days the squalls had blown over and the sky shone crisp and clear with early autumn. The gulls had returned, wheeling around the mast and diving for scraps of fish on the deck. They terrorized poor Marcio for their own enjoyment, sending him hissing and spitting for the hatch as fast as his awkward legs could carry him. The sun lightened Asta's mood. Ranmiro had been especially polite and considerate around her since she had told him the story of her father's death, not pressuring her for any more tales. Now, seeing her luxuriating with the sun on her limbs, he grinned.

"You're looking better. Nearly there now!"

"How can you tell?" she asked. The sea was as flat and

featureless as ever, with not even an island to break the monotony.

"The gulls." He waved his arm. "Where there are gulls, there's land nearby. Wind willing, we should sight Inyesta by this evening." He looked at her curiously. "What will you do then?"

"Start looking, I suppose," Asta said. "What about you?"

Ranmiro grinned. "I trade where wind and fortune take me. But we'll meet again, lady of Atrath. You can rely on that."

She caught his smile. "My name is Asta."

"So you trust me now, do you?" He laughed. "You're a hard one to win over, and stubborn. May that help you find your kin."

"Obstinacy is in my blood," she told him.

"From what you told me of your father, I can well believe it." The sail flapped overhead and he glared up at it. "Pull that line in, will you? While I still have you on board you might as well make yourself useful!"

The winds picked up around the Inyestan coast, blowing squally rain before it. The *Aguia* was buffeted and tossed about, bobbing like a cork in a barrel. To Asta, it felt as if the elements were conspiring to prevent her from reaching shore. Was this some Inyestan magic, some trick? She didn't have time to brood on it, as Ranmiro sent her scurrying up and down the ship pulling in the sail while he hung grimly to the tiller, olive eyes glittering beneath his deep seal-skin rain hood. Eventually he threw up his hands.

"Drop anchor," he commanded. "We'll have to ride this out."

Asta hurled the anchor into the waves with venom, wishing she could hurl Ranmiro and his stupid cat in after it. She was so close to land now, yet still Inyesta remained tantalisingly, frustratingly, out of reach. If she could see the coastline, she might have risked swimming, but to the south lay only a thick bank of cloud and fog. Inyesta remained as elusive as ever.

"Tomorrow," Ranmiro assured her. "These late summer squalls never last long, and the morning will be beautiful. You'll see."

"Ugly and stinking, you said," she reminded him. She couldn't find beauty in the land that had taken her kin. She sat on deck until it was so dark she couldn't see her hand in front of her face, hoping that the clouds would unfurl the moons and stars and bathe the southern coast in silvery light. But she was cheated, and not even Marcio's purring could comfort her in her restless sleep.

She slept badly and woke late, to the morning sun streaming through the open hatch. The boat was under sail, rocking beneath her feet as she made her unsteady way through the galley and out on deck. After the previous day's gloom, the sunlight was dazzling. She was forced to screw up her eyes, unable to see anything but reflected light.

Ranmiro grunted. "After all your grumbling, I thought you'd be more excited," he said.

"What are you talking about?" Asta's vision was clearing, slowly, enough for her to see him point at something far beyond their bows. Her eyes followed the line of his finger.

The sun slanted across the deck of the ship, and beyond the beams of gold and white lay a dark shape. As she stared as it the blurred mass came into focus. She saw the high peaks of mountains, the soft curve of the tree-lined shore, the spires and turrets of a great, sprawling city, and for the first time, she looked on the fabled land of Inyesta. Somewhere out there, on that brooding, bruised shore of greys and purples, her people were enslaved, and she was going to find them and bring them home.

FIFTEEN

THE SWEEPING BAY of Abonnae thronged with ships. The black-hulled beasts of Inyesta disgorged their wretched cargo on to the shore and swept away, greedy for more spoils. Asta watched from the deck as the *Aguia* jostled towards her allotted mooring, Ranmiro exchanging cheerful curses and shouted scraps of news with his fellow sailors. Marcio had sprung up into the prow and sat bolt upright, exuberant tail wrapped around his front paws, like a figurehead on a far grander vessel. As soon as the boat touched the pontoon, he sprang for the shore in a graceful, fluid arch that belied his weight and arthritic legs, and limped off towards the city. Asta was about to follow him when Ranmiro's hand on her arm held her back.

"Don't you want me to fetch him back?" she asked.

"He's a smart old boy. He'll come back when he's hungry. He knows his way around. You," he rapped her smartly on the head with his knuckles, "don't. And you'll want to lose the shadow-cloak too. Claiming to be an assassin is a serious crime."

"Will you keep it for me?"

"Keep it, sell it, whichever turns the best profit. Winding Street for the slave auctions, stay away from the Red Temple. And Punishment House, you don't want to end up there. Try not to attract attention!"

"Any more advice?" Now the moment had come, she didn't

want to leave the boat. It had been a haven for a few days, a place to regain her strength and courage. It had, at last, given her the time she needed to come to terms with what had happened to her since she was taken from her village.

"None that I can think of. Be careful, lady of Atrath. I'll be watching over you. I hope you find what you're looking for in Abonnae."

"Me too." As Ranmiro assisted her on to the dock she leaned over and kissed him lightly on his cheek, just above where his beard sprouted. "Thank you for everything, Ranmiro."

"Get on with you!" He gave her a little push, but his eyes sparkled. "What did I say about not attracting attention? Run, run and find your family!"

She hastened towards the shore, following Marcio's damp paw prints, trying not to look back. As her feet hit the stone wharf she looked around to get her bearings.

Well, said the dry voice in the back of her mind, *here we are.*

Decided to talk to me, have you? Finn had been worryingly silent since Asta had told Ranmiro of their father's death, but she had caught a sense of betrayal from him.

Only because I have to, was the acid rejoinder.

Asta rolled her eyes. *The sooner we find Rhodan and Lefalli and I'm rid of you the better, little brother!*

Finn fell back into baleful silence, but she felt him lurking, sulking, in the darkness behind her eyes. She hoped he would help her out if she needed him. A snaking line of chained slaves passed her on the opposite side of the road, and she scanned their faces, looking for her tribe, her people. But none of these wretches were even Atrathene, much less of her tribe. Wondering if they were headed to Winding Street, she decided to follow, keeping a careful distance.

The buildings along the harbour were fronted with tapering, fluted columns, and it was easy to sneak from one shadow to the next, far enough not to be able to smell the fresh-unloaded slaves, but close enough to hear their cries, the lash of the whip against bare backs, the shouts of abuse directed at them. Every time the whips cracked she winced. There were women in that column, children little older than Rhodan, and she could see the lash come down, searing his flesh, reopening old wounds and laying a fresh pattern of scars across his shoulders. She wanted to rush out, snatch the whip from the hand of the overseer, hurl it into the harbour with all her strength . . .

Don't.

Her brother's reminder stayed her hand, but only just. She dug her nails into her palms, holding her breath, a living shadow trailing the traders of misery. She hardly noticed the Inyestans around her except as gaudy birds fluttering in the corners of her eyes. There would be time for them later. Her eyes now were only for the cargo, the living rags blown in from the surrounding nations, and maybe from further lands.

They must have walked a mile or more. The houses on the sea front were more widely spaced now, their walls bordering the road on one side, with the sea on the other. The stone of the docks gave way to shallow cliffs, no higher than a man was tall, and below them were wide, shelving beaches of white sand, where the Inyestans played or sunned themselves. It was far from the stinking city Ranmiro had described, but then again she hadn't seen a tenth of what Abonnae had to throw at her.

Another few miles. Her feet ached now, heels blistering in her thin-soled boots. Another mile and she would be limping as badly as Marcio. There was nowhere to hide; the houses had fallen behind her and the sandy beach petered out into a flat expanse of mud and grey-green slime that looked ready to gulp her down the instant she set foot on it. The slave column was far ahead, a crawling dot on the horizon. If she felt exhausted, drained of energy by the hot, damp air, how must the chained prisoners feel?

She had her answer a few hundred yards further on. A slave thrown to the marsh, lifeless hands tangled in the rough grasses as if even in death he was trying to pull himself free. His legs had already vanished into the ravenous, foul-smelling mud, and the flies buzzed around his staring eyes.

Asta stopped. She had to; that hopeless gaze compelled her. She started towards him with the thought that if only she could reach him, she could close his eyes to the horrors around him, give him a tiny bit of respect.

Don't! Finn's voice was commanding, and it froze her in her tracks. *The marsh won't take your weight.*

But –

He's dead, Finn said sternly. *Save your strength to help the living.*

Asta balled her fists, breathing hard through her nose to keep from vomiting. "What should I do then?" she asked, hardly aware that she had spoken out loud.

Leave him. Follow the slaves before you lose them. By the spirits, she felt his shudder, *this is a desolate hole!*

Asta dropped to her haunches, addressing the dead man.

"May your ancestors watch over you, and may you ride a better trail in the Spirit Realm than the one that brought you here." She felt Finn's grumble, and she checked him. *That could be Rhodan lying there.*

You think I haven't thought of that? But he fell silent, chastened, as she resumed her journey. By now the slave-chain was nowhere in sight. She swore under her breath. They couldn't have gone far. If she carried on down this road she was bound to catch up.

There was a stand of trees ahead, a line slicing across the flat fenland, too straight to be natural. They were dull green and drooping, blasted by the sea wind. Seeing no other landmark in the vicinity, Asta decided to head towards them. They ran inland from the shore , stopping abruptly as if the line had been sheared.

Beneath the trees, nothing moved. Water dripped from the branches and splashed on Asta's skin, making her shudder. The ground underfoot was soft and spongy, and brackish water stood in every footprint she made. There were no sounds of birds, or animals, only the soft squelch of her footprints and the relentless dripping from the trees. Finn whimpered. She was inclined to agree with him. There was nothing natural about this place. The air smelled cold, tainted with smoke and a sour, unpleasant scent that clogged her throat.

The line of trees was only a few hundred paces across, and it ended as abruptly as it had started. On the far side was a deep, stagnant ditch, and beyond that a high stone wall, green with moss and lichen. The only way to follow the wall was to hitch up her shift, remove her boots, and drop knee-deep into the ditch. The water was cold, thick with slime that tangled around her calves, and the bottom was ankle-deep in mud. She bit back a squeal as something slippery slithered between her toes, and she tried not to think of leeches. There were bogs at home, but they were living places, heather-dusted and sharp with the scent of peat. This stinking marsh was a world away from Atrath.

She turned her back on the sea and headed inland, following the line of the wall, trying not to stumble as the mud squirmed beneath her soles and her gorge rose. The wall ended in a sharp corner, the ditch sloping up to meet the drier ground under the trees, which crept up until their needle-leaves pressed against the stone. Asta stripped a handful and used them to dry her feet as best she could before pulling her boots back on, but the mud was thick and gloopy, staining her legs almost black up to her knees. There *were* leeches, black eyeless slugs that clung to her calves and ankles, growing fat on her blood. She prised them off with her thumbnail. The wounds weren't big, but they bled freely, and she sat under a tree and wadded the ends of her shift against the incisions until the blood slowed to a trickle. She vowed not to return down this path. Who knew what else lived in the ditch that might be stirred up by the smell of fresh blood?

Shuddering, she pushed herself to her feet and pressed on, feet gritty and itching inside her boots. The sooner she was away from this place, the better. The very air around her felt tainted, and the brush of wind made her skin crawl. It was a relief when her boots met stone, a broad sweep of white. A road, and roads led to civilisation. There were few roads in Atrath, no cities to speak of, but even tracks made by the ruts of passing carts led to and from somewhere, and this was no cart track. It looked like it was well-trafficked, a paved avenue shielded on either side by the sombre evergreens. It led up to the wall. And in the wall, the blank wall she had been following for what seemed like days, was a gate of barred iron, big enough for two carts passing side-by-side. Asta sidled up to it and risked a glance through the bars. She saw buildings in the compound, people walking about, some milling, others moving with purpose. She shrank back as she saw a line of shackled slaves being herded from one side of the courtyard to the other, vanishing through a black, gaping door.

Finn?

His mind stretched out, questing. She wished they could spirit walk through the gate, into the huts, touching the minds of the people within, but in these morbid woods it would be too dangerous to leave her body. She felt Finn's frustration, his disappointment, like a crushing weight in her belly. *I don't think they're there,* he said at length.

Asta was reluctant to leave without finding out more about the camp. She had walked so far, and it was a long trudge back to the city with empty hands. She sighed. *What now?*

Someone is looking at you.

She glanced up, startled, to meet the eyes of a black-clad man striding towards her on the far side of the gate, his hand resting on the hilt of his short sword. She felt a moment of panic as he addressed her, before Finn stepped in smoothly, translating the words as they reached her mind and ensuring the speech that left her mouth could be understood. He was getting good at this.

"What are you doing here, horse-girl? Are you with a customer?"

Asta blinked. It was the last thing she expected to be asked at a concealed camp in the wilderness by a man gripping a sword.

"If you're not here with a customer, you need to leave . . ." He rattled the lock on the gate, and Asta found her tongue.

"I'm a customer." The Inyestan tripped easily from her lips.

He looked her up and down, taking in her mud-streaked calves, her crumpled shift, two weeks growth of brine-matted hair standing up at every angle on her head. His lip curled. "You don't look like a customer, horse-girl."

"Here!" In the recesses of her bag Asta had found a wad of paper money. Heylan must have hidden it there. She had no idea of its value, but she thrust the bundle towards the guard, hoping it would look like enough. "I have money. I'm here to buy." She wondered fleetingly what she would be buying, but he had released the grip on his sword and was fumbling with the lock on the gate.

"We get some strange ones around here," he said. It didn't sound much like an apology. "It's good you showed me your money, or I would have turned you away. Come in." He locked the gate behind her, and pointed to a hut huddled against the fence. "Wait here. Someone will be with you shortly. What's your name?"

"My name?" He looked curious at her hesitation. Should she give an Inyestan name, or trust him with hers? She drew in a deep breath. "My name is – is Heylan." She hoped Syven's wife wouldn't mind the liberty.

"Have you come from Abonnae?"

This time she was on more steady ground. "Yes. From Abonnae."

"Wait here," the guard repeated, closing the door behind him. The room was bare but for a bench that ran along three of the walls. Asta sat down and scratched some of the dried mud off her knees, feeling it crack as she bent and straightened her legs. She clawed her fingers through her hair to brush out the dirt, and tried to smooth the creases from her shift. It seemed that waving money around was a pass in Inyesta, no matter how filthy or exhausted you were. She just hoped she had enough to grease the wheels of information.

The door opened and she looked up, startled. The man in front of her was tall and slender, eyes like two peach stones that darted from side to side. Unlike the guard, he was dressed in garish purple and green, with a lavishly patterned surcoat that brushed the floor. Asta noticed how muddy it was at the hem, how clammy his palm was as he gripped her hand and pumped it up and down in overenthusiastic welcome. There were beads of sweat gleaming in his hairline and gathering at the edges of his sharply-pointed beard.

He's scared of you, Finn muttered. *Find out why.*

Asta forced a smile, and extracted her hand the moment she considered it polite to do so. The newcomer slid a greasy palm under her elbow.

"My name is Catmael," he said. "Come across to my office. We can talk about your needs in comfort."

The office was a short walk across the flagstones to the far side of the compound, up a flight of wooden steps that ran around the outside of the building, and through a pair of wooden-slatted doors that looked out on to a wide balcony. "Normally I'd invite you to sit in the sun," Catmael apologised, "but the weather has taken a turn for the chill. Would you like a drink?" He poured a glass of wine without waiting for a response, and Asta sipped it, watching him over the top of her glass, waiting for him to speak. Her heart was thumping, and she gripped the glass so hard she feared it might crack under the pressure.

"So," he said at length, "you came here to buy? You're not our usual sort of customer . . ."

"I might be buying." She sipped the wine, trying not to shake her head at the dryness. "It depends what you have to sell me . . ."

"What kind of slave are you looking for? Is it for the Red Temple, or for your personal use?"

"I'm looking for a boy." She evaded the question. "About six years old. I'd like to train him as . . ." she trailed off. She had no idea what boy-slaves were used for in Inyesta, and her mind was suddenly alive with horrors.

"As a house boy?" Catmael supplied. "Gardener's boy, maybe?"

"Yes," she said, relieved. "My gardener needs more help.

Someone to look after the horses and run errands." Belatedly, she wondered if they had horses in Inyesta. She hadn't seen any so far. "Do you have any boys who are skilled with horses? I could use an older woman too, to take care of children."

"And the boy is for your household?" Catmael persisted. "Not for the Temple?"

Asta caught the urgency in his tone, decided to see how far she could string him along, in case he let something slip. "He would be spending time at the Red Temple, yes. I have close ties with that place."

The wine bottle rattled against the glass as Catmael poured himself another measure and drank it quickly. "We are always happy to be in the favour of the Red Temple," he said.

"I'm glad to hear it." Asta forced a smile.

"We have some women available, and some boys that might suit. I'll have them brought out for your inspection." He rose, and Asta moved to follow, but he gestured her to sit back down again. "Finish your wine. I won't be long."

The moment the door closed behind him Asta rifled through the papers on his desk, trying to find anything in a script she recognised. Finn could change her words, but even he couldn't read Inyestan, and she sank back, frustrated. Catmael had been scared, a little of her, but far more by her mention of the Red Temple. Scared, and desperate to please. That must be where some of the power in Inyesta lay.

Finn was indifferent. The politics of Inyesta were none of their affair. Her charge was to find Rhodan and Lefalli, and the other stolen women and children if they were here, and get out. Leave Inyesta to the Inyestans, go back to the Beehive Village and let the peoples of the Eastern Sea fight amongst themselves.

Asta tidied the papers with a sweep of her hand and slumped back into the chair, frustrated. *They're not here.* Finn sounded crushed. *We're wasting time.*

Not if we're learning, she told him sharply. *Where else do you suggest we start looking?*

He fell silent. He had no answer to that, and she wished he did. She drained her glass, and was about to walk over to the window to look out when the door squeaked open and Catmael returned, rubbing his soft paws over each other and smiling in a greasy manner.

"I have some slaves ready for your inspection, Lady of the Red Temple," he said, holding the door open for her. "Shall we?"

Asta inclined her head as he ushered her out on to the balcony and down the steps. The slaves were lined up in miserable formation, and it took only a sweeping glance to tell her that Finn was right. Rhodan was not here. Disappointment settled like a heavy fist in her stomach. The boys in the line were all too old.

She made a show of inspecting them anyway, walking slowly up and down the line, listening with half an ear as Catmael made a play of their virtues, squeezing muscles and drawing back their lips so she could see their teeth, as if they were colts and it was trading season. The whole charade made her feel sick, and the whip marks she saw on their skin, knitting to neat pink scars that would eventually turn white but would never entirely fade, made her feel even sicker.

There were people of all races in the line, young white men like her father, Scattering women, Atrathenes . . . She hesitated, scanning them closely. No one she knew, but they were people of the tribes all the same, and her heart ached for them. Most of them kept their eyes downcast, but one woman glanced up, her mouth opening in surprise. Asta waited until Catmael was distracted for an instant and edged in closer, talking in her own language under her breath.

"How much to buy you?"

The woman's hand moved against her shift, displaying three fingers, and Asta gave her a small nod. The slave was of the fisher tribes to the south, her forearms laced with ritual scars that had been inked to create a bruised lattice on her skin.

Asta stepped back as Catmael returned his attention to her. Finn was grumbling at the back of her mind, but she couldn't spare him the attention right now. "Have you seen anything you like?" he asked.

"This one." Asta indicated the fisher. "How much is she?"

His nervous smile broadened. "An excellent choice. The people of the horse tribes are known for their strength."

"I heard they were strong-willed." Asta struggled to keep the bite out of her voice.

"They can be broken, as horses can. Shall we say five?"

You think you can break us, but you're wrong. "Two?"

"Four?"

Asta shook her head. "I won't go higher than three."

Catmael extended his hand. "Three it is, then."

Asta peeled off three of the notes and slapped them into his open palm. She could not meet the eyes of the other slaves in the line. She wished she had the money to buy them all and free them.

"Are you sure you don't have any other boys?" she pressed again. "The Temple would prefer a younger boy if you have one . . ."

Catmael tugged at his shirt collar. "The Temple always does. You've already taken most of our younger boys; I have none of that age to show you. There was one last moon . . ." His eyes narrowed as he looked at her. "Yes, he was about six. One of your horse folk." He flicked his fingers towards Asta's purchase. "I remember him because he was quite pale, for an Atrathene. He stuck in my mind. But he's long gone."

Of course, she thought. He would not see her as an Atrathene. He would not be expecting to see a free Atrathene in Inyesta, and he saw her people only as obstinate slaves. Still, she took a step away from the woman she had bought, lest he remark on any resemblance and start asking deeper questions. She felt a long quiver, as if a cold hand had snatched her in its grip and then let go. Finn stirred in her mind, demanding, and she had to shut him down. She couldn't think with all that chatter in her head.

"Where?" She tried not to sound too eager, knew she had failed as Catmael's eyes widened in surprise. "Where did he go?

Did the Temple already buy a child like that?" She pressed her lips, tried to calm down by taking a few deep breaths. "I'd hate to think I'd wasted my journey, when I could have spent my time in service to the Temple. They're very keen to purchase a young boy. They won't be happy with this timewasting."

She wondered what women did in the Temple. She hoped Catmael wouldn't press her on that score.

Catmael rubbed his neck, and wiped his sweaty palm down his robe. "I don't think he went to the Temple," he said. "I'd have to check the records. I'm sure I could get in another child to fit your specifications, if that's what the Temple requires . . ."

Asta felt a surge of anger from Finn, struggled to keep it contained. Her own fury was rising. If she didn't get out of here soon she would do or say something that would get her into trouble.

"I didn't realise you could . . . *acquire* . . . children to order?"

"We give our requests to our buyers, and they do their best to supply them. All kinds of people pass through the slave markets on the Scattering. Have you ever been there?"

"Yes." Her nails dug into her palms. "Yes, I've been there. You said you were going to check the records? Perhaps I could purchase this boy from his current owners, rather than waste any more time. I've been here a while, and it's a long journey back to Abonnae on foot."

Catmael nodded, appearing to understand. "The life of a penitent is hard. How you people live like that is beyond me. And we must finalise your purchase for this one."

"Yes." He had lost her now, and she was eager to grab the information and get away from this miserable prison camp. "Let's seal this purchase."

"Come back to my office." His sticky hand gripped her elbow and escorted her up the steps, while below, most of the slaves drifted away, leaving the woman she had bought standing alone. She wondered aloud if they ever tried to escape.

"Sometimes." Catmael chuckled. "But where would they go?

They're marked, everyone knows they're slaves. It's easier just to stay here and wait to be purchased. I don't know why they bother, really."

Asta looked over the camp, at the high walls, the watchtowers, the enslaved men and women squatting in the shade of the buildings. Beyond, to the north, she could see the ocean; to the east lay the vast flat expanse of the marshes, and freedom. The freedom to live without walls, without owners or shackles or the scalding tongue of the whip. She sighed. "Oh no. Why would anyone want to do that?"

Catmael appeared deaf to her sarcasm as he drew her chair out for her and offered her another glass of wine, which she refused. It was hard enough to keep a clear head. He vanished from the office and she heard him tramping down the steps, presumably to fetch the records that would show her where Rhodan was. If it was Rhodan the paper trail led to, if she wasn't following a wild mustang down the wrong path. And if she was, what then? What if she couldn't find any of her lost tribe? Did she give up and try and get home, break her promise to her people back in the village? Would Finn live in her head forever, sullenly reminding her of her guilt, her failure?

She felt his embrace. *Don't give up, sister. We'll find him. You'll bring him home, and Lefalli. You'll bring them all home. I trust you.*

I'm doing my best. The ring of boots on the stairs warned her that Catmael was returning. He had not been gone long, and in his hand he clutched two small, tightly wound scrolls.

"This is your purchase," he said, unrolling it on the table in front of her. Asta perused it as if the words and numbers made sense to her.

"What do I do," she asked, hoping it wasn't the wrong question, "if I want to sell her on to someone else? Or free her?"

"Why would you want to free her?" He looked baffled at the concept.

"Sometimes the Temple acts in ways that are beyond all of us." She hoped bringing up the mysterious Temple again would stop him asking too many questions.

"Have you been a penitent long?" he countered.

"Not long." Asta forced a smile. "Is my inexperience showing?"

"A little." Catmael ran his finger down the page. "These are her ownership documents. If you want to transfer ownership of her, you pass them on to her new owner. If for some reason you want to set them free, you give them to her. Or sell them to her. Does that make sense?"

"I think so."

"You'll need your thumbprint here," he indicated a spot on the document. It had already been printed a few times, she noticed, and she dipped her finger in the pad of ink her offered her and added her own mark. "Now you own her. All you need to do to pass her on is add the thumbprint of her next owner."

She watched as he transferred the valuable scroll to a thin leather case, which he handed to her. "And . . . the boy?"

"This is the address of his last owners." A second scroll. It seemed simpler than the first. At least, there was less writing on it, and no thumbprints.

"May I take this with me?" she asked, hoping she could find someone to translate.

Catmael frowned. "It's against policy . . ."

"I think the Temple would like to see it." She would cast this hand as often as she had to, making a play of sighing and shaking her head. "I shouldn't tell you this, but . . . The Temple is very interested in this particular boy. I can't tell you why, but he's vital to our faith, and we must find him." She rolled up the scroll and tightened her hand around it, daring him to protest. "I can pay . . ."

Catmael twitched, nodded. She felt his tension lift as she pushed another sheet of the paper money across the table towards him, and it vanished into the purse on his belt. "Thank you," she said. "I won't trouble you further."

"Nothing is too much trouble for the Red Temple."

"Your generosity will be remembered." Asta hoped that was

the right thing to say. Probably not; Catmael looked as if he was about to vomit.

He likes the Temple's money, but not its attention, Finn observed. Asta agreed.

She rose. "I need to leave now. My new slave and I have a long road back to the city."

Catmael raised her hand to his moist lips. "May you find what you're looking for, lady of the Red Temple."

"That is all I desire in life," she said. "Isn't that all any of us can ask for?"

"Indeed." He steered her towards the door, one hand in the small of her back. "Do you need me to walk you to the gate? Your purchase will be there for you to receive it. I have other customers waiting . . ." He sounded apologetic.

"I can walk by myself. I'd hate to get in the way of your commerce." She forced a smile, but he had already turned away, mentally dismissing her and hurrying to greet the young man jumping down from the carriage that had drawn up before the office, drawn by a pair of matched chestnut geldings. She shrugged.

Cock, Finn muttered.

Salesman. She didn't care about Catmael. He had given her what she wanted. She was more interested in the carriage. If a carriage had driven here without much sign of mud on its wheels, there must be a better road back to Abonnae than the one she had taken to get here. And it lifted her heart to see a horse.

The woman she had bought was standing outside the gate-house, her hands tied loosely in front of her, the trailing end of the rope in the grip of one of the gate guards. From a distance she looked demure, but as Asta approached she could see the fisher-woman was watching her through narrowed eyes. She took the rope from the guard, who gave her a blunt nod, and led the woman – her purchase – out of the gate.

She called back to the guard as she was leaving. "Could you point me back in the direction of the city, please? I walked the penitent's path here," she added, at his doubtful look, "but now that I have what I came for I should take the quickest road back to the Temple."

He directed her towards the dusty track, rutted with the imprints of carriage wheels. It was a better road than the route across the marshes, but her legs were already sore from the earlier journey, and after a mile her blisters were bleeding and every step was painful. The woman walked behind her, not dragging on the end of the rope, neither complaining nor speaking. Asta wondered what had been done to her to make her so compliant.

She judged, by the state of her feet, that they were probably far enough from the camp now, and she drew the woman back from the side of the road, through the ditch and to the far side of the straggle of rough pines that fringed the path. Once she was reasonable sure they couldn't be seen, she untied the rope from the woman's wrists and let it fall to the ground.

The fisher-woman stared at her, rubbing her arms where her tattoos ended. "Who are you?" she asked at length.

"I'm from the Beehive tribe. We used to be the Plains Hawk."

There was recognition at that. Of course. The Plains Hawk were legendary, mainly thanks to Asta's father.

"Why are you here?"

"I'm looking for some people from my tribe. They were taken, back in the spring. Have you seen any of them?"

The woman shrugged. "I've seen people of the tribes, but I couldn't say if any of them were yours. Sorry."

"My nephew? He's a little boy. Quite fair-skinned? He might be with his mother . . ."

Again the mournful shrug. "I wish I could help you."

"I wish you could too."

An awkward silence hung between them for a moment, and then Asta held out the scroll tube. "Here, take this. It's yours."

The woman stared down at the leather cylinder. "What is it?"

"Your freedom papers. You'll need to put a thumbprint on them. Here—" She shook out the scroll, indicated her mark.

The woman cast about for a moment, then pressed her thumb into the mud at her feet and forced it down onto the page. It blurred – her hand was shaking – but is was still recognisable as a print. A transfer of sale.

"Is that right?" she asked.

Asta nodded. "If anyone questions you, just show them this deed," she said.

"Are you sure?" The fisher-woman blew out her cheeks, and grinned, a smile that lit up her rather dour face. "I had hoped, but then you didn't say anything so I thought I'd better keep my mouth shut . . ."

"I'm sure. I might not be able to find my own tribe yet, but I can free you, at least."

The woman looked around, at the heathland that spread out before her, at the rustling trees that shadowed the road back to the city. She shook out her shoulders and inhaled deeply.

"Even the air smells better now!" She turned back to Asta. "How can I thank you? There must be something I can do."

"There's one thing. If you make it back to Atrath, find my tribe. We're settled on the coast. Tell them," she hesitated over her words, "tell them I'm alive, and I'm still looking. Tell them I'm doing all I can to keep my promise."

"I'll tell them." The woman gripped Asta's wrist firmly, her eyes shining. "My name is Dilantay."

"Asta." Asta returned the grip. She half-expected the woman to react to her name, to the fame of her father, but her name was common enough. The fisher let it go without remark.

"So," she said, "where do I go now?"

"The sea is that way." Asta pointed across the stretch of moorland. "Or you could come back with me to Abonnae?"

Dilantay shuddered. "Not me. I've seen enough of that place for my lifetime. And if you're wise you'll stay away too. People go into their temples, they don't come out. Everyone knows it, but no one talks about it. Their priests have too much power."

"I have to go. I think that's where my nephew is. I have to

try and get him back."

"Then good luck to you. I'll tell your people of your kindness, when I find them."

"Good luck to you too, Dilantay."

She stood for a long moment, watching the tall tattooed woman striding away from her. Finn watched her too; she could feel his brooding presence behind her eyes.

Problem, little brother?

Are you going to waste all our money saving strangers? What if we need it to free our own people?

Shut up, Finn. It was hardly a fortune. She could have led us to Rhodan –

She didn't though, did she? His thoughts were harsh.

What would you have done, if you were me? Left them all there? If I had enough coin to free every slave in Inyesta, don't you think I would?

You're soft, sister. But his voice was calmer and she felt the gentle mental pressure of his embrace. *Let's head on to the city, shall we?*

Asta had stopped to ease the leather of her boot away from her mangled heel when she heard the rumble of carriage wheels on the track behind her, and she retreated from the road to let it pass. It was the carriage she had seen outside Catmael's office, the paired chestnuts trotting with a high gait. Asta watched them with envy. If she had a ride, she would have been back in Abonnae by now. She wasn't used to walking.

The cart slowed, and crunched to a halt on the road ahead. The young man opened the door and hailed her, waving his arm. "Are you going back to Abonnae? Would you like a ride?"

For a moment she thought he meant she could take one of the horses, before she realised he meant for her to join him in the carriage. She nodded and smiled her thanks as he extended a hand to help her scramble aboard, while the woman he was with shuffled up to make room on the high forward-facing seat. On the opposite, lower seat, huddled into the corner so silent and still that Asta didn't see him for a moment, was their new slave.

He had the copper skin and hair that marked him as being from the Scattering, and he was no more than sixteen, with stick-thin legs shackled at the ankle and a heavy collar around his neck that forced his chin up. His eyes were wide with fear, and his fists clenched tightly in his lap. Thinking of Dilantay walking towards her uncertain freedom, Asta felt sick for him. She dropped her eyes as she realised she was staring, and turned to thank the young couple once more for their assistance.

"I'm Fernande," the man introduced himself, "and this is my wife, Inesh. Are you a penitent? We wondered whether we should stop for you."

Asta shook her head. "I have been a penitent, but not now."

Fernande and Inesh exchanged a nervous glance. "Are you going back to the Red Temple?" Inesh asked.

"I'm looking for someone." Asta stilled Finn's warning voice in her head. "I've come from overseas. Can you help me out?"

Fernande looked doubtful. "We don't meet many people from overseas." She seemed to be discounting slaves as "people", to Asta's eyes. "Who are you looking for?"

"My brother's son. He's gone missing in Abonnae." The slave twitched in the corner. "We just want him back. Can you read something for me, an address?"

She gave Fernande the parchment, saw his hand still as he moved to unroll it. "This is a slave deed," he said.

"My brother and nephew are in the trade." As what, she did not say, and hoped he wouldn't ask.

He shrugged. "That makes sense. Is it this address here?" He pointed at the marks, and went on before she could reply. "Must be, the only other addresses on it are Winding Street and the camp. Will you be able to remember it?"

"I can." Finn muttered additional reassurance in the back

of her mind, and she trusted him not to forget, even if she did.

Fernande gave her the address in the city and a name, Marisse Delacatour. He rolled up the parchment and returned it, wishing her luck. They fell to talking. Fernande and Inesh were recently married, and setting up their home together. The miserable Scattering boy was their first slave, bought to help around the house and in the field where Fernande intended to grow peppers. They talked about the boy as if he was as useful, as expendable and inanimate, as a new mop or hoe. Asta longed to talk to him, to try and offer reassurance or sympathy, but she felt she couldn't without alienating her genial ride, and her feet rebelled at the prospect of being dumped back on the side of the road again. Besides, the more they talked the more she might learn about the ways of Inyesta. But she couldn't help being curious.

"What's his name?" she asked. If the boy had a name, at least he could retain that tiny shred of humanity.

Inesh shook her head. "We haven't decided on a name yet. We were going to get him and see if anything came to us."

Finn hissed, and Asta had to clutch the lip of the seat to prevent herself from recoiling in horror. Names were so important to her tribe, but this poor boy had been stripped of even that. She mentally groped for Finn's hand. *That won't happen to Rhodan.*

If they've taken my son's name, I'll burn their fucking city to the ground!

Steady, little brother. She tried to calm him as she felt his rage and frustration spill over, kicking and thumping inside her skull, making her head ache. She stared out of the carriage window, at the flickering sunlight. They were approaching the city through farming country, and she saw men and women working in the fields, swinging hoes and bending backs. Were they all slaves? Why didn't they run, with no one to supervise them? Did any of them cling on to their own names, their own culture?

Opposite her, the nameless slave whimpered, the first sound she had heard him make. Her hand twitched towards him, before she remembered where she was and stilled it. The carriage swept on, towards Abonnae. Towards Rhodan.

SIXTEEN

FERNANDE DROPPED ASTA off outside the Red Temple, the crimson heart of Abonnae, with directions to the house where Rhodan might be. It was the first time she had seen the Temple, beyond a glimpse from the harbour as the *Aguia* came into port. It stood on a hill in the very centre of the city, at the crossroads of two wide, bustling streets. The surrounding buildings were white and cream, but the Red Temple was constructed from pink-tinted sandstone and crimson marble. On either side of the grand entrance was a high tower, battlements casting a shadow like jagged teeth on the pavement. Shallow steps led up to an arch that loomed high over her head. Ten men could have walked abreast through it and not touched the sides. The arch was decorated with stone carvings, curlicues, little faces laughing and crying, horses, cats . . .

As if summoned by the thought, a plump black cat walked down the steps, flicking his paws with a disdainful air, and curled around her ankles. She scratched him between the ears. "Marcio? Is that you?"

The cat sat in a pool of sunlight and licked his shoulder, not responding to the name. When Asta looked through the arch she saw more cats, sunning their sides and bellies in a courtyard dotted with fountains and benches. Figures in red robes, hooded so that only their eyes were visible, moved among them, mingling with men and women in bright garb. The Temple seemed to have no defence, and she couldn't see any slaves.

Finn twitched, and she realised she was wasting time. Whatever the Red Temple was to the Inyestans, it was nothing to do with her. She followed Fernande's directions, past the Temple, counting off the streets until she reached the seventh on the left, and turned down it. There were not many people about; a few women leading slaves on chains around their necks, a couple of men talking animatedly on a street corner, a few beggars that everyone seemed to be ignoring. No one spoke to Asta, but some, she noticed, crossed the road to avoid her, or stared in open curiosity as she passed. She paid them no heed.

The road swept in a long southward curve, changing gradually from shops selling icons and religious paraphernalia, to warehouses, to compact houses with neat yards facing the road. None of the buildings were numbered. Finn counted them off, and she hoped he was right. It was a long road, and she didn't want to miss the house.

I think it's this one. Finn's voice brought Asta to a halt in front of a house with a wooden gate, painted white, but flaking to expose the wood underneath. The yard beyond was neglected, weeds growing through cracks in the stone and clogging the once-neat flower beds. There was a stone bench in the yard, and anyone sitting there would be able to see a long way up and down the street.

The gate squeaked a protest as she swung it open, and her feet snagged in the tangled greenery that straggled across the narrow path leading to a door painted the same flaking white as the gate. She knocked with her fist.

Shuffling footsteps, and the door opened with a rattle of chain, just wide enough for Asta to stick her foot in and prevent it closing. "I'm sorry to bother you," she said. "Are you Marisse Delacatour?"

"I'm Lusha. Marisse is asleep. What do you want?" The voice was high and quavery.

"I need to speak to Marisse. Please. It's important; I've come a long way." Asta debated whether she should mention the Temple. It seemed to open some doors.

"Let me see if she's awake." Asta moved her foot, allowing the old lady to shut the door. She ignored Finn's snort of derision. If they didn't let her in she would find her own entrance. There were many ways to skin a horse.

Is he here, Finn?

I don't know. He's been here recently, but he's not in the house now. He might come back. Finn was trying to keep his voice calm, but Asta sensed the tension, the urgency, behind his words. Her own heart thundered as the chain slid back and Lusha opened the door.

She was a small woman, bent-backed, her face as cracked and leathery as old hide. Her eyes were dull brown, with no iris or pupil. Asta found it hard to tell where Inyestans were looking, with their strange eyes, but she had no doubt the full force of Lusha's glare was turned on her. She smiled.

"I'm sorry to bother you. This won't take long."

"In there." Lusha nodded to a door off the entrance hall. "I'd give her a moment to wake up. Would you like a drink?"

"Please, if it's no trouble."

"Why would it be trouble to extend hospitality?" Lusha shuffled away, presumably to fetch the drinks, and Asta ventured into the sitting room.

The room was gloomy, panelled with dark wood, and even the bright sun outside struggled to penetrate the dimness. There was a table at one end made of similar wood, and on the opposite wall was a fireplace. A vase crammed with softly wilting blooms stood in the grate, and over the mantle, above the clutter of dusty candles and trinkets and a blue mug with a broken handle, was an expansive painting. Asta took a step back, trying to focus on the image, which seemed too large for the room. There were hooded figures, prostrate or kneeling, offering gifts with outstretched hands, but the painting had no perspective. It was impossible to tell whether they stretched out to each other, or to the Red

Temple which appeared several times, or to the night-black hand that dripped blood in the middle of the scene. She felt that was important, a candle was painted below it, presumably to illuminate it, and in the lower third of the picture were the figures of slaves, with chains around their necks and bright red, false, smiles.

"You can sit down, you know?"

Asta jumped at the voice, coming from the deep chair to the right of the window that looked out onto the front yard. The chair had high wings, and the woman sunk between them with a frayed blanket pulled up to her chin and a small, elderly dog wheezing on her lap was tiny, even smaller than Lusha. Silver eyes like water-splashed pebbles watched Asta as she walked across the room and lifted the cushion from the identical, facing seat.

"Not there. That's Lusha's chair."

"Sorry." Finn tutted his irritation, chafing at the delay. He wanted to look around, but Asta picked up one of the chairs around the table and brought it back to sit between Marisse's chair and Lusha's. "Please, are you Marisse Delacatour?"

The old lady sucked her gums, fingers working through the dog's fur. "You're not Inyestan, are you? Where are you from?"

Asta was saved from having to reply by the re-appearance of Lusha, carrying a tray with a long-necked flask and three delicate cups on it. The flask was filled with cloudy orange juice, and a dish on the tray held crackers and slices of hard-boiled egg. Lusha set the tray down on the low table below the window, before taking a cracker and a slice of egg and placing them reverently in a dish on the mantelpiece, just below the painting.

Marisse poured Asta a measure of the juice. It was thick and pulpy, but delicious, and she was grateful for the cooling sensation as she swallowed.

With much thumping of cushions, Lusha settled into her own chair, and motioned for Asta to help herself to food, and more juice if she wanted it.

"What did you want of Marisse?" she demanded.

Asta set her plate down and drew the scroll Catmael had given her from the pocket of her shift. "I'm looking for a relative," she explained. "He was enslaved. I spoke to a man named Catmael, who says you own him now." She laid the scroll case down on the table between the two elderly women. "I have money. I want to buy him back."

Lusha picked up the paper, squinted at it, then handed it to Marisse. "I told you we shouldn't have bought the boy," she said. "This is your doing."

"You agreed we needed more help around the house, and in the yard." Marisse's rebuke was mild. "We worked all our lives. We deserve a break."

Her tired voice suggested this was an old disagreement. "Where is the boy now?" Asta asked.

"He said his name was Rhodan, kept insisting it."

Her heart leapt. It must be him. It had to be.

"We called him Snipe." Lusha added. "He was a stubborn boy, wouldn't answer to it."

Finn snarled. *Shut it,* Asta warned him. *You sound like Mother.* Aloud, she said, "I've travelled a long way, and I'll pay good paper. I just want him back. Where is he?" Wherever he was, he clearly hadn't done much in the way of yard work. Or dusting.

Lusha blinked. "Well he's gone, my dear."

"Gone? Gone where?" *Not dead, Finn, he can't be dead. We've come all this way . . . .*

"We sold him. He wouldn't do as he was told, and he kept trying to run away," Marisse said, breaking off a scrap of cracker and absently feeding it to the dog. "Stubborn, he was, like Lusha said. Never known a boy like it for obstinacy. Couldn't beat it out of him, nor starve it. Gave up in the end."

The matter-of-fact way she spoke sent the heat rushing to Asta's face, and she snatched up the scroll case with a shaking hand. She was shocked into silence, but Finn raged enough for both of them, beating against the walls of her skull, fighting to control her body, to wrap his hands around the throat of the frail old lady and choke the life out of her. He snatched at her hands and she twisted them in her lap, wrestling him down into the dark of her mind, holding him there.

Finn! Not now! We'll find him, we'll find him and we'll burn the city. She's an old lady, Finn. This whole fucking culture is diseased, not her!

This place is fucked, Asta. Let's find him and get out.

We will.

"Are you all right, dear?" Lusha peered at Asta. "You look a bit upset."

"I'm fine." Asta poured a drink and swallowed it quickly, to cover her anxiety, to buy time to think. "Who did you sell him to?"

Lusha swivelled her eyes reverentially up to the painting. "To the Red Temple, to the service of the Deity."

Always the bloody Temple! There's something going on there, Asta. I don't want my son to be part of it.

Asta ignored him. She had her own fears regarding the Temple. "Who is the Deity? What will he do there?"

"The Deity watches over all of us," Lusha said, piously. "He needs people to serve him. Snipe will have a good life there."

"Rhodan. His *name* is Rhodan."

Marisse gummed her cracker, sucking it to make it soft, and swallowed. "You're Atrathene, then. Never known a people set such store by names. You're a long way from home."

"Please," Asta broke under her silver stare. "My brother is dead. Rhodan and his mother were taken, with many of my people. I just want to bring him home."

Marisse pushed to her feet with a creak of old bones, depositing the hound at her feet with a squeak of protest. She motioned for Lusha to stay sitting. "You'll want the Temple, and quick. I'd only take a switch to a stubborn boy, but the Red Maids . . . They'll be harsher than me, if he hasn't learned his place. I'll see her out, Lusha." Her hand with its yellowed nails lingered on her companion's wrist, and Lusha patted it.

"The Deity will protect him," she said. "Even if he is a heathen."

"Of course he will," Marisse assured her. "Come with me, Atrathene child."

The sun was close to setting as she opened the door. It seemed to move faster, here in the south, and the hot winds had faded away, swirling dust settling in patterns on the driveway. The cloudless sky told Asta it would be cold at night, and she had nowhere to sleep. She hoped the Temple had at least put a roof over Rhodan's head.

"Thank you," she said to Marisse. The old lady's hand darted out and caught her wrist in a crab-like grip.

"You be careful," she said, in an undertone. "Lusha doesn't remember, but I do. She thinks the Deity is benevolent, the Temple is kind. Get your boy out of there and get back to Atrath."

Asta stared at her, startled into silence. Marisse spoke in heavily accented but fluent Atrathene.

"I travelled when I was young. I've seen a lot of the world, a lot of gods."

She found her tongue. "What – has Lusha forgotten?"

"The stonings, the fires, the whispers on street corners. Now they have more subtle methods. They come and take you away in the night, I've heard. Not us; we're old, we don't cause any trouble now. You cause trouble, you ride outside the herd, and they'll come for you too."

"The shadow-cloaks?"

"Not them. They're on the other side." Marisse pressed her lips together. "I've said too much, even in your tongue. The birds of the air have eyes that watch. Get Rhodan, and get out, before—"

She broke off, turning back to the house, to her wing-backed chair and to Lusha, who had forgotten what she was meant to remember. She left Asta staring at a closed door, with nowhere to go and the chill of evening on her back.

By the time she reached the main road it was dark, and a few stars gleamed overhead. The cold raised goosebumps on her arms. It wasn't as cold as winter nights could be in the Beehive Village, but there she always had somewhere to go, someone to bed down with. Here, she was alone.

Where do we go, Finn?

The Temple. He sounded scathing. *I would have thought that was obvious.*

I don't want to go tonight. I want to check it out first, with you. I need to find a safe place to meditate—"

There's nowhere safe in this fucking swamp of a city, Asta!

She dug her heels in. *I'm not going to the Temple unprepared. It's too dangerous. I have paper; let's find an inn or lodging house—"*

You'd waste our paper on inns, as well as fisher-girls? What if we can't afford to buy Rhodan back? I'm telling you, Asta, go to the Temple. If they're as godly as Lusha believed, they'll at least put you up for the night.

While they were talking she was blindly following her feet, weaving in and out of pedestrians and carriages without noticing them. The cooler evening air brought more people out on the streets, parading in their gaudy clothes, laughing too loudly as they flocked like butterflies between the shops and eating houses. There was an edge to the laughter, an undercurrent, as if everything in Abonnae was painted a shade too bright, to conceal the darkness that lurked beneath.

A crowd of men poured out of a nearby building and raced past her, yelling cheerfully and pushing her aside without consideration. She held herself tight against the wall, seeking the reassurance of solid stone under her fingers, until they passed. There were too many people, the noise and bright colours hurt her head, and she struggled against a surge of panic. She needed to get off the street, away from everybody.

Asta? Is something wrong?

There was nowhere safe, nowhere she could hide. She and her brother were utterly alone, the narrow alleys of Abonnae leaning in to each other about her head. It was like being locked in a room, suffocating in the dark. Drowning, while everyone around her could still breathe.

Get me out of here, Finn!

Her throat was closing. She fought for breath, trying to suck air into her lungs.

I've got you. Walk with me. Keep putting one foot in front of the other, you'll be fine.

Clinging to the reassurance of her brother, walking where he told her to, taking deep breaths, Asta let go of the security of the wall and let him guide her through the streets, focussing on the echo of his voice in her head. She ignored the jostling crowds, let the shouting and music fade away until there was nothing but her and Finn, until she felt fluted marble under her hands, cool air blowing from an open space ahead, and realised where he had led her.

You treacherous piece of shit . . .

I'm sorry. He really was, she could feel it. *I couldn't think of anywhere else to take you. What happened back there? It happened before, in Heylan's warehouse . . .*

I panicked. It happens every now and then. Since Father died . . .

Why didn't you tell me?

Asta shook her head. She didn't want to think back to that time; her father dead, her mother banished, the cloak of leadership thrown around her shoulders, which were too frail to bear the weight alone. How she had woken up in the darkness so many times, choking in fear, until she learned that having someone with her, a calming figure at her side, reduced the terror and made it easier to face down the panic.

What could you have done? You refused the leader's robes.

If I'd known . . . He let the statement hang.

As if I'd tell you, little brother! Asta was feeling better now, her chest eased, and the Temple steps were quiet enough for her to look around without being jostled and nudged. Even her momentary anger with Finn was fading. *Now we're here, we might as well go in.*

She took a deep breath, and stepped through the open metal doors that bracketed the arch into the Red Temple.

Seventeen

The courtyard in front of the Red Temple was dusky pink under soft moonlight. Cats prowled the arena, darting in and out of patches of light on their own private business, caring nothing for gods or the sanctity of the space they ran in. Eyes, green and amber, flashed in the moonlight, watching Asta walk across the courtyard, and she thought uncomfortably of spies. Could they see Finn, nestled inside her head?

On the far side of the square was a second, smaller arch, human sized, barred by a door of beaten bronze. Torches on either side illuminated a small hatch with a bell hanging beside it. At Finn's nudge, Asta raised her hand to the bell and pulled the cord.

The clamour was loud in the silent courtyard, sending cats yowling in all directions. From the far side of the door came a staccato rattle of footsteps, and it took all Asta's courage not to turn tail and flee as the cats had done.

The hatch slid back. In the darkness beyond, Inyestan eyes gleamed sliver. "What brings you to the house of the Deity?"

"Please, I'm cold, I have nowhere to sleep." The woman behind the door seemed to expect something more. "I ask for the Deity's mercy."

Jewel-bright eyes scanned her. "You are not Inyestan?"

"I'm a traveller."

"You have no money?"

The paper was concealed in her shift. She hoped no one would search her.

"No money, and no place to stay. Can you help me?"

The hatch closed, and for a moment she thought she was shut out for the night, before there was a rattle and the door swung inward to reveal a long tunnel, illuminated with torches. The Inyestan woman was dressed in a floor-sweeping crimson robe with no sleeves, a light cloak thrown over it to ward off the night's chill. "Follow me," she said.

She led the way down the corridor, and unlocked a room on the right hand side. In the darkness, Asta heard breathing, and faint snores, and felt the warmth of sleeping bodies clustered together. The woman's hand on her shoulder steered her into the room.

"I'll come and let you out in the morning," she said. "There will be a meal for you then. Sleep well."

Before Asta could ask any questions the door closed behind her, leaving her in utter darkness. The key turned in the lock.

Finn?

Not here. It's not safe.

With his night eyes, he guided her to an empty spot among the blankets and straw mattresses on the floor. She lay down, listening to the little noises of the sleepers in the dark around her, the mutters and sighs, the muted grunts and squeaks as two of the women made love. Feeling suddenly lonely in the crowded room, she pulled the blanket over her ears to muffle the sound. *I'll never sleep in here, Finn.*

At least we're in. He sounded smug. She sensed he was enjoying himself, even if she wasn't. *Let me have a look around.*

Leave them alone, you dirty bastard.

He snorted. *You wouldn't say no to a bit of warming up like that, would you?*

I'm warm enough. It was stuffy in the room. The walls glittered with condensation, the heat rising from huddled bodies. She lay on her back, one hand pressed to her stomach, feeling the swelling beneath her palm. She would not be able to hide it for much longer.

Finn? What was it like, when Rhodan was born?

She heard the smile in his thought. *The first time Lefalli put him in my arms . . . At that moment it was as if I had scattered into a thousand pieces and been put back together again in a whole new way. I looked the same, but everything about me, and the world, had changed forever. I loved him instantly, with all that I was.*

Would she love her children, knowing they had been conceived for such a foul purpose? At the moment she felt so distanced from the processes going on in her body, so concerned with staying alive and finding her kin, it was hard to imagine those tiny wriggling bodies nestling in her arms. How could she love them?

You'll love them.

Her brother's words lifted her, and despite Asta's protests that she would never sleep, the warmth and comfort was enticing. It had been such a long day.

I'll wake you if anything happens.

Finn's promise was the last thing she heard before her eyes closed.

Asta woke with a stiff neck and calves that screamed in protest as she tried to move. The blood had caked on her battered heels, and she vowed never to walk any distance again if she could possibly avoid it. There was a reason the Ancestors had tamed horses for the tribes.

All around her, other women were stirring. She wondered if the Temple only let women in, or whether the men were confined to a separate sleeping room. A quick glance around suggested the rest of the women here were Inyestan, and they gave her curious glances as they rose from their beds. She supposed she should be talking to them, but she was too tired, too sore and hungry to do much more than grunt as she smoothed herself down and checked the folding money was still safely concealed in her inside pocket.

The door rattled and swung open. A different red-robed woman was waiting for them outside, and the scent of cooking and clatter of plates drifted down the corridor. Asta hadn't realised how hungry she was, but the hollow gurgle in her belly told her that she was starving. She would be able to think more clearly after she'd eaten. Lusha's boiled egg and cracker seemed a long time ago.

The priestess led the women who had slept in the Temple overnight to a hall filled with row upon row of long benches. About half of them were filled with men and women with pinched faces and faded clothes, their hair still haphazard from sleep. Asta ran her hand over her own spiky crop as she took a seat, in between two women whose curious glances took her in and then dismissed her.

There was little chatter in the dining hall. The Inyestan priests and priestesses moved among the diners, issuing soft instruction to the white clad, barefoot servers. As one set a plate in front of her Asta glanced at his ear to see if it was clipped, but his lobes were smooth and unblemished. She reached for her fork to spear a chunk of fish, and without looking, the woman next to her snaked out a hand and caught her wrist.

"Don't," she muttered, lips barely moving, eyes fixed on her own dish.

Asta looked down the length of the table. The scent of the meal was torturing her empty stomach, but no one at the table, not even the thinnest of the women, was eating. She wanted to ask why not, but she sensed she wouldn't get a reply. She watched as one of the priestesses moved along the table, muttering a few words to every woman as she passed, and gesticulating over every plate. As she moved on, as if freed from a spell the women she passed fell on their food like starving dogs.

Finn bristled with suspicion, an innate distaste for authority that had led him to reject the leader's robes that bowed his sister's shoulders. She shut him out, concentrating on the priestess, her graceful gestures and husky voice, the way the smell of incense clung to her robes and was released in fragrant clouds as she moved. Her eyes were pearls of flawless pale blue, shadowed by the hood of her cloak.

She stopped in front of Asta and their eyes met, the Inyestan blinking in surprise. "You're a long way from home," she said.

"I have no home." She wondered if there was a formal way to address the priests of the Red Temple.

"What brings you to Abonnae?"

"I'm looking for something."

The priestess smiled. "You might have found it. Could you wait behind for me after the meal? I'd like to talk to you about your homeland." She made a pass over Asta's plate and moved on, her voice so low Asta couldn't make out what she said to her neighbour. Instead she bowed her head over her meal; chunks of fish in a creamy sauce and a small glass of watered wine; trying not to guzzle it down and make herself sick. In her mind, Finn was quietly exultant, but she didn't share his confidence. This was a big place, and Rhodan could be anywhere. If she found him, how would she get him out?

The women around her finished eating and scattered without saying a word. Unsure of when she would see another meal, Asta forced herself to eat slowly, lingering over the dregs of her wine until the hall was almost deserted. When she pushed her plate away and looked up, a red-clad figure was waiting by the door, beckoning to her. Across the vastness of the hall, she couldn't make out if it was the same woman, but she followed the call.

The priestess said nothing, merely nodded and indicated for her to follow, down the corridor, across a small inner courtyard and through a modest door. They emerged between two vast pillars, as thick round as tree trunks, stretching up until their heads were lost in the shadowy rafters. On the far side of the pillars, row after row of red-clad clerics and penitents in their duller robes knelt, foreheads pressed to bare stone, before a grand altar. Other priests moved among them, swinging fragrant, smoking censers on long, delicate chains. The scent made Asta's eyes water, making it hard to pick out the shape of the room or the design of the altar.

The silent priestess led Asta through an iron gate set in the stone wall of the Temple and up a flight of stairs to a galleried landing that looked down on the worshippers. Up here the air was clearer, but Asta could still hear the low hum of the faithful as they chanted. It was a relief when the priestess led her into a side room and closed the door behind her, cutting off the unsettling noise.

The room was bare but for a table and two chairs, one occupied by a fluffy white cat. The walls were decorated with a frieze similar to the one Asta had studied at Lusha's house. The priestess indicated for her to sit before she could see if they were actually the same, and turfed the cat out of the other chair. She leaned on the table with her chin resting in her hands, studying Asta until she squirmed under the scrutiny. That strange blank gaze made her skin crawl.

"What are you looking for, sister?"

For a moment Asta was confused by the familiarity. She wasn't this woman's sister, so why call her that? Was this her veiled way of saying that she knew about Finn?

The woman smiled. She seemed to sense Asta's bewilderment. "We are all brothers and sisters here, children of our Deity and of Chesserai, who is our Holy Mother. Even you horse-children of the north. I am Sister Margoli." She arched her thin brows, waiting for Asta to provide her own name.

She hesitated. "You can call me Heylan."

"Was that so hard, sister?" Margoli smiled.

"Where I come from, our names are valued."

Margoli's smile broadened. She had almost no top lip. "But you're not where you come from, are you? What brought you here? What are you looking for?"

"Family. I'm looking for . . . family. Something I've lost, that's important to me." It wasn't untrue, not exactly. Her mother had always impressed on her that it was a great wrong to lie. It seemed that since she had been in Inyesta she had done nothing but lie.

"You think you will find family in the Red Temple?"

"You called me 'sister.' What does that mean, if not family?"

"I suppose we are a family, in a way," Margoli said thoughtfully. "We're always looking for new members. It's a life of service, of penitence, and it's not for everyone. Do you think you could embrace that?"

"I'm not afraid of hard work," Asta told her.

Margoli leaned back, regarding her for a long time, thin lips twitching. "If you stay, that's what you will find. If you think you can have free meals and a roof over your head, without accepting the Deity into your heart, you will suffer greatly."

Asta shuffled under her level gaze. "I don't know much about any Deity," she confessed. "Where I come from we have no gods." Only the spirits of her ancestors, generation after generation, looking down on her now. She felt their scrutiny more keenly than she felt Margoli's, and it was them she needed to please, to pacify. Not this scarlet-clad cleric.

"I'm aware of that. That's why I wanted to talk to you particularly. We feel your people have suffered through their lack of faith. Do you agree?"

"I think my people have suffered, more than you know."

"Could you be an ambassador to your people? Take the word of the Deity back to them, that they may see the true ways?"

"I could certainly bring word of the Red Temple back to my people, although whether they would listen . . ." Asta shrugged. "You will have to teach me . . . sister."

"I must talk to the Holy Mother. You understand what you're taking on?" Her smooth fingers gripped Asta's wrist. "It will be hard. You must be a penitent, from the first. Your sins must be driven from your flesh by humility. Only then, when you have learned humility, when you understand our ways to your very soul, will you be fit to carry the word of the Deity to your people.

If you don't think you can manage the task, say so now and I'll let you be on your way."

"How long will it take before you consider me humbled?" She was sure the Red Temple would not countenance her pregnancy, as much as the Scattering had encouraged it. She could not have her children here, in Inyesta. They would never be safe.

"It takes as long as it takes. Are you agreeable?"

It seemed like the best chance she had to track down Rhodan. Asta nodded, and Margoli rose. "Wait here," she said. "I must talk to Chesserai. I won't be long."

The key clicked in the lock behind her as she left, and that soft sound told Asta what Margoli's gentle words and smooth touch had kept silent; that Asta was a stranger here, yet to earn her trust. She stretched in her seat, massaging the ache that had settled in the small of her back.

You handled that well. Finn's voice held grudging respect. *Mother would be proud of you.*

She might be more proud of what we're doing if you'd ever let her see Rhodan.

He said nothing, but she knew that if she could have seen him, he would be glaring.

Come on, Finn. She lost Father, she lost you, she was driven out of the village, and then you deprived her of her only grandchild. It's hardly fair.

She killed our da, Asta.

A simple, harsh fact that had sliced their family in two as cleanly as a blade. But Asta knew, and it had taken the blood pouring over her own hands to realise it, that the cut was raw-edged and unhealed, even after all this time.

She acted from mercy. I found out how hard that can be, that day on the beach. Would you have had him live, knowing he couldn't ride, or even walk? Would you want to live like that?

He snarled. He sounded like their mother. *I would have liked the option.*

Asta had no reply to that. They lapsed into silence, broken

only by the faint drum of her fingers on the desk. There was no air in this stuffy chamber, and she longed for a window, a patch of blue sky. She was sick of living behind walls.

Asta? Finn's voice was small.

What?

When you get Rhodan back, take him to see Mother. I think I owe her that much.

She didn't have time to reply. The smart echo of footsteps on stone sounded in the corridor outside and she straightened, pushing her brother, and his concession, to the back of her mind.

"She's in here." Margoli had opened the door and was speaking over her shoulder to someone Asta couldn't see. Then she moved aside, bowing her head respectfully. "Shall I leave her to you, Holy Mother?"

The Holy Mother, Chesserai, made a sharp gesture of dismissal. She was a tall woman, probably around a decade older than Asta, with short dark hair that was swept forward to frame her olive-skinned face. Her lips were too red, and her eyes, heavily painted in blues and greens, were as smooth and blue-white as moonstone. She wore the same floor-length, sleeveless red robe as Margoli, under a light cloak with a deep hood that furled around her shoulders. She did not sit down. Asta wondered if she should stand to greet her, but decided against it.

Chesserai held her gaze for what seemed like an age, daring Asta to lower her eyes. Asta would not be cowed, and Finn's hostility blazed bright in her skull, a savage firecracker erupting behind her eyes.

She's seen Rhodan, Asta! She knows where he is!

Shut up! She didn't discount the possibility that this Holy Mother could read minds. There could be anything going on behind that blank gaze.

Chesserai inclined her head. Her earlobes were laden with gold hoops, and they chinked together faintly as she moved. She slid into the chair opposite Asta with feline grace, and held her gaze for another long moment, as if waiting for her to speak.

When Asta said nothing, she cleared her throat. "What do you want here, daughter of Atrath? Many races come through our halls, but it's rare to see a horse-woman walking freely in Abonnae." Her brow creased, a faint trickle of powder drifting down onto the surface of the table. "Not just Atrathene, though. I can see it in the shape of your face."

Asta said nothing. She hoped Chesserai's perceptiveness would not link her to Rhodan, not yet. Not before she had the chance to work out how the land lay beneath her feet.

"Margoli seems to think highly of you. Do you think you could live as a penitent, until your sins are scourged?"

In reply, Asta slipped her foot free from her boot and extrended it, filthy and blistered, raw from walking. Chesserai looked at it with distaste.

"I chose to walk here. I gave up my horse, so the Red Temple could see how serious I was. I'll be penitent; I'll do whatever it takes. I need this, Holy Mother."

Chesserai's fingertips brushed the skin of Asta's ankle, and for the first time, she smiled. A genuine smile, the mask slipping away to reveal the woman beneath. "You're courageous. I think you'll do well here. Do you want to join us?"

"More than anything."

"I'm glad." Chesserai rose. The inspection appeared to be over. "Margoli will show you around, and give you your penitents' robes. She'll tell you what to do. Wait for her here."

"Yes, Holy Mother. And . . . thank you."

"You won't thank me when your fingers are worn to blisters! Though I think perhaps it will not be as hard for you as it is for some, daughter of Atrath. Not if you can swallow your pride."

She swept from the room in a swirl of scarlet before Asta could find her tongue to reply. In the dark recesses of her mind, Finn chuckled.

She's got the measure of you without even trying!

Asta stretched her legs out before her, revelling in a rare moment of triumph. *Sounds like we're in, little brother!*

You watch her. I don't trust her. She might smile, but behind her eyes . . . it's like looking into an empty house.

Oh hush! The door swung open. Margoli returning, all smiles now her Holy Mother had granted Asta permission to stay. She led Asta to a dormitory with beds stacked on top of each other four high, wooden ladders running up their sides. The spaces between were no higher than the fruit boxes in Heylan's warehouse; it would be impossible to sit up, awkward even to roll over once in bed. The adept patted one of the middle bunks.

"You'll sleep here," she said. "I'll bring you your robes, and when you're changed I'll show you around."

"When do I start my penitence?" Asta asked.

"You've started it already, sister. You're one of us now."

Margoli left her while she went to fetch Asta's new robes. There was no way to sit on the beds, and she hung on to the ladder as a wave of tiredness washed over her.

You'd better not get any fatter, or you won't be able to fit in those beds!

I'm not planning on staying here until I'm fat. Asta wished she could sit down, lose herself in Finn's spirit for a while and let him take the strain of looking for Rhodan. There might be a small chance to meditate here, in her bunk at night. It was worth a go. If she stayed here too long she would once again feel the suffocation of imprisonment behind these red stone walls.

She straightened as Margoli came back, a sheath of grey cloth draped across her arms. Asta wriggled into it, keeping herself turned away so the curve of her belly was obscured from view. The priestess chuckled.

"No room for modesty here, sister Heylan! Any more than there is room for pride. Come on, you can help me prepare the evening meal, and then the temple must be swept. There's always much to do."

There were other penitents already hard at work in the kitchen when she arrived. Margoli set her to chopping tiny, fiery peppers, and the juices stung her hands and eyes until they streamed so hard she could barely see. She tried to wipe her inflamed eyes on the shoulder of her robe, but it only made them itch and sting more. The kitchen was crowded, but no one spoke, and the only sounds were the thud of knives against chopping boards, and the bubble of the pots of stew, steaming over the long fire trench in the middle of the room. Around half-a-dozen cats sprawled around the fire, or begged at the feet of the penitents who were chopping meat to add to the stew.

Margoli came to fetch her, looking with approval at her blistered hands and red-raw eyes. She carried a small pot of salve, and she took Asta's hands between both of her own and massaged the ointment into her skin, dabbing a few spots around her eyes. "Is that better?" she asked.

"Much better. Thank you." Asta blinked away the tears, fighting the urge to rub her sore eyes. Away from the kitchen, the air was cooler, and the salve calmed the orbs of fire in her head. By the time they reached the ground floor of the Temple, where she had watched worshippers bent in supplication the day before, her vision had cleared. There were no people here today. Only cats.

"Why are there so many cats in the Temple?" she asked, as Margoli handed her a short-handled brush and a pan to sweep the dust into.

"They are attracted to the scent of the Deity. We regard them as manifestations of his ever-changing will. The Feline is unknowable, as the Deity is. Also," she grinned, "they keep the rats and mice away!"

Asta nodded, thinking of her mother, who was as unknowably feline as a woman could get while still retaining a semblance of humanity. She wondered what Margoli meant by "the scent of the Deity." The candles and incense burning in the Temple, presumably; she knew there were some scents that made cats behave like drunken humans. She was about to ask, but Margoli gestured impatiently at the brush in her hands.

"The Temple must be swept before evening worship, Sister.

Every inch of it. And you must not disturb the cats."

"Is there a bigger brush?"

Margoli merely raised an eyebrow.

"But the Temple is huge! I can't—"

"You are a penitent, Sister Heylan. You can, and you will. I will be watching."

She moved aside to tend the candles fluttering on the altar. Asta contented herself with glaring at her back, then dropped to her knees and began to sweep.

The Temple might be vast, but she wasn't alone. There were other penitents engaged in the same duty. The floor was dusty with dirt tramped in off the street, with cat hair where they rolled in patches of sunlight, and cat shit in dark corners, along with the occasional beheaded rat or disembowelled mouse, half-eaten and toyed with. All the Temple cats looked well-fed, and Asta suspected they killed for fun, or out of boredom. She tried not to disturb them, but some of them ran playfully before her brush, or butted against her hand demanding fuss, and in her head she gave them names and chatted to them. It helped relieve the monotony of cleaning, especially as Finn seemed distracted. When she tried to talk to him, she got no reply.

She crossed paths with another penitent, an older man, while she was shaking out her dustpan in the courtyard. The humid air glued her shift to her back and there were damp, sticky patches under her arms, so she was grateful for a moment's respite. She stretched, kneading her hands into her back and craning her neck left and right to stretch aching muscles.

"Don't be too long," the man muttered out of the corner of his mouth, keeping his eyes downcast. "They have eyes everywhere."

"Thank you." She kept her own voice low. He had obviously been here a while. "Listen, I'm looking for—" but he shook his head and quickly moved away before she could finish the question. Talking amongst penitents was discouraged.

So how am I supposed to find him, Finn?

Finn said nothing, but she felt his shrug.

You're a lot of fucking help, little brother. She dropped back to her knees and continued to scrub, conscious all the while of the unblinking eyes of dozens of cats, all fixed on her, waiting for her to make her move.

EIGHTEEN

THE DAYS PASSED slowly, too slowly for Asta. She was never alone for more than a few moments, never long enough to drop into a meditative trance. The penitents exchanged a few muttered words when they could, but nothing that seemed relevant to her quest. They seemed passive, content to work through their lot in anticipation of some greater reward in the future. But Asta didn't have time to be complacent.

The larger of the twin moons was fat, low over a horizon banded with blush-pink and gold, while in the east, the first hint of sun was visible over the wall of the Temple. Dawn was bright, and the stifling heat of the day had yet to burn away the clouds of sunrise. Asta was feeling nauseous, and on the pretext of running an errand for Margoli, she had slipped away from serving breakfast to the beggars and the homeless that crowded the steps of the Temple every evening. For a prosperous city, Abonnae seemed to be full of people unable to feed themselves. Asta had felt the pinch of hunger, in the famine season, but she would never have lowered herself to begging from a strangely benevolent god. Not before she came to Inyesta.

She sat on one of the benches in the courtyard, absently caressing a black fluffy cat that poured himself into her lap with treadling paws and a deep vibrating purr. He looked like

Marcio, and she wondered where Ranmiro and his cat were now, and if she would ever see them again. She felt small, and very alone. It felt like she was stumbling from one prison to the next, wherever she went, exchanging one set of enclosing walls for another. The high battlements of the Red Temple closed around her, and she was unable even to walk in the Spirit Realm or take to the streets in the ghostly body of her brother. She picked at the calloused skin on her palms, blisters swollen and burst until the old skin hung loose and the new was pink and tender underneath. She wished she could just walk away. Despite Finn's insistence that Rhodan was here, she had seen no sign of him, or of any Atrathene child. If he was here, he was well hidden.

"Are you rested, daughter Heylan?"

Asta sprang to her feet at the sound of Chesserai's voice behind her, dumping the cat on the ground with a yowl of protest. It pounced away from her a few feet and sat, licking one upraised paw, whiskers quivering and tail fluffed up in indignation. Chesserai looked after the cat, and a furrow appeared between her brows.

"I didn't hurt it, Holy Mother. Cats always land on their feet."

Her attempt at humour rebounded off the blank wall of Chesserai's expression. "Do you sew?" she asked. "Margoli tells me you have some skill with a needle."

"I have a little, Holy Mother." She had sewn often, back in the tribe. Fixing Finn's clothes after their mother had fled for the mountains, and fashioning clothes and horse blankets for herself and for Rhodan. Everyone in the tribe could sew, but Asta had more patience for the task than Lefalli. She found that keeping her hands busy helped her think.

"Could you sew this?" Chesserai lifted her sleeve. There was a long rent in the fabric, along one of the seams.

"Do you have a needle and thread, Holy Mother?"

Chesserai smiled lightly, tapping her belt. "I do, but my eyes aren't up to the task of stitching myself. The children are always ripping their clothes, or growing out of them."

The children. Chesserai's children? Or children from outside the Temple?

"Let's sit in the sun, the light is better over there." Asta indicated one of the benches in the courtyard, one that wasn't currently occupied by cats. The black cat padded after them, twisting in and out of her ankles as she sat down. "I didn't know you had children, Holy Mother?"

Chesserai handed her the needle and thread. "Everyone in the city is my child, dearest daughter."

"And are you responsible for all their clothes?" Asta kept her eyes firmly on the crimson thread, slipping it through the eye of the needle.

Chesserai laughed, smothering her hand with her mouth as though giggles were unbecoming to one of her status. "Of course not! But the children here at the Red Temple . . . yes, they are in my charge."

Asta's needle flashed back and forth, placing tiny, neat stitches in the torn sleeve, willing her hands not to shake. "I haven't seen any children in the Temple," she said.

"We don't let them just run around, getting under the feet of the penitents. But there are children here."

"Really? I would like to meet them, Holy Mother. I was . . ." she lied quickly, "in my tribe, I was a teacher. I miss that."

"A teacher? I didn't think the savage tribes set much store by learning." Chesserai sounded surprised. "Can they even read and write?"

"We have a tradition of storytelling. If I can learn the stories of your faith—"

"*Our* faith, daughter," Chesserai reminded her.

"Our faith, sorry." Asta mentally cursed herself for her slip. "If I can learn those stories, I can pass them on, as you asked me to. Spread the word among my people."

Chesserai leaned back on the bench. "I had not considered that," she admitted. "Oral storytelling as a way to impart knowledge and encourage faith. How clever you are, daughter. And what a neat job of sewing." She twisted her sleeve to admire Asta's handiwork. "Perhaps I shall call on you again. You have given me something to consider, after all."

Asta inclined her head. "I'm very keen to serve the Temple, in any way I can," she said.

"Ambition will always be rewarded here, daughter. Now," she rose, and looked pointedly at the broom Asta had left abandoned against the wall, "I believe you were sweeping the courtyard?"

"Yes, Holy Mother."

"Then I will leave you to your work, daughter. We will speak more on this."

Asta kept a watchful eye on Chesserai over the next few days, taking care to position herself where she hoped the Holy Mother would see her working. There was still no sign of any children. Finn chafed and Asta wondered. Was it possible Chesserai had lied about there being children in the Temple? Was it a test of some kind?

She was scrubbing down the walls of the women's dormitory ready for the night's intake when she heard a soft throat-clearing in the doorway, and looked up to see Chesserai watching her with an expression of mild amusement. Her eyes flicked up and down, taking in the soap scum that flecked her up to the elbows, and the damp patches on her shift. "Daughter Heylan, will you clean yourself up and join me at the altar?"

"Of course, Holy Mother." It was the work of a few minutes to find a clean shift and sluice her arms, drying them on the fabric of the old one and stuffing it under a bench. Let some other penitent clean up after her, for a change.

When she emerged in the great hall where the services were held, Chesserai was standing by the open door, silhouetted by the sunlight behind her.

"Come with me," she said, clicking her fingers and gliding

ahead, without looking back to see if Asta was following. She led the way through the Temple, heels echoing on the floor Asta had crippled her back cleaning. A couple of penitents were laying down ornate rugs for the evening's worship, and Chesserai deftly stepped over them as they unrolled towards her, never breaking stride. She bowed to the altar and stepped behind it, into a dim alcove. The ornate fascia of stone was topped with intricately worked bronze and silver which let the candlelight in to fall in geometric patterns. Behind it were three doors. Two of them were small, unremarkable portals, flanking a central door which was banded with iron, the wood in between carved with the same images that adorned the outer walls of the Red Temple. It stretched high above Asta's head, as big as the main gate of the Temple, bigger. Asta brushed her fingers against the metal. It was warm, and vibrated faintly under her hand, like a distant purring.

"This way." Chesserai opened the smaller door on the right, and ushered Asta through into a long, narrow corridor that curved away in front of her. There were doors at regular intervals on either side of the passage, all firmly closed. This was a part of the Red Temple Asta had yet to explore. Finn's excitement mounted, and she hushed him sharply, trying to concentrate on what Chesserai was saying.

"As you've proved your prowess with the needle, I could use your help. It's just through here."

Chesserai opened one of the doors. The room beyond was light, dazzling white and as hot as fire. Panes of glass in the roof allowed sunlight to stream in, highlighting a long table piled high with cloth robes of the same the delicate pink hue she had seen inside shells on the beach. Beyond the table, almost lost in the glare, was a bench running around two sides of the wedge-shaped room. On the bench sat around half-a-dozen boys, of Rhodan's age and older. Asta started forward before she could stop herself, but only one of these boys was Atrathene, and he had a good three years on Rhodan. He was not of her tribe, and her heart sank as her eyes skimmed over him. A few of the children were

Inyestan, with their impenetrable eyes, while some had the brass or copper colouring of The Scattering and some were of races she did not even recognise. She hesitated, crestfallen, and Chesserai gripped her elbow and steered her towards a seat at the table.

"If they try on their robes, you can adjust the seams to fit. You did say you wanted to help out with the children?"

"Of course, Holy Mother."

The boys all seemed beyond caring about the state of their robes. They were curiously subdued; even under Chesserai's watchful eye there was none of the joshing or elbowing Asta expected from a pack of boys of their age. Their eyes were dulled, their movements rigid as they stripped down to vests and little shorts and pulled the robes over their heads.

Asta saw at once what the High Priestess meant. The robes were supposed to fall to mid-calf, but the older boys were reaching that gangly stage, and bony, scabbed knees were exposed beneath the hemmed fabric. It was easier to let down the wide hems on the bottoms of the robes after she had loosened and re-sewn the generous seams. The robes seemed designed to accommodate the boys as they filled out, but not as they grew taller. The smaller ones looked swamped by the excess of fabric.

She had finished the first hem on one of the Scattering boys, trying not to look at his clipped ear that reminded her of Syven. She broke off the thread with her teeth and was double-knotting it when there was a faint squeak as the door opened. She looked up, her vision obscured by cloth and skinny, bruised legs. She nudged the boy in front of her aside—

And he was there, twisting awkwardly in the doorway with his fingers knotted in front of him. He was speaking to Chesserai, but Asta could hear nothing over Finn's roaring in her head. She reeled before the surge of wild emotion, and she had to clench her hands against the floor to hold back from throwing herself at him, snatching him up in her arms and running, running until the Temple and the whole damn city were far behind them and they were free again.

Asta! What are you waiting for?

But something was not right. Asta battled with Finn, forcing him to shut up, to listen to what Rhodan was saying, to let her look at him with her own eyes. She felt his distress as she pushed him, whimpering, to the back of her mind, kicking and scratching against her.

Do you want to fuck this up? Do you want her to know?

Asta, for fuck's sake . . .

Shut up!

He fell back, letting her think clearly. Chesserai was berating Rhodan and he stared at the floor, fists clenched tight at his sides. Asta willed him to look up, to meet her eyes. That would be enough for now, to let him know she was here, working on a way to get him out.

"Daughter, don't let this disruption distract you from your work. Snipe, join the back of the line. I'll see you in my office after tonight's service." Chesserai stepped back, and Rhodan looked up. His eyes met Asta's, and slid over her as if she wasn't there, no hint of surprise or even recognition in his face as he walked past her to take his place on the bench. She couldn't see him now; he was behind her, and the other boys shuffled impatiently as Chesserai tapped her foot.

"Daughter Heylan?"

"I dropped my needle . . ." Asta groped for it on the floor, keeping her head down so the Holy Mother wouldn't see the tears swimming in her eyes. Rhodan didn't know her any more. It hadn't been so long; what had they done to him? Had she changed so much, or had he?

Finn was crying, soft and broken, in the back of her mind. She wished she could fall into the Spirit realm, see him face to face, but there was no chance of that now. She found the needle, a cold sliver of metal under her fingers, and she drove it into the soft skin at the base of her thumb. She gasped at the pain, but it helped her to focus at least for a while on what had to be done.

She sat back on her heels, and sucked the blood from her hand, hoping it didn't drip on the robes she was altering. Chesserai saw the gesture, and handed her a strip of cloth from the table to wrap around her hand. "Are you fit to carry on, my child?"

Asta nodded. If she could get close to Rhodan she might be able to penetrate that blank wall he was hiding behind. The makeshift bandage rendered her slow, and clumsy, and the sun had moved some way across the glass roof before she got to the end of the line. She tried not to think about the thinness of the boys, the scrapes and cuts on their young skin, the fading whip scars across some of the older boys shoulders. But it was hard. The brightness of the room and the thumping of her heart made her head ache, shot little flashes of brilliance into the corners of her eyes.

And then suddenly Rhodan stood in front of her, skinny in vest and shorts, robe hanging over his arm. Her nausea rose as she scanned him, seeing the layers of bruising on his torso, fresh red and purple marks laid over fading yellow and green. She took the robe from him and dropped it over his head, letting the tip of her forefinger brush his spiky hair, just above his clipped ear, his slave mark from the markets of the Scattering. He didn't react.

The seams needed no adjusting around his upper arms, but she unpicked and re-sewed them anyway, hoping he would react to her. His eyes were blank. It was as if she was a stranger. She couldn't even whisper in his ear with Chesserai so close by. All she could hope was that her touch would awaken him from whatever trance he was under.

Talk to him!

I can't, Finn!

Talk to him about something casual. See if your voice gets through. Find out what they've done to him.

Asta dropped back to her knees to adjust the hem. "It's always hot here, isn't it?" she said. "Not like where I came from, over the sea. The horselands . . ."

"Daughter, much as I appreciate the potential value of story-telling, now is not the time for chat," Chesserai butted in. "Maybe later we can arrange a class for you to practice on?"

"Yes, Holy Mother." Rhodan had not flickered at the sound of her voice. Asta felt hot and sick, and she sewed as slowly as she could. Trying to prolong the contact, willing him to say anything, to touch her arm, even to blink or smile. Her nephew was a blank slate, wiped clean of personality, and she couldn't make the sewing last forever.

"Are you finished, my daughter?"

Asta nodded, throat too tight to speak.

"You may go." As she rose, Chesserai caught her arm. Her eyes, half-lidded, gleamed pale as the moons. "Make sure you come to evening service tonight. I would speak with you afterwards."

Dismissed, Asta stumbled out into the corridor and leant for a moment against the wall, face buried in her hands, and allowed herself the luxury of a few tears.

Don't cry.

Finn hugged her spirit, a brief squeeze.

I was so close, Finn! If she hadn't been there I would have grabbed him! He's under a spell, or drugged. How do I break that?

Find out more about it. He's here, and he's alive. His voice grew cold. *Give me time alone with that bitch who's been beating him . . .*

And you'll do what? Haunt her to death? Besides, you don't know it was Chesserai. It could have been anyone.

You find out. You can be my mortal fists. I'll drag her to the Spirit Realm and have it out with her there. What does she want to see you for?

Asta sniffed hard, swallowing the last of her snot. *No idea. What's your grand plan for getting us out of here, little brother?*

I'm working on it. Trust me, and keep your head. It won't be long now. You should be asking yourself something, though.

What? She was tired, and her head throbbed. She didn't want to play mind games with Finn.

Why the temple needs so many slave boys. What are they doing here? They're not penitents, or worshippers, and they're obviously kept out of public view. If you can find out why that is, you might just have something to bargain with.

Although Asta had been a penitent in the Red Temple almost half a moon, she had yet to attend a service. Penitents were not obliged to attend; their worship of the Deity was couched in hard work and sacrifice. If they were doing chores around the Temple, that was considered supplication enough. And Asta felt she knew all there was to know of sacrifice.

She joined the crowd thronging into the heart of the Red Temple, past the heavy armed guards that lurked by the doors, one anonymous face among hundreds. Those keenest to express their faith pushed forward until they were in the front rows, lying prostrate on the rugs laid out on the temple floor and howling for forgiveness for sins real and imaginary. Their cries mingled with the insistent jangle of bells far above and the yowling of the cats, who knew they were to be fed after the service. The noise combined to make Asta's head ache. She lay face down on the rug, one hand cradling her belly, the other lifting her head so she could breathe through the dusty fibres that tickled her nose and made her eyes water. She wished she could look up, but she didn't know if it was permitted.

The man lying next to her was fat, spilling off his own rug, sweaty thigh pressed up against hers. He muttered his penitence into the stifling carpet, and she uttered some fabricated sins of her own, concealing her greater misdeeds of thought, if not of action.

I thought about killing my Holy Mother. I came here full of lies, and if I could, I would burn this temple and everyone in it. I don't believe in any Deity, but if I did believe in you, I hope this prayer reaches you, whoever you are. Just so you understand what a mistake you made when you ruined my life.

In the back of her mind, Finn chuckled.

The bells stopped, and with them, the supplication. There was silence in the Red Temple, so thick and heavy with expectation Asta could taste the air around her, through the miasma of dust and sweat. She heard feet tripping up and down the hall, but the man next to her hadn't moved and she was taking her cue from him.

In front of her, in the direction of the altar, Chesserai's voice rang out in the quiet of the Temple. She was chanting, so fast even Finn couldn't keep up to translate, but he muttered that he didn't recognise the tongue as Inyestan. He suspected it was a far older language.

The prostrate crowd uttered a groaning echo, and Chesserai clapped her hands, just once.

"You may sit," she said.

Asta's neighbour grunted as he shifted into a cross-legged position on his mat. He had smuts of dust hanging off his beard, and Asta wondered, briefly and irritably, why she wasted so many hours cleaning the floor of the temple if the worship rugs were still so dusty. She brushed the dirt from the front of her own gown, and tried to listen to what Chesserai was saying.

She had never seen the Holy Mother in full regalia before. She only recognised Chesserai by her voice. Only the two pale ovals of her eyes were visible behind a mask fashioned into the image of a horned feline, richly decorated with gold thread and paint on the leather, picking out swirls and patterns that shifted eerily in the light from the candles on the altar. When she turned the right way, her eyes flashed gold and flame, and her body was wreathed in the smoke from the incense braziers glowing at either end of the altar. Robed priests moved among the supplicants, swinging their censers on their gently chiming chains, chanting in a throbbing undertone. Asta couldn't make out the words, but they wormed their way under her skin, matching her pulse beat for beat. The rhythm, the smoke, the soft padding of feet, all combined to make her eyelids heavy, her attention drift until she hovered on the edge of sleep.

Asta! Wake up!

Her head had fallen onto her shoulder, and she jerked upright at Finn's nudge, looking around guiltily. There were no priests near her. Chesserai held a golden flagon aloft and intoned deeply, and her worshippers mumbled a response. Asta sneaked a glance at the fat man. His eyes were as blank as all Inyestans', but a thin strand of drool hung from his beard and he didn't seem to have noticed it.

They're in a trance. Keep me awake, Finn.

Easy. She looked around, knowing he was watching through her eyes. The worshippers were dulled, the priests moved like ghosts. Chesserai poured the water in the flagon onto the ground at her feet. It was arcane, and strange, and Asta could make neither head nor tail of it. She had walked the shaman's path with her father, but there hadn't been this endless, meaningless ritual. Just the flatness of the Spirit Realm, the rope around her wrist, and, when a sacrifice was needed, the hot gush and copper tang of blood over her hands and in her mouth. Nothing like this droning, that went on and on . . .

Losing you again, sister? You're meant to be looking for Rhodan.

Asta wanted to rub her face with her palm, slap her cheeks to drive away the lassitude, but that would have brought unwelcome attention down on her. There was music, drifting like dust motes in sunlight from the galleries above, and the man next to her stirred, shook his head and wiped his chin, blinking as if emerging from a cave. All around people shifted position, easing cramped muscles, rubbing their eyes and looking up, seeking the source of the music and the glow that accompanied it. Light, golden as sunshine, gleamed out from the galleries, and behind it Asta saw figures moving, shadows against the glare. And now there was singing to accompany the melody, the high, piping voices of boys who had yet to reach manhood.

Asta tipped her head back and let the music fall around her. High above the shadows moved, resolving themselves into skinny forms that drifted down impossibly from the high galleries, landing with soft, bare feet, the light shining through the robes she had mended that afternoon so she could see the frail stick-forms of arms and legs. Not spirits fallen from the sky, but real, human flesh and blood. The drugged slave boys transformed to shining, flying beings. Rhodan.

He was so close that if she reached out she could brush his robes. The light threw a halo around him, making her squint as he dropped to his knees and lay his forehead on the ground. The music died away, leaving silence in the temple once more.

Chesserai held her hands high, a gesture that could be benediction, or surrender. "Go with the Deity," she said.

Her words broke the spell. All around Asta people scrambled to their feet, brushing smudges of dust off their gaudy clothes, turning to their neighbours and exchanging greetings as if they hadn't been sitting next to each other for what felt like the longest time imaginable. The fat man wrapped a sweaty paw around her elbow and hauled her upright before she could protest. He smiled, and she realised he was younger than she was, behind the beard that aged him. She tried to look past him at Rhodan, but now people were streaming out of the temple around her. She nearly lost her footing as she was buffeted by the human tide.

"Careful!" The bearded Inyestan gripped her arm again, pulling her against his side. "Are you all right? You look dizzy. Come and get some air."

"I—" But the crowd was dispersing, and Rhodan had vanished. She hadn't even seen him go. Numbed, she let the stranger lead her into the courtyard, past a couple of the silent, heavy-set guards that were always lurking unacknowledged around the temple. He chased a couple of cats off a stone bench so she could sit down, before patting her on the shoulder and hurrying off towards the gate. She watched the last of the stragglers make their leisurely way from the Temple, chatting and laughing together as if a burden had been lifted. She wished she shared that sentiment.

The bearded man was back before the last of the worshippers had made their way down the steps. He clutched a glass full of thick fruity liquid poured over crushed ice, which he pressed into her hand. "Drink this. The afternoon heat can be too much if you're not used to it."

Asta muttered her thanks and took a gulp. The juice was smooth, the ice points of sharpness on her dry tongue.

"Have you been at the Temple long? I haven't seen you at worship before, I would have noticed . . ." He smiled shyly over the rim of his own glass.

"Not long." Asta indicated her robes. "I'm a penitent."

"I can see that. Do you have aspirations?"

"Aspirations?"

"To go far in the service of the Deity. Would you like to be High Priestess one day?"

"Me? No." Asta thought of Chesserai's blank eyes under the mask and shuddered inwardly. "I'm happy doing my penance for now."

"I'm glad to hear that." His smile broadened. "Maybe I could meet you one evening, when you're feeling a bit less penitent? I could show you around the city . . ."

Finn sniggered. *He wants to stick you, sister! Watch it, he's fatter than you will be in a few moons!*

His teasing was a welcome break from the tension of the service, but Asta wasn't about to allow it to continue. She rose smoothly, keen to break off the flirtation before it got even more awkward. "Maybe," she said. "I'm not going anywhere for the time being. But I have to attend my Holy Mother now. Look out for me at the next service."

"I'll make a point of it!" He took back her empty glass. When she looked back from the door to the Temple, he was still watching her. She waved.

What are you up to, Asta?

Cultivating a potential ally.

Not a potential fuck?

Possibly that too. She allowed herself a small smile.

You'd have to go on top, or he'd crush you like a bug.

I could live with that.

Whore. Asta felt the warmth of her brother's affection in the teasing.

Dead bastard.

Semi-dead bastard, thank you very much! She laughed openly at his response, the sound echoing around the empty room. By the altar, someone stirred. It was Chesserai, still wearing her mask.

"Is something amusing you, daughter?"

Asta inclined her head in immediate humility. "Just the cats playing in the courtyard, Holy Mother." She turned at the clip of heels on the floor behind her, to see another priest, in a far less ornate mask. He was accompanied by Safie, one of the other penitents who had been at the Red Temple longer than Asta. She was leading a girl of no more than four summers by the hand. An Atrathene girl. From the movements of her jaw, she looked like she was sucking on a sweet.

Chesserai clapped her hands. "Good, we're all here. Now we can proceed with the second part of the service."

Asta looked around. The Temple was deserted apart from the five of them, though footsteps echoed down from the high galleries above. "I thought that was it?" she ventured. "The service is over, surely?"

"The public face of the service. We still have duties to perform. And you have a special opportunity to demonstrate your faith, my daughter. A rare opportunity, one that is not extended to everyone. Follow me."

"An opportunity?" But Chesserai would be drawn no further, merely smiling mysteriously. Asta fell into step at the back as Chesserai led the quintet behind the altar, right up to the enormous reinforced door. She placed her hand on the intricate central lock, and it glowed, light seeping between her fingers. When she lifted it, she left behind the shining imprint of her palm.

"Quickly now!" Chesserai's devotees hastened through a small portal that had opened in the base of the door, ducking their heads to pass through. Asta wanted to hang back and get a good look at the locking mechanism, but Chesserai hustled them ahead of her, and the portal whispered shut behind them, leaving no trace that it had ever been there.

The tunnel that led past the sewing room had curved around

to the right, but the one Asta stood in now was arrow straight and sloping downwards, so sharply that in places the packed-earth floor gave way to rough steps. It was so wide ten men could have walked abreast, and so high Asta couldn't see the roof when she glanced up, only yawning darkness. It was hot, and as the route led downwards through a number of right-angled bends, it grew hotter. The little girl stumbled, tired or overcome by heat. Asta darted towards her, but before she could reach her Safie picked her up and carried her in her arms.

Asta tugged at her shift, pulling it free from where sweat moulded the linen to her skin. The faith of her father's people spoke of many hells; hot underground caverns where demons crawled. Was that where Chesserai led them, into some Western hell? Asta clenched her fists, scraping at her clammy palms with broken fingernails, and longed for a knife.

The passage ended in another immense door, similar to the first but banded with more iron, so hot it blistered Asta's fingers as she touched it. She wondered how the wood didn't burst into flame around it. Beyond it, the corridor levelled out through a series of iron gates, five in all, and through them, she could see a room. Chesserai opened a portal in each gate and door and sealed them shut behind them before she opened the next one.

They really don't want anyone getting in here, do they? Asta muttered to Finn.

That's one explanation. The other one . . . doesn't bear thinking about.

And now he had put the idea in her head that was *all* Asta could think about. That the gates, the barred doors, the locks that responded magically to Chesserai's touch, were not designed to keep people out, but to keep something *in*.

The last gate vanished behind them. The masked priest and Safie had obviously been here before; they headed straight for the noisy stream of water that ran down the left hand wall to disappear into a hole in the floor. The priest pushed up his mask and drank eagerly from his cupped hands, and Safie filled her water bottle and let the dark-haired girl drink from it. The little girl seemed fascinated by the play of candlelight on the water, and the way the spray burst against her hands. She watched the water, and Asta watched her, trying to identify her tribe, wishing she could get close enough to whisper to her without being overheard.

"You can drink, Heylan. It's a thirsty journey, especially if you haven't made it before."

Asta shook off her fears about what could be lurking behind the gates and locked doors. "Thank you, Holy Mother," she said, hastening to the waterfall to drink and splash water across her heat-tightened skin. It was delightfully cold, and she shivered deliciously. "How does the water stay cold? It's so hot in here."

"It runs through our ice room," Chesserai explained. "The Red Temple has a monopoly over all the ice in the city. If people want ice, they have to buy it from us. Just an extra stream of income for the Deity, and for the Temple." She smiled. As she had been talking she lit fresh candles, each as long and thick as a man's arm, that were stored in a chest against the wall opposite the waterfall. In their fresh light Asta could see the room properly for the first time. She longed for a proper look around, but Chesserai drew her aside and spoke to her in a low voice.

"You have shown ambition," she said. "I value that. But ambition alone will not carry you as far in the Deity's service as it might."

Asta licked her lips. "What more do I need, Holy Mother?"

"Patience. Acceptance." She flashed a tight smile. "Discretion, maybe. Obedience, certainly . . ." She stepped back as the priest approached, leaving Asta wondering what she meant. Was this part of the test the Holy Mother had alluded to?

There was another altar, wider than the one upstairs, made of smooth obsidian. The rood screen was separate from the altar, set back against the wall. It was a massive grid wrought of black iron, and it looked more functional than the delicate screen in the Temple above. Asta had a brief vision, that behind it was another barred door, another tunnel leading down, and another, over and over until they reached the core of the earth. And what lay beyond that?

There was a strong smell of cat-herb in the room. She could taste it on her tongue even after drinking the water, a cool, citrus fragrance, not unpleasant but heavy enough to induce a mild headache. Asta wondered if it was in the drink Chesserai heated up over a low brazier to the right of the altar, but it felt stronger than that. Safie and the masked priest were both relaxed, watching the little girl playing under the waterfall. She pushed her hair back, and Asta saw the notch clipped from her earlobe that told her that she too, like so many before her, had passed through the Scattering.

The smoke from the brazier stung her eyes, and Asta moved closer to the rood screen to get away from it. The cat-herb smell was even stronger here. The screen was up against the wall, and behind it was solid rock, for the most part. There were a few black, gaping holes in the rock wall, and the smell came from them. She crouched and put her face to one of the holes, squinting in the gloom.

In the blackness beyond the wall, something moved.

"I wouldn't put my face there, if I were you."

Asta looked around. The three clerics were staring at her. Safie's eyes and mouth were perfectly round, and she shook her head urgently. "Come away, sister. He doesn't like it if you look through there."

"Who doesn't?" There was a rush of air at Asta's back, and a roar that set the metal screen, and the stone wall behind it, vibrating like a drum skin. Asta sprang back with a yell, forgetting her penitent manners. "What the fuck was that?"

"That was our Deity, my daughter. You've woken him up." Chesserai spoke calmly, as if this was an everyday occurrence, as she took the metal pan from the heat to allow the tea to brew.

"The . . . Deity? You keep your Deity . . . down here? Under the Temple?"

"Of course we do. Haven't you been paying attention? The

Red Temple is the House of the Deity. We are his followers, his worshippers." In the reflected light from the candles, Chesserai's eyes glowed orange. "One day soon, I will be his bride."

"His what?" Asta could hear the creature, whatever it was, crashing around behind the wall. The little girl screwed up her face and burst into tears.

"I'll tell you all about it after the ceremony." Chesserai had to raise her voice over the snarls and crashing. She beckoned to Safie and mouthed, "Bring her to me."

Safie led the girl up to the brazier, where Chesserai blew gently on the terracotta mug of tea. Asta was close enough to inhale the steam rising from it, and it made her head swim. She retreated a step.

Chesserai crouched, until her eyes were level with the Atrathene girl's, and kissed her on the forehead. "Don't cry, little one. Have a drink to make you feel better." She wrapped her hand around the back of the child's neck and raised the mug to her lips.

Asta watched the change come over her, saw her dark eyes glaze and her shoulders droop. It was as if she had fallen asleep, while still standing and drinking. Chesserai straightened with a satisfied smile.

"I think we're ready to begin now," she said. "Heylan, if you take her arms . . ."

The girl was limp, showing no resistance as Asta and the silent priest lifted her between them and laid her out on the black slab. Asta cradled her cheek with one hand, smoothing her hair away from her forehead, wondering if she had people in her tribe who were missing her, even looking for her, right now. Her unease was growing by the second, and the noises from behind the wall were hideous, slavering and thumping until the whole room seemed to vibrate in time with the thunder in Asta's skull. She reached out for Finn, but he had retreated. All she could sense was his anxiety, and it did nothing to calm her own fears.

The girl stared at the ceiling with wide, blank eyes. Her skin felt cool under Asta's hands, despite the heat of the cavern, and her fingers embraced the slender flesh and bone of her upper arms. She was younger than Rhodan, smaller and thinner, and Asta wondered how long she had been a slave, whether she could somehow rescue her, as well as Rhodan, how she would get them home . . .

With a soft rustle of fabric, Chesserai let her cloak drop to the floor. Beneath it, she wore a floor-length sleeveless dress that left one olive shoulder bare and exposed the curve of her right breast. A leather sheath strapped around her forearm held a jewel-hilted knife, and tiny images of flame danced in her opalescent eyes. She held her arms out, palms upward as if in supplication, and Safie stepped forward and drew the blade.

Asta gripped tighter. She willed the Atrathene girl to struggle, to show fear, but she seemed to be in a trance, unresisting and helpless as a rag doll. The priest watched Asta warily, blank eyes concealing his thoughts.

They won't . . .

Asta wasn't sure if she caught Finn's thought, or her own. Surely they wouldn't . . . Just a ritual cutting, a symbol. Chesserai was chanting, a low sound on the edge of hearing. She had chanted in the Temple high above, but now her words had a harsher edge. They seemed to still everything in the room; the trickle of water, the crackle of the brazier, Asta's own ragged breathing. Even the sounds behind the wall were muted; the gods themselves held their breath and listened to the Holy Mother as she intoned her prayer.

Safie bowed low and handed her the blade, hilt first. Candle fire slipped off the blood-red stones in Chesserai's palm, making them flash in Asta's vision. Red as sunset, as a signal fire. Red as blood spilt on the sand.

Asta!

Finn struggled to keep her alert. The chanting, the scent of the candles, the heat, all conspired to dull Asta's wits. She saw, without understanding what she was seeing, as Chesserai raised the blade and slammed it down.

And then her hands were wet and red. She lost her grip on the girl's arms as the tide engulfed her, as Chesserai slit her from throat to hips. The girl twitched, just once, but she never made a sound, and the twitch was that of a dreamer, not a child struggling for life. Blood streamed down the sides of the altar, into the deep gulley that ran around the edges of the stone, and through a narrow culvert that ran under the wall that held back Chesserai's Deity.

Asta raised her bloodied hand towards the little girl's face, wanting to close her staring eyes, to hold her close, to say sorry for what had been done to her. Her throat was so tight she could barely breathe, and Safie tapped her elbow.

"You're struggling," she said, in an undertone. "Let me take over."

Asta relinquished her place at the altar, pressing her palm to her mouth in an effort to keep her vomit down. She could not stop staring, at the darkness of blood on the girl's skin, at Chesserai's arm, bloodied to the elbow, shaking the knife until ruby drops spattered in a wide arc across the floor. The Holy Mother smiled. She looked as benign and calm as a summer morning, as if this butchery was nothing but part of her day's work.

"Daughter, could you fetch some water please?"

Asta moved without thinking, filling up a bucket beside the waterfall, bringing it back so Chesserai could rinse the gore from her skin, watching it turn from crystal to swirling red. Inside, Finn was calling to her, trying to break through the wall. It was hard to hear anything over the noise in her head, and she knew if she did think about it she would break, she would snatch the knife from Chesserai's fingers and plunge it hilt-deep into her throat. They would never let her get away after that, and Rhodan . . .

Oh shit, Rhodan . . .

He would end up on the slab, he would drink the drugged tea and go to his death without a fight, and the creature behind the wall would gorge itself on his blood . . .

Asta, hold it together. For the sake of our family . . .

Finn's voice calmed her. He was there, his fingers entwined with hers, his arm around her shoulders, steering her as she fetched fresh water and watched Safie and the masked priest lift the little broken body down from the slab and lay her, very precisely, on a spot on the floor. The priest straightened and pressed a place on the wall, a part of the grid that looked no different from the rest. There was a grating sound as the slab the girl lay on sloped downwards, and with a nudge of Safie's foot she rolled towards the wall and vanished beneath the floor of the cavern. There was a snarl, the scrape of claws on stone, and a hideous crack of bone as the Deity began to feed.

NINETEEN

I T'S ALL RIGHT, sister. It takes some people like this. Try and keep your head between your knees."

Asta was dimly aware of Safie's voice, a hand rubbing her between her shoulder blades, a cold mug of water pressed to her lips. She was lying on the floor, looking at feet. Chesserai's feet, metal-tipped toe and three-inch pointed heel, straps embracing her calves. There was a spot of blood on the front of her ankle, clinging on as she moved, and that red filled Asta's vision until it was all she could see.

"She's fainting again! Steady her head!"

The voices came from a long way away. Down a tunnel, a tunnel filled with blood that gurgled away into darkness. But the gurgle was water, pouring into her dry mouth, and she swallowed eagerly, washing away the bile, the raw red pain from holding in her screams.

"Can you sit up?" Safie's hand was still on her back, pressing her upright. Asta forced the heels of her hands against her eyes, not wanting to see the chamber, the red smears on the stone, the blood on her own hands. When Safie pressed her hands down into her lap, everything was spotted black and red.

"My first time," Safie's voice was low in her ear, "I threw up all over the Holy Mother! It gets better."

"Better?" Asta managed to choke. It felt like the inside of her throat had been scraped with a paring knife. "How can you—?"

Safie patted her on the back. "I know it's hard," she said. "Try to remember, they're only slaves. It's not like we give real people to the Deity, not any more."

"Real people?" The anger flared like heat in her chest, and she had to swallow more water to quench the flames.

"There must be much you don't understand, little daughter." Chesserai crouched. "I'll explain everything to you, back upstairs. Sit quiet now while we clean up. Would you like some tea to calm your nerves?"

Tea. Tea to make her dead-eyed and compliant, so she wouldn't scream under the knife. Asta shook her head. She shuffled back against the wall, watching as her companions sluiced the blood from the stone, washed the tea-kettle and packed it away, let the brazier burn down and returned the buckets to their stack near the waterfall. By the time they were done, there was no sign that the room had seen such bloody sacrifice, and even the beast behind the wall had fallen silent. But the image was branded into Asta's memory, and there was blood under her broken nails that she could not scrub off.

The candles were left burning. Asta estimated that by their size they could burn for seven days or more. Presumably someone had to come down here to replenish them. How often did Chesserai wield the knife to keep her god sated? How many hundreds, thousands, of slaves had passed through this room over the years?

Oh, holy fucking hells . . .

Asta clutched the wall behind her to steady herself. The Inyestan appetite for slaves was insatiable. They had taken people from the lands around the eastern ocean, year after year. They had blackmailed and cajoled the men of the Scattering into helping them with their sordid trade, and did any of them even know what went on below the Red Temple?

We thought they were buying them to work their farms, to hoe their gardens and pour their drinks. Not to feed their god.

And was it just the Red Temple? There were dozens of smaller temples in Abonnae; there must be hundreds throughout the country. Did they all have a secret room, an imprisoned god that needed feeding? Surely not . . .

"Sister, are you well?"

It was the first time the priest had spoken to her. His mask was pushed up to the top of his head, and his curly hair sprung out from either side of it like a fuzzy crown, greying at the edges. He was a big man; she felt the strength of his arm as he hauled her to her feet.

"I'm fine."

He gave her a cheery grin. How could they be so *normal*, so friendly? As if they had done nothing more serious than butcher an animal, rather than a human child. It all seemed so sickeningly casual. Not for the priests of the Red Temple the significant sacrifice the people of the Scattering had wanted Asta to be. Not a single death to give life to a nation, but an endless parade of corpses to feed a ravenous beast, down here in the dark. And was that so different, after all, to the sacrifices of goats or chickens that her own people made, to bring luck for important undertakings, or to honour their dead?

It was a mess, and wherever Asta turned all she could see was blood. She was adrift on a crimson sea, far from land and reason. It was too much. Better, now, to focus on Rhodan. To get him away from here before the knife came down on him in turn.

The priest ushered her out into the tunnel and closed the door behind her, on the candles, the brazier still glowing faintly, and the waterfall where the little girl of the tribes had played in the last few moments of her life. Asta could not suppress a shudder.

Safie and the priest seemed lighter on their journey back up to the Temple, their sombre duty behind them. They were joking between themselves, and even Chesserai joined in with the laughter. Asta forced a smile as they included her in their jokes, but her heart was hot and sick and she wanted to rage against them, to beat down the walls of the Red Temple with her bare fists.

We get out. Finn kept saying it. It had become his mantra, and she sensed it was the only thing keeping him under control, when she felt her own rein might slip at any moment. *We get Rhodan, we get out.*

Where to?

Anywhere!

When? And how? You said you had a plan?

Tonight . . . He trailed off. She knew the *how* was as far beyond him as it was her, right now. She didn't even know where the boys slept, what they did all day. She never saw them around the Temple when she was working, and they must eat at different times.

I'll find him, little brother. I haven't come all this way to let him – She couldn't finish the thought. Rhodan, drugged and cut open on the black altar . . . It wouldn't happen. Not while she still breathed.

She was still trying to work out how she would get him out, when he didn't even recognise her and she didn't know where he was, when they reached the huge iron door that led back into the great hall of the Temple, and Chesserai held her hand against it to lock the portal securely behind them. She reached out, her hands clutching the wrists of Safie and the priest.

"Thank you, my children. The Deity blesses you. May you walk ever in sunshine."

"May cooling waters help you on your path," said Safie.

"And may the seas carry you ever homeward," the priest added. There was a moment of silence, as if something passed between them that could not be spoken aloud, and then the contact broke. Safie smoothed her robe. "Sister Margoli will want me to help with the evening meal," she said.

"And I have lessons to give," the priest excused himself, taking his mask from the top of his head and handing it to Chesserai. "I'll let you know how those boys are getting on. Did you still want me to send that one to your office?"

"Please. He makes trouble." Chesserai inclined her head,

and grasped Asta's elbow. "Come with me," she said. "You must have many questions, and I hope I can give you some answers."

Chesserai's office was right at the top of the temple, up a tightly winding stair with ropes nailed to the wall for handholds. As they passed the window slits Asta could see the dizzying view of the city below, and she thought briefly of how her mother would have hated it when she was human. She had no head for heights, but they didn't bother Asta, whose father used to take her climbing. The Holy Mother seemed immune to the view. By the time they reached the top of the stairs, and a small, circular landing, richly carpeted, Asta was panting for breath.

Chesserai smiled. "Not many people have the energy to bother me up here," she said. "It feels like my little sanctuary in the sky. Come in and have a drink."

Chesserai's sanctuary was perfectly round, a circle of rooms that enclosed the tiny landing, and all the walls were made of glass. It soared above the city like a soap bubble that had come to rest on the tip of the tower. The roof, all wrought iron and brass, overhung the banks of windows like an outsized hat. Asta could see the curve of the dome above, and hear the faint throbbing calls of pigeons on the tiles outside.

Chesserai had her arms folded, one eyebrow raised. She was watching to see how Asta reacted to the light, the height, and the hundred foot drop all around her.

Asta didn't blink. She had disliked the sway of the topmost point of the ship, when she had first been brought to the Scattering, but the floor here was solid beneath her feet. And she would show no more fear in front of Chesserai, nor any sign of weakness. There was a wide sill, calf height, in front of the window and she stepped up onto it. The glass in front of her leaned in towards the roof, throwing her slightly off balance, adding to the sense of vertigo. She looked down onto the street in front of the Temple, Inyestans moving like brightly-coloured insects far below. She could see all the way to the harbour, where black ships no bigger than gulls nestled on the water. Beyond was the open sea. Beyond that was home. If she could have pressed her palms to the window and willed herself there she would have done it in a heartbeat. Instead she stepped down.

"Nice view."

"I can see the whole city from here," Chesserai said, moving to her brazier and stoking the heat with a poker. "Tea?"

Like a fucking spider in the middle of her web. I wouldn't drink anything she offers you, Asta.

"No thank you."

Chesserai smiled. "Think I'm trying to make you docile and compliant, daughter?"

"Something like that."

"Come and sit down." There were fruits on the desk, and Chesserai peeled one with a delicate blade and handed it to Asta. "You can sniff it if you like," she said, seeing her hesitation. "It's not poisoned. You should trust me."

Finn snarled. Asta ate. The fruit was juicy, and it smelled fresh. There was no taint on it as far as she could tell. "Thank you, Holy Mother."

Chesserai peeled her own fruit, slicing it into small, neat chunks on the plate before her. "I don't blame you for being upset," she said. "It's always unsettling, the first time. But I have high hopes for you, Heylan."

"Really?" Asta kept her face carefully composed.

"Of course. You want to spread our message to your people, and that pleases me greatly. We have never had a temple in Atrath. And I know you have more than just Atrathene blood in your veins . . ."

Their creature wants to drink your mixed blood, Asta. A special treat for him . . .

Be quiet!

She kept her face fixed. "My father was from one of the

Western Kingdoms." That was all she would say of her da. His story was not for Chesserai and her kind. It was for Asta's people alone.

"You have some questions?" Chesserai sat back, wiping the last of the fruit from her lips with a long-nailed thumb.

"What's in the tea?" Asta didn't know why, of all the things she could ask, that was the first question to pop into her mind. Finn snorted his derision.

"A mixture of herbs, to dull pain."

"Just pain?"

"Wit and memory . . . I'm sure there are things you are more interested in discussing than herbal concoctions. My ears are open to you, child. Ask the questions you're afraid to ask. You have this one chance."

"The Deity – what is it?"

"*He* is our God." The way Chesserai's lips pressed together indicated that the question had been answered, and more information would not be forthcoming.

Useful, muttered Finn.

"You have many temples in the city. Do they all have a . . . *Deity* in the basement?"

"Of course not. There is only one Deity, though he has many mouths."

"And all those mouths need feeding?"

Chesserai steepled her hands. "You're asking if what you witnessed under the temple is repeated in other houses of worship, across Abonnae, across Inyesta?"

"Yes."

"The Deity has many mouths. They all need feeding."

"Literally?" Asta asked. She had a vision of the beast with myriad tentacles stretching below the earth, to emerge in every temple on every street corner. Each one with a gaping mouth that demanded food.

"Metaphorically."

"And you feed them all? With slaves?"

Chesserai scoffed. "Would you prefer we used people?"

"Slaves are people! Why not use your own race, rather than—" she drew in a breath, fighting back the words that leapt to her tongue. *Rather than coming to my shore and stealing my people?* "Rather than the people the Scattering bring you, I mean?"

Chesserai frowned. "There has been a change in policy," she said.

"Policy?"

"It was thought, in some quarters, that perhaps the Deity was taking too many of our own people. There was . . . discontent. We were requested by a higher authority to look elsewhere. It seems even that may not be satisfactory now." Her lips pursed, as if she tasted lemon on her tongue. "It did not used to be this way. But we adapt, my daughter. By taking more of those from other lands, and by holding tight to our faith, even in the face of opposition."

"There is a higher authority than you, Holy Mother?"

Chesserai smiled tightly, without humour. "Not in Abonnae." She reached out and patted Asta's wrist. "Daughter, if you're going to carry our word back to your savage lands, you must understand one thing. The Deity created us, and he created other races to serve us. That is fundamental to our faith."

Her touch was cold, like a snake crawling over Asta's skin. She drew in a deep breath, tried not to recoil from the contact. "You want me," she said, "to go back to my people and convince them they were created to serve yours?"

"You must show them the right path, and in such a way that they will come to us and serve us willingly, with love in their hearts. Just as the people of the Scattering have done."

"The Scattering has its own gods."

Chesserai's eyes flashed. "False gods! They will learn the error of their ways, if they think they can defy the Emperor and the Deity by making their own sacrifice! They—"

She broke off at a timid knock at the door, and at once she was smooth again, the unruffled Holy Mother once more. "We will talk more of this later, daughter. I know you can do as I ask."

She raised her voice. "Come in!"

The door swung open. Rhodan stood on the threshold, twisting the bottom of his shirt in his hands. "You wanted to see me, Holy Mother?"

Chesserai rose, a study in elegance, and beckoned him closer. He came, dragging his feet on the rich chestnut-and-gold-swirled carpet. He frowned at Asta, bottom lip pushing forward as it did when he was trying to remember something. He stood at the end of the desk, looking between the two women, picking a scab on his wrist and digging one toe into the carpet.

"Brother Juann tells me you're refusing instruction again, Snipe."

Rhodan stared at the floor.

"Well?"

"That's not my name."

Chesserai's breathing was loud in the silence. In the rafters above, pigeons fluttered and cooed. Asta's heart was in her throat. If she reached out she could take Rhodan's hand. She didn't dare to move.

"What is your name then, Snipe?" the Holy Mother asked softly. "Why don't you tell me?"

His frown deepened. Asta held her breath, willing him to break the spell Chesserai had cast on him, to remember his own name, and hers.

Chesserai slid to her feet, and moved over to the brazier, letting the air feed the fire through the open hatch in the front, and moving the iron kettle onto the hot plate. "You see," she spoke to Asta as if Rhodan wasn't there, "even regular doses aren't always enough to keep the more rebellious slaves in check. Some will not do as they are bid, or try and resist the will of the Deity. Those that resist can still serve, in a different capacity."

Asta found her voice. "The girl this morning, below the Temple . . . Did she resist?"

"She was . . . reluctant to do as she was told, yes."

"But she was . . ." *She was no more than a baby.*

"She was a slave, the possession of the Red Temple, as this boy is." She flicked her fingers towards Rhodan and sighed, as if explaining to a child who struggled to grasp the concept. "When someone becomes a slave, even if they are Inyestan, they cease to be human. They become . . . a *thing*."

"They become food."

"Not all of them. They sweep our streets, they work our smallholdings. They give us more time to devote to our faith."

"You can't sweep your own streets? The penitents sweep the Temple . . ."

Chesserai chose to ignore her. The kettle hissed and steamed, and she moved it off the heat, pouring the hot water into a mug. Asta scented the herbs brewing in the cup as the Holy Mother stirred it, and she tried not to inhale too deeply.

Rhodan took a step back. Chesserai lashed out, pinning his wrist to the table with her hand. He squeaked in pain, and Asta started forward.

"Sit down, Heylan. This is none of your affair."

Asta remained half-standing, nails digging into the tabletop, Finn yelling in her head, as Chesserai picked up the cup. She held it to Rhodan's lips, her other hand transferring from his wrist to the back of his neck, long nails digging in above his life vein so he couldn't pull away.

He pressed his lips tight and squirmed. Blood trickled down his neck, and his eyes were wide and terrified. He kicked out, and Chesserai dodged away from his flying feet. "Heylan! Hold him for me, will you?"

"Don't make me drink!" Rhodan twisted in her grip, trying to bite her. "Go away!"

Asta!

"No!" She flipped the table, slamming it against the brazier. The little door flew open, hot metal catching Chesserai across her calves. She shrieked and let go of Rhodan, spilling the drugged tea down his shirt as he writhed in her grip and sank his teeth into her wrist.

She drew back her free hand and slapped him round the head.

Asta scrambled over the upturned table and threw an arm around Chesserai's throat, straining to drag her away from Rhodan. Chesserai spat, clawing at her arm, raking blood from her skin. She arched her back to try and throw Asta off, and as she swung around the brazier went over with a spark and hiss of flame. Rhodan scrambled away from their feet as they fought, snatching up the splintered chair leg and brandishing it before him like a club. "You leave her alone!"

"Rhodan, get out of the way!"

Chesserai was stronger than she looked, and Asta was tired. She grunted in pain as the Holy Mother slammed her spine against the metal frame that ran between the windows, and her grip faltered. Chesserai's elbow caught her in the gut and the air exploded from her lungs as she dropped to the floor.

On hands and knees, she gasped, helplessly trying to find her breath. Chesserai glared down at her as she drew the knife from her sleeve.

"Child, I don't know what's wrong with you, but what you've done," she tapped the naked blade against her palm, "is unforgivable."

Asta sat back on her heels, wiping away a string of drool with the back of her hand. "Let him go," she croaked.

"Let him go? Who? Oh . . ." her eyes slipped beyond Asta to Rhodan, backed up against the window, holding his makeshift club before him like a shield. "Is he your son? Is that it? I had wondered, when I saw the two of you together in the sewing room. And now I know for sure. How *noble* of you, to travel all this way to find one lost child."

Not one lost child. All of them. Asta shook her head, but Chesserai was ignoring her. She strode across to Rhodan, seized his chin and twisted his face into the full glare of the afternoon sunlight. He flinched and tried to back against the glass, but she held him firm.

"Mixed blood. Interesting . . ."

I told you! Finn's cry was a mixture of triumph and alarm.

Asta forced herself to her feet, breath tight. The blade was too close to Rhodan's throat.

"Let go of him."

"Don't tell me—"

"I said let *go!*"

Asta lunged forward, barging into Chesserai, throwing her off-balance. She grappled for the knife, straining against Chesserai's arm as the Holy Mother twisted it out of reach. It caught the inside of her arm and scored a line of fire, and she hissed at the pain.

Chesserai reversed the blade and slammed the hilt down on the bridge of Asta's nose. She lurched back, seeing stars, fighting to keep her balance.

Asta, behind you! The kettle!

Finn snatched her hand, twisted it back until she felt smooth, warm metal under her palm. Her fist closed on the handle, and her brother lent her his weight, his strength, to swing the heavy kettle around and smash it into the side of Chesserai's skull.

She went down as if felled with an axe, throwing a hand up against the splash of scalding water against her face. Asta leapt over her, and grabbed Rhodan's hand, clutching it tight.

"Run!"

She jerked him towards her as he tried to hang back, clutching the chair leg with one white-knuckled hand. His eyes narrowed.

"Where? Who are you?"

"Do you want to stay here?" She could taste the blood now, bubbling from her nose and down her throat. She spat. "Because I don't."

He let the weapon fall. "No, but . . ."

"Then run with me." Chesserai rolled over, dragging herself across the carpet. "Now!"

He tightened his grip on her hand, and they ran.

TWENTY

ASTA'S FEET CLATTERED on the tight spiral of the stairs, one hand clinging to Rhodan's, the other burning down the rope that stopped her falling headlong. From above, an alarm bell clamoured urgently. Rhodan stumbled, striking his knee against rough stone, pushing himself up without a whimper. He limped a few more steps, and Asta snatched him up into her arms. She grunted at the effort as he stiffened in resistance.

"Please, Rhodan, trust me!"

Perhaps hearing his name triggered a memory in his dulled mind, or perhaps it was the desperation in Asta's voice, but Rhodan went limp, his head falling against her collar, skull jarring against her with every step. If they missed a step, and fell, would their broken bodies be fed to the beast below the Temple? Her head was full of the clash of bells, and Finn's repeated exhortations to run, as if she wasn't running already . . .

Asta stumbled as the floor flattened beneath her feet, widening out into a corridor. She looked wildly left and right, panting. She barely knew this part of the sprawling Temple complex, but there had to be a way out. There was shouting from the corridor to the left, a second alarm bell ringing, so she headed right. Her arms were heavy from Rhodan's leaden weight, and she had to set him down, to blow out her clogged nostrils in a spray that spattered her shift, and to catch her breath.

"Can you run?" she asked him.

He nodded, and shook out his sleeve. "I took this from her. Do you want it?"

Asta looked down at Chesserai's knife clutched in her nephew's hand. She could have kissed him. She took it from him and stuffed it in her belt.

"Run then, you clever boy!"

They hurried down the corridor, trotting now as they didn't seem to be in immediate danger, although distant shouts echoed through the halls and the bells still peeled. Asta stopped at every corner, glancing round, falling back if there were people ahead of her. She could try to brazen it out, but her bleeding, swollen nose was a dead giveaway.

Rhodan pointed. "We're going towards the hall," he said. "There's a door that comes out near the Robing Room. Does that help?"

Asta nodded. "More than you know."

"Where are we going?"

She listened at the door to the curving corridor, waiting for hurrying feet to pass. "I'm taking you home."

He hung back, scowling. "I don't know you . . ."

"Listen." She dropped to one knee in front of him. "I know you don't remember me, but I loved your ma and da very much. I promised your da I'd find you and look after you. When we get out of here I'll tell you all about it." *And maybe when you get that fucking poison out of your system you'll know me again.* "But for now I'm asking you to trust me. You don't want to go back to the Holy Mother, do you?"

He raised his hand to his head, the red brand on his scalp where Chesserai had hit him. "No . . ."

"Then come on!" The footsteps had passed. Asta lifted the latch and opened the door slowly, hoping it wouldn't squeak on its hinges and give them away. Her heartbeat was so loud it would mask any approaching footsteps.

"Not far now," she muttered, more to reassure herself than Rhodan.

She was barely ten steps down the corridor towards the hall when the shout rang out behind them. "You there! Stop!"

"Go on!" Asta pushed Rhodan in front of her as he hesitated, glancing back. "Keep running!"

She tried to stay behind him, to shield him from any blow that might fall, but he was too slow, his legs tired from the flight. She hoisted him onto her hip, his feet kicking against her knee, arms around her neck.

"I said stop!" A missile cracked against the stone wall in front of her, an explosion of plaster dust that stung her eyes, but the door ahead stood mercifully open, and light streamed through the altar grille. She heard voices raised in excitement and anger. There was no turning back now.

She dived through the door and slammed it shut behind her, crushing Rhodan against the wood, fumbling for the bolt that wouldn't hold anyone for long.

"How are you holding up, little cub?"

He frowned. "I'm not scared."

"Then I'm not scared either! We walk now, pretend you know me and I'll take you out."

"Why?"

"Because . . ." Knives flashing, candlefire, the beast in the darkness beyond the wall. "Because trust me, is why! Can you do that?"

He shrugged and sniffed. "S'pose so."

"Come on, then."

They stepped out from behind the altar into chaos. People ran back and forth, robes flapping, bells ringing. Cats fled squalling before their flying feet. Someone had upturned a stand of candles and a fire burned between the pillars, sending a miasma of smoke across the room. Even the Deity in his pit far below must be able to hear the noise. And it was all for Asta, and Rhodan.

"Stay close to me," she urged, as they darted from shadow to shadow, shielded by the smoke. No one seemed to be in charge. The doors to the courtyard lay open and inviting, throwing ruddy sunlight across the scrubbed floor. She crouched in the darkness between two pillars and pointed towards the light. "Go. Wait for me by the door."

She watched him dart away, one small boy among dozens of hurrying, confused figures, until she lost him in the crowd. He had got this far, he was smart. If anything happened to her he could still escape the Temple.

"Sister Heylan?"

Asta straightened, brushing the knife at her belt. She would cut her way out if she had to, but she'd rather bluff if she could.

"Sister Margoli!" She feigned relief. "What's going on?"

Margoli's eyes narrowed to blue crescents. "Where have you been? What happened to your nose?"

"I fell on the stairs, rushing to get here." Her whole face throbbed, and the darkness under her eyes ached. She must look hellish. "What's happening?"

"I think you know, *sister*."

Her heart sank. To have come this far, to see the sunlight from the world outside, to have Rhodan in her arms and fail to carry him to freedom . . . Her hand tightened on the stolen blade.

The air was very still, a bubble of calm around the two of them that the noise of the temple could not penetrate.

"Is he your son?"

"My nephew." Her fingers were sweaty around the knife hilt. Suddenly she wanted to explain, to Margoli, to anyone who would listen. "My brother died trying to protect him. I swore on his spirit that I'd bring his boy home safe." Her eyes blurred. "I've come so far. Please, sister, let us go."

Margoli reached out, a gentle gesture. "I wish I could . . ."

"Chesserai was going to feed him to the Deity! She stole his memories, she took his name. I couldn't stand there and let that happen . . ."

"I'm sorry for your loss. But—"

"Stay away from me!" Asta lashed out, the tip of the blade searing a scarlet rent in the fabric over Margoli's breast. She staggered back, mouth dropping open in shock and hurt, and Asta turned and fled.

The smoke was thicker now, the heat increasing. She pushed her way through, ignoring the voices that shouted to restore order. A man grabbed her elbow, yelled in her face that penitents were to man the fire buckets, but she shook him off, staggered down the steps into the merciful evening shade of the courtyard, stumbled over a cat, swore, and wiped her streaming eyes. "Rhodan! Snipe!"

She hated his false name, but it was the one he recognised, and in the shadows under the pillared colonnade, a small figure stirred. His face was smudged with dirt and his nose was streaming. He sniffed hard. "Can we go now?"

They dodged past the bucket chain. All the water running through the fountains in the courtyard was diverted towards the fire, and smoke roiled out of the Temple door. No one paid any attention to a penitent and a dirty little slave boy, and Asta felt a flicker of hope. A fluffy black cat bounded ahead of them as they strode through the courtyard, Asta walking as her father had taught her to walk into danger; head up, shoulders back, as if she had an absolute right to be there.

We're going to make it, Finn!

In front of her, the gates to the courtyard, the gates that the Temple boasted were never closed to those in need, swung shut with a deep clang of metal that sent a cold jar down her spine. Rhodan clutched her arm, fingers digging into the wound Chesserai had carved. From behind them, a voice rang out.

"Take them alive."

Asta whirled around, back to the metal gate, arms wrapped protectively around Rhodan, who had his face turned to her belly. She felt him shudder, and the small movement made her sick with fear and frustration.

Margoli emerged through the smoke, a wad of blood-soaked cloth clapped to her breast. She looked unsteady, but she moved without the support of the hefty men that flanked her. The Temple Guard. Asta had seen their brooding presence in the dining hall or at the back of services, but she had never spoken to one of them, and their presence was never acknowledged. It was as if the order was ashamed to have need of such heavies. She wasn't convinced they needed them now, against a pregnant woman and a little boy.

She retreated. The metal of the gate was still body-warm against her back, and she could go no further. She pushed Rhodan behind her, and stepped forward, knife heavy in her hand.

"I won't let you take him, Margoli."

The guard advanced. Asta held her ground.

"Be sensible, Heylan. Hand him over and neither of you will get hurt."

"Until your god gets hungry again, is that it? You can't have him!"

Margoli nodded at her guards. "Try not to hurt her."

Asta struck out as the men closed in, fleeting blade catching and tearing open the nearest throat. The dead man made no sound, slumping to his knees, bright arterial blood spraying through his fingers. The guards' silence was unnerving. Asta expected them to yell, but they approached with the quiet menace of an approaching storm, and there were too many to fight. Her knife caught another in the upper arm, but he twisted away, wrenching the blade free of her grip, and fists and teeth were not enough, not when one of the guards grabbed Rhodan and held him up in the air, dangling by one arm, kicking ineffectually and swearing. The guard brandished his ugly, hooked blade and looked questioningly at Margoli.

"Sister?"

Her arms were pinned to her sides, tears mingling with the sweat and blood on her face. So close . . .

I did my best, little brother. I did everything I could.

She sagged, broken. "Let him go. We'll do whatever you want, if you let us stay together. We'll even go to the Deity, both of us."

All of us. "Don't take him away from me." Her voice cracked. She hated herself for sounding so small. "I came so far . . ."

Margoli's hand lifted her chin, brushed over her cheek. Her eyes were so bright against the gathering dusk Asta found it hard to look at them, and her voice was only a breath.

"I had a little girl once."

Margoli let go and stepped back, as if nothing had passed between them, as if Asta was driftwood she had picked up, mused over and then cast aside.

"It's late," she declared, to the courtyard at large. "Take them to the holding cell. In the morning, we'll sell them both to Winding Street. Foul-blooded foreigners are no use to us."

Asta kicked out, but she could do nothing as her hands were bound and she was prodded and kicked across the courtyard and through a small gate tucked into the eastern wall, half-hidden by greenery. The cats watched her from the top of the wall, fluffed up, reluctant to brave the impact of her lashing feet. She couldn't see Rhodan, and that was worse than the violence, that emptiness in her vision. She twisted, trying to look back, and was rewarded with a slap that made her ears ring. "Rhodan! Where are you?"

"I'm here . . ." He sounded uncertain, his voice muffled, and she wished she could reach him and reassure him.

"Everything will be all right. I'll look after you, I swear—" Another blow to her head drove her teeth painfully into her tongue, and the taste of fresh blood warned her to shut up.

Finn? How do we get out of this? Finn?

No reply, and she couldn't search her mind for him with so much going on around her. Spitting and stumbling, she was forced down a steep flight of steps, through a plain iron door with a small barred grille set at head-height. Rhodan was shoved in behind her and she caught him as he fell, clutching him to her breast. She flinched at the iron clash of the door slamming behind him, and the rattle of heavy bolts shooting home.

The light shining through the grille darkened, and Asta heard Margoli's urgent whisper. "Sister? Can you hear me? I spared you into slavery for the daughter I lost. I can't extend my mercy any further. Do you understand?"

"Mercy . . ." To live as a slave seemed a warped kind of mercy. Her father's brand of mercy she could understand, but this felt like exchanging a quick death for a slow one.

"The Holy Mother would have you killed. She's . . . dangerous. You'll be out of here in the morning."

She moved away; Asta heard the clip of her heels on the stairs, and a door closed, plunging them into darkness.

Finn! I need you, little brother!

He wasn't there. Not speaking, not sulking in the dark recesses of her mind, where she had always been able to find him. He was absent, the way she could tell a hut was empty without being able to see every corner of it.

Finn!

If she walked in the Spirit Realm, maybe she could find him, bring him back to her. If there was nothing to tie her lead rein to, Rhodan would have to help her, even though he had never done it before. She needed her brother, she couldn't deal with Inyesta without him. Why had he chosen this moment to abandon her? The panic at being in the dark, enclosed, rose within her.

In the darkness, Rhodan sniffed. The simple sound cut through the rising tide of fear. She could not lose herself, not now. He needed her.

"Tante Asta? You are Tante Asta, aren't you?"

"You remember me?" Relief flooded through her, pushing aside the darkness. They had not taken his memories after all, merely suppressed them.

"I – I think so . . ." He crept close to her, snuggling under the crook of her arm, and she felt his bones digging into her side.

"Do you remember your own name?"

"They called me Snipe. I kept trying to tell them that wasn't my name, but they wouldn't listen."

"Who wouldn't listen?"

"The two old ladies. Then that nasty woman made me drink

tea and then I couldn't remember anything. It was all straw in my head." He squirmed in closer. "Have you really come to take me home?"

She kissed the top of his head with bruised lips. "I came halfway round the world to find you, little cub. I'm not leaving you here."

"Will my da be there, when we get back?"

Asta felt her heart crack right across at his plea. She stroked up and down his cold arm, fragile as a twig under her touch. "No . . . he won't be there. He—" she swallowed, looking for the right words. "He rides the Spirit Trail now, Rhodan."

"Oh." There was a small silence. "When will he come back?"

"He can't come back. Do you remember when Tante Siralane was sick, and we put her in the ground and sacrificed a hen for her?" She was forcing herself into contortions, trying to avoid the word *dead*.

Against her arm, she felt Rhodan nod. The fact that she couldn't see his face made it a little easier.

"The day the men took you, and your ma, Finn tried to save you, and some men killed him." She blinked hard. She wouldn't cry, not again. Not until they were on safer shores.

"Oh." Rhodan seemed to mull this over. She didn't want to push him, but he spoke of his own accord. "Tante Asta, when we were on the big boat . . . ?"

"Yes?"

"Ma got sick, and the men put her over the side. Is she in the Spirit Realm as well?"

Oh Lefalli. I'm so sorry. No child should have to suffer this. "You saw them do that?"

He nodded, and the hope that Lefalli still lived faded and died within her. Asta had almost resigned herself to never seeing her brother's wife again, but she had held a small flame inside her, that she was working on a farm or in a grand Inyestan house. Not cast into the sea as Finn had been, dying while her son was still in chains. *Finn, if you can hear me . . . I'm sorry. I'll break them for what they've done to you.*

"Can I visit them there, in the Spirit Realm?"

"We'll see." A trained shaman might be able to take him, and protect him from the dangers of spirit-walking. Asta didn't have the skill, and she didn't want to make the Walk in Abonnae, where nowhere was safe. Her idea of searching for Finn and dragging him back would leave Rhodan exposed, and she couldn't do that, not now. She was all he had.

He leaned his head against her shoulder. "Tante Asta, what will happen to us now?"

"I don't know, sweet. I wish I did."

"Will they split us up?"

"I'll kill them if they try."

In the blackness of the cell, his little fingers crept through hers, holding them tight until morning.

TWENTY-ONE

A STA WOKE FROM her doze, neck twisted and stiff from leaning against cold stone. Rhodan lay curled up against her side, still holding her hand, his mouth slightly agape. She noticed one of his front teeth was loose, and realised there was more light in the cell than when the door had slammed shut at Margoli's heels. There was a draft coming through the grille. She rose, careful not to disturb her nephew, and made her way over to the door.

The cell was a cube, six foot square in every direction. A tall man would have difficulty standing up, or lying down flat. The floor was bare stone, the walls craggy. She could see nothing in here that would help them escape.

The light in the corridor had a flickering quality and she felt the warmth from a torch or lantern that must be placed just out of sight. She could see the bottom of the stairs, but no sign of life, and no one responded to her soft call. She wondered how long they had been locked up. It was impossible to judge the passage of time, hidden away from the sun, but the gurgle in her belly told her it was past breakfast. She pressed a hand to her stomach to try and silence it . . .

And *felt*. Beneath her palm was a faint rumbling, a stirring. The dam burst, unleashing a tide of emotion, of confusion. She sank against the wall, wanting to cry for no reason, as a key turned in her head. The light shone in, and she understood.

Finn, you fucking bastard, what did you do to me?

She realised now what he had done. He had concealed her pregnancy from Gerhild, back on the Scattering – it seemed a lifetime ago, was it really only a few weeks? – but he had done more, and worse, than that. He had concealed it from Asta herself, cut off her feelings for her own body, so she could concentrate on looking for his son.

You selfish bastard, how could you?

He was gone, and she could only rage silently at what he had hidden from her. She wiped her bruised eyes hastily as footsteps echoed on the stairs. Rhodan raised his head.

"Are they coming for us, Tante Asta?"

"I think so." She rose, bringing him close to her. They would face whatever came next as warriors, not prisoners grubbing on the floor. "Are you feeling brave?"

"My tooth is wobbly." She took that to mean "no".

"Can you pretend?" She wrapped her arms around his chest as the bolts barring the door scraped back and it opened to reveal four of Margoli's heavies and a priest. They obviously weren't taking any chances, their blades levelled as one at Asta and Rhodan.

The priest regarded them with scorn. "Tie them," he said. "The mouthpiece of our Holy Mother has decreed they be sold as slaves. They are to be taken to Winding Street."

"Are you talking to us, or them?" Asta demanded. His blank eyes, the contempt in his voice, stung her into defiance. "Can't Chesserai speak for herself any more?"

"The Holy Mother sleeps, thanks to the Atrathene whore. She should be grateful for Sister Margoli's clemency."

"Is she dead, then? Is Chesserai dead?"

The priest spat on the floor at her feet, but would not dignify her question with a reply. The guards bound her hands tightly behind her back and threw another loop around her waist. One of them pulled out a thick leather collar and drew it tight around Rhodan's throat, grabbing him as he tried to back away.

"Don't collar him, he's not a bloody horse!"

"If the Atrathene whore continues to talk, she will be muzzled." The priest's gaze was implacable.

"It's all right, Tante Asta." Rhodan jutted out his chin over the collar. "I'm not scared. My grandfather was a hero, I can be like him."

He didn't struggle as the rope leading from Asta's waist was looped through the collar. She stretched her arms back as far as the restraint allowed, and brushed his fingers with hers. "Little hero," she whispered.

The priest led them back up the stairs, through the courtyard and onto the street, flanked every step of the way by the silent, glowering Temple guards. There were a few stares and mutters as they made their way out of the Red Temple, but no one on the street gave them a second glance. They were invisible, the crowds parting and flowing around them without one person looking Asta in the face. It was as if she travelled in spirit, the way she had done with Finn, and she had to look down at her body to check that she was still solid flesh.

The business of the Temple carried on whether Chesserai lived or died. It was a service day, and many of the people thronging the streets were heading in the opposite direction, towards the Temple, perhaps innocent of the sickness that went on deep beneath the marbled halls. Or perhaps not.

She started as she saw a face she recognised in the crowd. The fat man who had worshipped at her side, the one Finn joked had been trying to talk her into bed. She wanted to call out to him, but she didn't know his name. Their eyes met, and his slid away without acknowledgement or even recognition as he neatly sidestepped to avoid colliding with the guards. He had seen her, but he looked on her as if she was nothing, a goddess of air and shadows.

This, Asta realised with crushing suddenness, was the fate of a slave. To be nothing, to be property, to be spoken of as if she was an object. To lose her name, along with a chunk of her ear.

This was how it began. And this was what Rhodan, what all her people, had lived with since they were snatched from the beach. What so many people, all across the eastern sea, had to live with every day under the yoke of Inyesta and her ever-hungry god. She shivered as the priest quickened their pace.

Winding Street was only a short walk from the Temple, and the Slave Market dominated one side of the road. It looked almost like a temple itself, with its long arched frontage extending into blackness, but the smell that wafted from the portals was animalistic, shit and sweat, blood and fear. Asta tried to swerve away, but the nearest guard caught her and steered her back in line, none too gently. The priest led them between two of the arches and into the heart of the market.

It was quieter than she expected. The market back on the Scattering was built for spectacle, tiered seats around a central arena. Here there was no spectacle, only business. There was no sales ring, but small podiums set in a grid of iron railings and wooden partitions. There were around half-a-dozen auctions going on, the bidding conducted by hand-gestures and nodding. The slaves were driven through the barriers and partitions, encouraged by cracking whips in the hands of overseers, their echoing snap the loudest sound in the muted, miserable quiet.

Rhodan whimpered. He had passed through this hall before, and he crept closer to her and clutched her bound hands with his free ones, seeking a comfort she could not give him. The priest said nothing, leading them round the alleys at the side of the market, through the hall and out into the back yard, past a line of reeking privies to a large hut, a lean-to against the back wall. There were more slaves here, corralled like horses, and the wall, high and crowned with savage shards of glass, forestalled any thoughts of escape. The slaves sat or squatted in the dust, many staring blankly ahead, but splashes of blood on the walls suggested that some who passed through here hadn't given in to the torpor of despair. Even as the priest hammered on the door of the hut, Asta was looking around for potential escape routes.

A man emerged, tall and heavily built, his stomach falling to a paunch that suggested he was fond of rich food and ale, and he had a slight limp. Under a drooping moustache, his lips hung in a frown which deepened as he saw the priest.

"Brother Gonzaluo, what trash have you brought me this time?"

"Bernaldus, you old fraud, would I ever bring you trash?" The priest spread his hands in a supplicating gesture, and the slave dealer burst out laughing, clapping his meaty hands on both of Gonzaluo's upper arms.

"My friend, you bring me nothing but! Can you stay for a drink?"

Gonzaluo sighed, shaking his head. "I have to get back. This one," he shook Asta's rope, "has caused all manner of chaos. Sister Margoli in her mercy sends her to you to spare her life."

"Margoli the fanatic? She didn't want to throw them onto a sacrificial knife?"

"It would seem not, this time. Perhaps just to spite the Holy Mother. You know how Margoli envies her position. I'll tell you all about it over a drink, but it's best for all concerned if the horse-children were to . . . *vanish.*"

Bernaldus' eyes lit up. "You'll be keen to get rid of her then?"

"For a *decent* price. There are other markets . . ."

Bernaldus pouted. "You know that you, *personally*, won't get a better deal than you would from me. Let's see the goods."

He nudged the guards aside and stared at Asta, pulling her lips back with thick fingers that tasted of smoke. He studied her teeth. "What happened to her nose?"

"Temple business."

"She broke her nose on Temple business? Fine, don't tell me." He rubbed his fingers over the swelling. Asta winced. "It's not as bad as it looks, she'll have a bit of a lump there, but if I *just—*" He seized the end of her nose between thumb and forefinger and gave it a sharp twist to the right, cracking it back into place. Asta screamed, her foot lashing out to kick him in the shin, but he darted back with surprising nimbleness before she could make contact.

"She won't be too ugly, once the swelling goes down." His grubby finger jabbed her lower eyelid. "We can powder over most of the bruises. What's her stock?"

"I can talk for myself." Asta spoke thickly, voice distorted by the fresh blood flowing from her nostrils. "I'm not a horse to be bartered over."

Both men ignored her, and Rhodan tugged her hand.

"They won't talk to you unless they have to," he whispered. "You're not a person any more."

She didn't have the opportunity to reply. Bernaldus was running his hands over her in a way that made her queasy. There was nothing sexual in the contact, but it felt like a violation, knowing he could do as he pleased with her, and act without fear of retaliation. She recalled the way Olafur had touched her – there had been lust there, but also a kind of reverence. This touch was just part of so much horse-trading.

Bernaldus glanced sharply at Gonzaluo. "She's half-Atrathene, right? What's the other half?"

Gonzaluo shrugged. "One of those little barbarian kingdoms to the far west, I think. Does it matter? I'm in a hurry. There's a mess to sort out back at the Temple. How much for her and the boy?"

"Let's see the boy." He whipped out a knife and cut the rope that bound Asta and Rhodan together, drawing him forward at the end of his tether as his feet dragged in the dirt. He fingered the boy's clipped ear. "What's the story on this one? It's not often the little ones get returned."

"He was sold to an old couple who couldn't control him. They passed him on to us. He's her son or her cousin, or something . . ."

"Looks like the Western blood flows stronger in him. I could sell him as an exotic if he won't be trained." Bernaldus straightened. "I can give you three hundred for the pair."

"Three? The Temple wants at least five. If I go back with

three—" Gonzaluo made a cutting gesture across his throat, "I might as well not go back at all. I thought we were friends?"

As the two men fell to haggling, Rhodan crept closer to Asta. "Tante Asta, you won't get sold without me, will you?"

"No, I promise I won't." She still had the paper money, sewn into her shift. She could buy their freedom as soon as Gonzaluo was gone, if she could make the slave-trader listen.

The haggling was reaching a climax, insults about people's mothers and parentage being thrown, and eventually with ill humour Bernaldus pulled out a sheaf of notes, counted off a number, slapped them down into Gonzaluo's hand, and spat to seal the deal. The priest peeled off three notes which vanished inside his own robe, the rest went in the purse at his belt.

"Pleasure," he said. "I should say something about you not attending Temple regularly. Deliver you some spiritual chastisement."

Bernaldus chuckled. "I consider myself chastised! Some sugar-ale will ease my guilt, I'm sure."

"I'll join you in that next time my duties permit. For now, I have to go back and see to the chaos she caused, before some jumped-up bureaucrat from Kishtawar decides to jump in and interfere." Gonzaluo jerked his thumb sharply at Asta. "Don't be too soft on her, will you?"

He clicked his fingers, and the silent guards fell into step behind him. They vanished under the arch, back into the softly sorrowing hall of the slave market.

"Tarese!" Bernaldus bellowed back towards the hut. "Come out here, woman! One for you!"

"Listen," Asta tried to grab his attention, "I have paper. How much would it cost to buy our freedom?"

"Tarese!" He flicked a keen eye at Asta. "How much paper? Where?"

"You'll talk to me now?"

"I couldn't do my job if I didn't. Where's the paper?"

"Loose my hands and I'll show you."

He chuckled, but did as she asked. Asta crouched, ripped open the re-sewn hem of her shift with ragged nails, drew out the tight-rolled bundle and pressed it into the slave-traders hand. "This must be enough. It's all I have."

Bernaldus unrolled the money and flicked through it. "Not hardly, my girl. There's less than a hundred here."

"Is it enough to at least buy Rhodan free?"

"The boy?" He brayed with laughter. "He's worth twice what you are to me, even if you are breeding." He pocketed the money. "Slaves don't carry paper. Tarese!"

"Coming!"

A woman emerged from the hut, tall and craggy-faced, greying hair swept back into a loose straggly bun. She frowned as her eyes fell on Rhodan. "Him again? I told you we should have sold him as an exotic first off. You're too bloody soft."

Bernaldus shrugged. "Twice the sales, twice the profit. You know I don't like exotics, or the perverts who buy them, but I suppose it's better than having him keep coming back. I'll take him to the kids' pens; you sort her out. Careful, she's breeding."

"No!" Rhodan threw his arms around Asta's waist. "You're not taking me!"

Asta backed up as Bernaldus and Tarese advanced, trying not to stumble over Rhodan's feet, until she felt the rough stone of the wall against her spine. The wall was topped by spikes of glass two hands high. If she tried to hoist him over he'd be cut to ribbons. She would lay down her own life rather than live as a slave, but she couldn't take his.

"Please . . ."

Bernaldus ran his hand over his jowls. "I'll throw him in with the women," he said. "It won't be for long. He'll get snapped up soon enough."

"What did I say? Too bloody soft," Tarese crowed, as the paunchy man tried to pry Rhodan loose from Asta. "Don't break his arm, or we'll be stuck with him for an age."

"Come on, boy, I don't want to hurt you." Bernaldus' hands,

heavy and calloused, wrenched Rhodan's arm, and he squeaked. "You'll be back with her soon. I'll give you that much."

"You promise?" Asta asked.

"Swear on the Deity. I'm not the shit you think I am."

"Go with him, Rhodan." She pushed his arms down. "I won't be long."

Rhodan let go, dragging his fingers against the coarse cloth of her shift. "You'll come for me, Tante Asta?"

"Always do." She could not watch him being led away. She turned to Tarese, who eyed her warily.

"Too soft," she muttered. "It just makes it worse in the long run. You know you won't get sold together?"

Asta would jump that fence when she reached it. She would find a way out of here, long before any more paper changed hands.

Tarese rubbed her hands together. "Let's get started. Take off your dress."

Asta glared at her. "No."

"Oh for the love of the Deity! You stink. It looks like you rolled around in shit. You are not *saleable*. It's my job to make you that way. Take the dress off before I cut it off you. I don't care if you are breeding. Breeders are ten for a leaf, whatever Bernaldus might say."

Tarese had a pair of scissors at her belt and a gleam in her eye, as Gerhild had done, back on the Scattering, a lifetime ago. Slaves and Goddesses seemed to come in for the same treatment, the world over. This woman looked like she would relish stripping Asta down in the yard. She pulled the dress over her head and let it fall. Tarese caught it before it hit the ground, and stuffed it into a small burner next to the hut. "I'll get you something else to wear. Was that so hard?" She sniffed. "Go to the pump and wash that muck off, so I can see you properly."

The water from the pump was cool, a relief from the searing mid-morning heat in the shadeless yard, and it made Asta shiver as it sluiced over her bare shoulders and down her back, soaking through her underthings until they were almost transparent. She tried to cover herself with her arms, painfully conscious of the way the fabric stuck to the curve of her belly. Tarese threw her a towelling rag so she could dry off.

"You pretty up nice, under the dirt," she said. "How far along are you?"

"Two moons, I think." Only two? Had Finn stopped the babies growing inside her, another of his interferences? Or had she lost track of time, as the days and nights in the Temple blurred into one?

"That's early. We'll give you extra eggs and milk, grow your baby strong! Don't worry," she casually hitched up Asta's skirt, "Bernaldus won't sell you to a hard master, unless it's for good coin."

"What will happen to Rhodan? What's an exotic?"

"Nothing you need to worry about." From a leather belt around her thigh, Tarese drew out a flat metal box. She flipped open the lid, and took hold of Asta's chin with strong fingers. "Let's cover up those bruises," she said. "What happened? You resist being taken?"

"There was a fight." That was all Asta was prepared to admit. What Gonzaluo told Bernaldus in their cups would probably reach Tarese soon enough; she wasn't going to make things easier for the slave dealers.

"Easier if you go down gentle. You get a better price, you get treated better. You might as well—"

"Might as well what? Surrender?" The chalky powder Tarese was dusting on Asta's face trickled into her mouth, and she coughed.

"Eventually every country on the ocean will come under Inyestan rule. You might as well get used to it." Tarese spoke matter-of-factly, as if it was inevitable, as incontrovertible and unstoppable as the sunrise.

"People will resist your rule. The Scattering—"

Tarese laughed. "The Scattering? What can they do? A bankrupt little cluster of rocks. I hear they tried to raise a God to fight us, and they failed. They always do, these little countries. But you're not from there, so why do you care about them?"

Asta didn't reply.

"Suit yourself. It doesn't matter anyway, I was just trying to be friendly. Want me to lighten your skin?"

"No, why?"

Tarese shrugged. "Some do. If they're going for a certain type of master. Makes no difference to your price."

"I like my skin the way it is."

Another shrug. "Your bruises look better now. There's salve in the powder; that should take down the swelling."

Asta's skin tingled faintly, Tarese's potion getting to work. She hoped it would take the ache out of her skull.

"Wait here." Tarese vanished into the hut. Asta considered running, but that would leave Rhodan to the mercy of these strangers. She had made him a promise, and she wasn't going to break it.

I'm doing my best, Finn. I wish you were still here.

The grey-haired woman emerged with a dress draped over her arm. She quirked an eyebrow. "I wondered if you might try and run. There are guards all over the market; you wouldn't get ten yards."

"I wouldn't leave Rhodan."

"Pull this on, then." Asta caught the dress as Tarese tossed it. It was similar to her penitent's shift, almost as shapeless, with a tie around the middle to draw the waist in. The material was coarse and dull brown, scratchy against her fingers. As she pulled it over her head she smelled the whiff of old roots impregnated into the fabric. At least it wasn't onions. She would never be able to breathe in the scent of onions again without thinking of Heylan, of all Syven's wife had done for her. Only for her to end up in an Inyestan slave market. It seemed there was little justice on the ocean for Asta.

"This used to be a sack, didn't it?"

Tarese flashed her teeth. "No expense spared, girl! Come on," she looped a stout length of chain around Asta's wrists. "One last thing, and then I'm done with you." She wrapped the chain around a post in the yard and pulled it tight, so Asta couldn't back away. "Try and keep still."

She flung a dirty, brown-stained towel around Asta's neck, and pulled out a short, razor-sharp blade on a thin handle. She pinched Asta's earlobe in her other hand and made two swift cuts, moving so fast her hand was a blur. It wasn't until she threw the neat triangle of flesh to the ground at her feet that the pain kicked in, and Asta reeled, tasting bile and swallowing it back down. The towel was soaked with blood and Tarese pressed it hard against her ear as she retched.

"It'll stop bleeding quickly. Hold still a moment." She caught Asta round the waist as a wave of dizziness washed over her and she slumped, her knees giving way. "Here you go."

The nausea passed, and the cup of warm wine Tarese tipped down her throat seemed to help. Asta forced herself upright, cheeks burning at showing such weakness. If Rhodan had borne this, then she could. She had thought only the Scattering cut their slaves, but the pain told her she was very wrong. She elbowed Tarese's arm away. "I can stand on my own."

"Don't kill yourself with pride, girl." The Inyestan woman let go. "Can you walk? Then I'll take you to the holding pens. What the buyers will make of you is in Bernaldus' hands."

I used to be a leader. I used to be a Goddess. Not much of either, maybe, but I'm more than this; more than they think I am. She had to tell herself, a litany of silent encouragement. She didn't have Finn to prop her up any more. She would stand or fall on her own courage, and Rhodan would stand or fall with her. Her blood was her strength, the blood that was pouring from her mutilated earlobe, staining the shoulder of her sacking gown. They might cut her ears, try and change her skin, but what was inside her was still true.

The holding pens were through a gate, down a narrow smooth-walled alley, and into a neighbouring yard. This one was bigger than the courtyard behind the market, noisier and more pungent, divided into rough squares by high walls, punctuated with iron gates. Beyond the gate that Tarese led her to, listless figures shifted in the heat. Someone was wailing, a broken ululation that went on and on, and made the hairs at the back of her neck crackle. Shouting and scuffling came from a neighbouring pen, and she flinched at the sharp crack of a whip, and the screech that followed it.

Tarese unlocked the gate with a bronze key that hung around her neck, top and bottom locks clicking smoothly open. There were two gates, with a gap between them just large enough for two women to stand in, and Tarese locked the first behind her before she opened the second. She gave Asta a light shove into the pen, and as she stepped through, momentarily confused by the sharp transition from light into shadow, she heard her name called, running feet, and a little body slammed into her arms.

"Tante Asta! Are you hurt?"

"I'm fine. Are you?" She pushed him away and looked around, trying to get her bearings as the gates clattered shut behind her, locking them in. A quick glance around the pen confirmed that there were only women here, seven of them, the youngest a girl of no more than fourteen who lay listlessly with her back pressed to the stone wall, staring at nothing. The oldest was an Inyestan woman in her late forties, with deep scars on her well-muscled forearms, squatting in the dust with an air of resignation. There were even a couple of white women who might be from her father's country, clinging together. One of them was the girl that was wailing, and the sound made her ears ring.

"Stop that!" A woman pushed herself out of the shadows by the gate. She was dark, darker than Asta, and a bright red scarf was wound defiantly around her head, covering her ears. "Even I can hear you howling! What good will it do?"

The western girl's crying increasing in pitch. Asta felt her head might split, and Rhodan clapped his hands to his ears, face darkening. Red Scarf drew back her hand, and slapped the crying girl hard around the face, smacking her head against her companion's jaw with a frightening crack of bone meeting bone.

It had the desired effect, cutting her off mid-cry and throwing her into shocked silence. The woman with the red scarf straightened, massaging the palm of her hand, and turned to Asta. "You new?"

Asta could only nod. The woman looked at Rhodan, and her eyes softened. "Is he yours?"

"I suppose he is now."

She nodded a greeting. "I'm Saheen. They call me Red, but I've had half-a-hundred names. You?" She cocked her head on one side, waiting for an answer, watching Asta's mouth.

"I'm Asta. This is Rhodan."

"Where you from?"

"I've been a few places." She didn't want to share everything until she knew whether Red could be trusted. "You?"

"South of the south, from what I remember." Red sat in the dust, legs crossed, and patted the ground before her in invitation, holding that intense gaze. Asta sat. Rhodan remained standing, watching her with his brow furrowed in deep suspicion. "I was no older than him when they took me. I've made a career out of running away!" She laughed, raw and throaty, and snapped her fingers at the scarred Inyestan woman. "Get us a drink, will you?"

The woman pushed to her feet with a sigh, like an old dog disturbed from the fire, and slunk over to the bucket in the corner. She returned with a small leather purse slopping with dusty water. Red took two quick swallows and handed it to Asta. "They keep you dry out here. There's times I would have sold my eyes for a drink of water." She chuckled again. "But what use is a blind slave?"

"You've escaped a lot?" Asta eyed Red speculatively. If she was an escape artist, maybe she would know how to get them out. "From here?"

"I'm the reason they put glass on the walls," Red said, with a touch of pride.

"Could you get us out? Or even Rhodan on his own?"

Rhodan's attention snapped back to her. "I'm not going nowhere without you, Tante Asta."

"Anywhere," she corrected automatically. "I'm not going anywhere."

Red snorted. "Too right you're not! You can't get out of these yards, I've been back twice since they put the glass in and I can't figure it out yet. I will, but you don't want to risk the boy, do you?"

Rhodan sat, all of a sudden, as if his legs were tired of holding him up. "I don't want to be a slave any more," he said.

"Would you rather be dead?" Red asked sharply, her head whipping round to face him. "Or whipped?"

"I don't want to be whipped. My ma's dead . . ." He trailed off as if considering the possibility.

"If they caught him, would they whip him?" Asta asked.

"Would they what?"

Asta repeated the question while Red watched her lips.

"Probably not. Pretty smooth boy like that, an exotic . . ." She raised her hands to her topknot and untied it, unwinding the scarf from her head. Her skull was shaved to the skin, only a light dusting of stubble showing through. The shaving had been rough; there were scabbed cuts and darker patches of bruising on her scalp, but it was the sight of her ears that made Asta gasp. The flesh of her earlobes had been pared back until there was nothing left but a nub of bone and a dark hole that oozed fluid. The skin around the holes was puckered and scarred, red stripes over faded white ones. Asta couldn't look away.

"Bernaldus did that, for my escapes. Later on they take your lips, and any other parts they think you don't need, or that are no use to them. That was when I was younger; they whip you more when you're older and less attractive!" She laughed again.

"Who whip you?" Asta was trying not to be sick. She was relieved when Red wound the scarf back round her head, concealing her wounds.

"Punishment House. The Deity doesn't let Inyestan masters

sully their own hands by beating their slaves!" She spat, and nodded at Rhodan. "I thought you were his mother?"

"I'm his aunt." Asta wondered if she should explain further, when there was a yell from the scarred Inyestan woman.

"Cat!"

Red sprang to her feet, fist closing on a pebble. The Inyestan was pointing, and the other women in the pen were leaping up all around her, grabbing whatever missiles they could find and launching them at the black cat that balanced precariously on top of the wall, one paw lifted to avoid the stabbing glass.

Red's throw caught it on the shoulder, and with a yowl the cat sprang down and vanished behind the wall. The women sank into their previous torpor as if nothing had happened. Red dusted off her hands.

"Fucking cats," she said. "You'd think they wouldn't need to spy on us any more. It's not like we can plan anything. You were saying?"

"I promised my brother I'd bring him home."

Red snorted. "You'll need the Deity's own luck. Better to strangle him now, rather than see him taken as an exotic." Asta expected her to laugh again, but Red's face was deadly earnest.

"Strangle him? I'm not going to—"

"I did it to my girl. She was four, and they were going to send her up to those sick bastards the Hill, after they let me keep her for so long." She stared into the middle distance. "I took her to the fountain and held her under water until she stopped kicking."

Rhodan tightened his grip on Asta's arm, eyes wide. Asta didn't know how much of the conversation he really understood, but she suspected it was too much.

"The Hill?" She didn't want to ask, she saw the raw pain behind Red's clenched teeth. But she had to know, for Rhodan, who might be allocated the same fate.

"She'd be an exotic, like your boy." The muscles twitched in Red's jaw with the effort of holding something back, pain, or anger, or both. "They like interesting skin, coloured eyes, red hair . . . Anything a bit different. And some men on the Hill like them young. Too young for most people's taste. The Hill will pay in heavy gold for a mixed-blood boy like yours to take to bed—"

Asta cut her off with a gesture. She had heard enough, and she didn't want Rhodan hearing any more. The prospect brought the sting of bile to her throat.

Red snorted. "Better off dead," she muttered. "All of us. I wouldn't wish it on anyone." She shivered, and it seemed she shook something off with the gesture. "Lunch soon," she said, looking at the sky. "There might be a sale this afternoon. Bernaldus won't sell a slave that looks hungry."

As if on cue the gates rattled. It was the bulky slave trader, arriving with two buckets of food and one of water, juggled in his hands as he manoeuvred his way through the double set of gates. He set them down and pulled a stout club from his belt in the same smooth movement, watching the caged women warily. None of them made a move towards him, and he relaxed.

"There's boiled eggs," he announced, "and liver. You can thank the breeder for that, and hope she brings in more than I'm spending this afternoon!" He flashed a grin and left, locking the gates behind him.

The other women were watching Red. She was obviously the leader of the herd, and she got to eat first. Asta understood that without being told; it was obvious in the confident way she prowled towards the buckets and lifted the lids, letting the smell of warm meat waft across the pen. She bared her teeth in a grin. "We *have* got lucky! Grab it where you find it, I say!" She beckoned Asta towards her, and pressed a chunk of wobbly liver and a hard-boiled egg into her hand. "I supposed we've got you to thank for this," she said. "Usually it's gruel or stew, but Bernaldus can't resist a breeder. He's got a soft spot; Tarese is barren as the desert."

"You can see that in her face. She looks like all the spring water's been sucked out of her." It was the first time the Inyestan woman had spoken. She had a soft voice, at odds with her heavy frame, and she ate delicately, peeling back the shell of her egg with deft fingers. Asta wondered what her story was.

Rhodan was struggling with his egg, so she took it and peeled it for him while he chewed on the liver, cramming it into his mouth as if he wasn't sure when he might eat again. His crouching posture over the food reminded her of the stray dogs Finn used to take in as a child, who'd snarled and snapped if anyone approached while they were eating. The Temple must have fed him, but she didn't know if he had been starved elsewhere. All the women in the pen had a pinched, sallow look, as if they never got quite enough to eat.

She handed the egg back to him, and he snatched it from her fingers and crammed it into his mouth. Slavery had turned him feral, and it hurt to see the wildness in the eyes of the sensitive boy who had been taken from the beach. She ate her own food more slowly, forcing herself to make it last. She was still eating after everyone else had finished, their eyes fixed on her, watching every bite she took. She swallowed the last of the liver and wiped around her mouth, making sure she had consumed every speck of meat. It sat heavy in her empty belly, and she hoped she could keep it down.

She leaned back against the wall, and Rhodan crawled into the crook of her arm. Uninvited, Red sat down next to her, casting a baleful glance and flicking a stone at another cat that picked its way along the top of the wall opposite.

"Were you always a slave?" she asked Asta, watching her lips for the reply.

"I was a leader in my own tribe. I came here for Rhodan, and for his mother. The slavers took some of the women and children of my tribe, and I hoped . . ." It hurt to admit it to herself. "I hoped I could find them and bring them home. Not just this little cub, but all of them. I didn't realise then how wide the ocean was, or how many slaves the world held. Maybe I was naïve."

She felt the urge to talk, as she hadn't done since she was on the boat with Ranmiro, escaping the Scattering to something much worse than a sacrifice. "These slavers killed my brother, and his wife, and scattered the children of my village to the four winds. I don't know what I was thinking, that I could find them . . ."

"But you found this one?" Red patted Rhodan's arm. "Don't let go of him again. I lost so many little ones, even the one I was allowed to keep—" She broke off as the gate rattled again.

Bernaldus had returned, flanked by Tarese and three other men, each as bulky as he was, but rippling with muscle rather than fat. Between their meaty hands, they each held a stout length of chain.

Red sighed as she heaved to her feet. "Best get on with it then," she muttered loudly, tightening her scarf around her shaved scalp, pulling it down hard over her ruined ears. Her eyes were as blank as an Inyestan's, devoid of life.

Asta would not end up like that. She rose slowly, watching the nearest heavy as he advanced on her. He swung the chain easily between his hands, shackles weighing down either end of it. Rhodan muttered his defiance, and she shoved him behind her, backing up until he was cushioned between her and the wall. The stones were rough, pitted with handholds.

"When I tell you," she said, in their own tongue, "climb up the wall. Be careful of the glass. Drop down the other side and run to the harbour. Wait for me there!"

He looked up, doubtfully. "I can try, but the glass is really sharp . . . ."

"Go!" She laced her hands behind her and gave him a boost as the slaver lunged forward, chain stretched taut between his fists. She saw it coming for her neck and kicked out, her long leg catching him under the kneecap. He fell back with a grunt of surprise, and she ducked under his arm and grabbed the length of chain as it loosened in his grip. She couldn't look at Rhodan, as the man's bulk filled her vision. All she could do was pull on the chain with all her weight, to prevent him using it on her.

It looped around his wrist, and as she pulled the flesh of his hand darkened, tendons standing out like knotted wire. Her palms burned with friction, and her heels kicked up dust as she was dragged slowly forwards.

She stumbled, and the thug seized on the momentary loosening of the chain to throw the slack around the knuckles of his left hand. He drew back his fist.

"Not the face!" Bernaldus threw himself between them, moving swiftly for a man of his bulk. He shoved the man's arm aside and the punch landed on her bicep, spinning her off her feet to land face-down on the sun-baked earth. She tried to scramble up, and felt the chill kiss of a blade slide beneath her throat as her skull was seized and pulled back to expose the veins in her neck. She tried not to breathe.

"I don't care if you are a breeder." Tarese's voice was soft, almost chatty, a tickle against Asta's marked ear. "The boy's worth more to us than you and your baby. Tell him to come down."

The knife pressed harder. Sweat prickled Asta's armpits, and her throat, where steel met skin. Rhodan clung to the top of the wall, and he was swearing, all the words he was too young to know. The spikes of glass were higher than his head and he kicked at them, trying to force his way though.

Tarese shifted the knife as she changed tack. "He's bleeding up there. Do you want him to gut himself trying to get away?" Bernaldus had fetched a ladder from outside the compound, and held it steady while one of the big men ascended slowly, step by step, thick chain clenched between his gold-capped teeth.

"Rhodan, keep going!"

One of the glass spikes shattered. Rhodan's arms were streaming blood as he turned his attention to the ladder, kicking at it, trying to push it away. Tarese raised her voice.

"Hey, kid! Pack it in, or I'll draw your mother here a bright new smile! Is that what you want?"

Rhodan went still.

"Well?" Tarese pressed the blade tighter. "Is it?"

"Rhodan, don't listen to her—" the knife tight across her windpipe choked off Asta's words. The man with gold toothcaps was nearly at the top of the wall.

"Come down or I kill your mother. She means nothing to us."

"She's not my ma." He spoke quietly, but Asta could hear every word. "My ma's dead."

"Rhodan—"

"She's dead because of you!" He twisted to try and wriggle through the gap in the glass, but too late. Gold-tooth's hand closed on his ankle, ignoring the blow from Rhodan's bare foot that caught him under the chin. He threw the boy over his shoulder like a feed-sack and slid down the ladder, barely touching the rungs. Asta felt the pressure at her throat ease as Tarese withdrew the knife. She tried to lunge forward, but the older woman caught her arm in a crab-like grip as Gold-tooth hefted Rhodan towards Bernaldus, who swung a bag down over his head in one expert manoeuvre.

"Give him back!" Asta smashed her elbow back and upwards, colliding with the bone of Tarese's jutting chin, jarring her arm numb as Tarese released her hold. She dived for Rhodan, but too late. Gold-tooth was between her and the gate as Bernaldus shoved Rhodan though it, snatching Tarese's arm and pulling her with him. Blood poured down her chin, and the blank grey eyes she turned on Asta were narrowed with loathing. As the gate slammed behind her she spat through the bars, and then she was gone. They were all gone. Asta was alone, on her knees in the dust, sick with bitter failure and with only the distant cries of circling birds for company.

TWENTY-TWO

HERE WAS NO way out under the gate. The earth was packed hard as stone, refusing to yield to her digging fingers, and the gate was solid as she rattled it. No one came to heed her cries of desperation, and finally she lapsed into silence and tears, sinking down with her back pressed to the metal bars.

Finn? Finn, I'm sorry. I had him, and he slipped through my fingers like a handful of sand.

Finn was gone, as lost to her as Rhodan was. Taken as he had been that black day on the beach, with the gulls screaming and the blood pooling in every footprint she left. She felt the rip of his death from her spirit all over again. Worse; she had lost him twice over now, and she never had a chance to say goodbye. He had been her consolation, her guide, her light in the shadows of Inyesta. How would she ever find Rhodan again without him?

I need you, little brother. Please. Come back.

There was only silence in her mind, a chill steppe wind blowing over the grave.

Finn?

If he was lost to her, did that mean Rhodan was lost too? How could she ever find him, without Finn in the back of her mind, pushing her on, lifting her when she fell? Rhodan was gone; he would vanish into one of the houses on the Hill to be used and abused until his youth and looks were gone, and then what? To be sold again and again, while she wandered these Southern lands in a never-ending, futile search for him?

There were no answers to her questions, nor her pleas to Finn to come back to her.

If she listened hard, she could hear the rumble of the auction house, buying and selling, trading human lives as if they were horses. Less than horses; horses were valued and treated with respect. There was no respect in the slave markets of Inyesta, or the Scattering.

She scrabbled in the parched earth again, but it was a fruitless effort and she flung herself back against the wall, waiting to be sold, waiting for Bernaldus to slice her ears from her head for insubordination. Her freshly-clipped earlobe throbbed in time with her heartbeat and the ache in her skull that was her only constant companion.

Footsteps thudded against the dirt, two sets, one heavy, one scrabbling. She raised her head in sudden wild hope that Rhodan had been rejected, to be thrown back into her arms. But it was only Bernaldus, hauling Red by the arm as she dragged her feet. He shoved her through the double gates and stood on the far side glaring at her, hands on hips, puffing at the effort.

"I should just give you to the fucking Temple," he snapped. "Save the cost of feeding you. Who'd buy an earless murderer anyway?" He spat through the bars, saliva frothing on the ground between Red and Asta, and turned on his heel. Asta rattled the gate to get his attention.

"What about Rhodan?" she demanded. "Where is he?"

Bernaldus spread his hands in a shrug. "Gone," he said.

"Gone where?" Asta slammed the heel of her hand against the gate. "Gone where, fuck you?" But he was already walking away and she collapsed, head against the unyielding bars, the tears she had been too proud to shed flowing freely down her cheeks.

Red padded up behind her and rested a cool hand on the back of her neck. "Better give up on him," she said. "He's gone to the Hill. You want to keep your ears, you won't run away to look for him." She crouched to pick up a stone and hurled it at a cat that was prowling across the yard outside the gate. "Me, I'm for the Temple now. Burned my last bridge. The Deity be merciful to me!"

Asta shifted around so Red could see her talking, and wiped a shaking hand across her face. Talking was better than feeling like this, the yawning emptiness that threatened to engulf her. "What do you know about the Deity?" she asked.

Red scratched under her scarf, picking away at scabs and flicking them from her fingers. "Our god is a hungry god," she muttered.

"You're telling me. I've seen him."

Red shook her head, lips pressed tight. "No one has seen the Deity. Not even the High Priest."

"Is that what they tell you at worship? What do they say in the markets and the taverns?"

"Nothing, if they're smart. Haven't you learned yet there are spies everywhere? The Shadow Cloaks are in on it, right up to their hips. Everything in Abonnae is corrupt, everyone's dirty, and those not out for what they can get are paddling just to stay alive. You start asking questions, you're going to lose more than your ears, girl!"

"I've seen him." Asta kept her voice low, so Red had to lean right in to hear her, her brow furrowing with the effort.

"Who?"

"What they call their deity. I've seen him. Under the Temple."

"Like shit you have!" Red sat back on her heels, blowing out her cheeks and flicking her hands in a gesture of contempt.

"Swear on my father's spirit. He's—" Red darted forward and clamped a hand across her mouth.

"What did I *just* say?" she hissed. "You want to die too? Listen good, you seem a fair smart girl. Too hung up on the kid, but he's cute, and your blood after all. If you want to keep living, stop talking, keep your head down and your nose away from Temple business! Get a decent master, work hard, stop the babies coming if you don't want to lose them, and you'll be golden. Otherwise, you'll be *dead*. You get me?"

Behind the hard set of her jaw, Asta saw a flash of genuine terror in Red's eyes. Maybe the fear that had made her drown her baby; maybe that fear would close her hand too hard around Asta's throat. She nodded, carefully, and Red sat back, her face a mask once more.

"I reckon you shouldn't talk for a bit," she said.

Asta nodded. Red curled up beside the water bucket, her cheek pressed to the ground, eyes slitted in the streaming afternoon sunlight. Asta huddled into the shadow of the wall, watching as it lengthened. The heat was suffocating. The afternoon rain had yet to fall, hanging in the air like a sheen of sweat on the sky. She tasted the moisture every time she breathed in, but it did nothing to slake her thirst. The sky seemed to be buzzing, a low-level drone like a swarm of insects passing far overhead, and the pressure was building, pressing down on the front of her skull. No matter which way she moved, she was lying on a bruise, and her sweat-stained smock clung to her skin. There was nothing to do but lie here. Wait to be sold, wait to bake in the blinding sun, wait to die. Wait for something, or nothing, to happen.

Red shifted, grunting, and dragged herself back over to the pitiful scratches in the earth Asta had made by the gate. "Fuck this," she muttered, spitting on her hands before she started to dig again, trying to widen the impressions in the dry, packed earth.

Asta watched her. There seemed little else she could do.

"You're not going to help me?"

Asta shook her head. Red sat back on her heels and blew the yellow dust from her palms. "You giving up on me, girl?"

"What's the point? There's no way out."

Red twisted her wrist and forced it under the metal gate, touching freedom on the other side. "That's quitting talk. You give up, you're as good as dead. You know that, right. If you give up, where's it going to get you?"

"Where has it got *you*?" Asta's words were savage, she knew it, and uncalled for.

"It's kept me alive so far, just about. You want to find your boy?"

Asta closed her eyes against the glare, the ache in her head, the bitterness that filled her mouth. "He's gone. Even if he was still here . . . being alive isn't the same as being free."

"They both beat dying, girl. Which is what'll happen if you lay here staring into the dust. While you live, you've got hope."

No matter how she twisted it in her mind, Asta couldn't see that. She had lost Rhodan, lost her people. She had lost Finn twice over, and everywhere she turned there was darkness. Darkness and chains, closing around her, dragging her down.

"Watch out!" Red shifted to sit over the hole she had scraped in the dirt as the gate compound rattled. Asta watched Bernaldus approach through grief-dulled eyes, wondering what he could possibly do this time that could make things worse than they already were. He was accompanied by two tall, slender women. Despite the heat of the Inyestan afternoon, they both wore black cloaks that covered their heads and swept to their ankles, and their faces were concealed with fabric masks, leaving only their eyes visible. As the shorter of the pair turned to look through the gate, Asta saw the distinctive outline of a blade riding on her hip.

Red spat. "Shadow Cloaks. Now we're in the shit." She stood up, brushing her hands down her thighs, and gripped Asta's shoulder firmly. "On your feet. Show respect."

Asta clambered up, clutching the bars of the gate for support. It felt like she was moving though tar. She watched the assassins as they approached, flanking Bernaldus on either side. He was sweating heavily, dabbing at his face with a cloth, eyes darting left and right as if he anticipated a sudden assault. The women moved with the smooth confidence of warriors, and the taller one pointed at the gate. At Asta.

"That one," she said. "We'll take a look at her."

Bernaldus glared through the bars. "Are you sure? She's wilful, and the other one even worse. I can get you a nice Inyestan girl for only a little more paper . . ."

The woman shook out her gloved hands. The gesture must have carried some meaning, for Bernaldus edged away from her, heavy brows drawing together in anxiety. He yelled over his shoulder for Tarese, and his wife froze, just for a moment, as she hurried into the compound and saw the company that Bernaldus kept.

"I was about to say, it's not sale hours . . ."

"We can make an exception," he told her firmly. "These two ladies are interested in the Atrathene breeder."

"We won't pay extra for a breeder," the taller woman said flatly. "No tricks."

"I wouldn't dream of it." To Asta's ears, Bernaldus sounded more sincere than he ever had.

"And no double-crosses. We know you, slave dealer."

He shook his head. He seemed, for once, to be short of words.

"Have your woman bring her out." The taller woman pulled off her glove and inspected her nails while her companion leaned against the wall, her hand never far from the hilt of her sword. Red fell back, giving Asta's shoulder a squeeze as Tarese unlocked the gates, looped a wire around her wrists, and drew her out into the yard. "Don't kick up a fuss," she hissed. "Too many weapons around!"

Asta didn't feel she had the strength to kick up a fuss. If these women bought her, they might take her anywhere. Right out of the city, across the sea even. She could see Rhodan falling away, further and further from her grip with every moment that passed. She tried to pull away, and only succeeded in tightening the wire against the flesh of her wrists.

The shadow-cloak prowled around her, moving with a delicacy and grace that reminded Asta of her mother, and brought a painful lump to her throat. If she had Nasira's skills, she would have been over the wall and away with Rhodan clamped in her jaws. If she had been her father, she could have talked her way out of it. Even Finn would have made a better job of Rhodan's rescue than she could, and he was dead, and at the thought of her brother she was forced to fight back her despair.

The woman tapped the back of Asta's knees with her sheathed sword hilt, sending a flare of pain over her sunburned skin. "What are these red marks?" she asked.

Bernaldus shrugged. "She had them when I bought her. I think they're natural."

The marks of a Goddess, the Scattering believed. Some goddess. Asta could have laughed in scorn, but she thought of that other god, kept caged and fed on human flesh, and shivered. That could have been her. It still could be; these two armed women obviously had their own agenda, and her search for Rhodan would not figure in their plans.

The woman squeezed Asta's biceps, pulled back her lips so she could inspect her teeth, cradled the curve of her stomach in her hand. Asta tried to back away at this invasion, but was brought up short by the wire around her wrists and Tarese's urgent hiss. The woman glanced at her companion and raised an eyebrow. "What do you think, Ilu?"

Ilu was running a length of steel wire between her hands with a soft swishing sound. She shrugged. "Up to you. Does she look like a hard worker? Does she have a tongue?"

"Can you speak?" the assassin asked.

Asta nodded.

"Speak, then." Her blank golden eyes didn't waver in their scrutiny.

"What do you want me to say?"

Tarese jerked the wire as Bernaldus uttered a soft moan of fear. Asta's heart was in her throat, but she met that steady gaze with her own, as befitted a leader in her own tribe, for all her heart was racing.

Ilu snorted, apparently amused. "She'll do, Som," she said, stashing the wire beneath her cloak. "Let's go. Things to do."

A ridge formed between Som's eyebrows, the only expression

Asta could see on the visible fragment of her face. "I'm not sure she's worth any price the fat man asks for her, Ilu."

"The fat man would be wise to remember who he's haggling with."

The sweat was pouring off Bernaldus now, soaking a blood-dark stain into his shirt. The hand he placed on Asta's shoulder was slippery as a fish. She recoiled from the touch.

"You fine ladies must understand, I have to earn a living, same as you. Our businesses aren't so different. Let's keep it friendly."

Som's eyes hardened. "For mercy, I'll pretend you didn't say that. I'll pretend you gave me a price of four hundred, and I haggled you down to three."

"Saves time," Ilu added. "And sweat."

"But that's less than—" Bernaldus knew he was defeated, by the way he crumpled. "She's caused me nothing but grief. Take her. The last thing I wanted was attention from . . ."

"From the likes of us?" Ilu's eyes, a honey-shade deeper than her companion's, looked grim as she pushed away from the wall. "Don't worry. You won't see us for a while. Not until you don't expect it."

"That's what worries me!" Bernaldus tried to laugh, but the sound that emerged was a squeaky splutter.

"It should." Som's eyes showed no hint of humour as she reached under her night-velvet cloak and withdrew a tight roll of paper. She counted off a few of the notes and handed them to Bernaldus with her fingertips, avoiding his greasy palm.

"Make her ready and have her brought to our carriage at once," she ordered. "Then forget we ever had this conversation."

Bernaldus tugged his collar. "Well that's a trick, isn't it? Might cost a little more paper to make me lose my memory, and as for finding it again—"

There was the soft scrape of blades being drawn. Som and Ilu moved as one, as synchronised as dancers, as twins. Bernaldus' eyes swivelled as he tried to look at both weapons at once, the tips of their swords lying delicately, one on each side of his jowly neck. Asta felt Tarese's indrawn breath. She wasn't sure if she was breathing either. She had barely seen the women move.

Som quirked her eyebrows. The slave trader nodded, carefully, bright spots of blood welling at the sides of his throat. Ilu took a step back, and Som followed, lowering her sword.

"We'll be in the carriage," she said. "We'd prefer not to hang about."

"Not at all." Bernaldus raised his hand to his neck and stared at the crimson staining his fingertips as if it belonged to another man and he was wondering how it got there. "I'll send her out . . ."

"Do." Som sheathed her blade, turned, and vanished back into the darkness of the auction hall. Ilu nodded tersely towards the slave trader and followed her. In the silence, the flies buzzing around the courtyard, and the faint drip of water, were suddenly very loud.

Tarese shook off her trance, loosening the wire around Asta's wrists and taking her arm. "Can't say you got lucky," she muttered, "but there's worse than Shadow Cloaks, I suppose. Let's get you cleaned up for them."

Asta looked back at the compound, at Red standing in the shadows behind the gate, thick fingers gripping the bars. The deaf slave inclined her head in sullen farewell. Asta wondered what would happen to her. She wondered what would happen to all of them, now she was alone.

The carriage belonging to Som and Ilu stood opposite the entrance to the slave market. Despite Asta's fear, her sorrow was lifted a fraction by the sight of the pair of matched black geldings that drew the carriage. She recognised Atrathene horses when she saw them. She took a clanking step towards them, the shackles dragging heavy at her ankles, and Bernaldus seized the chain that ran between her wrists and steered her back on course. The setting sun washed the stones of the street the colour of blood, and the black carriage was trimmed in the same colour, completely enclosed, with scarlet drapes covering the windows. She could see no driver, no life at all within, and the men and women walking in the street avoided the carriage as if it was a phantom. It seemed to take no effort; the crowds flowed around it without a glance or an acknowledgement that it was there at all, the way the people of the Scattering avoided beggars. Inyestans, like all the city folk she had met, were skilled at avoiding things they didn't want to see.

Bernaldus shuddered, and nudged her forward through the invisible line that formed an empty circle around the carriage. Asta expected there to be a muting of sound, a tingle in the air as if a spell had been cast over it, but everything was reassuringly, yet frighteningly, normal. One of the geldings farted and she fought back the urge to giggle, knowing she was already close to hysteria, to panic. If she lost her composure she would never be able to regain it. She would spiral into darkness and be lost.

Bernaldus stopped walking and the chain jerked her wrists sharply.

"What happens now?" She didn't know why she was whispering, but as if in reply the carriage door opened and a long, black-clad arm beckoned her into the darkness of the interior.

She hung back, losing her nerve, and Bernaldus gave her a hefty shove from behind. It was climb the step or fall flat on her face, but the shackles gained weight as she climbed. She thought of the slave boy, chained on the floor of Inesh and Fernande's carriage on the way back to Abonnae.

I'd like to stab this whole fucking city, Finn.

Maybe he could still hear her thoughts, even if he couldn't reply. The prospect was a slim comfort. Silken fingers closed around her shackled wrist to draw her forward, and the door slammed behind her, cutting off the evening sunlight and throwing her into stuffy darkness. She blinked in confusion.

"Sit down." She couldn't tell if it was Som or Ilu who spoke, but the hand drew her forward and down until she was sitting on a velvet-padded bench. There was a scratch, and the flare of a small oil-lamp, so bright it scalded her eyes and threw the rest of the interior of the carriage into deeper blackness.

"That's better." Another scratch, a smaller flame. By the light Asta could at last look on the faces of her new owners.

They were sisters, they had to be sisters, with their dark olive skin. Their hair was incongrouously fair, plaited and entwined around jewelled headpieces. Som, the taller of the two, had a pink scar running through her eyebrow, sweeping across her cheek to vanish in the shadows beneath her chin. It narrowed her right eye, making it look as if she was constantly on the verge of winking. Her blemished face was illuminated by the glowing bowl of a pipe as she brought it to her lips and drew on it, releasing the aromatic smoke with a long sigh. Ilu sat next to her, and she finally relinquished her grip on Asta's wrist and sat back, appraising her from under lazily lowered eyelids. Asta opened her mouth to ask a question, and Ilu pressed a finger to her lips.

"Not now," she said." Let my sister have her time. It takes the sting off."

"Plenty of time for talking later," Som muttered in a sleepy voice, lips still clamped around the pipe stem. "My, that eases my joints . . ."

Asta couldn't see the pleasure in the smoke. Her cuts and bruises still ached, and the heavy sorrow in her gut was not eased by the miasma drifting around the inside of the carriage. If anything it made her even more nauseous. Unable to lean against the wall and show weakness before these strange, deadly women, she longed to rip the heavy drapes aside to see the streets of Abonnae passing by the window. But Ilu watched her every move, and she had the wire in her hands again, running it through her fingers as if the motion was as soothing to her as Som's pipe. Asta sat, staring at the manacled hands resting in her lap, her shackled feet that didn't reach the floor. They swung back and forth with every bump in the road. If she swung her legs up she could kick the wire from Ilu's hands, maybe break her wrist, but she couldn't run, and she had seen how quickly those swords moved into action. Caution dictated she sit still, and sorrow pressed her into her seat. Her limbs were too heavy to run, even if there had been somewhere she could run to.

The sounds outside the carriage changed, becoming less muffled, and the wheels smoothed over a better surface. Asta had the sensation that they were climbing, not steeply but steadily. Som's pipe flickered and died, but the smoke remained, and Ilu coughed gently.

"Nearly there," Som said, speaking to the fuggy carriage at large. The words were barely from her mouth when the carriage slowed, and came to a stop. The three women looked at each other, the Shadow-Cloaks and their new possession. No one spoke.

Outside a door slammed, and the noise lifted Som from her semi-trance. She sat for a moment, unscrewing and cleaning the pipe, packing each separate piece away in a velvet case as black as her cloak. Her scarred face was riven with concentration. Only when it was tidied away to her satisfaction did she look up, with a lopsided smile. "Sorry, were you waiting for me?"

Asta was awkward in her chains, and Ilu took a firm grip on her elbow to help her down from the carriage. They were in a vaulted stone hall, and the carriage they had just left was one of four of varying sizes, from a two-man gig to a coach-and six bigger than some of the huts in the Beehive village. In front of the carriages were stone arches, blocked by wooden doors twice as tall as Asta, and on the opposite wall was a smaller door, standing open. Yellow light spilled through it, casting a path across the dusty floor.

Ilu tugged the manacles as Asta's feet locked. "Come on then," she said.

"I'm not going anywhere until you tell me where we are."

Som laughed, without rancour. "Hard words for a slave. We'll talk, Atrathene, but we'll talk indoors, in comfort and safety."

Asta hung back. "We'll talk here."

"Don't be stupid. We don't want to hurt you."

"What do you want then?"

Ilu shook out her wire, with pointed movements. "We don't want to hurt you," she echoed her sister, "but we can. Do you understand who we are, what we do? We kill, silently, and we leave no trace. That's all we do. We could kill you right now, and you'd die never knowing what happened to your little boy." She took a menacing step forward. "It would be easy."

"Do you think I wouldn't fight?"

Ilu stared at her for a moment, then she threw her head back and roared with laughter at Asta's ludicrous defiance. Asta felt her face burn. She looked down at her feet, hot and humiliated as she walked behind Som, with Ilu and her razor-sharp wire uncomfortably close to her back.

They passed through the door and up a wide staircase that veered to the right at a small half-landing, light spearing in through a narrow window-slit. They reached a door at the top and Som fished beneath her cloak and brought out a silvered key. She weighed it in her palm as she pressed her ear to the door, and Asta caught her breath. Maybe this wasn't the womens' house after all? Maybe they were intruders, and they had brought her with them as – what? A sacrifice? Bait?

Som ran her hands down either side of the door frame, light as a lover's touch. "All clear, I think," she muttered.

"Can't be too cautious. You want the slave to go first?"

Som shook her head, turning the key smoothly in the lock. She opened the door to reveal a lighted gallery beyond. Doors to her left, with paintings between them, portraits and landscapes, faces and places Asta did not recognise. The doors were trimmed with gold, and in the alcoves stood marble tables laden with trinkets, pottery and glass sculpture and vases as tall as a man, spilling over with bright blooms. They filled the air with their scent, honey and sea-thyme and fresh spring grass, and from somewhere there was a breeze, an actual breeze. It felt like the first time cool air had brushed her face since she stepped onto the dock in Abonnae, and she inhaled deeply.

"This way." On Asta's right was a balcony, a two-storey drop to the floor below. The room was full of light and golden gleaming, and it was hard to make out any detail as they descended the stairs at the far end of the galleried landing. Som moved ahead, a black cut-out shape moving through the light, like a shadow roaming free of its host. Behind Asta, Ilu's breath close to her neck reminded her of the blades, told her not to hesitate, not to try and double back.

There was a sunken area in the middle of the floor, like the bath back at the manse in Mikligard. It was reached by a few descending steps. Sofas lined the walls of the well, and in the middle was a long marble table, a tray of glasses, and a heavy jug of the peachy juice, poured over ice. Som sunk onto the nearest sofa, hands drifting to the pouch that held her pipe, while Ilu poured three glasses. Asta remained standing. She didn't know if she was allowed to sit, or whether it should be her serving the drinks. Her hands twisted one over the other, battling anxiety, rage, and the overwhelming urge to run. There were doors in the walls of this lower room, and they must lead somewhere.

"Sit down, girl." Som set her pipe on the table and released the pin on her cloak, letting it pool around her on the tapestried seat. Beneath it she wore more black, a shirt open at the throat, black tight-legged trousers, and a belt hung either side with sheathed daggers. Around her neck, vanishing under her shirt, was a leather thong, maybe holding a pendant. She sucked her pipe and tucked a stray wisp of honey-hued hair neatly behind her ear with her free hand.

"In that case . . ." Ilu shucked her own cloak, and with it the frown that drew a deep line between her eyebrows. Underneath she was dressed identically to her sister, but she wore tiny gold drops in her ears and a plain band of gold around the smallest finger of her left hand. Asta saw it as she removed her gloves, shook them out and threw them down on the table. "It's grand to be home!" She grinned, as if she had thrown off some burden along with the black velvet cloak. She looked almost friendly as she pointed to the sofa opposite. "Sit down, Atrathene. We don't murder our guests!"

"Ugly word, murder," Som muttered over her pipe, still more on edge than her sister. "Where are they? I thought they'd be here?"

"Maybe they're getting food," Ilu suggested, and her smile dimmed. "Are you going to sit down?"

"Is that an order?" Asta asked.

"It's a request. I don't want to crick my neck while I'm talking to you, and I'm sure you have questions. We have things we want to ask you too, Asta."

That made her sit down, fast, her knees swept from under her. Ilu took her wrists and unlocked the shackles, letting her free her own feet. "You know my name?" Asta asked as she straightened.

"We've been watching you a while, haven't we, Som?"

Som grunted and leaned back, one long arm trailing along the back of the sofa, the other pulling on her pipe. She left the talking to her sister.

Ilu and Asta eyed each other warily over the expanse of table top. Asta's secrets were all she had now, and she didn't want to give them up to this stranger. But she had to learn more.

"Where are we?" she asked.

"Som and I live here, along with . . . some other people."

That was no help. "Are we still in Abonnae?"

"Yes. We're on The Hill; do you know of it?"

"I've heard of it." She tried to hold back a surge of excitement, of renewed hope. It was likely Rhodan had been taken to the Hill. Maybe there was a slim chance . . .

"Money lives here," Som remarked.

"How do you know my name?" Asta didn't care about money, didn't know if Som meant it as bragging, or a simple statement of fact.

"I told you, we've been watching. The smuggler told us you were in trouble. He told us a lot about you. He's kept a close pair of eyes on you since you landed."

"Ranmiro? I never saw him. Why didn't he say anything?"

Ilu chuckled. "He didn't need to. He left his cat to watch over you, and he watched you through his eyes. The cat followed you all over the city, into the heart of the Red Temple, and when you landed in serious trouble, Ranmiro came to us for help. We're old acquaintances; he's helped us out in the past, and favours should always be returned."

"The cat – oh!" Marcio, running along the dock ahead of her, mingling with the Temple cats. One fluffy black cat looked very much like another; she couldn't tell them apart the way she could horses. And the cats had tiptoed along the high, glass-speared wall of the slave compound, and suffered stonings and abuse for their temerity. Had they all been spies, other men and women watching through their eyes? "I had no idea . . ."

"Everyone spies on everyone else in Inyesta," Som remarked. "The Emperor's men, and the priests, all spying on each other. It's our national pastime. Makes our job that little bit more challenging."

"You're . . ." Asta sought the word, "hired killers?"

Ilu sipped her drink, and smiled behind her glass as Som tutted. "You make it sound so vulgar. It's a calling, not a job anyone can do for love of money. If all you're interested in is paper, you won't last ten minutes."

"We are Inyestan Shadow Cloaks," Som added severely. "We are bred apart from other men, and our name sends fear into the heart of even the Red Temple. Even the high priest bows to the Shadow Cloaks."

Ilu sniggered. It seemed most unbecoming, after what Som had said. "We're also human. We piss the same as anyone else."

"Could I hire you?"

"Slaves don't have paper," Som said, but Ilu leaned forward. "To kill?" she asked.

"To find someone."

"How would you pay?"

"My village has many horses . . ."

"You can't fold a horse up tight and pop it in your pocket, Asta. Paper up front."

"Ilu—" Som broke off at the sound of a door opening and closing on the upper floor. Even divested of their cloaks, both women were fully alert at once, daggers sliding into their hands smooth as silk. Asta bunched her own fists, and wished for a blade.

"Sisters? Are you here?" The male voice drifted down from the gallery above, and a head appeared. Ilu sheathed her dagger with her previous ill grace.

"Where have you been, Gartzea?" she demanded. "Sucking cock behind some tavern?"

"I went to get food. You two would starve if folks didn't wait on you!" He seemed impervious to the insult, bounding down the stairs two at a time, long-legged and keen-eyed, hair thinning around a bald spot he was obviously trying to conceal. He carried a heavy canvas bag, and he tossed it on the table and extended a hand to Asta, but she wasn't looking at him. Behind him, moving at a slower pace but with just as broad a grin, was Ranmiro. Marcio was draped around his neck, kneading paws against his chest.

"Ranmiro!" Asta started forward, barking her shins painfully against the low table.

"Little goddess!" He caught both her hands in his, frowning at the cuts and bruises left by the chains. "You look like shit, but at least you don't stink of onions. I see you found your boy."

"Found him and lost him again." She sighed. She wanted to huddle against his chest in the cabin of the *Aguia* and let herself cry until she felt better.

"If you've found him once you can find him again. Why are your eyes wet? I thought you were the daughter of heroes? Come," he patted the table, "let's eat and talk. Maybe we find your boy that way? Seems as good as any other!"

"Ranmiro, don't be cruel." The other man, Gartzea, took her arm and studied her face for a long, uncomfortable moment. "An exotic," he said, almost to himself.

She shook free. "That's what they called my nephew. The traders, the other slaves. They said that made him worth more paper." She struggled to keep from spitting on the polished wood floor. "He's my blood, my brother's son. How is that less important than pieces of paper?"

Gartzea looked past her to Som, who sat on the sofa in a haze of pipe-smoke, a black figure surrounded by blue cloud. "How long has she been here, that she still doesn't understand how things work?"

Som shrugged. Gartzea took her arm again. "Come upstairs with me now."

She tried to shake him off with a curse, but his grip was stronger than his appearance suggested. "Come," he urged, tugging her arm. Everyone was staring at her. Even Ranmiro, even his stupid cat.

"Why? Because I belong to one of you, you think you can take me to bed any time you like?" Her face burned. "I'm not your fucking whore!"

"But you are property. I'm not going to hurt you." Gartzea was floundering, looking at Ilu for support. She tapped her unsheathed dagger against her palm and raised her eyebrows, as if Asta was a naughty child making a scene.

"Go with him, little Goddess." Ranmiro smirked. A moment ago she had been so pleased to see him; now she wanted to punch his smug face until the bones shattered beneath her fist. "It won't take long, I'm sure!"

Ilu snorted. Gartzea's eyes were wide and innocent, but his grip was like rock grinding shut around her wrist. As she looked down she noticed the outline of a dagger concealed in his sleeve, and another hilt poking from the top of his boot. Shit, was she completely surrounded by murderers-for-hire? If she got him in a vulnerable position she could make a grab for one of the blades, take him hostage, fight her way free. She forced herself to relax, muscle by muscle, letting Gartzea draw her towards the stairs. Her eyes never left the blade concealed under the width of his lacy cuff.

He led her back up to the second floor, the way they had come in, never relinquishing his grip on her forearm. Every step brought them closer to the door to the carriage house, to possible freedom. Asta held her breath, waiting for a chance that didn't come.

Gartzea opened the second last door before the exit, fumbling at the catch with his left hand. Asta caught a glimpse of the bed in the darkened room, and her legs locked as she clamped her free hand around the door frame. If he wanted her, he would have to drag her there.

"By the Deity, Asta, stop being such a fool!" Gartzea spoke in a furious whisper. "He's been through enough; do you want to wake him up?"

"What are you talking about?" She found herself whispering back.

"Him!" He wrenched her arm free, her fingers scraping across painted wood. Gartzea twitched back the thin netting that draped over the bed like a tented canopy.

Rhodan lay curled up on his side beneath a silken sheet, hands pillowing his head as if he was only pretending to sleep. Dark lashes fluttered against his bruised cheek with every breath, and there was a smudge of red, of blood maybe, just above his mouth. His arm and shoulder, above the sheet, were bare.

Asta was cold. She couldn't touch him, even to wipe away the blood. Her breath sounded too loud in her lungs. The patterns on the bed sheet were too bright, the sound of a fly buzzing against the window like a saw through her skull. All she could see was the splash of blood, the naked arm, the glint of steel through a lace cuff out of the very corner of her eye. Gartzea was talking, but his words and movement seemed slowed, like specks of dust spiralling lazily down through a sunbeam, and she couldn't make out what he said. He stretched his hand towards Rhodan and she lunged forward, unthinking, unconscious, seizing his forearm and sinking her teeth through lace and skin, deep into the flesh beneath. Like a dog, and like a dog he howled, thrashing to break free, groping with his weaker hand for one of his other blades as the knife on his bleeding arm dropped onto the bed next to Rhodan's sleeping face.

Asta saw it fall, ripped her teeth free. She spat out a chunk of flesh and bloodied cloth and dived for it, snatching it away from Gartzea and dropping into a fighting crouch.

"Come at me then, you fuck! What did you do to him?"

He fumbled the grip on his second blade, dropping it with a curse, and clutched his right arm as the blood welled through his fingers. "You mad bitch! What are you saying? Look what you did!"

Asta wiped her mouth with the back of her hand, a blood red smear across her skin. She spat again. "What did you do to him?" She realised in her fury she had spoken in her native tongue before.

"Nothing, I swear! What are you talking about?"

"Liar!" Feet on the stairs now, running towards the fight. "I heard what they do to exotic slaves, here on the Hill . . . ."

"You think I—?" He lashed out as she came at him, dodging her awkward thrust and backhanding her across the jaw, so hard her teeth rattled. "Are you mad? We're trying to *help* you!"

Even with a wounded arm, his turn of speed was frightening. While Asta was reeling from the blow, he had the knife from his boot in his left hand, parrying her stabs and thrusts, leaping back to avoid a long slash that left a dripping red score across the bottom of his ribcage. He grunted in surprise, but the move had Asta stumbling off balance and inside his reach.

Metal clashed in front of her eyes, filling her sight with sparks, and she felt a sting above her right eye. Red dripped in her vision as she pressed against Gartzea, snarling and sweating, looking for an opening to drive the blade home. Gartzea held firm, bloody right hand straining for her face, to force his fingers into her eye sockets, to wrap a hand in her hair and pull her head back to expose her throat. Her feet slipped on the floor as he pushed her back, inch by painful inch, and she felt hands on her shoulders, on her arms, tearing them apart, shouting words she couldn't hear over the ringing in her skull.

"Let go, both of you! What's going on?"

Asta tried to tear free, to lunge once more at Gartzea as Ranmiro held him back, but Som gripped her firmly. The Shadow Cloak's breathing was steady and calm, the point of her blade a cold spot below Asta's ear sucking the heat from her skin, leaving her suddenly drained and shivering. The bloodied knife tumbled from her hands, and Gartzea let his own blade fall, shaking his head and looking at his arm in disgust.

"She bit me! Fucking dog slave, after all we did! These primitives—"

"That's the Temple speaking," Ilu said sharply, moving over to the bed and checking the occupant. "He's still asleep. The drugs are holding."

Asta's mouth tasted of metal as she spoke. "You drugged him. So you could roll him over for your own pleasure?"

"There you go again!" Gartzea, breathing heavily, tried to staunch the cut across his ribs with his shirt. "Som, you tell her. Maybe she'll believe you."

Som let her blade drop and wrapped her arm around Asta's chest from behind, a gesture that was as much comforting as it was restraining. "We knew he was yours. We brought him here to keep him safe. We would have bought you too, but you weren't in the sale. We had to get more paper and come back for you. We outbid every man who wanted an exotic today, to protect him."

Asta desperately wanted to believe her. "Why drug him, then?"

"He's been through so much. He screamed all the way here, he must have heard something . . ."

Asta thought back to Red's words, and nodded reluctantly.

"We thought it best to let him sleep his fears away, so when he woke up you'd be here for him. I'm sorry we didn't tell you straight out." She looked challengingly at Gartzea. "I had no idea she'd react like that. Are you hurt?"

The blood was clotting on his ribs, little more than a scratch. It was his arm he regarded ruefully. The lace was torn and hung ragged and bloodied, and the flesh beneath was swelling. "I'll need to get some sugar-ale on that."

"We could all use a drink," Ilu suggested. "Leave the boy to his dreams. We still have much to talk about with this runaway *sumri gudienne* of the Scattering."

TWENTY-THREE

THEY SAT AROUND the table in the sunken well, and Ilu poured a generous measure of sugar-ale for Asta, Ranmiro and Gartzea. Neither she nor her sister appeared to be drinking. Asta sipped hers, more to be polite than out of any desire. She wanted to keep a clear head, and the sharp taste of the spirit, swallowed neat, made her shudder. Ranmiro added a generous splash of fruit juice to his and rummaged in the bag Gartzea had brought, looking for food, while Ilu tended Gartzea's arm and Som fiddled with her pipe. For a moment, silence reigned. Asta's ears were alert for movement or cries from upstairs. She would speak to Rhodan first, before she trusted any of these people who claimed to have rescued him. Even Ranmiro, who might have betrayed her to the Shadow Cloaks for his own reasons. Perhaps for paper.

"Why did you buy us?" She broke the silence. "You know who I am, obviously. What do you want from me? To sell me back to the Scattering?" She would throw herself into the sea, and take Rhodan with her, before she let that happen.

Ilu snorted. "The people of Mikligard think they can bring down the Empire with their superstitions and their sacrifices. They're dreaming, and they waste all our time. Don't think we haven't tried talking to them."

"About me?"

"About a lot of things."

"I won't go back there."

"No one's asking you to." Ilu poured a small glass of the fruit juice, and took a morsel, crunchy and battered, from the bag, popping it into her mouth and offering the bag to Asta. "Try these, they're nice."

Asta took one. There was meat inside the warm batter, and rice and beans. It crunched pleasantly in her mouth. "What, then?" she asked, with her mouth full. "What do you want? Are you with the Temple?"

Som and Ilu exchanged a loaded glance. "Not exactly," Som said.

Ilu rose, checked the doors and the windows, slapping a fly to pulp against the glass with a violence that made Asta jump. No one spoke until she returned to the table and refilled her glass.

"We're clear," she said. "Som?"

Still Som spoke in a hushed voice, twisting the stem of her pipe between her fingers.

"You've been in the Red Temple, Atrathene. Are you of the faith?"

Asta chose her words carefully. "I believe in the spirits of my ancestors. I was in the Temple looking for Rhodan. That's the only reason I came to Inyesta, to find my kin. I don't care for your gods, or their appetites."

Gartzea snorted. "You're not the only one. Can't say I care much for your appetite, either!"

Asta tightened her lips. If he wanted an apology he could whistle until his face was blue.

Ranmiro, who was being uncharacteristically quiet, leant forward for the first time.

"Lady of Atrath, I watched you through Marcio's eyes. I heard you with his ears. I know you penetrated the darkest sanctum of the Red Temple. I know you came face to face with our God."

"I came face to face with something. I don't think I would call it a god."

Som sat back, eyes wide, pipe dangling forgotten in her fingers. She let out a long, slow breath. "You don't understand, do you?"

"Understand what?"

"No one outside the Temple sees the Deity, only the priests, and their sacrifices. They should never have let you in, and they certainly shouldn't have let you leave the Temple. What happened?"

Asta pressed her lips tight while she considered her answer. "It was a test," she said at length. "A test of my loyalty to the Temple. They wanted to see if I could accept the sacrifice of my own kin."

"And could you?" Som asked sharply.

"Could I accept it? Why do you think I'm here, and not there?"

"Why did they let you go?"

"An act of mercy, I suppose. Or internal politics." Asta had doubted Margoli's mercy at the time, now she could see the older priestess had taken a fearful risk to save her, whether for Asta's benefit or her own. "Why does it matter?"

Ilu took up the explanation. "There are certain . . . powerful factions, I suppose, within the Empire who believe the church has too much power. They want it curtailed. Of course, these factions can't take on the Temple openly. To do that risk civil war, and these . . . factions . . . Their position is not as strong as it looks to the man on the street. We have been contracted—"

"—are happy to oblige," Som butted in.

"—consider it our duty, to break the power of the Red Temple. The church has grown too strong, too authoritarian, too greedy. Greedy for money, and for blood."

Asta sat back, arms folded. "Why should I help you? Because you're holding my nephew to ransom?"

"Better than buying him to fuck him," Gartzea muttered.

"Our faction," Ilu licked her lips, "would like to reduce the Empire's dependency on . . . outside sources . . ."

"For fucks sake, Ilu, stop being cagey about it." Gartzea curled his lip in scorn. "Slaves are the backbone of the Temple's strength. They started buying more and more slaves when the Inyestan people protested against the idea of sacrificing their own kind. Plenty of people beyond the sea, all different from us. Let's throw them into the maw of our god, and spare our own children the same fate. They're only *slaves*, after all . . ."

"Break the Temple, and you reduce much of the Empire's reliance on slavery. We can rebuild our trade, legitimate trade, with other nations. That's what our master believes," Som said.

"So you Inyestans will have to tend your own fields and wipe your own arses? How will you manage?"

Ilu laughed at Asta's scorn. "I've always managed to wipe my own arse!"

Som took over, her scarred face cast in a serious light. "You can help us, Asta. We've signed a contract. We're pledged to kill a god."

Asta was saved from having to reply by a thin, high wail from upstairs. She sprang to her feet. "I'm doing nothing for you until I've spoken to Rhodan. In *private*. Maybe not even then, depending on what he says. I'm not your slave, however much paper you handed over for me. I act as I choose."

Som nodded. "Go to him," she said. "Then we'll talk."

The room was still dark. The insect nets around the bed were torn down and tangled around Rhodan's body as he thrashed, legs kicking against the softness of sheets. Asta rushed to his side, pulled him free of the nets, held him hot skin against skin until he fought off the nightmare and his hands unclenched on her dirty smock. He looked up into her face, his eyes red.

"Tante Asta? I didn't know you were here."

"You were asleep, little cub."

"The lady with a cut face gave me a drink." He shuddered down the length of his body. "I don't remember much after that."

She lifted his chin and scanned his face. She couldn't see any extra bruises. "Still hanging on to that tooth, I see!"

He wiggled it from side to side with the tip of his tongue. "I don't want it to fall out here."

"Why not?"

"Because when we go home, I'd be leaving part of me behind. I want all of me to go home."

"I want all of you to go home too. If it falls out here, you'll have to pop it in your pocket and hang on to it until we get back to the village. Then you can show everyone the gap!"

"When are we going home, Tante Asta? Will it be soon?"

"As soon as I can find a boat to take us."

His lower lip quivered. "I don't think I want to go on a boat again."

"A flying horse, then, to carry us over the ocean!"

Rhodan pouted. "Don't be silly, Tante Asta. You know horses can't fly."

"Your grandfather's horse could fly."

He stuck his tongue out. "Don't believe you."

"It'll have to be a boat, then, if you don't believe in flying horses. Or you could swim?"

"I reckon I could swim home."

"Your arms would get too tired. Listen, Rhodan," she hated to drag the conversation back round to such serious matters, but she had to ask. "Since you've been here, has anyone hurt you? Has anyone got into bed with you or touched you where you pee?"

He frowned. It made him look even more like Finn. "No. Why would they do that?"

Asta didn't have it in her to answer the question. "No reason. I just wondered. Do you want to come downstairs with me? There's juice."

He held up his arms for her to carry him, and she grunted as she hefted him onto her hip, his arms around her neck. "You're getting too big for this."

"That's what Da says."

Oh, Finn. How could she be mother and father to her brother's child, without the tribe around her to catch her when she stumbled and dropped him? She needed to get him home. The problems of Inyesta were insignificant compared to the fate of this one little boy.

He wriggled out of her arms as she reached the bottom of the stairs, and she was grateful as her back was beginning to ache. He hung back from approaching the table, toes digging into the carpet defiantly. His nose twitched as he inhaled the greasy scent of the food, but he would not move. She tapped him lightly on the shoulder. "You can eat. It's allowed."

Rhodan glared at Ilu as she pushed the bag of rice-and-bean morsels towards him. He snatched it from her hand and fell on it, hunching up in a corner of the room with his back to everyone, only a rustle of paper betraying the fact that he was still present. It hurt Asta to see him so wary, so hostile.

Gartzea tugged the bandage on his arm, where the blood soaked through. "You got what you wanted?" he asked.

"I want a boat." Asta replied to him, but her gaze was directed at Ranmiro. "If I tell you what you need to know, will you take us home?"

He shrugged. "Telling is not much payment, Atrathene goddess."

"It's all I have. *I'm* all he has. If I die helping you change the world, who looks after my nephew? You people?"

Ilu reached out, and the hand that bore the ring closed gently around Asta's forearm. "We're not just about killing and revolution," she said. "If anything happened to you, we'd get him home to your tribe."

"Not good enough. My brother gave his life to protect Rhodan. My brother's wife died in the guts of one of your slave-ships. I'm not going to be parted from him. Finn's spirit would never forgive me."

She sensed the puzzled nature of the silence following this remark. Outsiders never understood.

"I'll give you what I can," she clarified. "I'm grateful you spent your paper on him, rather than let him go . . . *elsewhere*. But this isn't our fight. It's not what I came here to do. I have other people who need me, need me more than you do. I'm a warrior, not an assassin, and I fight with the tribe at my back. I'm not what you need."

Som nodded slowly, rolling down the paper on her bag of snacks and placing it neatly on the table in front of her. "I think that's fair," she said, raising a hand to forestall her sister's protest. "She's been through a lot, after all. Just tell us what you know, Asta."

"About the Deity?" Som nodded, and Asta took a gulp of juice and swirled it round her dry mouth, buying time to gather her thoughts.

"There's a door behind the high altar. Three doors. The iron one in the middle leads down a long tunnel, deep underground. It switchbacks on itself, I don't know how far down it goes. There are lots of gates, thick iron, before you come to a room . . ." Despite the heat of the evening, she shuddered. "They take the children there."

Ilu leaned forward. "What was the room like? Tell us everything you remember."

Asta told, skimming over the grisly details for Rhodan's benefit. He had finished eating and now he crept closer to her, sitting on the floor leaning against her calf. She stroked her fingers over his scalp as she talked, and the contact kept her grounded. Her companions had many questions, wanting to know this detail and that, going over and over the layout of the room until she was dizzy and tired, and until she was no longer sure what she had seen and what were false memories, everything mixed up in her head. Rhodan's head fell heavy against her knee, and she lifted him unprotesting into her lap.

"Rhodan needs to sleep," she said. "I've told you everything I know, sometimes twice. Do I get my boat?"

Ilu raised an eyebrow towards Ranmiro, who nodded. "The

tide is mid-morning tomorrow, and the wind should be favourable for the Atrath shore. The *Aguia* stands ready for when the Goddess needs her."

Asta felt the tension flow from her shoulders. They weren't going to keep her here. Once they were clear of the harbour, tomorrow afternoon, they would be free and on their way home. She may not have been able to find all her scattered tribe, but at least she had found Rhodan. She needed to get him away from here, get him to safety. That was her primary concern now.

Asta was woken by urgent voices on the landing. She had slept under the insect nets with Rhodan, curled tight around him so the bones of his spine dug into her stomach. He twitched in his sleep, and she smoothed his hair to try and calm him. When she slept, she dreamed of waves crashing at the base of the tower. Lefalli was there, her hands overflowing with straw that blew across the surface of the sea no matter how she tried to clutch on to it. Asta didn't care about the straw, she was looking for Finn, and she woke with a smothering pang of loss, and a sob that made her turn her face to the sheets so she wouldn't wake Rhodan.

She lay there for a moment, gathering her courage, restoring her equilibrium, listening to the rustle of low, urgent voices in the hall until her curiosity overwhelmed her. She slipped out of bed, holding her breath as Rhodan stirred and then settled again. Som had lent her a shift to sleep in, and she pulled it down around her knees and padded across to the door. She half-expected it to be locked, but the handle moved under her palm.

There was no one on the landing. It was still dark outside, but lights glowed from the door of the coach house and from the big lounge downstairs. The coach house was nearer, so she headed that way.

One of the doors to the yard stood open, and the gig was missing. Moonlight spilled across the floor, fading and returning as the clouds parted and closed again. Asta hesitated, tempted, one hand resting lightly on the side of the night-black coach. If she grabbed Rhodan, they would be able to run . . .

She shook her head. She was too used to running. Som and Ilu, and their tribe, seemed willing to help them. If they ran, they would be no better off. She fought down the instinct, but she advanced with caution, wary of walking into a trap.

The gig stood in the yard, which was illuminated by torches. Ranmiro stood by the horse's head. His frown deepened as he saw her.

"You shouldn't be here. Go back to bed."

"What's going on?" she asked.

"Gartzea has taken sick. I'm driving him to the nearest temple."

She moved in closer, breathing in the homely scent of the horse. "Do the Inyestans sacrifice their sick, then?"

Ramiro snorted. "Why would they do that? They go to the temple for healing. The priests see you, and it's the will of the Deity whether you recover or not."

"Surely you don't believe that?"

"The alternative is to cast yourself into the hands of a back-street butcher. At least the priests know how to treat a sick man."

Asta had her doubts, but chose not to voice them. "What's wrong with him, anyway?"

There were heavy footsteps behind her, in the coach house. Som and Ilu carried their stricken co-conspirator between them, his head cradled against Som's breast, his ankles tucked under Ilu's armpits. One arm hung limp by his side, the other, the one Asta had bitten, was strapped tight across his chest. Even in the dim light she could see the swelling. Sweat beaded his brow, and his teeth were gritted in a rictus of pain. He groaned as Som and Ilu jogged him as they lifted him into the gig. Neither of them acknowledged Asta.

Ranmiro mounted the carriage behind the horse, and took up the reins. "What do I tell them?" he asked.

"Tell them it was a tavern brawl, if they ask. Hopefully it's nothing serious, they can break the fever and we'll have him back by noon." Som already had her pipe in her hands, filling it by touch alone.

"And if they don't?" Asta asked.

"Then you miss the boat." Ilu snorted, striking a match and holding it up for Som to light her pipe. "Next time keep your teeth to yourself."

Gartzea and Ranmiro were not back by noon. The tide came and went, and the *Aguia* did not sail. Som and Ilu played endless games of dice, polished their weapons, and filled the downstairs room with a fug of pipe smoke that only added to the oppressive heat. Rhodan lay on the kitchen floor with a damp sheet draped across his back, drawing horses on a scrap of paper and wobbling his tooth with his tongue. Asta prowled the gardens, always within earshot of his cry, looking for something to do. Dice bored her; the smoke stung her lungs, the sight of Rhodan pushing his tongue into the roots of his tooth made her feel sick. She tried to sleep under the shade of a plant with waxy leaves as long and broad as her arm, cooled her feet in the fountains and artificial streams that kept the garden green, and watched Marcio leaping at insects like an excited kitten, before he remembered his station, threw her a haughty glare, and sat down in the dust to have a wash. She wondered if Ranmiro could see her.

"What's going on, cat?"

The cat flicked his whiskers and turned his attention to his inside leg. She grinned as she thought of the view Ranmiro might be getting now.

There was a cry from the house. "Tante Asta! Tante Asta, come quick!"

Asta sprang up, startling the cat and sending him limping into the bushes as fast as his legs would take him. She raced back to the kitchen, expecting to see blood, or slavers, or a corpse. Rhodan stood with the sheet around his shoulders, one hand proudly extended, lips drawn back to reveal the gummy gap where his tooth had been. "Look!"

"Have you still got it?"

The tooth was a white fragment balanced on the tip of his finger, impossibly small.

"Don't lose it. We need to wrap it up in something."

"Here." Ilu leaned in the kitchen doorway watching the drama. "I thought someone was being murdered in here! Take this." She held out a velvet bag, no bigger than her forefinger and only twice as wide. It reeked of smoking herb.

"You can keep it safe in there and hang it round your neck, kid. That way it won't get lost."

"What do you say, Rhodan?" Asta prodded him. He muttered his thanks.

"First tooth?"

"I think so," Asta said. Rhodan shook his head. "Apparently not, then."

"My boy was no older when he lost his first one. You've never heard such fuss!" Ilu flashed a tight grin, and patted Rhodan on the shoulder. "Why don't you run and play? There are five secret fountains in the garden; if you find them all I'll give you a sweet!"

She watched him run off, and her smile faded.

"We've been called to the local temple," she said. "Gartzea is asking for us. Do you want to come?"

"Do you think I should?" If Gartzea was asking for his friends he must be feeling better, to Asta's relief.

"I don't want to leave you here."

"What about Rhodan? I don't want to take him near any temple."

"He'll be safe. Ranmiro will keep an eye on him."

Asta watched Rhodan charge down the garden, Marcio trotting at his heels. In the tribe, children were rarely left alone. Everyone had a hand in bringing up every child, and no doors were locked to them. If she had left Rhodan there, half the village would watch over him. It didn't seem right to leave his security to a cat.

"What if someone comes?"

"He can't get out of the garden, and no one can get in. He's our property now, even the Holy Mother herself couldn't just come in and take him. No one would dare break into the house of a Shadow Cloak. Come on!" as Asta hung back. "The sooner we leave, the sooner we'll be back." She shut the kitchen door before Asta could utter any further protest, and shot the bolt home.

In the lounge, Som was already wearing her cloak, hood thrown back, and she held out a spare one for Asta. It was lighter in her arms than the heavy velvet she wore the night she escaped the Scattering, silk flowing down smooth as water around her hips and calves as she flung it around her shoulders. The hood was light too, sweeping low over her eyebrows, and Som drew the mask across to conceal her face. Only her eyes were on display. Her Atrathene eyes, with their white irises . . .

"No one will look closely at you." Som covered her own scarred face, solid gold eyes shadowed by the cloth. "We walk. The local temple isn't far. Stay quiet and everything will be fine."

The masked trio headed up the stairs, out through the coach house entrance into the suffocating post-noon heat that rebounded off the white pavements and hurt Asta's eyes. The heat drove most of the people of Abonnae indoors at this time of day. Babies wailed from behind closed shutters, dogs yapped at their passage, voices were raised in hot, tired irritation. The few people on the streets, eyes downcast, crossed the street to avoid the Shadow Cloaks. They moved without appearing to hurry in the searing heat, but there was no doubt they were getting out of the way.

The temple Ranmiro had taken Gartzea to was around half a mile away, but the journey seemed longer, on foot, under the blazing sun. Asta wished they could ride, but nobody rode in

Abonnae, and her left heel had developed a nagging blister by the time they arrived. The chapel was far smaller than the Red Temple, and much less imposing. She would have walked past it without noticing if Som hadn't stopped in the middle of the street of shuttered shops, and gestured.

"Here we are."

A pair of roughly carved columns indicated the entrance to the hall. Flush with the shops beside them, they exhibited little of the skill that decorated the outside of the Red Temple. There was no gate, just an arch leading to a plain courtyard where a few cats lounged in what little shade the walls cast. On the far side of the courtyard was a plain-looking door, standing ajar to catch a breeze that wasn't blowing.

Som and Ilu exchanged a glance, and it was as if their features shifted, even though Asta couldn't see them. Their stance changed, Ilu's hand dropping to rest lightly on the blade at her hip as she fell in behind her sister. Som stood more upright, her brow furrowing slightly as a spasm of joint-ache ran through her. Her hand twitched towards her own sword.

Beyond the door, the corridor was shady, markedly cooler than the streets outside. There was a desk beside the door, a plump little man sprawled across it, dozing in a bar of sunshine like a cat. Som raised an eyebrow, drew her dagger, and slammed it into the desk between his splayed fingers.

The man lurched backwards with a startled grunt, smacking his head against the wall behind him, and made a noise that sounded like "hnurgh!" He blinked furiously, eyes clearing as they focused on the black cloak, the hilt of the blade still quivering, the tip buried an inch into the soft wood. His lips trembled, but all that emerged was a faint squeak.

"We're here to see a man who was brought in early this morning," Som said, her voice clear despite the mask.

The receptionist gulped. "The dog bite?"

Ilu nudged Asta hard in the ribs, and her eyes gleamed.

"The bite, yes. We'll see him now."

"I don't know if . . ."

He craned back as Som leaned forward, until he was pressed against the wall.

"I said we'll see him now. Where is he?"

He pointed with shaking hand. "Down the corridor, turn left and it's the first door. But you can't—"

"Don't tell me what I can't do." Som wrenched her knife free of the tabletop and slid it back into the sheath at the nape of her neck. "Come on, my sisters."

Ilu swirled her cloak with a touch more drama than necessary, letting the light catch the hilt of her sword. Asta stuck to the shadows. The man behind the reception desk, if not a priest, was someone who worked for priests, and she had a distinctive face in this part of the world, even if it was covered right now. She didn't want it getting back to Chesserai, or whoever ran the Red Temple now, that she had been here.

"He won't see you, you know," Ilu said in an undertone as they strode down the corridor.

"What do you mean?"

"The cloaks. If you stick to the shadows, people's eyes sort of . . . slide off them. That's the best way to describe it. Some magic in the fabric makes it hard to see in even a little darkness, as long as you're careful. And you strike me as excessively careful, Asta."

Asta shrugged. "Better to be cautious than dead."

"My philosophy too. We'll make an assassin of you soon enough."

Asta had no desire to be an assassin. She said nothing, following in Ilu's footsteps, keeping to the shadow of the wall. Som and Ilu's midnight-black cloaks played tricks with her eyes, flickering in and out of her vision. She had to concentrate to keep them slipping from the corners of her eyes, and the effort made her head ache. She was relieved when they passed from the darkened corridor into a bright white room, where there were no shadows to hide in.

The sides of the room were open to the humid air. Everything was thrown into too-sharp relief, buildings outlined against the wine-dark sky as the clouds piled up before the sun, and, with a rustle that swiftly grew into a roar, the skies tore open.

Asta backed away from the open wall as the lightning speared down, and Som's words were lost under a roll of thunder. She was gesturing towards a tall woman who approached them, her face twisted into a frown of consternation. She wore priest's robes, her long hair twisted into buns that rode high on either side of her head, like the ears of a small dog. She offered no gesture of respect beyond the merest inclination of her head.

"Can I help you?"

Som waited for the next rumble of thunder to pass before she replied.

"We're looking for our friend. He was brought here this morning. A dog bite."

The woman's upper lip twitched. "We don't have any *dog* bites . . ."

Ilu leant in beside her sister. "He was bitten by a vicious foreign *dog*. Maybe we have it leashed, for now . . . She could slip that lead, couldn't she, sister?"

Asta glared. How dare Ilu use her to threaten this woman? She wasn't their slave, and she wouldn't kill on demand.

The priestess bristled. "Are you threatening me?"

"We never threaten. We only promise. Where is our friend?"

"I warn you, your black ways have no authority here. The Temple—"

"The Temple grows arrogant. There's nowhere beyond the reach of the Shadow Cloaks, and you'd be wise to remember that," Som told her. "Our friend?"

"He's down there." The priestess pointed to a bed at the far end of the room. "And you call *us* arrogant. The Deity knows all. The day will come when he will crush you and your master underfoot—"

"This way, is it?" Asta wanted to hear nothing of the Deity.

All she wanted was to confirm Gartzea was well and then get out of here, away from the crushing humidity that made her scalp itch like fury under her hood. She raised her voice over the sound of the rain as it sheeted down, only kept out of the room by younger priests wielding mops. She supposed having open walls to catch the slightest draft put them at a disadvantage every time the rains came, but they had a well-rehearsed routine, as choreographed as a line of dancers, moving as one to hold back the invasive water that tried to creep between the high beds and across the well-scrubbed floor.

Around half the beds were occupied, and she tried not to stare at the invalids as they passed, hoping none of them were infectious. She was grateful for the mask that covered her mouth and nose, no matter how hot it was. Gartzea's was the last bed on the right, and she tucked into the gap between the bed and the outside wall, grateful he wasn't beside an open wall, and away from the damp.

As the shadows of the three women fell across him, his eyelids fluttered. They looked bruised in the murky light, and his arm, held across his body outside of the thin sheet that covered him, was still swollen, the bandage damp with fluid. His eyes were too bright; fever bright. Som glanced around to check they weren't overlooked and let her own mask fall, bending to give her friend a swift kiss on the cheek before she covered up again. He looked at her in confusion. "Som? Why are you here?"

"You asked for us. What's happening?" She remained standing while Ilu sat cross-legged on the end of the bed. She had her cutting wire in her hands, polishing the thin strand with a soft cloth, but all the while her eyes scanned the room for trouble. Asta, feeling awkward, leaned against the wall. She wished she had something to do with her hands. She buried them beneath her silken cloak and hoped Som would hurry up. There might still be a chance they could retrieve Rhodan and catch the next tide.

Gartzea rolled his head to one side and caught Asta's eye. His face tightened. "Dirty bitch," he muttered.

"Leave her, Gartzea," Ilu said calmly. "She's under my protection."

"Since when?"

"Since I said so."

"She wasn't to know this would happen," Som added. "She was protecting her boy."

"I can speak for myself," Asta insisted.

Ilu curled her lip. "Speak, then."

Asta dropped to her haunches so her face was level with Gartzea's. The heat poured off his skin, and sweat dappled his creased brow and lodged in his eyelashes, as if he was crying. "Gartzea? I'm sorry I bit you. I didn't think it would come to this."

She realised he was crying; what she had taken for drops of sweat were tears, falling unheeded on the sheet, although he made no sound. His lips were dry, and she poured some tepid water from the night stand into a glass and held it to his mouth, watching as he swallowed. His voice was so low she had to almost press her ear to his mouth.

"They're taking my sword hand."

"What?"

"They're taking my *sword* hand, you fucking bitch!" With shocking speed he lunged forward, teeth snapping at her earlobe. She heard the click as his teeth came together, felt the rush of his breath in her ear. She raised her fist to slam him down, but he had fallen back on the bed, panting, eyes wide and furious.

"They might not," Som said amicably, as if the incident had never happened.

"They told me they were. Tomorrow afternoon. Fucking Atrathene!" His voice was too loud, and Som hushed him with a gesture. "They want to cripple us all, Som. They know—" He turned his head to the side, broken. "Ederon didn't come. I thought he would come . . ."

"It's too dangerous for him to come here. You know that. It could blow all our cover." Som stroked his hand.

"They don't know anything," Ilu said sharply. "We'll get you

337

out; get you to a decent healer. What about Salbador? Is he still in town?"

Som shook her head. "Temple came looking for him, and he left town. He's in Malancha du Roan, last I heard."

Ilu flicked her wire. "We have a boat."

"You think he can be moved?"

"What other choice—" Ilu lowered her voice as one of the priests tending the sick looked around, noticed them, and dropped his gaze to the floor "—do we have?"

"They won't let him walk out of here freely. We'll have to negotiate. And what about Asta?"

"What about me?" Asta demanded. "I thought Rhodan and I were sailing today?"

Som shook her head. "Tomorrow. I'll talk to the priest here, and Ranmiro. I'll get Gartzea out, with *both* his hands." She smiled down at him. "We'll set them on the early tide for Malancha du Roan, and then on to Atrath. Does that sound like a plan?"

Ilu snorted. "Not much of one. We could have used a fighting man. Or woman."

"We'll have to get by with what we've got. Asta's given us a better chance than we had before. Let her live her life now."

Ilu whistled through her teeth, but said nothing. Gartzea's bruised eyes closed again, lashes dark against waxen cheeks. His lips moved in fevered prayer, and from behind Ilu, there was a gentle cough.

"I think you should leave now. Your friend needs to rest and regain his strength. The Deity will help him."

Ilu stashed the wire in her sleeve with dazzling sleight-of-hand. "Is there a chance he could keep his hand?" she asked the priest.

He was wheeling a small portable burner on a trolley in front of him, and he leaned on the handle and gave her a long, appraising look. "If the Deity is willing, anything can happen. Will you pray for your friend?"

"Do you think it will help?"

"Rest will help as much as prayer. Probably more." He poured some water into an earthenware mug, and the familiar scent of herbal tea rose up. "Now, if you could excuse me?"

"I don't think—" But Som, rising to leave, shook her head in quick warning. The priest was nodding and smiling, ushering them on their way. As they left Asta looked back over her shoulder to see him raising the drink to Gartzea's lips with infinite care and tenderness.

"Are we going now, Tante Asta?"

It was the fourth time in a row Rhodan had asked that question. Asta could have cheerfully throttled him. He bounced next to her in the gig, crammed up against her side, and every squirm set off fresh aches on her bruised skin.

"I just told you, yes!"

"Are we going on a boat? Will it be a big boat, like last time?"

"A small boat. And it won't be like last time. Now button it." The prospect of being trapped in the tight confines of the *Aguia* with both Gartzea and an excitable Rhodan for the duration of the journey to Malancha was not a prospect Asta relished.

"Will there be horses?" He stared at the black gelding pulling the gig, his voice full of longing.

"I miss riding too. This boat's too small, but when we get home all the horses in the world will be there, waiting for you."

"How long will it take, Tante Asta?"

"I don't know. Not long, I hope."

They rounded a corner and the broad sweep of the harbour unfurled before them as the salt tang of the ocean sharpened. Rhodan tugged Asta's sleeve excitedly. "It smells like home!"

"It does a bit. Is this where they took you, when you got off the big boat?"

He frowned. "I had a bag over my head. They made us walk a hundred miles before they took the bags off, and then they took us to a wet place in the woods. There were lots of people there. We slept in stables. I wanted my ma, but she was in the sea . . ." he trailed off.

"I went there looking for you. I walked all the way from the harbour. It was a very long way."

"Hundreds of miles?"

"Very nearly."

Ilu, driving the gig, glanced over her shoulder as she slowed the black to a halt. "I hate to interrupt this cheerful reminiscence, but we walk from here."

Asta lifted Rhodan down onto the sun-warmed pavement. The full heat of the day had yet to kick in, and the morning air was pleasant. The strong breeze blew spray off the ocean, cooling her limbs and face. Street hawkers lined the harbour, selling everything from chilled drinks to icons of the Red Temple carved from pink coral, squabbling with the warehouse owners whose doors they were blocking. Most of the carts had little wheels, and rolled aside to let cargoes pass, but sometimes they didn't roll quick enough, and then the dock-workers would provide a too-hearty shove. This led to inevitable quarrels, but the presence of the liveried Temple Guards, lurking now on every street corner, ensured fisticuffs were kept to a minimum.

Ilu followed Asta's line of sight. "It's not them you have to worry about."

"Who, then?" Asta muttered back. She walked a pace behind, rope knotted loosely around her wrists, Rhodan's hand tucked in the crook of her arm. Ilu had suggested it would be safer if they still appeared to be slaves, but no amount of cajoling or threats could persuade Rhodan to be bound. He was as obstinate as his father when the occasion demanded it.

"Temple spies. They're everywhere. Animal and human. Why do you think everyone is so well behaved? You never know who's watching."

Asta felt a cold shudder at the prospect. That seagull, standing on a stanchion surveying the harbour; were Chesserai's eyes watching her above that malevolent curved beak? Would a human hand clamp down on her shoulder at any moment, escorting her back to the Red Temple to face bloody justice? She wished she was wearing a shadow-cloak, that she might take Rhodan under its folds, protect both of them from prying eyes. "Can't we go any faster?" she hissed.

"And draw attention to ourselves? Smart. Besides," Ilu shrugged," we're nearly there."

Rhodan tugged Asta's arm. "Can I get a drink?"

"No."

"Please, I'm really thirsty!"

Ilu fished in her purse, eyes snapping above her mask. "Get him his bloody drink. We've got time." She released the loose rope. Asta gathered it over her arm and steered Rhodan across the street to a vendor selling jewellery, curios and a side line in lime juice over crushed ice. The ice was melting in the heat, and while she watched him spoon it into a cup and crush the limes, Rhodan investigated the stall. She heard him give a little squeak of excitement, and stilled him with her hand. When they were away from the stall she handed him the drink. "What was that about?" she asked.

Rhodan had an object clasped tightly in his hand. "He had this." He held it out, shyly. "It's you, isn't it?"

Asta took the cameo. The carving was cruder than the ones she had seen on the Scattering, when she and Finn had ghosted through the streets, but there was no mistaking the source. She frowned. "Did you steal this, Rhodan?"

"It's you!"

"I know it's me. It's wrong to steal. Wait here while I give it back."

"But—"

"You're not in trouble. Go and wait with Ilu. Let me talk to the man."

The stallholder watched her as she approached. He had a broad, open face, and he didn't seem to care that she was a slave.

"Problem with your drink, miss?"

She shook her head. "My son took this from your stall. I was returning it. You know how kids are."

"Got four of my own, little beggars." He took the cameo from her and placed it back on the stall without looking at it, to her relief.

"They're interesting pieces. I think the colour caught his eye. Did you make them yourself?"

He shook his head. "Got them off a copperhead trader."

"The Scattering?"

"Right enough. I think it's one of their queens or something." He shrugged. "I thought they'd make good paper. Your mistress want to buy it?"

"No thanks." She caught his flicker of disappointment. "But she will have a drink. I've got the paper for that."

She returned to Ilu and Rhodan with the drink in its reed-woven cup sending a pleasant chill through her palm. Rhodan had finished his, his upper lip stained with juice. He frowned, and dragged the back of his hand across his mouth. "Sorry, Tante Asta."

"No harm done. But don't steal anything else!" She shook her head at Ilu. "I was never made to be a parent."

"Everyone thinks that before they become one. I've found the *Aguia*, she's this way."

Ilu led the way down a long pontoon. Beneath their feet, the sea was visible through gaps in the planking, gurgling around the piles that held the edifice up. There were small vessels tied up on either side, mostly pleasure yachts, but a few fishing boats jostled against them, bouncing on the tide. As the *Aguia* hove into view Asta felt her heart lift. It didn't matter how long the journey took, or what diversions they had to make on the way, or even that she would be sleeping shoulder to shoulder with Gartzea, who hated her. They were going home.

I told you I could do it, little brother!

Even the gaping hole Finn had left in her life didn't feel so terrible at that moment, with Rhodan tugging her hand and Marcio yowling a welcome from the stern. She tickled him under the chin as she stepped onto the deck, and fussed him behind his ears. "Clever little spy!"

The cat purred, and butted her hand as Ranmiro emerged from below decks.

"Is Gartzea here yet?" she asked him.

"Not yet." His face clouded. "He should be. The tide has already turned. I don't want to be stuck here."

"I'll walk down and see if I can spot them," Ilu suggested, stepping neatly over Rhodan, who lay on his stomach fussing the cat. Asta sat on deck, watching Ranmiro humming to himself as he prepared to leave.

"Ranmiro? How far is it to Malancha du Roan?"

"Four days, with a fair wind. Not too long to be stuck with Gartzea!" He grinned. "Is that what you're worried about?"

"Something like that." It was taking longer than she wanted, the tide moving more swiftly than she expected, and she had lost sight of dark-cloaked Ilu on the wharf. The nape of her neck prickled, and she couldn't keep her hands still.

"Here they are." Ranmiro, standing, saw what she couldn't. Som and Ilu walked on either side of Gartzea. They were holding him up, and even from this distance Asta noticed his face was a sickly hue and he struggled to keep his footing. As they approached the boat he reeled, and Ranmiro leapt out and caught him before he fell. His sleeve fell back, and Asta stared at the bandaged stump where, only yesterday, his right arm had been. He still had around four inches of heavily-swathed flesh below his elbow, then there was nothing but that horrible, yawning gap.

She shook her head, sure she was seeing it wrong, as Gartzea fumbled wrong-handed for the gunwale and the two sisters lifted him bodily into the boat and pressed him into a seated position on the deck, taking their places on either side of him. Asta wasn't sure whether their stance was to support their friend, or to protect her from his anger, but either way she was grateful for it.

He curled in on himself, nursing his stump with his left hand, groaning softly.

"What happened?" Asta asked. "They weren't meant to take it until this afternoon!"

"There was a mix up." Som's voice was a low snarl. "A misunderstanding, or a decision made at some *higher level*."

"Higher level? Oh!" It dawned on Asta. "The priests crippled him because he's a friend of yours. Because you're Shadow-cloaks, or because you're helping me?"

"Could be either," Ilu said grimly. "We'll have to assume the worst."

"That means they could be coming here, right now. Som, were you followed?"

Som's eyes hardened. She reached for her pipe pouch, then let her hands fall. "Not by any human," she said.

The sky was full of eyes, the gulls of the air, the fish of the ocean, the cats of the temple grounds. All watching their every move.

"I suggest we set sail," Ranmiro said, "as soon as possible. Am I still taking Gartzea to Malancha?"

"I can talk." Gartzea's voice was slurred, though whether through drink or herb or too much pain, Asta couldn't tell.

"Talk, then," Ranmiro said. "What do you want to do?"

"There's little fucking point going to Salbador, is there? He can't grow me a new hand . . ."

"You want to stay here?" Ilu asked. "After what the Temple did to you? Shit, Ranmiro, maybe we should have taken him to a street-butcher after all."

"Do you really think Malancha will be free of priests and their kind? The Deity has a thousand mouths, remember . . ."

"And they all need feeding," Asta finished for him. He rewarded her with a glare.

"I want revenge. I lost my arm—"

"We've all lost things," Som remarked. "And people. You'll go to Malancha –."

"I'm going nowhere," Gartzea insisted.

"Stay here then, but cool your head and learn to fight left handed. Let the heat die down for a while."

She had filled her pipe as she spoke, and she passed it to him to suck on. He held it awkwardly, head wreathed in smoke, the creases smoothing from his face. He sighed. "You're a good woman, Som."

"Everything looks better over a pipe." She watched him smoke, hand twitching in her lap. "I think that's enough now . . ."

He passed it back with reluctance. "I know you're right," he said. "Doesn't mean I have to feel good about it. It's going to be hard to learn."

"This is the life we chose, Gartzea," Ilu said. "But Asta didn't. She gets to go home. One day, we all will."

Asta looked around at her companions, seeing them with fresh eyes. It had never occurred to her, and they had never let on, that they might be far from home, or missing family. Ilu had mentioned a son, but that was as far as it went. She really knew very little about them beyond the fact that they killed for money, and men like Bernaldus were scared of them.

Ilu was the first to shake off the moment. "We should go," she said. "Let Ranmiro catch the tide." She extended her hand to Asta. "Have a safe journey. I hope you find your way back to your people."

As Asta gripped her wrist in a friendly gesture, a bell began chiming from the high tower that stood on a promontory at one end of the harbour. The tone was picked up and echoed, first by the temple bells, then the watchtower on the opposite point, and bells in the warehouses and on the streets. Within a few moments the whole of Abonnae echoed with urgent clamour.

"What's that?" Asta had to shout over the noise, it reverberated down her breastbone and rattled her ribs. Rhodan scowled, and clapped his hands over his ears in silent protest. "Is that because of us?"

"No!" Ilu hollered back. "That's the Sea Bell! The city is under attack!"

"Attack? From where?"

"From the sea!"

"The sea?"

Ranmiro leapt from his seat and bounded over to the mast, scaling it hand over hand, lithe and agile as a cat. He swayed in the topmost rigging, scanning the horizon with one hand shielding his eyes, and Asta saw him start in surprise. He slithered back down to the deck so fast the descent left rope-burns on his palms.

"Copperheads," he said, rubbing his hands and wincing. "Dozens of them, and white-hairs and some I don't recognise, but mainly Scattering ships. They're heading this way. Lucky they're against the wind. We might be able to slip out under their forward bows, but only if we leave right now. And it's risky either way. What's it to be?"

"Why would the Scattering come here?" Gartzea asked.

Asta had a horrible feeling she knew, and when she caught Ilu's eye, she could see the Shadow Cloak thought the same way.

"I think they've come for me."

"They couldn't come up with another goddess to sacrifice?" Gartzea was obviously feeling better; his sarcastic tone was back.

"They think I'm the real *sumri gudienne*, from what I gathered. I don't know what's been happening in their tribe since I left, but this might be a last-gasp effort to get me back, or destroy themselves in the doing of it. They have nothing to lose now."

"What do you want to do?" Ranmiro insisted again. "Leave now, or get caught up in a war? Because I'm going. Being trapped in a harbour under siege is no place for a man of my talents. Gartzea? Sure you want to stay here?"

Gartzea rose, swaying slightly. "Som's right," he said. "I can throw a punch with my left hand, and I've still got a head on my shoulders. My place is here."

Ilu helped him out of the boat and onto the pontoon. Som followed, grunting at the pain in her joints. Asta looked at the three of them, standing together, caught between the Scattering assault and the machinations of the Temple. They had been good to her. They had saved Rhodan, they had asked no more than she could give, and now they were letting her go.

She turned to Ranmiro. "Can you do something for me?"

"For a Goddess? Almost anything."

"Will you take Rhodan to Malancha du Roan, and look after him there until I arrive? I'll pay good paper."

"Tante Asta—?"

"Quiet!" She pulled him into her arms. "You must be good, understand?"

Ranmiro's eyebrow quirked. "And where will you be?"

"I'll be here. I've got two good fighting hands, and I know the Red Temple well. I can be useful. I owe the sisters a great debt, and Gartzea a greater one. But Rhodan needs to be protected. I promised my brother."

"Tante Asta!" He squirmed in her embrace. "I'm not going on the boat without you! I want to help!"

"You'll go on the boat, Rhodan. I told your da I'd keep you safe. Ranmiro will look after you."

"I'm staying with you!" He clung to her, fiery and obstinate. She had to prise his hands off her shirt and pass them to Ranmiro, first one and then the other. She couldn't look at him, squirming, wrists held firmly, his face reddening as if he was about to cry. "Just . . . look after him, will you?"

"As if he was my own. You are a courageous Goddess. The blood of heroes flows within you."

Asta turned away. She had never felt less like a hero. "Shall I cast you off?"

"If you would!" The bells were clamouring, Rhodan was yelling his indignation, and Asta knew that somewhere in the Spirit Realm, Finn was cursing her with all the foul names he knew. Her head was splitting apart from all the noise as she found the mooring rope, loosed it, and let it fall into the sea before stepping into Som's comforting embrace.

I can't watch him go. Forgive me, Finn. Would you have him stay in a city under attack?

Som guided her down the pontoon, away from the sea. They were halfway to shore when instinct, a kick to her brain that must have come from Finn, made her look back.

The *Aguia* was on her way out of the harbour. Ranmiro hunched over the tiller, focussed on avoiding the dozens of small boats that jostled each other as they fled the port before the oncoming wave of Scattering ships, now visible as a menacing line on the horizon. A little figure standing on the bow rail had to be Rhodan, and she watched as he curled, stretched, and then all at once, he was gone, a sleek black shape diving into the crowded waters of the harbour.

"Rhodan!" She moved without thought, kicking off her light shoes as she ran the length of the pontoon and dived head-first into the choppy sea.

The first few inches of water were sun warmed, hot as blood, but the chill below stole her breath with its suddenness. She surfaced, eyes streaming, and struck out hard for the *Aguia,* for the spot where Rhodan had vanished. The waters were less crowded here, the pleasure craft and fishing boats already scattering, but the outgoing tide dragged at her limbs, and the surge made it hard to see.

"Rhodan!"

He could have been dragged under by the current, or the wake of a departing ship. She couldn't see him anywhere. Limbs aching and skin stinging with salt, Asta trod water as best she could, trying to regain her bearings.

"Rhodan!"

Looking back, she could see the jetty where Som and Ilu waited, dark figures against the sky. They had been joined by a small crowd, curiosity overcoming natural caution and the desire to flee. She had drifted closer to another pontoon, longer and wider, for larger ships. Most of them were still in place, slower to escape than their more nimble sisters. The water sucked at the dark spaces between their hulls, a confusion of light and darkness and ever shifting tide.

"Rhodan, where are you?"

"Over here!" The cry ended in a croak, but it made Asta's heart leap. She swam, a slow breast stroke, trying to see where the little voice had come from.

"Where?"

"Under the pier. Come quick!"

She swam between two of the looming ships, their intersecting shadows throwing the water below into deep blackness and even greater cold. Their bulk blotted out the sky. It was like swimming down a long, dark tunnel.

"Rhodan, I can't see! Keep talking and I'll find you."

His voice was small and scared. "My fingers are slipping . . ."

"Hang on!" She saw the struts of the pier rising through the darkness, and a paler shape clinging to one of them, bounced up and down by the rhythm of the waves. As she reached for him he let go, and her hand caught his barnacle-torn fingers before he could be ripped away from her once more. She wrapped her other arm around the wooden piling and hung there, trying to regain her breath.

"Tante Asta, I'm sorry . . ."

"Are you hurt?"

His hands were bleeding, and he looked bruised and battered, but as far as she could tell he had no broken bones. He shook his head.

"Then let's get out of here before you do get hurt." She drew in a deep breath, and bellowed. "Hoy! The ship! Down here!"

The scramble of footsteps directly overhead, and an upside down face appeared, level with Asta's. As far as she could tell, the sailor looked surprised.

"What are you doing down here?"

"Looking for a way up. Can you help us?"

"Hang on!"

Asta grinned at that. There didn't seem to be any other option. "Can you hang on, Rhodan?"

He had one arm around the piling, the other gripping her

thickening waist, fingers digging in above her hip. He nodded. "I won't let go of you, Tante Asta. You're safe now."

"I might let go of you! What were you thinking, you stupid boy?"

He was spared from having to reply by the slither of a rope with a sliding loop on the end, snaking over the side of the jetty. Asta let go of him and made a grab for it, working it down over Rhodan's head and shoulders and tightening it under his armpits. She gave the rope a few sharp tugs.

"Wait for me on the jetty. No running off!"

Rhodan frowned, kicking off from the piling and using his hands to help his ascent as he was lifted by unseen helpers, legs thrashing as he vanished from sight. Asta tightened her grip on the wooden support. The muscles in her shoulders burned, and there was an unfamiliar churning deep in her belly.

You hang on too. She sent the whispered thought to her children, wondering if they felt her cold, her fatigue. She hoped not. She hoped they were warm, and safe, and unaware.

There was a thump, like the kick of a coney, against her kidneys. It startled her so much she almost let go of the pier. One of her twins had made their presence felt for the very first time.

Asta felt a slow glow of happiness spreading through her chest as the rope descended once more. *Nice of you to say hello, little one!* She hoped Finn, wherever he was, still had a protective arm around them, just as she had one around Rhodan.

She had to let go of the jetty and tread water while she pulled the rope over her head, tightening it around her bruised ribs. She tugged it, and was lifted free of the water. It streamed off her skin and out of her clothes as she was hauled back towards solid ground, towards the light. Her shoulder crashed into the edge of the pier as she swung round, and she bit back a cry of pain, but then half a dozen hands were on her, pulling her up and setting her down. The damp wood beneath her bare feet steamed as the sun warmed it. Rhodan stood before her, shame-faced, and she was across to him in two strides to deliver a ringing slap around the face. He didn't try and dodge the blow, but his face darkened and his eyes were suspiciously bright.

"Don't you ever do anything that stupid again! What were you thinking?" She gave him a hard shake. "What would your da say if you drowned?"

"I'm sorry!" The tears were creeping from his eyes now. "I wanted to stay with you!"

"I told you, it's not safe! Why didn't you go with Ranmiro?"

Rhodan sniffed hard. Snot dripped from his nose, and he wiped it with a bleeding hand. "Because I want to *help*," he insisted.

"Rhodan, you're six. How much help can you be?"

His face was scarlet. "I don't want you to die like everyone else!"

The cry melted away her anger. She gathered him in her arms, pressing him close as he resisted. "I'm not going to die, Rhodan."

"That's what Ma said!" He pushed against her, fighting free. "On the boat. She promised me, but she still died!"

Oh Rhodan . . . "It's not a promise anyone can make, Rhodan. Your ma did her best, and that's what I'm doing. We've been good at staying alive so far, haven't we?" She touseled his hair and he nodded reluctantly. "So let's carry on doing what we're doing, and we'll both get to go home." She straightened, keeping him close against her leg. "Thank the nice men who rescued you. It's important to be polite."

Their rescuers were at the far end of the jetty, talking to Som and Ilu, and Asta saw paper change hands. Ilu's voice raised to carry to her. "Thank you for rescuing my slaves. I'll see they're disciplined when I get them home."

Asta nudged Rhodan in the back, and he immediately looked suitably contrite, hanging his head and letting his shoulders slump. The men who had rescued them barely spared her a glance as they headed back up the jetty towards their ship. They had returned some lost property, that was all, not saved two human lives.

"Come on." Som loosely tied her hands, and delivered Rhodan a light cuff around the head. "Let's get back to the carriage."

"Where's Gartzea?" Asta asked.

"He thought it wise to make himself scarce. But it looks like you're in charge of Ranmiro's cat!"

Marcio had jumped ship and was wrapped around her ankles, purring. He must have jumped unnoticed from the *Aguia* before she had cast off from the jetty, as his fur was still dry. Rhodan picked him up and held him to his shoulder, cradling him like a baby. "Where are we going now?" he asked.

Asta turned to look back over the harbour. The *Aguia* was a quickly vanishing dot, one vessel among many. Ranmiro would not be back. He was a pragmatist, not a romantic. And she wouldn't trust anyone else to take Rhodan to the end of the street and back, let alone halfway down the coast. They were stranded in Abonnae, caught between the Red Temple and the approaching copperhead ships that had crossed the ocean to hunt her down. She clutched Rhodan closer to her, and shivered.

TWENTY-FOUR

FOR THREE DAYS the Scattering ships had ringed the harbour. Nothing got in, nothing got out, and Abonnae, caught by surprise, was feeling the pinch. The temple guard were everywhere, watching as the stores emptied, quelling quarrels with the judicious application of violence. The Red Temple declared that daily prayer and offerings were compulsory for everyone, with dire punishments hinted at for anyone judged to be lax in their devotions. Asta and Ilu, in their cloaks, had already dodged two patrols on their long walk back to the slave market on Winding Street.

Asta kept her back to the warm stones of the wall, breathing softly as the heavy tramp of the patrol passed by a few feet away. The shadows enveloped her, protected her, but she couldn't quiet the hammering of her heart and she feared it would give them away. She could barely see Ilu, poised against the opposite wall. Only the faint glint as she shook out her strangling wire, and only that because she knew where to look.

The steady footsteps passed into the distance. Ilu slid away from the wall, a shadow detaching itself from the darkness and walking alone. Her voice sounded close to Asta's ear.

"I am fucking *sick* of this!"

"Me too. I wish we still had the carriage." All the carriages, and the horses, had been seized the day before as 'assets'. They belonged to Gartzea, as did the house, and there was nothing anyone could do about it without drawing undue attention to themselves.

"Ah well, it's good to get our legs stretched. Better our legs than our necks!" They set off again, sticking to the shadows, watching out for patrols. The streets were almost deserted. The people who hadn't been corralled into one of the Temples were staying indoors, and those out on the streets moved as furtively as Ilu and Asta, pretending not to notice anyone else.

Asta's stride faltered as they approached the entrance to Winding Street. There was still a murmur from the slave market, but it was quieter, internal trade rather than the bustling, lucrative import and export that usually went on. The slave traders would soon feel the screws tightening as much as anyone, if the blockade wasn't lifted. She didn't care anything for their pockets, but she didn't think she could face Bernaldus again.

"Let me do the talking," Ilu muttered. "If you hang back and keep quiet, he's likely to mistake you for my sister. Unless you want to go all-in and stick a blade between his eyes? I wouldn't blame you . . ."

"It's tempting." Asta was doubly grateful for her mask as they passed between the slave-pens. No matter how they tried to disguise the stink with perfume and sea-water, it would never wholly fade, and it took her back in an instant to the hold of the slave-ship, the wretched human cargo dying in their chains. If she could help to end that, even in a small way, then Finn and Lefalli may not have died in vain, and the hole in her spirit might start to heal.

No one was watching, and she reached out and casually opened the bolts on the pens as they passed. A tiny, defiant gesture, and she wasn't sure any of the caged slaves even noticed, but it made her feel better. They emerged into the bright sunlight of the yard behind the market. Nothing here had changed; there were still the same high glass-topped walls and sturdy gates, and the shambolic hut leaning up against the wall. Tarese was washing down a naked male slave, an old man who crouched in the dirt with his hands thrown up defensively as she sluiced him with water. His back and shoulders were striped white with whip scars, and he shivered and wept under the barrage.

Tarese saw them, set the bucket down carefully, and walked over, keeping a wary distance. Her eyes flicked between them without any spark of recognition. "What can I do to help you two ladies?" she asked.

"We're looking for a slave. A woman. She might have passed through here a few days ago."

"The Atrathene? You're not the first to ask. She went off with some of your . . . *colleagues*. I told the others that."

"What others?" Asta asked sharply. Over her mask, Ilu shot her a glare.

"The copperheads. They were here yesterday, asking if we had any horse-women with white patches on their skin. They offered good paper. But anyway," she sniffed, "if you want her, she's long gone."

Asta was profoundly grateful for the cloak that swept to the floor. "Not her," Ilu said. "This was a Southern woman with no ears."

"Oh, that bitch. "Tarese's sullen lips curled in distaste. "You don't want her. We have plenty of better goods than that. That one's disobedient to the core. She'll end up god-fodder if she's not careful. What about," she prodded the bundle at her feet with her toe, and the old man groaned, "a nice biddable old gent to help you round the house? He's wiry, this one."

To Asta's eyes the old man was not so much wiry as emaciated. He didn't look capable of lifting his own head from the ground, let alone wielding a yard broom.

Ilu's eyes hardened. "We don't need yard help. We want the woman. It's business. Where is she?"

Tarese frowned. "You'll have to speak to my husband. Bernaldus!"

There was a sleepy rumble inside the hut. Tarese was about to go and wake her husband when Asta reached out and grabbed her arm. "How much for the old man?" she asked.

"Two hundred. Bernaldus might go as low as one-fifty, but no lower."

Ilu leaned in. "Why don't you go and get him," she suggested, in a bittersweet tone, "and we might negotiate. If you bring us the earless woman, that is."

As Tarese vanished into the hut, Ilu turned on Asta. "What are you doing? We're not made of paper, you know?"

"Ilu, he's an old man. We can't leave him here. If I had my way I wouldn't leave anyone here."

"Fucking soft, you are." Ilu fell silent as the door to the shed opened. Bernaldus emerged, shirtless and flabby, knuckling sleep from his eyes. Ilu swaggered forward, hand on her hip.

"Hello, fat man. Remember me?"

He stared into her opaque eyes, and blanched. "The one I sold you, I got her in good faith from the Temple. Whatever she's done, she's your responsibility now." He nodded at Tarese. "Get him dressed and take him to the pens. I'll handle this."

"Get him dressed and bring him back to us," Ilu said. "We'll pay seventy-five."

"He's worth two hundred."

She drew her blade with a weary sigh. "Eighty, and only if you tell us what we want to know. He looks like he'll be dead within a week anyway."

"One twen—" Ilu's blade twitched. "Ninety. Though I'm cutting my own throat there."

"Would you rather I cut it for you?" But she let her hand drop and Bernaldus visibly relaxed.

"What did you want to know?"

"Sister?" Ilu let Asta take the lead.

"There was a southern woman here a few days ago. She wore a red scarf, and she had no ears. We want her. Where did she go?"

He spat. "Why do you want her? Nothing but trouble."

Asta's hand closed around her dagger, and she spoke clearly, as if Bernaldus was a simpleton. "Is. She. Still. Here?"

"I sent her over to Punishment House. If they can't break her there, she's for the Temple. You still want to buy her? I've got better exotics than her, if that's what you're after. Younger, too."

"Exotics?" Ilu stepped back. "Young boys with dark skin, or northern eyes? That kind of exotic?"

He looked a little askance at her. "We get the best money for them. Did you want one?"

"And you sell them where? To rich old fat men from the Hill?"

"Sometimes. Some go to the Temple. The prettiest ones – there's a good trade with the brothels in Malancha. The priests don't look so closely into the business there. I've got some nice boys in stock. Girls too. Unmarked flesh and all under ten."

Ilu's lips curled in distaste. Asta could feel a deep quaking in her gut, a longing to wipe the money-hungry smile from Bernaldus' face.

"I think we've got what we came for, sister," Ilu said. "At least, I have. You still want something from the fat man?"

"I have something for the fat man, as it happens." Asta forced her voice to stay calm. She saw the acquisitive gleam in Bernaldus' eyes, greed overcoming caution. "Something from the *exotics* he sells like so much meat . . ."

She pushed her hood back and unclipped her mask, exposing her cropped hair, her dark eyes, her ear with the neat triangle of flesh clipped from it, still raw to the touch. "People like you killed my brother. You would have called him an exotic, too."

"There's no need to be hasty, horse-girl. I sold you to a pair of fine ladies.—"

"Flattery won't get you off the hook, fat man," Ilu remarked, lounging against the wall. "Besides, my friend is a free woman. She can do as she pleases. I'm not going to stop her."

"You're free, there you are! Look how lucky you are, to be freed by your masters! I did the right thing by you, you must admit . . ."

There was a ripple of silk as Asta drew her dagger. Bernaldus went cross-eyed as she levelled the point just below his sagging chin, digging it in until he squeaked.

"On your knees, fat man. Don't yell for your wife. I can cut your throat before she gets here."

Bernaldus dropped, heavy as a sack of oats falling to the floor, tilting his head backwards to avoid the tip of Asta's dagger. His eyes were wide and liquid, and froth bubbled at the corners of his lips, under his moustache. His thinning hair, loosened from its binding, straggled over one ear.

"Please, don't kill me. Wasn't I good to you? I gave you decent food, I let you stay with the boy . . ." He trailed off as she tightened the knife against his throat, and he gurgled softly.

"You were decent to me. That's why I won't kill you." She felt him relax as she trailed the dagger up his neck to rest with the point tucked in behind his ear. "But I can't forgive you. You need to remember me. Every time you look into the eyes of one of your exotic children, I want you to think of me."

She moved her mouth close to his ear, cradling his sweaty cheek in her free hand to keep his head still. She whispered.

"I am the Summer Goddess of the Scattering. The leader of my tribe, the daughter of a hero. I have the blood of the patchcat in my veins. I travelled halfway across the world to save my brother's son, and there's *nothing* I won't do to protect him. I'm no man's slave, and I don't forget easily. Nor will you."

She shifted her hand to clamp it across his mouth, muffling his squeals as she dug the knife in, slicing, paring flesh from flesh while he bucked and tried to twist his head away. Warm blood poured down her arm, pooled on the ground, sucked in by the thirsty earth below his knees.

Something gave, softly, like taut cloth tearing, and the slave dealer's ear fell away from the side of his head. Asta let go of him, and stepped back as he slumped forward with his mouth hanging open, gibbering in shock.

Ilu raised an eyebrow, and her lips quirked. "Neatly done," she said. "Want to get out of here?"

"I think that would be wise."

"What about the old man? Don't you want to free him?"

Asta increased her pace as the screaming started behind them. "I want to free *everyone*. Let's start with Red."

Punishment House was a forbidding building, square and functional. Built of dull slate-grey stone, it stood four stories high, casting a shadow over the market in the square below. It was surrounded by a high wall, and the only gate Asta could find was a small postern down a narrow alley at the side of the building that seemed to be used as an all-purpose refuse-tip and privy by visitors and market traders alike. It hummed with flies, and the stink made her gorge rise. "This can't be the only way in," she choked.

"It's designed to discourage casual visitors. If you want to see people suffering, you can pay to visit the mad house and poke the insane with sticks. We're squeamish about seeing our slaves beaten and crying. It erodes the idea that they're not really people, when the blood they spill is the same colour as ours." Ilu sounded scathing as she picked her way down the alley, cloak held high out of the dirt. "Are you sure your friend can help us? I don't want to get shit on my shoes for no reason."

"She told me she was good at breaking out of places. It seems logical that she'd be good at breaking into places too. And she has as much reason to hate the Temple as anyone I know."

Ilu shrugged, and adjusted her hood so the shadows cast deeper over her face. "I just hope you know what you're doing. A renegade slave with a grudge sounds like a spark in a powder-keg to me."

"A renegade slave with a grudge like me, you mean?"

"Ah," Ilu winked as she leant over to knock on the door to Punishment House, "but you're special. You're a *Goddess*."

A small hatch in the door slid open. All Asta could see behind it was the glint of eyes and metal, and a harsh voice demanded they state their business.

Ilu set back her shoulders and raised her head. "I am of the Shadow Cloaks. My business is my own. Will you let me pass?"

It was not a request, and the grunts who worked for Punishment House, or at least this particular grunt, did not have the arrogance of a priest. He stepped aside to let them through the gate, keeping his eyes downcast. Ilu caught him by the chin and lifted his face.

"We're looking for a slave. A woman. Who do we ask?"

"The governor might know. He's in his office. Through the main door and up the stairs to the right."

"Thank you." Ilu let him go. The small yard between the outer wall and the main door was deserted, and Asta felt the guard's eyes on her back as they crossed the courtyard. The guard on the larger door, who must have witnessed the exchange even if he was unable to hear their words, let them through without question.

They found themselves in a neat, if sparse, lobby, facing another barred door. High-backed upholstered chairs stood around the walls, and there was a table holding a glass bowl filled with richly-coloured pebbles. A dry water fountain recessed into the wall opposite the stairs, which were protected by a guard wearing livery, rather than the plain helms and breastplate of the two outer defenders.

Ilu walked straight up to him. "My sister and I are here to see the governor about a prisoner. You will take me to him."

The guard sniffed. "We don't have prisoners here."

"Slave brought in for correction, then. One fruit looks the same as another to me."

"The Governor's a busy man. You'll have to wait."

Ilu's hand drifted to her sleeve. "I think he'll see me. If not now, then later, when he's least expecting it . . ."

The guard blinked, and his cheek twitched. "I'll tell him you're here, Miss—?" He waited for Ilu to supply a name.

"You do that. We'll wait here." She sat neatly on one of the chairs, legs crossed at the ankle, and her wire dropped into her hand with practised ease. "Take a seat, sister."

Asta was too restless to sit. She paced the room, running her hand through the smoothed pebbles in the bowl, flicking the broken hand pump on the water fountain, listening at the door that led to the interior of Punishment House. She heard nothing, but she assumed the door was heavily soundproofed. No one in the waiting area would want to hear the cries of those undergoing punishment. The Inyestan way, after all, was to pretend that unpleasant things did not exist.

The guard was upstairs only a brief time, and he returned looking chastened. "The Governor will see you right away. Very top of the stairs. He apologises for the delay."

"As he should, and so should you." Ilu rose, the wire dangling loosely from her hand. The guard was about to say something about weapons, but a cool look from Asta changed his mind. He fell back and let them pass into the stairwell without another word.

The stairs were wide, short flights circling a central column of functional, undecorated grey stone. Ilu took the steps two at a time, leaving Asta puffing in her wake. At the top was a plain door, yet another guard who silently nodded them through, and another antechamber, similar to the one downstairs but more richly decorated. The chairs were less threadbare, there was a religious portrait on the wall, and the water fountain was working, though when Asta drank, the water was brackish and not as refreshing as it could have been.

Ilu waited for her to finish and wipe her mouth before she walked over to the door of the Governor's office and opened it without bothering to knock.

The man sitting behind his desk was in his mid-fifties, Asta guessed, but the pouches under his eyes and his careworn face added a decade to his looks. He sighed as he rose to greet them.

"Only a priest or a shadow-cloak would walk in here the way you did, ladies. I'm glad I'm not dealing with the clergy, at least. And don't worry," he added, as Ilu glanced around, "I keep my office as bug-free as I can. You're safe to talk here."

"Even so, Fytor" Ilu's voice hushed as she took the only other seat in the room and propped her feet up on the Governor's desk, "let's not take any risks." She pushed down her hood and let her mask fall, and at her signal Asta did the same. Refusing to stand in the doorway like a spare rein, she hitched up on the corner of the desk, pushing Ilu's feet out of the way. The Governor raised his eyebrows, but didn't protest the intrusion.

"Is your sister well?" he asked Ilu.

"The usual joint-aches. We've come on behalf of my friend here."

"The free Atrathene?" Fytor looked down at Asta's hand, bloody around the fingertips, resting on his papers. "News travels fast in the city. I've heard you're a woman in some demand."

"Have the Scattering been asking for me here too?"

"It's only a matter of time. I hear they're in discussion with the Red Temple. Rewards have been mentioned." Fytor grinned. "I have my own spies. What did you come here for?" He glanced sidelong at Ilu. "You're not on a job, are you?"

"If I was, I wouldn't come to you at work." Fytor relaxed visibly. "We're here about a slave, a friend of Asta's. What was her name, Asta?"

"Saheen, I think," Asta tried to remember. "She called herself Red. She'd lost her ears, so I guess she's passed through here a few times . . ."

Fytor frowned. "Dark-skinned woman? Darker than you, I mean. From the South?"

Asta nodded.

"I think I know who you mean. You're in luck, she's still here. I was going to sign her over to the Temple. I don't think she has any more sale value, if it's the woman I'm thinking of. Did she kill her daughter?"

The way he said it was so matter of fact, as if he was talking about nothing even as severe as beating a horse, or a dog. Asta's fist curled amid the papers on his desk. "That's what she told me," she said, guardedly. Didn't he *care*?

It would appear not.

"She's on the Transfer Wing. You're lucky I hadn't signed her over already. That would make things more complicated. I have her deeds somewhere here." He gave Asta a gentle shove, and she slipped off the edge of the desk and landed lightly on the balls of her feet. Fytor rummaged through the papers, tidying them into some semblance of the piles they had been in before Asta and Ilu arrived. He flicked through the smallest stack.

"Here we are, yes. Come with me and we'll find her."

Fytor led the way back down the long staircase, back to the waiting room with the dry fountain and the worried-looking guard. He gestured to the big door, with its three intricate locks and heavy iron bars. It might not be called a prison, but Asta knew a prison door when she saw one. It reminded her uncomfortably of great iron door that led to the sacrifice chamber below the Red Temple, the prison of a furious, hungry God.

Inside, the space was cavernous. They stood on a walkway at the edge of a two-story drop into the basement of the building, driven deep into the bedrock of Abonnae. At Asta's feet, on the opposite side of the waist high railing, a net stretched across the gap to the rail opposite. Looking up she saw more floors, more nets, and beyond them, hazy and grey through the curve of a dirty glass dome, the sky. The light that filtered through was greasy and dulled, but it illuminated the heart of Punishment House all the way down to the lowest depths. Sound was distorted by the immense size of the room; she couldn't tell if she heard small sounds close up, or loud ones far away, but she could hear the crack of whips, the groaning of machines and the distant splash of water. Few screams, and she wondered at that, until, as Fytor led them up long ramps to the upper floor, they passed a line of slaves being led in the opposite direction. Every one of them streamed blood from fresh whip scores across their backs and shoulders, and every one had a metal bit, like a horse would, crammed between their teeth and chained behind their heads, mouths forced open and muted, lips split. They couldn't have cried out even if they'd wanted to.

By the time they reached the topmost floor Asta was dreading what she might see. She hung back, leaning over the rail as if it was the gunwale of a ship, trying to hold in her nausea. She looked down into the bowels of the building, and it dawned on her for the first time what the nets were for. If anyone threw himself over the rail, the nets would catch him, stop him plummeting to his death. Life was forever sold cheaply in Inyesta, but even here the lowest slaves still had some monetary worth, and that value, it seemed, overrode even that last desperate snatching at self-determination. A dead slave was worth nothing, after all. To kill themselves, to take back the last right that belonged to them – even that was denied here.

There was a small line of what Fytor referred to as 'holding cells' on the top floor, lifted up out of the stink of blood and shit from below, with only the curve of the dome above them. It was lighter up here, and the air was cleaner. The cells had barred doors, not the solid iron of the lower floors, and slaves who were due to be delivered to the many temples around Abonnae sat or lay in hunched postures of despair. All except Red.

She was in the third cell from the end, crouching down, studying the lock on the barred door. At Fytor's approach, she looked up, and bared her remaining teeth. It was almost a smile.

"Come to toss me into the jaws of the Deity?" she asked caustically.

"Not quite. Looks like you've been thrown yet another final lifeline. If I was a gambling man, I'd wish for your luck."

She ran her tongue over her gums. "That's me. Born lucky."

Fytor wore a bunch of keys at his belt, and he flicked through them. "You might not think yourself so lucky," he warned, as he unlocked the door.

Red stretched as she got to her feet, looking beyond him to Asta and Ilu leaning against the rail, hooded and masked. Her eyes hardened. "I'm not going with them."

"It's them or the Temple. They're willing to pay good paper for your deeds." Fytor looked anxiously at Ilu. "You are, aren't you?"

Ilu nodded. "Why not? I saved some money this morning."

Still Red hung back. "I'd rather take my chances with the demon I know."

Asta pushed herself away from the rail. Her nausea had passed. "Let me talk to her," she said.

Red edged away as she approached, but something in Asta's face made her look back, and closer. Asta pushed her hood back a fraction to reveal her eyes. "Red, it's me. From Winding Street, remember? I had a little boy . . ."

Red narrowed her eyes. "I remember you. Why are you dressed like a Shadow Cloak?"

"It's complicated. But I promise, if you come with us you'll be safe. My friends need your skills."

Red laughed at this. "Skills? They need help to break out of somewhere?"

"Break in, more like. Isn't it better than going to the Temple?"

She shrugged. "Suppose so. Though I'm going to end up there anyway. No sense dragging it out."

Asta extended her hand, and Red regarded it warily. "Trust me. What have you got to lose?"

"Not much, I reckon." Red stood still, hands extended, while Fytor slapped a pair of manacles around her wrists. "Just a precaution," he said. "Legal requirement. You can take them off when you get outside." He handed the chain to Asta while he rustled through his sheaf of papers and presented them to Ilu to sign with her thumbprint. "Just there, and there, and this one . . . all done!" He rolled his own copies of the papers and stowed them inside his worn black jerkin, and Ilu concealed hers in her cloak. Asta caught the flash of steel as she tucked them in between two of her knives and drew out a wad of paper, peeling off some notes and slapping them into Fytor's outstretched palm.

"Pleasure trading with you," she said to him.

He smiled thinly. "And you, and I bet it's rare you hear anyone say that!"

"It's rare I hear anyone say anything much, after the transaction. You don't get to chat much in our line of work." Ilu nodded to Asta. "Let's go. We'll try and hire a carriage for the way back. It's a long walk, and I don't want your friend escaping on the way."

As the postern gate clanged shut behind them and they picked their way through the refuse-strewn alley, Asta kept a wary eye on Red. The slave woman straightened as they emerged on to the market square, looking around with keen interest. They had missed the afternoon storm while they were inside Punishment House, and the air was fresher, released from the humidity that dogged the morning. The market was beginning to pick up again after the break, and it would continue until sunset. Even though there wasn't much to sell with the blockade on the port, the coloured awnings still flapped and dripped, a defiant rainbow flying in the face of the Scattering attack.

Asta ducked as a shower of warm drops from an overhanging awning splattered on her hood, and a nearby slave who was packing boxes of glassware turned to grin at the sight. The box slipped in her arms, and Asta made a lunge for it. And found herself, a thousand miles from home, looking at last into a pair of familiar eyes.

"Asta? Asta, my leader, is that you?"

For an instant she floundered for the woman's name. "Cymion? It is Cymion, isn't it?" Cymion who had left a little boy behind, had an older daughter snatched with her from the beach on that bloody day. Cymion whose hair had been hacked back to neck-length, exposing her slave mark, and a fresh scar on her throat.

"What are you doing here, Asta?" Their hands clasped tight over the corner of the box.

"Looking for you. Looking for all of you."

Their hushed conversation was attracting the attention of the stallholder, who glared, making motions for his slave to speed up in her work. Cymion set the box down carefully, not looking directly at Asta, speaking out of the side of her mouth as she began to unpack the wine glasses and flagons from their bed of straw.

"You've found me. What now?"

"Asta!" Ilu was calling now, realising her companion was lagging behind.

"I can't talk to you. He'll beat me."

"Know I'm here. Take any chance you can get to get to the harbour. Look out for a boat, the *Aguia*. Tell Ranmiro I sent you. He'll get you home." She backed away as the stall holder, irritated, started to come round the side of his stand to berate Cymion for slacking. *Best I can do,* she mouthed, but she backed away with fresh hope. Another of her tribe, here, still alive despite everything. There could be more of them. It was a thin straw she was clutching, but it was all she had.

"What was that about?" Ilu asked as Asta joined her once more. "You look a bit shaken."

Asta glanced back, but Cymion was lost amid the crowds of the market. "One of my tribe," she said. "I was beginning to believe they were all dead."

There were still hire carriages running, but only a few, and the prices they asked made Ilu curse and shake her head in disgust. They walked instead, the two dark-cloaked, masked women trailing their fresh-purchased slave behind them on a stout length of chain. Red dragged her feet, constantly looking from side to side as if already seeking an escape route, and Asta began to see with fresh eyes how a box and a rain-pipe provided a path to the roofs, how a drain was large enough that a slim man might wriggle down it and evade capture, where the concealing shadows might hide a woman in a dark cloak. There were a thousand escape routes in the city, and she was sure Red's keen eyes saw every one of them.

"Oh, she's good," Ilu muttered. She had barely looked around, but she must be seeing the same thing. "She'll bear close watching, this friend of yours. How long have you known her?"

"We met in Bernaldus' slave pens, the day you bought me."

Ilu snorted. "Well, you certainly go back a long way! Are you sure we can trust her?"

"I'm not sure I can trust anyone."

The Inyestan woman's lips quirked. "Not even me?"

"Especially not you."

"You're smart for a horse-girl. It's kept you alive so far, I suppose."

"I suppose it has." And Rhodan too, though how long that would last without Finn's spiritual help was anyone's guess.

When they returned to the house, it was in chaos.

The first hint Asta had that anything was wrong was the gate which led to the carriage-yard, which wasn't latched properly. It swung open at Ilu's light push, and the glance she threw at her over her mask was meaningful. "Lash the woman here," she said. "Let's make sure the house is secure before we go blundering in there. It might be nothing."

Her sword was half-drawn. She might say she thought it was nothing, but her actions didn't echo her words.

Asta looped Red's chain around a hitching post, pulling it firm and feeling sick about doing it, and sicker at the thought that something had happened in the house. To Som, and to Rhodan. She drew her own short sword and followed Ilu through the darkness of the empty carriage house. The door to the upper landing stood wide open, spilling unexpected light across the dusty floor.

Inside, all the bedroom doors stood wide open. The covers were ripped from the beds and flung in a heap, and every cupboard was ransacked. Curtains were torn down, tables overturned, and a chair smashed against the wall in Rhodan's room. In the room that Ilu slept in, the mattress was ripped open, and paper money fluttered across the floor, like autumn leaves in the light breeze. Ilu stirred the notes with the tip of her sword.

"Whatever they were looking for, it wasn't money." She spoke in a low voice, and these were the first words she had uttered since entering the house, hushing Asta when she would have shouted for Rhodan. Asta stood on the landing, staring down at the overturned lounge below, alert for the slightest movement to tell her some stranger was at large in the house.

Something stirred, down in the wreckage of the sunken seating area. Asta shook off Ilu's cautious hand and was off at a run, taking the stairs two at a time, sword trailing carelessly against the banisters. She hurdled a broken chair, and before the man lying half-under the table could scramble away, the tip of her blade pressed down between his shoulder blades, hard enough to make him squirm.

"I told you, I don't know anything! Leave me alone!" he cried. His arms sprawled out either side of his body, one hand groping groggily for a discarded dagger, the other truncated, bandaged and still bloody. The back of his head was bloody too, his hair plastered around an ugly gash.

Asta lifted the blade a fraction. "Gartzea?"

He rolled over under the sword, until it pointed at his breastbone rather than his back. His eyes, as far as she could tell, were unfocussed, and there was vomit on his chin.

"What happened? Where's Rhodan?"

"Why're you pointing that at me?" he slurred, trying to push the blade away with his clumsy left hand.

Asta pressed it closer. "I asked you where Rhodan was."

"Fuck you!"

"There's no call for that, Asta." Ilu had come up behind her, and gently lifted her blade with the edge of her own sword.

"Just tell me!"

Gartzea ran a palsied hand over his face. "They were headed for the kitchen. I was defending the door . . ."

He frowned, looking puzzled, and his eyes glazed. Asta turned towards the kitchen door, which was kicked clean off its hinges. She clambered over the fallen door, clinging tight to the hilt of her short sword. If the intruders had hurt Rhodan, or taken him away, she would hunt them down and slit their throats. She wouldn't rest until they lay dead at her feet.

The kitchen was in the same chaotic state as the rest of the house, cupboards turned out, tiles ripped up, the ashes of the stove scattered in a wide black sweep across the floor. All the stores in the pantry was ruined, jars of preserved fruit and pickled fish smashed ruthlessly, and the floor was a hazardous carpet of ruined food and lethal shards of glass. Asta picked her way through it to the open back door, shoes crunching too loud in the silence. She could see no one in the garden, only Marcio sunning his belly in a golden patch on the path.

She slammed the door and shot the bolt home. The action made her feel no more secure.

Then she noticed the footprints. There were plenty of footprints around the kitchen. Booted feet, some muddy from the rain, some black from where they had ploughed through the scattered soot. At least two sets, overlapping and criss-crossing; a man's tread, and a smaller print that could be that of a child. Too big for Rhodan, and he didn't wear boots, only the flat shoes of an Inyestan child, when he wasn't running barefoot.

There were another set of prints. Paw prints, delicate, running arrow-straight between the deepest patch of soot and the stove. There were no other feline footprints in the kitchen.

"By the Deity!" Ilu stood in the doorway, wearing an expression of disgust. "They might as well have ripped up the floor and shat in the hole! Any sign of Som, or your boy?"

"Not sure." Asta waved Ilu back as the assassin advanced. "Careful, there's glass everywhere."

"I'll get a broom."

Asta nodded vaguely, half her attention on the stove. It was a sturdy metal edifice, standing three inches clear of the floor on four clawed feet, with a wide door at the front and a stout metal pipe as thick as a great tree trunk that led to the chimney. She imagined the heat it poured out; it must be roasting in the kitchen in the height of summer, with the stove going full blast. There was a deep drawer standing half-open below the main body of the oven, where the soot and ash had come from. Her breath disturbed the flakes that still drifted around it.

There was a depression in the soot on the lip of the drawer, so faint she wouldn't have noticed it if her eyes hadn't been led in that direction. The oven door stood slightly ajar, and she hooked her fingers around it and pulled it wide. There was nothing inside but a dark, sooty space, velvet black. Velvet . . .

Asta reached in and pulled out Som's shadow-cloak, pooling it around her feet like a patch of night sky fallen to earth. Behind her, she heard a clatter as Ilu returned with the broom, but she didn't look around. Instead she crouched, head and shoulders deep inside the stove, twisting around to peer up the chimney.

"Asta?" The crunch of broken glass, the whisper of feet swishing through soot. "Asta, what are you doing?"

Was that movement above? A shuffling motion, the faint glint of steel?

"Som? Rhodan? Are you up there?"

Definitely a shuffle.

"It's safe to come down. Are you stuck?"

Soot trickled into Asta's upturned mouth, more into her eyes, and she spat and hastily withdrew. Ilu was kneeling next to her. "Are they in there?" she asked. "Are they hurt?"

"I don't know." There was a slithering sound from inside the chimney, a bump, a metallic clang, and Som's flat-soled shoes emerged from inside the oven, stretching for uncertain purchase on the floor below. Between them, her sister and Asta helped her back out of the oven.

"Where's Rhodan?" Asta demanded, before Som could even regain her feet.

"He's safe, he's with me." Som was blackened from head to

foot, her face bleeding from an ugly scratch, and she shivered despite the warmth of the evening. She made a fruitless attempt to brush her clothes down, and called back into the oven. "You can come down now; your aunt's here!"

A faster slither, a softer bump, and a skinny, waving leg emerged from the stove. Asta pulled Rhodan out and into a hug, heedless of the fact that he was mired head to foot, from the roots of his hair down to the gaps between his toes. It made the whites of his eyes look wild, and he grinned, sticking his tongue through the gap in his teeth. "Did you see us, Tante Asta? We were up the chimney! How did you know where to find us?"

"The cat." Marcio had limped into the kitchen and sat in the doorway, washing a sooty front paw and quivering his whiskers in a smug fashion. "He left a trail of footprints. Who were the men—?"

"Holy mother of fuck, what happened here?"

Asta turned to see Red staring around with wide eyes. She frowned.

"How did you get loose?"

"I thought you bought me for my skills in that department?" Red's eyes flicking hungrily across the spilled food on the floor.

"In that case, why didn't you run away?"

"And miss all the fun?" She shrugged. "Besides, how far would I get? Every trader in the city knows my face, I've got no paper, and the copperheads are sinking every ship that tries to squeeze out between them. I was going to go south, overland, but," she spread her hands, an eloquent gesture. "You interest me, free horse-girl."

Ilu thrust the broom at her. "Sweep up in here," she said, slowly and clearly. "Throw away the spoiled food, and the glass. Then we can talk about freedom."

Asta picked up Rhodan and carried him over the broken glass. His skin was gritty and his eyes were sore. "Were you scared in the chimney?" she asked.

"No. Well, a little bit. Me and Tante Som looked after each other."

"What happened?" She let the honorific pass without comment. Let him feel close to Som. He had precious few people left he could trust.

"Some people came, and they were shouting. Som said we had to hide. She pushed me in the oven and up the chimney, and we stayed very quiet. They were moving about. And he—" he pointed at Gartzea as they emerged into the lounge, "he had a sword and he was going to fight them!" Rhodan's eyes were wide at the prospect. Gartzea, slumped on the couch, raised an eyebrow. He had a bloodied cloth clamped to the back of his head.

"Do you know who they were?" Asta asked.

Rhodan's face darkened. "They talked the same as those other ones."

"Which other ones?"

"The ones that took us off the beach." He squirmed in her arms. "Can I get down now?"

She let him go. "Go and wash. You smell of chimney."

"I'm not dirty," he insisted, despite the evidence to the contrary. "I want to stay and listen to you!"

"Wash first. Then food. You want those little things with the rice?"

He rubbed his mouth with the back of his hand. "Don't like them."

"You liked them yesterday. Go on, get going and I'll find you something else."

He grinned, white teeth flashing in the dirt, and took the stairs two steps at a time, leaving a trail of black footprints behind him.

Som had sunk into the chair and fumbled with her pipe, trying and failing to light it with shaking hands until Ilu took it from her and sparked it into life. She handed it back to her sister. "What happened, then?" she asked.

"Copperheads," Som said. "We were in the kitchen. Gartzea held them off while I hid the boy."

Gartzea snorted. "Not bad for a one-handed man. Pass me that pipe, Som. My head's throbbing something fierce."

She took a deep drag and handed it over. Her hands had stilled.

"What did they want?" Asta asked.

"You, apparently," Gartzea said. "I told them I'd seen no Atrathenes, I didn't know what they were talking about, that I lived here with my business partner . . ." A spasm crossed his face. "What if they go to Ederon? Threaten him?"

"I thought you were angry with him because he didn't come to the temple when you lost your hand?" Ilu's eyes were sharp. Som glared at her and leaned forward to stroke Gartzea's knee.

"They don't know he's with you, I'm sure," she said. "He's never met Asta. He can't tell them anything."

Asta leant across to Ilu. "Who's Ederon?" she mouthed.

"Gartzea's lover," Ilu whispered back. "He lives on the Hill, with his wife, keeping up a respectable front. The Temple doesn't approve of difference."

"The Temple doesn't approve of anything much," Som added.

"Who were the copperheads?" Asta asked Gartzea. "How did they get in here? I thought you shadow-cloaks were so cautious?"

Som's gaze dropped, and her fingers twitched towards the pipe. "My fault," she said, in a soft voice.

"How so?"

"My joints were flaring, and I'd run out of pipe herb. I was in such a hurry to get to some, down here . . . I got clumsy. They must have been watching the house, for a chance, for an unlocked door. They just came storming in."

She looked so momentarily frail Asta didn't want to upset her further. Instead she turned to Gartzea. "Did they give you their names?"

"Before or after they caved the back of my head in? They didn't leave a calling card, if that's what you're asking, and they all look alike to me." He sighed. "There were three men and a woman. They didn't address each other by name, as far as I could tell. They spoke Inyestan to me, and their own tongue amongst themselves. I think the woman was in charge. They asked me where you were, half a dozen times, then they smacked me on the head from behind, and when I woke up you were pointing a sword at me."

"Did you tell them where I was?"

He scowled. "What kind of a shit do you take me for? First you accuse me of abusing your boy, then you think I'd go against Som and Ilu and betray you? You took my fucking hand; what's the matter with you?"

"Look, I'm sorry about your hand . . ."

"You fucking should be." He lapsed into awkward, angry silence.

Som sucked her pipe. "We should leave," she said. "We have other safe houses in the city, ones they might not know about."

There was a yell of alarm from the kitchen, a muffled curse and the crash of breaking glass. Ilu sprang to her feet, Asta only a moment behind. "Red! What's going on?"

"Hey! You can't walk in here—" Red's words were cut off abruptly as the kitchen door burst open. There was a scream from upstairs. From Rhodan's room.

Asta spun around to run to him and found herself grabbed from behind, arms pinned to her sides. She kicked out, her foot coming into sharp contact with a bony shin. She jerked her head back, hoping to smash her assailant's nose. He twisted away with a curse, and she caught a silver flash as a wire dropped down over her head and snagged tight around her neck. She couldn't shake off his grip to get her hands up to her throat, and he twisted the wire until she gagged. Black spots swam before her eyes as she scrabbled helplessly at her neck. Her knees were liquid, her vision dark, and she sagged. Everything was fading. Through the mist she could see Finn, or someone who looked like Finn. He radiated disapproval, and as she stretched out for him he turned away . . .

"Not so tight." The woman's voice came from far away. "We don't want her to die here, do we?"

Here? Where do you want me to die?

There was something important, that would keep her alive,

at least until they reached the right place to kill her. She worked her mouth, and the pressure at her throat eased as she tried to remember the words in the tongue of the Scattering.

"Please . . . Please, I'm pregnant . . ."

But the darkness was gathering and the pressure tightened once more. The sea roared hungry in her ears. She felt her feet slip out from under her, but she didn't feel herself hit the floor.

TWENTY-FIVE

ASTA WAS LYING on her face, on warm fabric scented with spice and perfume and stale pipe-smoke. She couldn't remember how she got there, and she couldn't move her hands. She decided the safest thing to do was lie still, eyes closed, and listen to what was going on around her until she worked out where she was, where everyone else was, and what was going on. She heard Inyestan voices, and people moving around, but her head was pounding so hard that she couldn't make out their words. And where was Rhodan?

The thought of her nephew made her muscles tense, and she forced herself, inch by inch, to relax. She wished she could open her eyes.

"How long are you planning to keep us here?" Som's voice, smoke-slurred and filled with pain. The Shadow Cloaks must be restrained in some way. Asta couldn't imagine them submitting to capture without a fight.

"We just want what's ours. Then we'll let you go."

"Asta isn't ours." Ilu sounded tired. "She's a free woman. We don't make choices for her. And you've got some fucking nerve coming here, when even the Holy Mother wouldn't dare . . ."

The woman's voice was maddeningly familiar. "I care nothing for your Holy Mother. And you expect me to believe that an Atrathene woman walking the streets of Abonnae doesn't belong to anyone? I know your ways too well."

"She sure as shit doesn't belong to you, anyway."

"She'll do as we say." A man's voice. "We have the boy, after all."

"And she's awake, and she knows that."

Asta suppressed her intake of breath. She remembered now where she knew the woman's voice from. Back in the council chamber in Mikligard, warning her comrades that they were overheard, that Finn and Asta walked unseen through the walls of the manse, listening and learning. Erikah, that was her name, and she had some power that let her sense spirits, that told her Asta was listening right now.

Asta could feel the copper-haired woman come close; warm, sweet breath on her face. She opened her eyes.

Erikah smiled. "That's better," she said. "Can you sit up?"

Asta's hands were tied behind her. That was why she had been unable to move them, but she managed to shuffle into a sitting position. Gartzea was slumped on the sofa, restrained by a burly Scattering man. His chest heaved and his brow glistened with feverish sweat. The exertions of the morning must have been too much for him in his weakened state.

Ilu and Som sat back-to-back on the floor, bound together, stripped to their undergarments, and another red-haired man picked through the pile of gleaming weapons that had been taken from them, occasionally muttering exclamations of surprise or pleasure. Rhodan sat on Som's lap, his arms around her waist, his head against her breast. He was very quiet and still, but his eyes were wide and anxious, and as they caught Asta's he offered her a small, brave smile.

Red sat slightly apart from the rest of them. The Scattering contingent showed little interest in her. Perhaps they had taken her for a servant. She was bound hand and foot, but Asta noticed the subtle movements she was making to free herself.

Asta's neck burned. It was painful to force the words out, in a hoarse whisper that would barely carry to Erikah's ears. "How did you find me?"

"We have our spies, as the Inyestans do. They stole the magic from us in the first place, so why shouldn't we use it against them?"

If Asta could keep Erikah talking, she might be able to buy Red the time to break out. She doubted they would kill her, the time and the place were wrong, but her friends were expendable. Rhodan, she guessed, was expendable. "So did you come here, is all this—" she nodded in the vague direction of the harbour, tried not to cough, "because of me? Because you need me back for your sacrifice?"

Erikah sat back on her heels. "Either we take you back, or we stay here and throw everything we have at Inyesta. You were our last hope. Our land is dying; we have nothing left. If the *sumri gudienne* can't or won't save us, we have to take matters into our own hands. Every dead man of the Scattering is one less for the Inyestans to enslave, after all."

"So either I lay down my life, or everybody dies? There must be another way."

"There is no other way! That's why I'm here, as head of the council. I tried to speak with the priest in charge at the Temple, and she looked through me like I wasn't human. They despise anyone who's not the same as them. All we are is tools for their use, their work and pleasure. She had no interest in finding a runaway Atrathene slave."

Red had one hand free. "Is this Chesserai you spoke to?" Asta croaked

"I don't know the woman's name. She told me she was acting as High Priest, that the High Priestess is sick and won't see anyone."

"And what about Syven? What happened to him?"

Erikah's face darkened. "He betrayed his country. I argued with the council, fought for his life, but I was overruled. I'm sorry. There was nothing I could do . . ."

Asta felt a stab of loss. Syven had been good to her in her darkest hours, and his blood still stirred deep in her belly. "You knew he had children dependant on him, and you stood back and let him die. What about his little ones? Did you let them live, or did you take them up to your bloody stone . . ." She couldn't finish the thought.

"The children were sold into slavery. The twins will be well looked after; you of all people know how precious twins are." Erikah flicked her eyes down to Asta's belly.

"And Heylan?" Asta didn't want to hear the answer, but she had to know.

"She followed the same path as her husband. They died together, with courage, and I made sure their bodies were respected. That little, I could do for them. They didn't betray you as they betrayed the Scattering."

Som's head jerked up, almost smashing against her sister's. "Heylan? A little woman of Mikligard? Trades in vegetables?"

Heylan, who had been so kind when she had every reason to turn away, who had given Asta a precious shadow-cloak and found her a ship, concealed her in her office and introduced her to Ranmiro. Heylan with her soft laugh and her skin that smelled of onions, who had killed for Asta, and now it seemed, had died for her, all the while knowing that she carried her husband's children. For some reason, even after all the time she had spent with Syven, the loss of Heylan was a bigger kick to the gut.

"That's her," Erikah confirmed. "You knew her?"

Ilu's voice was bitter. "She was . . . an ally."

"An Inyestan spy. She betrayed us, for Asta."

"There's more to Inyesta than you know, copperhead." Ilu twisted in her bonds, and spat.

"I don't want to know anything more of Inyesta. I know enough." Erikah reached out. Her hand was cool against Asta's cheek. "It was you I felt that day, wasn't it? In the council chamber. You and someone close to you – your brother, maybe?"

Asta refused to answer, her hard black eyes staring back into Erikah's cool blue ones. The woman of Mikligard had a dusting of freckles across her nose, and her skin was reddened from the southern sun.

"He's still in there, you know. Finn, I mean. You thought he'd left you, but he hasn't, not entirely."

"What are you—?" but before she could get the words out there was a cry, like the whoop of an Atrathene war band, and a yell from one of Erikah's heavies as he tumbled from the couch, blood gushing from the side of his throat. He hit the floor and lay still, heels kicking faintly. There was a fragile moment of utter silence, then a burst of chaos.

Asta kicked out, her foot catching Erikah below the chin and tipping her backwards. She leapt up and over her, barging into the copperhead held at bay by Red's flickering blade. He stumbled into the wall and righted himself as Red made two quick slashes, scoring fire along the inside of Asta's forearm as the ropes that bound her hands fell away.

Red threw her a dagger, but her hands were wet and slippery. She fumbled her grip as the man she had shoulder-barged descended on her, hair and face flaming with rage. His fist slammed into her left shoulder, numbing her arm to the fingertips. Behind him Erikah shrieked instructions, and Som and Ilu were shouting too, at Red to free them, at Asta to watch out.

"Put the knife down, Goddess. I don't want to hurt you."

Red traded blows with a copperhead man, and Erikah scrambled forward, snatched Rhodan from Som's lap. She climbed on the table with him kicking and swearing in her arms, and pressed a stout knife to his throat.

"Give it up, Goddess! Or I kill him!"

Asta tried to dodge around the big man blocking her way. He had no blade but his fists were like hammers and his second punch, to her jaw, sent her staggering. Her mouth was full of blood, it ran down her arms and pounded in her skull, and it was all over her knife, mired hilt-deep in gore.

The big man blocking her way grunted in surprise as the red bloom flowered on his shirt. He clutched at it with both hands as his knees buckled, and he sat down hard, breath bursting from his lungs in an explosion of ale fumes and spittle.

Something whistled past Asta's ear and she ducked instinctively. It was no bigger than a large moth, but it flew with the speed and precision of an arrow, striking Erikah's upper arm and sticking, quivering and erect, in her flesh.

She glanced down at it, plucked it free and tossed it away. "Throw down your weapon, Goddess. I don't want to hurt anyone."

Asta glanced over her shoulder. Red was pinned, but her assailant bled from a dozen cuts and looked exhausted. The slave just looked calm, her teeth bared in a lopsided grin. On the sofa, Gartzea raised a pipe in salute. Erikah staggered backwards, shaking her head, her arms wrapping around Rhodan, who grabbed her sleeve and sank his teeth into the ball of her thumb.

She barely seemed to feel the bite, as the blood welled over his lips and down her wrist. She raised her other arm to try and push him away, but he scrambled out of reach. Asta caught him as he ran to her. "Stay here!" she urged.

"I want to help Som!"

"Do as you're told!" She pressed his face to her stomach, trying to shield him from the blood and death he had already seen. He may have experienced the horrors of a slave ship, but that didn't mean he needed to witness any more killing. He already had enough nightmares.

Erikah staggered, rubbing her hands over her face, smearing her cheeks with blood. One knee gave way and she lurched sideways off the edge of the table, stumbling as her foot twisted in the rumpled rug. The colour drained from her face, rendering it sickly grey under her sunburn, and, with the grace of a toppling tree, she collapsed.

Red seized the opportunity to stab her stunned captor in the thigh and smack him around the head with the hilt of his own sword, stepping aside neatly as he fell. Silence descended on the room.

Asta found her voice. "Is she dead, Gartzea?"

Gartzea was unconscious, pipe dangling from his limp hand.

"She shouldn't be." Som had hooked a fallen knife with her

toes and was trying to manoeuvre it towards her mouth. "It's just a sedative dart from the pipe. She'll be fine later."

Asta took the knife, and cut the ropes that bound the sisters together. "What do we do about this lot?" she asked.

One of the Scattering men was dead. The one Asta stabbed was unconscious, and the man Red had clobbered moaned and tried to lift his head. Red gave him another whack, just to make sure.

They trussed up the two unconscious men and laid them in front of the stove in the kitchen. Som found bandages and patched up the one with the gut wound, but her face was grim and she didn't have to say that his prospects weren't good. Red and Ilu carried the dead man out to the garden; the carrion birds would make short work of him. He wore a jade pendant on a thong around his neck, and Red ripped it off and weighed it in her hand. He didn't have any other valuables besides his boots.

"What are you going to do with that?" Asta asked her. "Send it back to his people?"

Red snorted. "Don't be daft. I can get good paper for this."

"Slaves don't carry paper."

"Then you can sell it for me, can't you?"

"Don't you think we should send it back to his family?"

"Why?" Red looked genuinely confused. "What good would it do them?"

Asta had no answer to that.

Gartzea was comatose on one sofa. Erikah sprawled on the other, her eyelids fluttering. Rhodan had been sent to bed, and the moons flew high and fat over the rooftops of Abonnae. The city was quiet, watchful under the cold glare of the Temple and the searching beams from the Scattering ships that ringed the harbour. The tension was so thick Asta could taste it when she ducked out of the carriage house to get away from the constant fumes of Som's pipe.

"It all hinges on you, you know."

Ilu's voice, coming out of the darkness behind her. It made her jump. "What does?"

The assassin stepped forward into the moonlight and pushed back her hood. With the shadow-cloak concealing her from the shoulders down, she looked like a disembodied head floating in the air. "I thought it was us." She carried on as if Asta hadn't spoken. "Som and I. He sent us here. We were his personal assassins; wherever he went, we were there, ready to do his bidding. He's not a murderous man, but in his position he has dangerous enemies. You've been a leader, you understand . . ."

Asta thought of Meyloy, selling her to the Scattering. Who led the Beehive tribe now? Could she go back, even if she wanted to, and walk into her old position without a fight? "I understand," she said. "Who do you work for, then? A man of power . . ."

"The church is out of control. You've seen that. The heart of it is in Abonnae, but the disease is spreading. Even as far as Kishtawar itself. The Emperor sent us to cut out the core of the rot. He said there was no one he trusted more, but it had to be done, quickly and in secret. Only since we've been here everything has gone wrong. When we heard word of you, an Atrathene who had been inside the inner sanctum and managed to escape the Temple alive, we hoped our luck was turning. We thought we could get the information from you and send you on your way. But now . . ." She sighed.

"Is Gartzea one of you? A Shadow-Cloak, I mean?"

"No, but he does things for us. He negotiates on our behalf. He makes travel arrangements, takes the money. He's our public face. If someone wants to hire me or Som, they approach Gartzea first. He was willing to come with us to the Temple. He wanted to strike a blow; he hates everything they stand for, their persecution of men like him. Only now he can't."

"Because of me."

Ilu, charitably, said nothing.

"If we do nothing, this will just carry on, won't it? More

children, more slaves sacrificed. The people of the Scattering, I've got no love for them, but they'll break themselves apart trying to stop it, and Inyesta will swat them away like a fly."

"They'll break *you* apart trying to stop it," said Ilu. "That's their belief."

"I don't share it."

Ilu smiled. "I didn't imagine for one moment that you did. But you can help save them, Asta, in your own way. You can be their *sumri gudienne*."

Asta rubbed her hands over her face, trying to ease the ache in her bruised jaw. She suddenly felt very tired. "If I do this, can I go home? Will you help me?"

There was a rustle of silk in the moonlight. Ilu knelt, extended the hilt of her blade towards Asta. "You have my sword. And I don't give it lightly. I'll get you home, you funny little Goddess. You and your boy."

Choked, Asta reached out and patted her on the shoulder. Ilu grinned up at her. "Maybe a touch over-dramatic," she admitted. "And kneeling around in the dirt kills no Gods."

"Fuck, Ilu, how are we supposed to kill a God?"

"You're a goddess, and I've seen you bleed." Ilu rose, wrapping an arm around Asta's shoulders. "My sister and I are the experts on killing. You get us into the Temple. We'll do the rest."

When they returned downstairs to the lounge, Erikah was stirring. Som and Red had carried Gartzea to a straw mattress in the corner, and reclaimed the other sofa. They were sharing a pipe, and Asta was struck by how alike they looked, not physically, but in their weary, pained expressions, as if they had both been wrung out and left to dry. Neither had made an effort to clean the blood staining the floor, but the rugs were rolled up and the furniture righted, and somehow they had retrieved enough unspoiled food from the kitchen to make a snack, thick slices of bread slathered with fish paste that crunched with grit as Asta bit into it. She wondered for a moment if it had been scraped off the floor, but she was hungry. A little dirt was the least likely thing to kill her.

Erikah groaned, and her eyelids fluttered open. Her wrists and ankles were bound loosely, so she had some freedom of movement. Asta had been all for wrapping the rope around her neck, but Som had dissuaded her. She glared at Erikah now, watching as she blinked and twitched and returned slowly to harsh reality. A look of alarm flashed across her face as she realised she was a prisoner, and her eyes widened as they met Asta's once more.

Asta was on her in a flash, dagger pressed to her throat, ignoring Som's murmured protest. Erikah snorted and tried to back up against the sofa, fingers clawing the rough fabric.

"What do you want?" Her voice was rough with sleep, and her lips were cracked.

"What do you know about my brother? Do you know where he is now?"

Erikah's eyes clouded. "He's still with you. I can feel him . . ."

"Liar!" Asta jabbed the blade harder against her pale throat, drawing out a thin red line. "You don't know anything—"

"Lay off her, Asta," Som said. "She can't talk with a slit throat, can she?"

Asta sat back on the table, pushing the plate of bread aside, and allowed Erikah to sit up. She kept her blade levelled at her throat. "Talk, then. What do you know about Finn?"

"I sensed both of you back in Mikligard, in the Council Chamber." Erikah spoke carefully, skin prickling over the twitching point of Asta's knife. "I didn't know at that time who you were, only that you were there. It took time to untangle, time and meditation. By the time I realised you and your brother were sharing a spirit, we had already lost you. Olafur was dead, and I had to take charge of the Council, to get you back. Both of you." She glanced significantly at Asta's stomach. *"All* of you."

Asta shook her head. "Finn's gone. He's not part of this collection of spirits you want to put under your knife."

Erikah's voice was soft. "He hasn't gone, *gudienne*."

"Where is he, then? I don't hear him any more, he doesn't speak to me—" She broke off, the void opening inside her, the aching chasm of his loss. "I lost my little brother. Your people killed him. They cut him down on the beach and stole his wife and son from his arms. Don't sit there and tell me he hasn't gone; you don't know anything about it!"

"His spirit is still within you, my goddess."

"Then why won't he *talk* to me?" Asta's frustration spilled over into tears. It was childish, she knew, and she hated herself for crying in front of Erikah, but she had been so alone. Finn had been there for as long as she could remember, her noisy, infuriating little brother, born before the Beehive village was built, who could remember travelling across the steppe in the back of her parents' wagon. It had always made them closer to each other than the other children in the village, the ones that came later. He could have moved on at any time, but he had chosen to stay, after their father died and their mother was driven from the village, and he had married a local girl, not traded out like many men did. She had lost him, but they had found each other again. Not even death had taken him from her, but now he was silent, and she couldn't reach him, no matter how hard she tried.

"I don't know." Erikah looked on her with compassion. "All I know is I can still sense him. He's proud of you."

"Horse shit. Next you'll be saying he wants me to go back to the Scattering and throw myself across the sacrifice stone. I know my brother. Tell me something he would have said, to convince me you can reach him."

Erikah sighed. "I can't reach him, I can only sense him. I know he's there. Why do you think your pregnancy is slowed, why you can still speak and understand the Inyestan tongue so easily? Your brother is responsible for that, even if he's withdrawn from the forefront of your mind."

"So you can sense him, but I can't?" Yet Erikah's words held a ring of truth. Fucking typical of Finn, to withdraw and let her fumble her own way through a crisis, just because he had what he wanted now Rhodan was safe. She desperately wanted to take a Spirit Walk, track him down and slap him senseless for abandoning her, but what if he wasn't there either? He had left the realm of the spirits to help her find Rhodan. What if he was trapped now, somewhere between the worlds of the living and the dead? She would rather cling to the crumb of comfort that he may still be somewhere deep inside her mind, silently manipulating and interfering, probably judging. It was better than imagining him lost to her for good.

Erikah nodded. She was pale. "So much anger . . . He doesn't want to help us."

"Us? You mean the people in this room? Or the Scattering?"

"The Scattering. He is unwilling to let you go under the knife. And a willing sacrifice is so much more potent."

"Get a lot of those, do you?" Ilu asked sardonically.

Erikah blinked her wide blue eyes. "More than you'd think. And we scoured the ocean for a Goddess with such symmetry—"

"Symmetry?" Ilu asked.

"The white patches on the backs of my knees," Asta explained. "They match. Apparently it's a sign from the ancestors or some such horse shit."

Erikah shifted in her bonds. "Don't talk that way about my faith."

"I'll talk how I please about a faith that wants to kill me."

"Please, Asta. We don't want a war. Come back with us, and we'll leave Inyesta in peace."

"Or . . . ?" Asta asked.

"You have to come back. Summer is nearly over. If we try to bring the Empire down ourselves, thousands will die. Better to die in fire and blood than to fade away, a few old people clinging to a barren rock, our children sold into slavery."

"You could leave the Scattering," Asta suggested. "Start again somewhere else, somewhere fertile."

"Who would have us? Your people? We have worked as slavers for the Inyestans for too long, staining our own hands with the blood they spilt. We've made ourselves hated across the width of the ocean. We have nowhere else to go."

"Killing me won't save you, no matter what you believe. Do you really, in your gut, think it will? Has it ever worked before? Look at me," Asta reached out and raised Erikah's chin. "With your power, you can see into my mind. You know I'm not a Goddess. I'm just a woman trying to look out for what's left of her family."

Erikah blinked in surprise. "I know that. Of course I know that. But to the ordinary people of Mikligard, you *are* the Goddess that they were promised. I have to be seen to act. What else can we do? It might work, after all . . ."

"It might not, and I'll still be dead, and the people of Mikligard might as well throw themselves into to sea."

Erikah's face flushed with anger. "What do you suggest? Because believe me, I've been wracking my skull for a way out of this that won't kill everyone."

"We don't have to kill everyone," Som said softly. "We just have to kill a God."

"What?" Erikah thrashed her bound hands. "You could at least untie me. I've spoken reasonably to you, and I'm not going anywhere."

"Asta?" Som asked.

Asta snicked through the ropes with her dagger and withdrew to sit on the edge of the table once more. Erikah massaged her wrists. "Thank you," she said. "I don't think I heard the lady right. They want to kill a God, but I'm not allowed to kill a Goddess?"

"This is an actual God," Asta explained. "Or at least, some creature they worship as a Deity. It's kept locked up underneath the Red Temple, and they sacrifice slaves to feed it. Thousands of them. Your children, the children of my tribe, my friend's children . . ." She indicated Red, who had sat quietly throughout, lips working as she strained to follow the conversation.

"Me? What?"

"You lost your little girl." Asta didn't dwell on the detail. It was all one; whether by murder or abuse or overwork or sacrifice, the Inyestan system killed the most vulnerable first. The sick, the elderly, children by the thousand. "You want to help us bring down this shitty system, get your freedom?"

"Bloody right." Red flashed her teeth, more of a snarl than a smile.

"You think by killing this God you can change things?" Erikah asked.

"As do you. It's a start, at least."

"The Emperor thinks it will," Ilu added. "He wishes it. If he can claw back some power from the church, he can start making things better. Killing their god will rob them of much of their authority. That's why my sister and I are here, but we can't do it alone. Asta knows the Temple well, and Red, she tells me, is a lock-breaker, an escape artist."

Erikah's eyes flicked over Red and Asta, clouded with doubt. Ilu pressed her point home. "Our unconscious friend over there," she nodded towards Gartzea, "was meant to help us, but he'd give his right arm to get out of it—"

"Ilu, that's not funny," Som interrupted. Ilu made a face, but Som was staring down at her pipe. The quiver in her hands was back.

"And I don't think you should go either."

Som looked up, eyes sharp. "Why not?"

"Because this fucking city is no good for your joint-ail. Because you've been smoking like there's no dawn since we arrived. Because you can't get through a meal, or a conversation, without sparking up, and your hands are shaking like a fresh-landed slave." *Because you left the door unlocked, and let the copperheads into our house.* She didn't say that, but she might as well have done, and Som squirmed beneath the unspoken accusation.

She set the pipe down. Asta saw she was trying to keep her movements slow and deliberate, but her fingers spasmed and the pipe weed blew like a scattering of brown earth across the table. She rose. "I should check on Rhodan."

"Som—"

"We'll talk later." She held up her hand to forestall her sister's protest, and walked silently from the room. Ilu watched her go up the stairs, and as the door to Rhodan's room clicked shut behind her she blew out her cheeks and shook her head.

"I'm going to catch it later," she muttered.

"Tell her someone needs to be here to look after Rhodan," Asta suggested. "Gartzea can't do it."

Ilu frowned. "We usually leave children on their own."

"I'd feel better if someone was here to get him home. Just in case—"

"In case what?" Red started up. "You're thinking we won't come back from this little trip, am I right?"

"There's a chance we won't. I thought you had nothing to lose."

"Nothing but my life! And girl, I've spent a lot of time preserving that."

"I'll come with you." Erikah said it so softly Asta thought at first she hadn't heard correctly. Certainly too softly for Red to hear.

"I'll get you in there. I'll unlock whatever you want unlocking. But if you're going to fight a god with nothing but swords and daggers and your bare teeth, count me far out. And I want passage out of here when it's all done, a boat or a horse, and paper. And a document to say I'm free. Otherwise I stay here, with the boy and the smoker and the cripple." She grinned. "Maybe eat all your food; you won't need it when you're dead!"

"You'll have all that afterwards," Ilu promised.

"Before. I want to see it before, so it's here and I can just grab it and go." She folded her arms across her narrow chest. "Else I'm not stirring from this couch."

Ilu's brow furrowed. "Gartzea usually sorts things like that out. With the blockade, it might take a few days."

"You in a big hurry?" Red wanted to know. "Got some pressing dinner appointment with the Deity? He's not going anywhere."

"But we are in a hurry." Erikah spoke more loudly this time, and Red heard her.

"Why?"

"Because if we fail, I have to take the *sumri gudienne* back to the Scattering for the last day of summer. If we fail, there will be no other choice."

Red snorted. "You said a whole lot of words there and I'm not sure I caught them right. If we fail, you have to kill the horse girl even though you don't believe it'll make the slightest difference, just to keep your people happy for a month until they realise it hasn't worked?"

"No," Erikah said. "Because the promise that I'll bring her back before the end of summer is the only thing stopping the Scattering launching a suicidal war against Inyesta. If we don't kill this god of theirs and change . . . *something*, I can't stop that attack, much as I might long to." She smiled sidelong at Asta. "I'd rather not see you die. You seem like a good woman. So if you want help to kill your god, let me know what I can do."

"You'd do that?" Asta was surprised. Erikah was thin and pale. She struck her as a diplomat, but the fact that she had taken down Som and Ilu . . . . Maybe she was more of a warrior than she appeared. "You came round to our way of thinking pretty bloody quick. What are you up to?"

Erikah flushed deeper. "I'm not *up to* anything. But I've got no lust for blood. Yours or anyone elses. Not all of us on the council agreed with Olafur's every word, you know?" She cast a dark look at Asta. "One condition. One. If we fail, you'll come back with me to the Scattering, willingly, and lay down your life on the White Altar."

Asta thought about it. If they failed, it was likely that they would die anyway at the hands of the Temple. One bloody sacrifice was the same as another. And there was the chance, the wafer-thin chance, that they would succeed, that they would be able to somehow destroy the Deity, rob the Temple of its power, break the chains of slavery that bound the eastern sea to Inyesta, and go home.

"My condition," she said. "If I die, by your hand or anyone else's, you get Rhodan back to my tribe. Promise me that, and I'll sacrifice myself willingly."

Erikah extended her hand. "I'll do my best."

It didn't seem an adequate promise, but it was all Asta had, and she took Erikah's hand and accepted her pledge.

Erikah sighed. "I don't know how much help I'll be, but I have certain abilities you could make use of . . . I can use a spy-fly, and you know I can sense things other people can't."

Ilu clapped her hands, too loud in the stillness. "That's settled, then," she declared, turning to Red and speaking clearly. "I'll sort out everything you wanted, and what everyone needs. Once that's in place, I suggest we move quickly. I don't think the Emperor will tolerate the Scattering blockade long, and if his troops arrive it will just add to the confusion. Let's kill this beast, this god or whatever it is, and then we can all go home."

Asta was woken early by the pressure of a soft hand against her neck, just below her ear. She grunted and kicked out, earning a sleepy protest from Rhodan as her foot made contact with his back. She would be glad to get her own space back when they got home, but for now she hated to let him out of her reach at night. Abonnae was crawling with kidnappers and assassins.

One of the worst of them crouched over her now, with a finger pressed to her lips. The light from the candle she held turned her blank eyes into twin mirrors embedded in her skull. A silent jerk of her head indicated Asta should follow her into the corridor.

"Are we going somewhere?" Asta whispered. Ilu had her cloak hung over one arm, and she shrugged easily into it, silk falling like cold water on her bare arms and legs. She shuddered. The grey light falling through the high, unshielded windows indicated that true dawn was not far off.

"I don't want my sister to see this," Ilu said, pulling her mask across her face and sweeping her hood up so only her eyes were visible. "She's anxious enough, and it makes her joint-ail worse. But you should see it." She had set the candle down, and her hands twisted an invisible wire. "We'll all know soon enough, but I needed to tell someone."

"What is it?" Ilu merely shook her head, and Asta followed her, slipping like dark phantoms through the carriage house, out into the eerily silent pre-dawn streets of the Hill. The lower districts of the city were under curfew, but money ruled on the hill, and enough money could blind all but the most fanatical Temple Guards. Even so, people kept to their houses, and told themselves it was out of choice.

The crescent streets of the Hill wound in a leisurely path up to the summit, the houses growing larger and more widely spaced the higher they climbed. The Hill was crowned by a park, an oasis of soft green in the heart of the dusty city, ringed by a crumbling wall. The iron gates to the park were locked at this hour, but the wall itself was only waist-high, easy enough to scramble over. Asta felt the cool of the grass through her light shoes as her feet touched down, and she longed to kneel on the ground and sink her face into the dew-dampened sward. She kicked off her shoes and let her hardened feet soak, wriggling her toes against the earth. Ilu watched her with a sardonic quirk of her lips.

"Having fun?"

"I'm tired of being alternately hot and dry, and hot and damp. Why is it so green here?"

"I believe the Temple store ice somewhere under here. Some of the cold water leaks out, and it greens the crown of the Hill. But come on," Ilu tugged Asta's sleeve, "I didn't bring you hear to show you the grass."

She moved ahead, and Asta followed, damp grass sticking to her ankles and heels, shoes swinging idly in her hand. Faint sounds drifted up from the city below, the day just waking up, for even a city under siege must trade. Looking back, she picked out the harbour in the grey distance, the Scattering ships like gulls perched on the surface of the sea. The winding streets were silver and white threads, woven between densely packed houses, and a brown pall hung over the tanneries that marked the edge of the city's sprawling slums, the Nidus, where even the Temple didn't bother to preach. From up here, it felt like a different world.

There was a tower on the brow of the hill, a tapering needle with a circular base and a formal garden laid out around its lower contours, gravel beds and paths sweeping around low bushes decked with flowers not yet gone to ripe fruit. The stones were already losing their morning chill. Ilu pushed open the door at the base of the tower. There was a smooth hole where the lock should be, as if it had been cut out, and the edges were darkened to the same rich patina as the door. There hadn't been a lock here for a long time. The opening revealed a tight spiral of steps, curling upwards.

"What is this place? Asta asked.

"Some rich man's whim. Or maybe an old watch tower. I don't know." Ilu's tread was silent on the stair. "All I know is that it's useful to us. I'm surprised more use hasn't been made of it."

It was cold inside the tower, the steps stained with old bird shit, and Asta was uncomfortably aware of how it tapered. It felt as if the walls were closing in above her head, an ever-tightening corkscrew that would crush her without remorse, and it brought the pressure of panic to her chest. She had to steady herself against the wall and will herself forward, step by step. Even Ilu seemed to sense it, tugging her mask down for a long intake of breath.

They emerged on a narrow walkway. The pinnacle of the tower jutted skyward in a sharp point only a few feet above them, and the view, of the ground below and the city below that, was momentarily dizzying.

"Come on." Ilu edged around the narrow walkway, her back pressed to the stone of the tower. It was too narrow to walk side-by-side up here; the ledge was not designed for casual viewing, and that seemed a waste. The sight of the city unfurled like a map on the parchment ground was breathtaking.

Ilu pointed. "There," was all she said.

"What?" Asta squinted. Her friend was pointing out of the city, beyond the stout wall that protected the landward side of the port from incursion. Little white villages huddled in its shadow, irrigated fields where slaves like stick figures moved slowly, starting work before the worst of the sun's heat drove them to seek shade, or drove them mad. Beyond them, the horizon was hazy, obliterated by a long cloud of dust that roiled and spun and seemed to have its own life independent of land and sky. "What am I looking at?"

"Do you see the dust cloud?"

"Of course."

"Look harder."

She stared until her temples ached. Something was moving, out past the villages. An anthill swarming. The sun glinted on sharpened metal, and Asta could almost feel the tremor through the stone under her feet. She knew then. She had lived her life a warrior on the steps of Atrath, and she knew heavy cavalry when it was approaching, not matter how far off it was. Coming at speed too, for an army that size. By her estimate they would reach the city in two, maybe three days.

"Who are they?" She found herself whispering, even though the approaching army was miles distant and couldn't possibly hear her, much less care about her words.

"The Imperial Army." Ilu's face was grim. "I received word before dawn. The Emperor has lost faith in us. He has decided to finish the job himself."

"The Emperor's coming here?" The sun dimmed. The blood would run ankle-deep through the streets of Abonnae if the Imperial Army and the Scattering clashed. Asta had no doubt the poorest of the city; the slaves, the sick, and the children, would be the first to be crushed between the opposing forces.

"I doubt he'll come himself," Ilu said. "He doesn't get his own hands bloody. That's what keeps my sister and me in paper, after all! But does it matter? There are enough men out there to sweep the city clean of priests and gods."

"And Erikah's men."

"Unless we do their job for them. We need to take down the Deity, Asta, and we need to do it today. We're saving the city from more than just blood-hungry gods now." Ilu turned away from the sight of the approaching army, working her way back round the tower to the entrance to the stairs. Asta lingered a moment, watching the dust swirl, wishing her father was here to advise her. Or for a horse of her own, to carry Rhodan far from a city that would become a slaughterhouse if she didn't kill a savage god.

TWENTY~SIX

WHEN ASTA AND Ilu returned to the house, they found Erikah in the kitchen preparing breakfast. Rhodan perched on the counter, claiming loudly that he was "helping", and Red sat at the table, arms folded, watching with interest but not lifting a finger to assist. She raised an insolent eyebrow at Ilu. "You going to tell me I should be cooking, and the copperhead should be sitting here?" she asked. "I told her that, she said she liked to cook!"

"I miss cooking." Erikah lifted the lid of a saucepan, and a whiff of oats and honey drifted across the table, filling Asta's mouth with moisture. "Back home, there used to be plenty of food, and we could cook all kinds of things. But the trees died, and the fish ran out, and then the goats. And imported food is so expensive, only the richest families could afford more than the basics. It's been a long time since I've eaten honey."

"I thought you were rich," Asta observed. "You're on the Council."

"I head the Council, since Olafur died. That doesn't make me rich. The richest men on the Scattering are the slave merchants."

"Of course they are." Asta felt a pang of gloom as she lifted Rhodan down, away from the hot stove. "There's too much money tied up in that foul trade. Even if the Inyestans don't need slaves to feed their god, they'll still need them to look after their horses and hoe the crops. It's not going to stop overnight. How do we make that," she waved her arm vaguely, "all the rest of it, go away?"

Red watched her lips intently as she spoke, following every word. She snorted. "You know, I reckon there's five slaves to every free man in Abonnae alone. That's a whole lot of bought flesh. Weighs more than free flesh, by my count. And you know what keeps them in line? Fear. Fear that if they don't keep their heads down and their backs bent, they'll walk the same path I did and end up dinner for some ever-hungry god. You take away the god, loudly, in public, you take away a lot of that fear. And it strikes me that a man who's lost his fear might find his anger filling the gap where fear used to be." She flashed her teeth. "Your revolution might come from the inside, horse girl."

"We can but hope," Ilu said, reaching for a bowl as Erikah ladled out the porridge. "Of course, if the Imperial Army get here first the slave-owners will hide behind a wall of human flesh until it's shredded and torn, before they have to pick up arms themselves." She hesitated, spoon hanging in the air as she let the impact of her words sink in.

Rhodan tugged Asta's arm. "What's she talking about?"

"Nothing. Grown-up talk. Eat your breakfast."

"What's a larmy?" He was trying to suck porridge through the gap in his teeth, getting it all over his face in the process.

"A what?" Asta asked.

"She," he pointed at Ilu with the clean end of the spoon, "was talking about an Imperia Larmy. Are they coming to get us?"

"Who's 'she'? The mare's mother? 'She' has a name. She was polite enough to share it with you, so you should use it."

He stuck his porridgy tongue out. "The mare's mother said . . ."

"Rhodan! That's so rude! Say sorry right now!"

He flushed. "Sorry, Tante Asta."

"Say sorry to Ilu, I meant."

He turned to Ilu, who hid her grin behind her spoon. "Sorry, Tante Ilu."

"Tante?" Ilu asked.

Asta gave up. "Run and play. Take your breakfast with you."

Rhodan hesitated. "Will you tell me what's going on later? You promise?"

"I promise. Go!"

He scampered off, out of the back door where Marcio was yowling. "Come on cat!" He scooped up the protesting feline. "Tante Asta said we have to go and play. But you can come with me when the Larmy gets here . . ." His high voice faded. Asta caught herself grinning at his chatter. If he wasn't afraid, she wouldn't be either.

"Does he think I'm his aunt?" Ilu asked, with a chuckle.

"It's polite for children in the tribe to call their elders Tante or Uncle," Asta told her. "Most of us are related anyway, it's just easier that why."

"But you're his real aunt? By blood, I mean?"

"He's my brother's son." At the mention of Finn, a great heaviness settled on her shoulders. The porridge felt gluey in her mouth, and she rose from the table. "I need a few hours alone to get ready," she said. "Will you watch Rhodan for me?"

Asta locked the bedroom door behind her. Maybe she shouldn't; if she became lost in the Spirit Realm no one would be able to get in to haul her out, but she didn't want to be interrupted. She took down one of the silken cords that held back the insect curtains, and bound one end around her wrist, the other to the carved wooden bed post. It had been so long since she'd done this. She felt a quiver deep in her guts as she let herself go, a crunching spasm of fear, and she rested a protective hand on her belly. It occurred to her as she sank into darkness that Spirit travel might harm the fragile unborn souls of her children, but by then it was too late.

When the light returned, she was on the beach below the

tower house, in the long shadow of the cliffs. But this was the Spirit Realm, where shadows didn't move, where the sand was as flat and featureless as a sheet of yellow silk. She stood for a long moment, her hand resting on a smooth rock, trying to get her breath back as she scanned the shore.

The beach was empty. No sign of Finn, and the featureless sand held no footprints. The water was calm, still as glass. She wondered if she should walk up the cliff path. Maybe he would be in the village, or by the tower? But she knew in her gut he wasn't here.

Where are you, little brother? Erikah says you're still in my head, but I can't reach you. I just want to talk.

What she wanted, if she was honest, was reassurance from him that she could do this terrible feat being asked of her, that she was taking care of Rhodan and teaching him the right things, that she could get him home safe. She wanted a hug, a good-natured ribbing, even an argument. Anything was better than the blank silence she encountered every time she reached for him.

"Finn! Where are you?"

Her words fell flat, muffled by the velvet stillness of the Spirit Realm, where there was no breeze to carry her call.

"Finn?"

The silence of the beach was unnerving. The glassy sea made no sound, her feet no crunch against patches of shingle, no birds mewled in the slate-grey sky above. But there was the faintest touch, like a gentle breath against the back of her neck, a whisper beyond the edge of hearing, deep inside her skull, urging her to remember . . .

Asta spun around, heart thundering loud as surf pounding the shore. There was no one there.

"Finn? Stop fucking about, if that's you!"

Remember . . . I know you can.

A beloved voice, so missed, so mourned, and the memory he gave her came flooding back. They had pitched the wagons at the top of the cliff, here at the end of the world where the land fell into greedy grey ocean. Here, her father declared, was a good place, with fresh air and good soil, the sea teaming with fish and the woods with game. He was tired of the life of a nomad. His people lived behind stone walls all year round, they didn't follow their herds, but tilled the soil and ate what they grew. It would be hard at first, but as time went on it would become an easier way of life. And because her father was a leader, a hero, his people fell in with his plan, and the Beehive Village was born from the rocks of the cove.

He had brought her down here that day, a girl of seven years old, leaving Finn with her mother. They clambered over rocks and he taught her how to skip stones over the surface of the water. He could make them skip five times, but no matter how she tried, and no matter that he picked her out the finest, flattest stones, she couldn't skip them as far as he did. He asked her if she would be happy living in the same place all year round, and she had tried, in her little-girl way, to get used to the idea.

But I did. She selected a flat pebble, and with a flick of her wrist sent it bounding across the still surface of the sea. One, two, three, concentric rings breaking the calm of the water, the only thing moving on that dead sea. *I got used to it. It's home now. I want to get back here.*

"You got better at that."

The unexpected voice behind her made her jump, her heart leaping to her throat. She turned, terrified in case there was no one there. But he was as real, more real, than the rock he sat on, idling tossing a pebble from hand to hand.

"I hope I taught you well."

"Da!" She was seven again, flying across the sand and into his arms, half-expecting him to vanish at her touch, but he was warm and solid, alive and comforting. Not grey and broken as she had last seen him, but freckle-dusted and smiling, the scent of horses clinging to his clothes and skin.

He held her tight, and she sensed he was battling his emotions. "My little girl," he whispered. "Look at you now!"

"What are you doing here?" She extracted herself from his embrace and sat by his side, snuggled under his arm, wanting to keep in contact. She hardly dared believe she had been given this opportunity, knew it could be taken away again at any moment.

"You brought me here. You needed me; I couldn't stay away. We don't have much time."

"I was looking for Finn. I can't find him."

Her father's face darkened. "He's not here, in the Spirit Realm." He tapped her forehead. "He's in here. He's . . . stuck, I think."

"Stuck? In my head?"

"Because of Rhodan. He's safe for now, but he's not out of danger. You got him back. That's what Finn crossed over to help you achieve. But he can't rest, not properly, until he's back with his tribe. My grandson . . ." His face took on a wondering look. He looked no older than he had that day on the beach, no older than thirty. Too young to be anyone's grandfather.

"Finn named him for you, you know. A break with tradition."

He laughed. "Our family always excelled at breaking traditions! I named you for my friend, after all." His face grew serious. "Finn is trapped between the realms. He can't move on, or back, until you get Rhodan home. But he is with you, as much as he can be. You're not on your own."

"Can you come with me?" She wanted his reassurance, his solid presence. More than anything, she missed his easy laugh.

"Three people in one head is two too many, Asta. I don't know what harm it would do you." He hugged her closer. "But I'm *always* with you."

She was silent for a moment, comfortable in the embrace. "Da, they want me to help kill a god. I don't know where to start. There are so many things that need to change . . . I'm drowning in a swamp, and people keep throwing rocks at me. What do I have to do?"

He tousled her close-cropped hair. "You have to do what you think is the right thing. Even if everyone tells you it isn't right at all. Even if it leads you down a dark path. Even if it means . . . walking away from everything you care about, from home and family, not knowing if you'll see them again. You've done it before, you can do it again. Things might not turn out the way you planned, but that's not always a bad thing. And you need to start now, by walking away from me, from this beach, back to the world of the living. Can you do that?"

She clung closer to him. "If I go, will I see you again?"

He pushed her arm down gently. "You're a grown woman, Asta. You're going to be a mother. You can't cling on to the past. But, should you need me . . ."

"I need you, Da! I can't do this on my own!"

His voice was growing faint. She felt him floating away from her. "Of course you can. You're my girl. You can do anything you set your mind to. Obstinacy is in our blood."

"Da! Don't leave me! Come back!" but the sand had shifted to hard wood beneath her. The sky transformed to the frescoed ceiling of the bedroom, the air taking on the stuffy heat of an Inyestan forenoon, and he was gone.

Asta lay on the bedroom floor for a long time, letting herself cry. It was a shameless indulgence; it wouldn't bring her father back, or solve anything in the world of the living, but the shock of seeing him again, talking to him, had shaken something deep in her core. It all came spilling out, until she felt sick and hollow, wobbly round the edges, but stronger than she had for a long time. She sat up, wiping her eyes on her sleeve, and untied the cord from around her wrist. She wouldn't need it for a while.

Well, Finn, you're as trapped as I am. Let's get us both out of here.

Even if he couldn't hear, it made her feel better to talk to him, knowing he was embedded deep in her consciousness. As a faint, hesitant knock came at the door she scrubbed her hands over her face, rubbing away the grit of tears, and ran them through her crop, spiking it up. Whatever lay ahead, she was ready to tackle it now.

Som was outside, Rhodan hanging off her arm. She looked drawn, lines of pain etched stark on her face. Her hair, usually intricately braided and pinned, was loose, a shaggy golden mane that hung past her shoulders. With her hair down she looked younger, but her face was that of a much older woman.

"Som? Are you ill?"

Som forced a grin. "I couldn't tie my hair. The joint-ail is too much, and I found this creature," she stroked the crown of Rhodan's head, "sleeping in the corridor. I thought I'd bring him to bed. Have I interrupted anything?"

Asta shook her head. "I'm done. Is it late, then?"

"Getting that way." Rhodan let her lift him into her arms with a sleepy mumble, and she transferred him to the bed, tucking the sheets over him. He was fast asleep before he could ask for a story, and Som smiled as she watched him roll onto his side and his thumb crept towards his mouth.

"Can I beg a favour before you go?" she asked. "Would you braid my hair?"

"You're not coming?" Asta knew as soon as she looked at Som's face that she wouldn't be able to cope with the rigours of breaking into the Temple, but it was a relief to hear it from the assassin's lips.

"I'll send a bug. I'll be able to keep an eye on you, at least!" Som tried to smile, but her face was strained. "You've time to do my hair before you go. I would ask Ilu, but . . ." She shrugged eloquently.

"Sisters, eh? Of course I'll do it. Sit down. You can tell me how this spy-fly magic works." It was niggling at Asta that everyone around her, Erikah, Ranmiro and now Som, could effortlessly look through the eyes of animals while the skill was denied to her. It would be so useful if she could master it.

"I suppose it's a little like your Spirit Walking." Som's hair was very soft, kinked from the constant braiding. It smelled faintly of honey and sun-warmed copper, under the miasma of smoke that clung to her skin. "The animals aren't dead, but we can ride in their consciousness, if we put our hands on them and meditate. It takes a lot of concentration, and it's easier with bigger animals, like dogs . . ."

"Or cats." Asta thought of jewelled eyes flashing in the Temple darkness.

"It takes a long time to learn, and not everyone can do it. Ilu can't, but I learned when I was sick." Her hand drifted to the scar on her face, and Asta noticed for the first time how Som wouldn't meet her own eyes in the mirror, keeping her face determinedly downcast.

She decided to let the matter drop. "Where do you keep your pins?"

"In the top drawer," Som said. "Thank you for doing this. You don't mind, do you?"

"My people braid our hair for battle. It's the sign of a warrior." Asta pulled Som's hair back into one long horse tail, and split it into three strands for braiding. "It's very important in my tribe."

Som stared at her in the mirror. She would meet the eyes of Asta's reflection, where she wouldn't meet her own. "They took your hair."

"They took a lot more than just my hair. My brother, for a start. But yes, they took my hair, my status as a warrior. They claimed they were elevating me as a goddess, but here I've been reduced to nothing more than property . . ." She pulled the braid tight and began to twist it into a bun.

"Even gods can be brought down, Asta. I would think that was a comfort to you."

Asta snorted, skewering the bun with a pair of lacquered wooden staves to keep it in place. "The difference is, I know I was never a god. I'm not even sure what that *thing* below the Temple is, god or monster."

"Maybe a little of both. Those who set themselves up as gods often become monsters in the end."

"Easier to kill a monster than a god, I suppose." As Asta brought her hands down Som reached back and gripped her wrist.

"Be careful, Asta. Whatever's under the Temple, god or monster, it won't go down easily. I don't want to have to tell Rhodan you're not coming back."

Asta gripped her hand. "You won't have to," she promised. "We have a way of talking to the dead. I'll write down what you must do, and I'll leave it in a sealed scroll under my pillow."

Silently Som handed her parchment and ink, and watched her write the instructions and seal them with wax heated in the flame of the lantern. She lifted Rhodan's sleeping head and tucked the scroll beneath the pillow, letting him down again with great tenderness.

"There you go," she said. "If I don't come back, give it to him when you think he's old enough. But trust me, I'm coming back. I won't let any god stop me going home. And obstinacy is in my blood, and Rhodan's." She patted her on the cheek. "Stay well, Som. Watch over us with your spy-fly, and you'll know how it goes."

Twenty~Seven

THE DAYS WERE hot in Inyesta, and the nights weren't much cooler. They were humid and muggy, inclined to slow-moving fogs that poured through the streets like syrup, grey fingers forcing their way down Asta's throat every time she breathed in. But she was grateful for the extra shield of darkness the fog threw over them as they huddled in the shadows opposite the Red Temple, watching the door. Normally at this hour there might be any number of beggars seeking shelter, but now, with the city under curfew, even the beggars had decided to try their luck elsewhere. Or perhaps they'd been imprisoned, or made to disappear in a more sinister fashion. The street was silent, the Temple shuttered and still. Two guards were on duty on the steps, one leaning against a pillar, the other shifting his weight from foot to foot, steel-tipped heels clicking faintly on the pavement.

Asta had gone over and over the layout of the Temple with her companions, the colonnade, the first courtyard, and the door beyond it, but she had not anticipated that it would be guarded. She turned to Ilu. "What do we do now?"

Ilu wasn't there. It was hard enough to see each other in the darkness, cloaked, hooded and masked, but one moment her eyes had been glittering through the mist at Asta's side, the next she had vanished, invisible and soundless.

"She'd better not have run out on us," Red muttered.

"I don't think—" There was a rustle from the steps, and a muffled thump. The fidgeting guard dropped to his knees, and slumped forward with barely a sound. The second guard started forward, opened his mouth to cry out and dropped like a sack of grain, groping for his throat. Asta held her breath, waiting for a yell, for the clamour of an alarm bell, but the street was once more as silent as the tomb.

"Come on, then!" The sudden voice in her ear made her jump, and snatch for her blade before she could control herself.

"Ilu, don't *do* that!"

"Sorry!" The Inyestan sounded not the slightest bit repentant. "When I work with my sister, we each know our part. We've been together so long we can anticipate each other's movements. It's hard to adjust to working with someone new." Her brows drew together. "And I've never worked with three other people before . . . Lead the way, Asta. You know where you're going better than the rest of us."

Asta squeezed Red's wrist and jerked her head towards the Temple, indicating that she should follow. She picked a path between the two slumped guards, unsure whether they were unconscious, or dead. She was reluctant to look close enough to find out one way or the other. Both prospects made her uncomfortable.

As she touched one of the pillars it flickered, just above her fingers, and she snatched her hand away in alarm. A huge pale moth, the size of her palms cupped together, fluttered over her hands and around her face. She raised an arm to brush it away, and Ilu caught her wrist.

"It's Som," she said. "She's watching out for us. Let her be."

Asta watched the moth fly a quick circuit around the four interlopers. She couldn't imagine what the world looked like through those eyes. "Are you sure it's her?"

"Sure as I can be. Come on." Ilu beckoned her into the deeper shadows of the Temple courtyard. Feline eyes flashed through the mist. Could cats' vision penetrate the magic of a shadow cloak? Were they being watched as they picked their way silently across to the door where Asta had thrown herself on the mercy of the Temple? If so, there was nothing she could do about it, but she loosened her blade in its scabbard and her fingers tightened around the hilt. She was prepared to fight. Shit, she was prepared to die, if it meant the Scattering could shake off the shackles that held Mikligard under Inyestan rule. If it meant Rhodan could go home, and not have to spend his life watching the horizon for white-sailed slave ships. She steeled herself for confrontation as Ilu stepped aside and motioned for Red to get to work on the lock.

Asta couldn't see what Red was doing, but she heard her sucking her teeth and cursing under her breath about the lack of light, the fiddly lock, the watching cats. The swearing had its own rhythm, a kind of poetry that helped her concentrate as the tumblers clicked under her skilled fingers.

Erikah leaned over to Asta, her whisper light against her ear. "Are you sure it won't be barred from inside?"

"I don't remember seeing any bars," Asta confirmed. "It's only the corridor that leads to the overnight dormitories. There's nothing of value until you get deeper into the Temple. And the place is designed more to keep people . . . *things* . . . in, not out." She felt a pang of doubt. If bars had been installed on the inside of the door to keep out the Scattering invaders, they would have to find another way in. She didn't want to chance the main Temple doors. Even this late at night, it was unlikely the hall would be quiet.

Red let out a hiss of triumph as the door gave beneath her hand. The corridor beyond was pitch black. The fog-clouded courtyard was as light as day by comparison. Ilu sighed with relief. "Dark for dark business, that's what I like to see. Go on then, Asta. You know your way around."

Asta stepped into the darkness, and it swirled around her. If she breathed in, it would pour down her throat and drown her. She stood still for a long moment, steadying herself against the wall, letting her eyes adjust. The spy-moth's pale wings fluttered just ahead of her, and it gave her the confidence to let go and follow the white shape, like a piece of paper whirling in an updraft. She led the way past the doors to the dormitories, round the corner of the corridor, and into the kitchen where the Temple served food to those in need. It was lighter in here, windows around the top of the room let in fragments of moonlight, and the banked cooking fires let out a ruddy glow. A couple of penitents curled up in front of the fires, the woman on her side with her mouth open, snoring faintly, while the man curled against her back.

The interlopers edged their way through the kitchen, sticking to the shadows. Som's moth darted ahead of them, and back, leading them deeper into the Temple, closer to the great hall where the worshippers gathered. Closer to the Deity they had come to kill.

They moved from room to room. Asta's heart was in her throat with every step. She wasn't sure she trusted the shadow-cloak she wore, not here, and she trusted herself even less. She was sure she would stumble, or cough, do something that would betray them all, and lead them to the Deity in the worst possible way. *Cat blood,* she tried to reassure herself. *I have cat blood in my veins. I can walk silently, and the night will hide me. Finn, I don't know if you can hear me, but our mother's blood will protect us—*

She started, gulping back a curse as the spy-moth darted towards her, powdered wings dashing against her face. She raised an unthinking hand to brush it away and caught herself, remembering just in time. The moth flew in again, driving her back, and from the room ahead came the faint rumble of voices. She held up her hand for quiet, though none of her followers were speaking or moving.

Ilu was beside her in a moment, soft-footed as a cat herself, her mouth close to Asta's ear. "What is it?"

"People in the next room. Som saw them. She warned me."

"Right." Ilu shook her sleeve, the slightest movement, and the strangling wire slid into her gloved hand. "How many?"

"At least two," Asta confirmed. Even through her glove, the hilt of the little dagger she wore felt sticky and slick.

"You remember what I told you?"

How to kill a man before he could scream, how to drop him so he hit the floor with the slightest sound, how to kill bloodlessly, with blowpipe and poisoned dart, but that took time to learn, time they didn't have. She nodded, feeling sick. Ilu waved for Red and Erikah to stay where they were as she crept towards the door. It stood open a crack, a thin wedge of yellow light bright in the grey darkness. No shadows to hide in, no way round that Asta knew of.

Ilu motioned her to stand back. She pushed the door, lightly, and it swung as if a breeze had taken it. Asta couldn't see into the room, but she heard the exclamation of surprise, the scrape of a chair and rapidly approaching footsteps as one of the hidden men got up to close it again.

On the opposite side of the doorway, Ilu nodded, just once. The priest looked out of the open door. "No one there," he confirmed.

Ilu was on him at once, striking like a snake. Her wire slipped over his neck and around his throat, drawn tight before he could squeak. He tried to kick out, but she hooked his heels from under him and dumped him on his knees on the floor. He had pale eyes, and they bulged out like two boiled eggs as they filled with blood. He tried to clutch the wire with thick, fumbling fingers. Ilu leant back, twisting the wooden handles ever tighter, cutting deeper and deeper into the skin of his throat. His face darkened, his hands went slack, and the smell of shit rose from his crotch as he voided his bowels in the moment of death.

Ilu let him go, and he slumped face-down on the floor. There was a moment of sickly silence before the call came from the room.

"Leo? What's going on out there?"

Ilu crouched over Leo's body, retrieving her wire. She glanced up, caught Asta's eye, and nodded.

The man who came to the door had his back to Asta. He cried out in alarm as he stumbled over the body of his friend, and the woman who had killed him, and it was the last sound he ever made. Asta curled an arm around his throat, close as any lover, and drove the dagger hard into his right kidney.

His mouth dropped open, but the only sound he made was a long wheeze. As she wrenched the blade free, she felt the heat of his blood through her gloves. He fell with a clatter that made her curse aloud.

"Asta!" Her name on Ilu's lips was a sibilant hiss, the snarl of an angry cat.

"I'm sorry!" The dagger falling from her bloodied hand made even more racket as it clattered on the stone floor. "Shit, what am I doing? Ilu, I didn't mean—"

"Hush!" Ilu gripped her by the shoulders. "It's all right. Be quiet now!"

"I can't . . . I mean . . . Fuck, I'm a warrior, I've killed men before . . . but not like this!" She looked down into Leo's upturned face, and realised with a sharp jolt that they had been penitents together, had worked side by side in the kitchen, barely speaking but aware of each other's presence. He had never done her any harm.

"What's wrong with the breeder?" Red demanded, emerging from the shadows.

"It's all right. Assassination takes some people like this, the first time. That's why I wanted my sister with me. A steady hand . . ." She laughed at the irony, and Asta found herself relaxing in her embrace, letting go of her panic the way Som let go of her pain when she inhaled her smoke. Ilu massaged her shoulder. "Feeling better?"

"I'm sorry. I lost myself for a moment. I don't know what happened. I know him—"

"It doesn't matter. Have you found yourself again?"

Asta nodded.

"Then let's get on. The night's not getting any younger." She stepped neatly over the bodies, holding up her cloak. Erikah made a little sound of distaste. "What? It's all right to kill in the name of your people, but not my Emperor?"

"We shouldn't leave them piled up like this," Erikah insisted. "It's disrespectful."

Ilu shrugged. "I'm sure when their people find them they'll bury them or throw them in the sea or chop them up into godfood. The dead are the dead. We can do no more for them. But let's make sure their deaths weren't for nothing, shall we?"

She strode on, putting an effective end to the discussion. Asta, Red and Erikah trailed behind her until she beckoned Asta forward once more. "Are you safe to lead now?"

"I'll be fine." They were approaching the hall where the worshippers gathered, where the great metal door was concealed behind the altar. Asta had led them onto one of the high galleries, to scan the room from above before they descended to the nave. She was glad she had; from the balcony she counted six guards around the altar, and more dotted around the room, in poses ranging from eager to half-asleep. There was no way they could reach the tunnel behind the altar, even shadow-cloaked and moving like ghosts.

"There must be another way in?" Erikah asked.

"There must be," Ilu urged. "Think, Asta! You've been down there and come back. Was there any other way into the sacrifice chamber? Some little overlooked hole?"

"There might be one . . ." Ice cold water, washing the blood from her hands and face, splashing down from the darkness of the roof above . . . "Of course! It's under the ice house! The run-off water from the ice. It's so hot in the chamber, but the ice-water runs down the wall. It cools it down. They use it . . ." she faltered, "they use it for washing down the altar."

"You think there's a way in through the ice house?" Ilu's voice was sombre. "Where is it?"

"Back through the kitchen, out of the back door. I should have thought of that while we were there."

"Not to worry," Ilu said. "The deeper it gets into night, the fewer people will be about. Is the ice house usually guarded?"

"I don't think so. Why guard it? Who would steal ice?"

Ilu laughed low in her throat. "Who wouldn't? The ice trade is worth a lot of paper round here, and the Temple controls every aspect of it. Trust me, there will be a guard. He might not be the youngest or fittest, but they won't leave the ice house unguarded."

Ilu was right. There was a guard on the ice house, sat against the wall with his chin slumped forward on his chest. His helmet lay by his side, and the shiny dome of his head gleamed in the blurry moonlight. Ilu drew one of her tiny, poisoned blades, the ones kept in a case strapped to her left arm, and dispatched him before he could even wake up. She left him propped against the wall, and returned his helmet to his head, drawing it low to conceal his swollen lips and protruding tongue.

"With a bit of luck no one will notice," she said. "Red, do you want to try the door?"

Red did not respond, and Ilu let her mask drop and tried again. "Red? Red!"

Red dropped to her haunches and studied the door. "Not locked," she said. "Are you done with having me along?"

Ilu threw a querying glance at Asta.

"We might need you to help us get out," she confessed, letting her own mask fall. "I hadn't thought much past getting into the Sacrifice Chamber."

"You'd thought to get in, but not out?" Red scoffed. "I guess with what we're doing there's not likely to be a return journey, is there?"

"It seems unlikely," Ilu said grimly.

Red threw up her hands. "Fuck it!"

"Fuck it, you're leaving?" Asta asked. Red hesitated. "You can go if you want. You've done more than enough, getting us this far. Som has your freedom papers, and some money. You can go wherever you want."

"Doesn't matter where I go, I can't get away from me." Red

looked pensive. "I'm tired. I'm done with this shit. If I die here, at least I'll die doing something to piss in the eye of the Temple. Fuck it, I'm still in, wherever that takes me."

"What about you, Erikah?" Ilu asked. "You're very quiet."

"I'm listening."

Asta listened too, but she couldn't hear anything. "What can you hear?" she asked.

"The thoughts of the Inyestan God. They're so jumbled, so full of pain, and hunger. They hurt my head." She rubbed her brow. "I think what we're doing here will be a mercy, and not just to the slaves."

Mercy was something Asta knew all about. She hitched her cloak higher on her shoulders, and sidestepped the dead guard outside the ice house. Inside, the cold whipped her breath away. The fine hairs on her arms prickled and stood to attention as the chill cut through her robes to the skin beneath, and she hugged herself as she looked up at the blocks of ice. They were sliced into rough blue-white chunks around the size of bricks, stacked halfway to the ceiling that domed high overhead. As she exhaled, her breath curled before her mouth like wisps of smoke from a pipe. Red stamped her feet, and pulled her scarf down further over her ruined ears. "Shiiit," she muttered, a long exhalation ending in a sigh. "Are we going to stand about admiring the ice all night?"

Asta shook off the paralysing chill, so shocking after the warm humidity outside. "I'm not," she said. "There must be a drain or a run-off in the floor. Let's look for it."

The pallor of the ice cast its own eerie shine, like filtered moonlight, making it brighter in the ice house than Asta had anticipated. They stood on a stone lip circling the edge of the building, level with the door, and in front of her was a drop of about six feet to the lower layers of ice. She lowered herself carefully off the edge, losing sight of her companions as they spread out, searching for the elusive way in that led to the sacrifice chamber.

Walking on the ice was perilous. Asta had to stretch up to hang on to the lip of the shelf above, or steady herself against the cold, damp wall to keep her footing. Several times she slipped, with a lurch that sent her stomach leaping into her mouth. The quiet of the ice house was eerie, punctuated only with the soft drip of melting ice and the distant rumble of Red cursing more loudly than she realised.

There was another layer of ice blocks below her, creating a step down to the damp stone floor of the building. The floor sloped faintly under her feet, and the ice towered above, smooth and impenetrable as a mountain face. She watched the faint blue shape of her own reflection in the white, a hooded phantom sliding over the glassy planes.

"Asta! Over here!"

Erikah had her hood pushed back, copper hair curling over her shoulders. She shifted from one foot to the other, and as Asta approached she realised the Scattering woman stood ankle-deep in water that was so cold she felt the chill over it even in this bitter place. She stumbled into the stream, and her curse sent an echo bouncing around the domed room as she tried to snatch her feet back. Her shout brought Ilu running.

"Be quiet!" she demanded. "What has Erikah found?"

"The way down, I think. I stumbled across it." She pointed to a raised grille set in the floor, just below the level of the water. "This is where the melt-water from the ice runs off. It's the lowest point of the floor. Do you think that's the source of your waterfall, *gudienne*?"

"It might be." Asta crouched, trying not to flinch at the freezing water swirling around her calves. The grille covered a square hole in the floor. It looked wide enough to get her shoulders through, but with the water and the uncertain play of light and shadow, she couldn't tell if it narrowed further down, or how far the drop was.

Silently, Red held out a chunk of ice, and Asta let it fall through the gaps in the grating. It made a reassuring "plink!"

as it landed, and she guessed it was only a few feet down before there was, at least, some kind of floor. She looked up to see Ilu looming over her, an anxious cast to her face.

"I think we should try it," she said. "I can't think of any other way in."

Ilu dropped to her haunches beside her. "Are you sure?" she said, in a low voice. "You don't know where it goes. I'd hate to get stuck down there." She shuddered. "Shit, this water is cold! I can barely feel my feet any more!"

"If it looks like it leads nowhere, we'll turn back," Asta assured her, trying not to let her own anxiety colour her voice. "I don't like it any more than you, but what's the alternative?"

Ilu straightened. "In that case, can we get that grate up?"

Asta rattled it. Even through her gloves her fingers were growing numb, and the cold iron cut into her palms. The grille gave a little, on the left hand side, but the other side was stuck firm. "I think we could lever it up," she said, "If we had anything—"

"Try it with your dagger," Ilu suggested.

"Use your own dagger. I need mine. You've got spares."

"Take mine." Erikah held out her own blade. Asta expected an elaborate sacrificial knife of the kind Olafur had worn, but the single-edged knife Erikah handed over was plain, solid and serviceable. It would not have looked out of place on a meal table, but the blade was stout. Asta inserted it under the grate and levered it slowly upwards, feeling the metal give in its bed of stone. The tempered steel of the blade bent under the pressure until she thought it would snap and she closed her eyes, turning her head away against the impact.

With a clang and a splash, the grate fell back, spattering water up into Asta's face. She shook it clear. The water gurgled into the black opening that yawned at her knees. It looked very dark, and very cold.

Asta looked up at Ilu. "You're the biggest," she said. "You go first."

"Like fuck I will!" The Emperor's assassin quailed before that dark hole in the floor. "I've been trapped in confined spaces before. I still wake up at night in a sweat thinking about it. I'll go down, but you have to go first. Besides, you know what we're dropping into."

"I hope I do." Asta pulled her wet cloak tighter around her body, and sat down with her legs hanging down the hole. The freezing water made her hips ache as if she was an old woman, and she wondered for a moment if her babes could feel it, if they clung to each other against the chill.

You'd better still be looking out for them, Finn.

She pushed off from the edge and dropped, smacking her elbow on the lip of the drain hard enough to bring tears to her eyes. Her feet jarred on the floor, and when she blinked away the water she was standing in a narrow passage, the roof low enough to scrape her skull, that sloped steeply downwards into the earth. She was also standing under a torrent of water that poured down the hole, and she stepped forward quickly, but not before it had run down her spine and made her squeal. She pulled her hood back up to avoid more drenching, and to hide from the walls that crowded in around her, pressed down on her skin. If she lost herself to panic down here, she would ruin everything.

She called up to the dim figures moving above, and to the moth flitting around their heads. "It looks safe, come down!"

Red landed beside her, shaking the water from her headscarf like a dog emerging from a pond. She peered down the tunnel, and flashed her teeth. "Homely," she remarked.

"Hopefully it won't be for long," Asta said.

"Shit, you think what's at the other end, it can go on for miles and I won't complain!" She moved aside as Erikah dropped down, wringing out her long hair and tucking it back under her hood. She had retrieved her knife, and weighed it in her hand, looking around as if she expected an assault from all sides.

"If we carry on that way," she pointed down the tunnel, "are we heading underneath the Red Temple?"

"What?" Red cocked her head. "You talking to me?"

"Did they name the Temple after you?" Erikah asked archly.

"Maybe they named it after your hair?" Red reached out, curled a loose strand of Erikah's hair around her finger, and sniffed it. "I recall I had long hair when I was a little girl. About the only thing I do remember."

Asta stroked a hand over her own hood, missing her braids, the honour that went with them. If she could bring down the Inyestan god, she deserved her braids back. If not, she would be dead and it wouldn't matter. And Rhodan, who had been so courageous – he was young to start growing his hair, but he deserved to be recognised for his bravery. If she got him home.

She shook out her shoulders, and stared down the passage ahead. It was dark, with only the white shape of Som's spy-moth's wings to guide them. She was losing the sensation in her feet as the water spilled over them. The longer they stood here, the harder it would be to walk. She glanced around at her companions, barely able to see their faces in the darkness. "Are you ready?"

There were murmurs of assent.

"Then let's move. I hope Som can see where we're going, because I sure as shit can't."

Asta kept her eyes fixed on the flicker of the moth as she followed the tunnel downwards. It wasn't a steady incline, in places it was so steep it was easier to slide on her backside and let the water help her along. There were a few sheer drops, none so high they couldn't be navigated, but unexpected and jarring on the ankles and knees. And always Som's moth hovered just ahead, white wings a light in the darkness, leading them on, and down, until at last she vanished altogether.

Erikah walked into Asta's heels with a splash as she stopped in confusion. Asta hushed her. There was light up ahead, a dim burning glow that diffused up through the floor, turning the water the same shade as Erikah's hair, illuminating a solid wall of rock ahead. They had reached the end of the tunnel; in front of her feet the water spilled through a long, wide crack in the floor. That was where the light came up from. She knelt, trying to squint through the rushing water into the chamber below.

Ilu dropped beside her. "What do you see? Anyone there?"

It was impossible to tell. Her eyes streamed with water, her ears full of the sound of the waterfall. "If there is anyone there," she whispered back, "there won't be more than a couple of them. We can take them if we have to. Or we can wait."

"Let's get it over with." The crack in the floor was wide enough to wriggle through. It was a long drop to the floor below, too far to climb back up again if anyone was to come into the room, and Asta, stepping out of the waterfall, felt uncomfortably exposed. The cloaks would hide them in the shadows, as long as they didn't move, but she doubted that would be enough.

Erikah staggered as she landed, clutching her head. "It's overwhelming to be this close," she confessed. "It's hard to shut out. A god's mind is so much more powerful than a human's. It's . . . primal." She shuddered. "I hope we can kill it quickly."

Ilu scanned the room. There was nowhere to hide, and from behind the latticed wall Asta heard low gruntings and the sound of massive weight shifting, claws scraping on stone.

"It's hungry," Erikah said.

Ilu rubbed her hands together. Her wet cloak steamed faintly in the heat. "Red, have a look at the door. Is it barred or just locked? Asta, how big is that creature?"

"It's hard to tell. Don't get too close," she cautioned, catching Ilu's sleeve as she took a step towards the wall with the holes. "What are you going to do? Stab it?"

"I thought poison. Though how much poison it would take to bring down a God . . ." she rubbed her chin thoughtfully. "I don't know the physiology, that's a problem. But if I can dart it with a strong enough poison that should take care of it while we blow the wall."

"While we – what?" No one had mentioned blowing anything up before.

"Just a little black powder. Enough to take down the wall, no more. Then . . . we take his head, as proof we've killed him. After that," she patted Asta on the shoulder, "we go home." She reached into her cloak for her blowpipe. "I already loaded a dart with the strongest poison I have. With luck, he won't know what hit him."

Erikah stiffened, like a hound on a scent. "Someone's coming!"

"Are you sure?" Ilu had the dart to her lips.

"Red? Red! Is someone coming?"

Red shrugged. "Can't hear anything, horse girl. But that doesn't mean—" She broke off, scuttled away from the door in a spider crouch. "I hear them now, right enough. What do we do?"

There was nowhere to hide, even if there had been time. There was barely time to draw a blade before the door rattled and the beast beyond the wall gave throat to a roar that set the ground trembling.

The door swung open. Asta had been expecting a couple of priests and a sacrifice, but instead she looked into the face of a phalanx of Temple guards, bristling with weapons, every blade ready and pointed at her. She felt the blood wash from her face at the sight.

Ilu's hand moved quicker than thought. There was a sigh, and a faint whizzing sound, like the hum of an insect, and one of the guards dropped with a clang of metal, as if he had been felled by a blow to the skull. The man next to him leapt forward, but he was stilled by a harsh command, barked from inside the cohort of armed men.

"Don't kill them yet. Our Deity will feast well tonight!"

Asta backed against the altar. She could hear the god behind her, shuffling restlessly, gusts of hot breath blasting her damp skin through the perforated wall. The guards spread out, weapons held steady, levelled at the four women, and behind them was a woman Asta had convinced herself was dead.

Chesserai wore a half-mask, the horned gold-swirled demon-cat, and the lower half of her face was swathed in bandages. She leant heavily on Margoli's arm, and she moved stiffly, hunched, as if her skin had shrunk and tightened over her sparse flesh. Her left hand was bandaged, and rested on a brass-topped cane of ebon wood. On her other side, drawn and pale, lips trembling, was Gartzea.

For a second the air hung still between them, as the poisoned guard gurgled his last at Chesserai's feet. Ilu moaned softly, a faint echo of unbearable grief, sword drooping in her hand as if it was too hard to hold it up. Asta looked from her to Gartzea, and back, trying to make sense of his presence here. "Gartzea?" she ventured. "You're meant to be with Rhodan, and Som . . ."

In reply he held out his fist, and opened it, palm upwards. The crushed remains of the moth stained his palm, and his fingers were thick with dust from her wings. "I'm sorry, Asta. You're on your own now."

"My *sister!*" Caution, training, were thrown to the wind as Ilu lunged forward in fury, to be felled by the butt end of a pikestaff slamming into her stomach. She doubled up even as one of her blades flicked out and ripped open her assailant's throat.

A second guard howled as Erikah's sturdy knife caught him below the hip, and the noise broke a spell. Asta ducked as Margoli lunged towards her, feeling the razor-sharp sacrificial blade shear her cloak and shave the skin from her shoulder. She rolled, came up in a fighting crouch in front of the latticed wall, feeling it shake at her back as the god battered against it, roaring his hunger.

Margoli circled her. Asta heard shouting, but all she saw was the lethal blade in the priest's hand. The blood trickled warm and wet down her back.

"Margoli, I don't want to fight you."

"Why did you come back? I gave you a chance to get away, even after what you did!" She lashed out. Asta sprang sideways, and the blade skittered across stone. Margoli's knuckles were bleeding, and her lips moved, but Asta heard nothing over the raging of the imprisoned god.

She lunged again. Asta fended her off with an elbow, cracking against her jaw. Margoli stumbled, gripping the altar for support, and Asta twisted the dagger and slammed it down into her hand.

Margoli howled, eyes wide and blue. She tried to break free but Asta was on her. She whipped a second dagger from the sheath at the back of her neck and pressed it to her throat.

"Chesserai! Call your dogs off or I'll kill her!"

Margoli squeaked.

"You're a good woman," Asta spoke to her in a lower voice. "You can't believe what happens here is right. I don't want to kill you."

The Inyestan woman bucked against her, trying to throw her off, but Asta held her firm. "You don't understand, do you?" Margoli spat. "Foreign bitch, you've got no soul, no faith . . . My God will protect me."

"Your god is a killer, a monster. Can't you see that?"

"Asta!" Ilu's voice was breathless. Asta couldn't look around, all her attention fixed on Margoli. The priest's lips twitched in a strained smile. "Asta, finish her and help Red!"

Margoli's lips stretched until she was beaming. "Yes, kill me. I'm willing to offer my blood to feed my Master, to make him strong enough to destroy you."

"Margoli, please, listen to me. Your god is insane. We came here to kill him. You need to let him go . . ."

"Heresy!" With unexpected strength Margoli shoved her away, long enough to drag the knife from her hand, leaving a ragged, bloody hole through her palm. She fumbled with the blade, catching Asta across her collarbone, a searing pain that drove her to her knees. The ground around her feet was slick with blood. It was seeping under the altar, down into the secret pipes beneath the floor, into the cave.

Margoli was all teeth and eyes, spittle gathering at the corners of her mouth. "He will feast on me. He will take me in, and I will be his bride."

"Margoli, stop it! Stop it, come away now! For fuck's sake . . ."

Margoli turned the blade round, bloodied tip pointed at her own throat. Her eyes rolled back in her head as Asta snatched it, too late. There was blood all over her hands, spurting in wet gouts across the altar. The blade was embedded in Margoli's throat and her hands twitched towards it, eyes glazing as she lost consciousness.

"Margoli!" There was thunder at Asta's back, the wall vibrating with trapped fury. The Deity sensed his food, could smell it, but it was denied to him. The trickle of blood running under the altar incited him to frenzy, and he slammed against the walls of his prison to reach the meat. No stone could withstand such a battering.

Asta felt the crack before she heard it, as a change in the air behind her. With a shriek and a rumble a section of wall gave way, showering her with crumbling stone and plaster. A chunk of falling masonry struck her bleeding shoulder, and her vision blurred with pain. Erikah screamed, and Red grabbed her arm and dragged her towards the door.

"Asta! Run!"

She looked back. She had to. A gaping hole was torn in the wall. She saw claws, curling around the stone, ripping it open wider and wider. Chesserai stood before the wall, arms thrown wide to receive the embrace of her divine husband as her guards fled. Only one had wit to grab her and throw her screaming over his shoulder as he ran for the door, almost knocking Asta from her feet in his desperation to escape.

The gap in the wall yawned wider, releasing the rank stench of the prison that contained the enraged god.

"Asta, come on!"

She spun round, bloodied shoes slipping on the stone floor of the passage. Gartzea and one of Chesserai's guards heaved against the iron doors, struggling to throw them closed as Red dragged her through. They clanged shut on her heels, but there was no time to shoot the bar home. From the room beyond came a ripping, roaring rumble, like the earth in motion, and a crash against the doors that buckled them outwards as if they were no thicker than paper.

"We have to keep it in!" Red raced for the next set of doors, dragging Erikah by the wrist. Asta followed, stumbling in the wake of the guard who bore Chesserai. She was kicking and punching, her shouts muffled against the soft cloth that covered his breastplate. Asta's head swam, and it was hard to breathe. Her left arm was numb from the shoulder down, and the pain spread across her back like consuming flame. From behind came the rhythmic clanging of metal, keeping perfect time with the clamour of her heart.

She half-turned to look back, stumbled, and her left shoulder collided with the unforgiving wall of the passage as the doors gave way under the beast's assault. There was a rush of air, of fire. The explosion erupted in her collar and sent fire searing down her arm, and up, through her skull, spearing into her mind, and then there was only darkness.

TWENTY-EIGHT

IT WAS COLD. Cold and dark, and Asta curled up on hard ground. When she tried to push up with her left hand, her arm gave way beneath her and she sprawled on her face, smacking her nose with such force it brought tears to her eyes. She lay there for a long moment, gathering her strength, assessing her surroundings, cursing herself for getting knocked out again. She needed to grow a harder head.

There was silence. No, not silence, but noise that was so distant she didn't fear it was approaching at any speed. A quick mental sweep of her own body confirmed that both legs were working, and the way she could move her arm told her it wasn't broken, just wrenched and sore. She laid her right hand on her belly and felt a reassuring rumble.

Thanks, Finn. You couldn't protect me from knocks in the same way?

Her shadow cloak pooled around her on the floor. The hood had fallen over her head when she fell, and she pushed it back cautiously, and sat up. She was alone in the corridor. Behind her, the iron doors to the sacrifice chamber were ripped from their hinges and thrown down like Rhodan's toys. Ahead was nothing but darkness, and a chill breeze blowing down from above, carrying those unnerving fragments of sound.

She staggered to her feet, swaying on wobbly legs, balancing against the wall for support. There seemed no choice but to carry on up the tunnel towards the hall of worship, to try and find her friends. She couldn't stay here, and the idea of going back into the sacrifice chamber to find a light turned her stomach. She would press on, in darkness, and hope that if she found death ahead it would be swift and painless.

She still had her sword. The hilt bruised her left hip when she fell, but it was just another pain to add to the horde. She wondered if this was how Som felt, all the time, and at the thought of Som she remembered the white moth, crushed in Gartzea's ruthless hand. Had Som died, in that instant, leaving Rhodan alone in the house on the Hill? How could she reach him now?

The next set of gates was smashed down. One hung creaking from a single twisted hinge, jagged metal reaching out to claw Asta as she climbed through. She pulled her cloak free and kept going. The disturbing echoes grew louder as she passed through gate after gate, all broken and twisted like scraps of paper. She kept expecting to see bodies; her friends, the guards, Chesserai.

The first bodies were further up the passage. One of the guards, his head neatly lopped from his shoulders and rolled a hundred yards up the corridor, and Gartzea. He lay on his face, his truncated arm curled beneath him, the other flung out across the floor. As Asta stepped over it, his fingers twitched against her ankle, and he groaned.

"Gartzea?" She dropped to her knees beside him and rolled him on to his back. His chest heaved, and there was blood on his temple. "What happened? Ilu . . . Red?"

He shook his head, dazed. "I'm sorry, Asta. I'm so, so sorry . . ."

"You fucking should be, you piece of shit! If they're dead, if Som's dead . . ." Her knife was in her hand, pressed into the bottom of his ribcage. If he tried to fight her, she would stick him.

"Why would Som be dead?" He was trying to focus on her face, tongue flicking over cracked lips.

"The moth . . . you crushed it . . ." Powder drifting from his hand to the chamber floor, a quiet moment of murderous stillness.

Gartzea tried to laugh, and winced as Asta's blade dug in harder.

"I'll kill you. Don't think I'll hesitate. How could you?"

"How could I what? Som," he coughed, curled in on himself, tried again. "Som isn't dead! I cut her contact with the moth, but that wouldn't kill her. Didn't she explain it to you?"

"Hardly. And that doesn't make up for what you did. How could you betray us to Chesserai?"

He squirmed. "It's not that simple. When I was in hospital . . ." His eyes flicked down to his arm. Asta felt a pang of guilt, but she wasn't going to let him off that easily. "The priests came. They took good care of me, and told me about the Deity. They reconnected me to my faith. At least, I thought they did. They seemed so charming, so caring, always bringing me drinks and listening to me raging—"

Drinks. "They drugged you, didn't they?"

"I don't know. I thought it was the pain, or the herbs I was taking for the pain. Everything was hazy. Still is." He massaged his forehead. "I was a fool. They asked me to repent my sins and I-I told them about Ederon. He came to the house after you left tonight and told me they'd threatened to kill him if I didn't do as they said." His eyes widened. "I can't lose him, Asta! I can't!"

She let the blade drop, at last. "You're a fucking idiot, you know that? Are you hurt badly?"

"I think I could stand now." Her arm tucked in the crook of his elbow, and the wall, helped him to his feet. He shook his head. "I've fucked up everything, haven't I?"

"Maybe. Maybe not. We can still kill this God."

He tottered a few steps. "I'm not fit for fighting, Asta. I'm sorry. What can I do?"

She peered out into the hall, screwing up her eyes against the sudden light. "Go home," she said. "Protect Rhodan. Help Som get him to safety if it all goes wrong. You might have to deal with the anger of the Shadow Cloaks later. I don't have time for you now."

He squeezed her hand. "Be safe, Asta."

"Fuck off!"

He darted one way from behind the great altar, she went the other, and she lost sight of him in the glare and the drifting smoke that stung her eyes. She hoped he got out alive, because if Ilu found him first he stood no chance.

She stumbled over something soft, yielding. One of the choir boys, lying twisted around the bottom of the altar. A chunk was torn from his torso, from hip to armpit, and the snapped-off ends of his ribs stuck out through the gore. She stepped over him, swallowing the bile in her throat.

Now her eyes were used to the glare, she could see other corpses littering the room, strewn like rag dolls, crumpled and broken and dropped where they had fallen. The light came through tears rent in the metal doors at the far end of the hall, throwing a halo around the huddled figure who knelt in supplication before the altar. The only sound in the room was the steady drip of blood and a monotonous litany, rhythmic chanting that never varied in tempo. In the distance she heard shouts and crashing, the clamour of bells, but in the temple all was still.

Asta took a step away from the altar, and the worshipper raised her head. It was Chesserai, and she looked at Asta blankly for a long moment, struggling to focus on her face. Her mask had fallen, and for the first time Asta saw the burn scars that puckered the left side of her face, shiny tightened skin pulling one side of her mouth upwards in a permanent leer.

"Asta . . . You lied to me about your name, but that doesn't matter now." Chesserai's tongue flickered. Her voice was an octave deeper than before, and in the depths of her opaque eyes tiny fires burned. She pushed herself away from the altar and stood erect, swaying as if buffeted by a strong wind. "You can't stop us. Don't even try."

"Us?" Asta took a step forward, wary of the knife in the hand of the High Priestess. "It's not me that's going to stop you, Chesserai. The Imperial Army are on their way to take down your god, and your Temple. It's over."

"It's over for you!" Her eyes were wild, looking at a spot far beyond Asta. "I ride in the head of my God. He carries me with him on his righteous crusade, to crush the unbelievers and the blasphemous."

"You ride in the head of your god? Chesserai, what have you done?" Asta edged around the altar as Chesserai backed away, her metal-tipped heels striking through the gore underfoot to the bare stone beneath.

"What have I done? Only the same as you and your ghost-brother. You of all people should understand."

"I'll never understand your faith, Chesserai." Something squelched under her feet. Asta dared not look down. All her attention was on her adversary. "You're ankle-deep in blood. Give it up." She shrugged the cloak from her shoulders. "Give it up and I'll give you my shadow cloak. You can get away. No one else has to die to feed your faith. What do you say?"

"They do not die!" Chesserai's protest was a high scream wrung from her twisted mouth. "They live in their god forever, as I will! You can't stop this, Atrathene!"

Asta was close enough to make a grab for her, but Chesserai twisted under her lunge, spun on her heel and ran. She splashed through pools of blood, her long stride taking her heedless over the crumpled remains of the dead. The sudden movement caught Asta off balance, and the satin fabric of the cloak slid from her arms. She hesitated for an instant, unsure whether she should leave it, but as Chesserai gained distance on her, her mind was made up. She ran after the priestess, after the trail of red footprints, as Chesserai vanished through the door that led to her tower.

The spiral was tight, and Asta breathless. She heard Chesserai above, panting and slipping on the stairs, and a shoe came flying down the helix and struck her hard in the shoulder. Asta ducked the second shoe and kept going. She was on Chesserai's heels as she crossed the landing and threw herself through the door of the soap-bubble chamber. The priest tried to slam the door, but Asta met it with a kick that threw it back on its hinges, and stumbled into the room.

Chesserai balanced on the high window ledge, where Asta had stood and looked down on the city the day she snatched Rhodan from the baleful influence of the Temple. She was not looking at Asta. Her face and hands were pressed to the glass, and she keened high in her throat. If Asta ran up behind her, she could push her through the fragile glass, to the pavement hundreds of feet below. The fall might take Asta with it, but –

"I wouldn't do that, if I were you."

Chesserai's voice was so calm, so reasonable, that Asta hesitated.

"You can if you want, but first come up here beside me, little daughter. Tell me what you see. Look, my knife is on the table. I have no weapon to strike you. If you still want to push me out of the window, go ahead. But I don't think you will."

"Why?" Despite herself, Asta was drawn towards the glass. Chesserai held out a hand to help her up, but Asta ignored it, and looked in the direction the High Priest pointed.

The Nidus was burning, the vast sprawling slum lost under a pall of brown smoke that towered a mile or more in the still air. And the god walked through the slums, through the haze, immune to fire, to blades, blind and deaf to all but its own insatiable hunger. He ripped open the roofs of the shanties as if they were the skins of ripe fruit, gouging out the contents and devouring them, human and animal both.

"I see through his eyes." Chesserai's voice was a breath in her ear. "I feel his hunger, his madness. I can control his mind. I can control my god. Look there."

She pointed northwards, and the Deity kicked out as he swung around, great bull head lowering.

"What we have done to the Nidus, we can do to the Hill. Isn't your little boy hidden on the Hill?"

"You wouldn't take on the Hill. Your own people live there."

Chesserai laughed, a high, strangled sound. She had bitten her lips until the blood flowed freely down her chin, mixing with the froth at the corner of her lips. Asta had seen a dog once with water fever, and Chesserai's rolling eyes and foaming lips reminded her of that. "What do I care for people?" She threw her arms wide. "Today, I am a god! Push me from the window, and my Lord will find your boy and tear him limb from limb. And you," Asta felt the cold prick of a knife at the back of her neck, "you're going to experience it. Every screaming second. You'll watch with me, inside the head of our god, and you'll understand. You'll welcome him into your foreign, blasphemous heart before you die."

"I will not!" But the knife pressed hard against the nape of her neck, digging into her spine, and Chesserai's lips were just as hard against her forehead, blood and spittle sinking into her cuts and scrapes. The room lurched under that venomous kiss . . .

Asta opened her eyes. The city was red-washed, multifaceted, small and weak under her great horned feet. She felt the power, the strength of anger flowing back into long-wasted muscles. They had hurt her. They had fed her blood and kept her imprisoned in the dark for so long she could remember little else. The light out here scalded her eyes, seared through her mind and exploded in a riot of colours in her skull. There was too much, too much light, too much noise, too much information bombarding her from every direction after too long in the dark. All she wanted was to get back there, to her darkness, her warmth, her stinking cell, away from the chaos in her head. But there was an itch . . .

The itch was deep inside her mind. It was familiar; she had felt it before, so many times in her long confinement. There had been different voices over the long years, but the words were always the same. And always, after, there was meat. There was meat now, she could reach out and snatch it from the streets and dwellings, but the voice, the itch, pushed her onwards. Upwards, to where the human dwellings were bigger, away from the miasma of smoke and stench that hung over the port.

The itch was deep in her mind, and even deeper, like a firefly seen against an explosion of stars, was Asta herself, her own awareness riding in the head of the furious, frightened god. And even deeper, so far down it was barely a spark of consciousness, was Finn.

Finn! She felt him stir, for the first time in an age, and the rush of love for her brother brought her own awareness flaring to the surface. The Deity hesitated, shaking his great head in confusion, trying to rid himself of the turmoil in his mind.

Well, you get yourself into some situations, sister. His voice was as wry as ever.

Finn, the god, he's going to kill Rhodan. Chesserai is controlling him. I don't know how to stop him. Help me?

I can hold her. But it means letting go of the twins. It means exposing them, to danger, and exposing you to them. Are you willing to take the risk?

What risk?

I don't know. He sounded worried. *I've been trying to protect them, and you, from everything I can.*

Plenty of women carry babies without a spirit protector, Finn.

Most of them don't ride around in the heads of gods!

Finn, let go of them. Stop Chesserai. Hundreds of people have died already. Do you want Rhodan to join them?

She felt him withdraw, first his consciousness, and then his presence from her form, draining away from her head. She felt a giddying rush, of love, of fear, of hunger. How much of that was her, and how much that of the god? She looked through his eyes, watching the houses of the Hill crumple like paper money before his furious passage, his face level with the upper storeys, claws dragging holes in masonry and marble.

Asta? Can you still hear me?

I hear you, Finn. She heard him, but she couldn't feel him. For the moment, they were two separate entities.

Take the reins, sister. Save my son.

Chesserai was gone. Asta felt her, muted, struggling as Finn threw the same net over her that had cradled Asta with such care while she looked for Rhodan. Suddenly she was alone in the mind of Chesserai's mad god, and it was overwhelming. She spiralled down into darkness as the Deity's mind threatened to overwhelm her. She was drowning in a deep pool, her feet striking out to seek purchase on the bottom, and finding none. She kicked and thrashed, and the world, spinning in four planes, swam back into focus. She saw the street now, where Gartzea's house stood, where Rhodan must be hiding. The God's shadow fell before him, elongated by the morning sunlight, and the darkness fell over the mansion. She could see the flat roof, the scarred woman standing, legs wide, sword held across her body. Som, not dead but determined, willing to throw herself into battle with a god.

Asta screamed a warning, but it was lost under the tempest of the god's roar. She fought to hold him back, clutch his mind, but he threw her off as easily as she would have brushed away a fly. He reached out, and she felt the sting, like a piercing insect bite through her own palm as Som sunk her sword through the creature's outstretched hand.

Crimson flared up before her eyes, rage and pain. No one had dared hurt her, not for a long time, and the shock hurt as much as the wound. The god shook his hand, and the blade skittered across the rooftop in a bright spray of blood. His other hand caught Som full across the body. Asta felt the crunch of bones giving way beneath her palm, the heat of blood as Som's chest caved in and she crumpled lifeless against the stone.

The god licked his hand. Asta taste blood, hot copper richness filling her mouth. It made her hungry, the familiar taste. There was meat after blood. Always meat. She reached for the broken woman, wanting to taste the flesh, the crack of marrow between her teeth, to sate the hunger that never left her.

"You leave her alone!"

The god turned, and Asta with him, to see what Som had died to protect. The sword was as long as Rodan was tall, and he could barely lift it. He staggered under the weight, point dragging on the ground as he struggled to brandish it.

"She was my friend! You killed her!" He waved the blade, and the god's nostrils flared. Young meat. Tender. He liked the young ones the best. He had told the woman that, and she had provided. So many young ones, over the years . . .

Finn! Oh shit, Finn, he's going to kill Rhodan, and I can't stop him!

The Deity took a step closer. Rhodan held his ground, face flushed with the effort, swearing. The sword caught the very tip of the god's claw and rebounded, and Rhodan staggered at the shock that must have numbed his arms. Still he hung on, grim and determined, stubborn as his blood.

Finn!

Asta was screaming, fighting. Fighting the hunger, the rage. There was better food, she pleaded. More meat, down in the city. The woman, the woman who had locked him up. She would have meat. She had kept him in that cell for so long.

Yes, the woman . . .

The god glanced back down to the city, distracted for an instant, and Rhodan darted in to hack clumsily at the wound Som had already made. The Deity snatched his hand back, wary of a second sting, and it was as if a hole opened, his distraction a gap that Asta used to dive deeper into the recesses of his mind and seize the reins. He *wanted* to go to the city, he *needed* meat from the woman. This stinging scrap on the rooftop, it was nothing. Beneath his contempt. There were better meats, meats that didn't sting and bite. Behind him, in the city . . .

Asta wrenched the god's attention away from the rooftop, from Rhodan who she dared not think about now. She could set the Deity on a new trail. Below them lay the heart of the city, the docks, the ships, the slave market on Winding Street with the roof half caved in and people fleeing in all directions, like termites from a cracked mound. Looming above the chaos she could see the stout red stone walls of the Temple, and above them, delicate as lace, fragile and sharp as a bone needle, she could see the tower of the High Priestess. The morning sun shone red through the glass bauble where her body lay, turning it to a bead of blood on the very tip of the needle.

Blood. She thought it hard, trying to send the image deep into the hungry god's psyche. She felt his interest spark. There was no edge to that hunger, only an insatiable gnawing desire, to feed and sleep and feed again. The god took a long stride towards the temple, then another, gaining speed.

In the darkness, Asta could hear Chesserai, kicking and screaming. Through the god's eyes, through the glass, she could see her body writhing on the floor of the bubble, the physical manifestation of her mental battle with Finn. She could see her own form, lying in the shade of the window ledge, twitching as if she was having a fit.

The Deity hesitated. Asta felt his confusion as his hand brushed over the glass of the dome, leaving a bloody smear. He had never seen glass before. She felt his frustration grow and she pushed it, as hard as she dared. The woman who had hurt him was behind that barrier, and if he smashed it, he could reach her.

Careful, Asta . . .

She heard her brother's warning, but there was nothing she could do as she pushed deeper into the god's mind, feeling the pain and rage of years, dammed up. The dam was cracking, and she thought hard about Chesserai, about all the things she'd done, about how she was lying only a few feet away from those red-stained claws, if only he could smash the glass.

The dam burst. The glass shattered. Asta felt a tide sweep over her, a wave of wild red fury like nothing she had ever felt before. She reeled before it, losing her grip on the fractured mind of Chesserai's god. She watched the glass splinter under the crushing blow of those claws, shards spinning away in the multiple planes of his vision. They crashed to the floor around the two women, and in that glittering instant, Asta felt Finn drag his protection from Chesserai and throw it over her, a stifling blanket that left the High Priestess alone and exposed under a lethal rain of glass.

She only screamed once, and the sound had an edge of joy to it, as she looked up into the whirling eyes of her master, and embraced her death.

Asta looked down through the god's eyes. Everything was red, but those two other insect bites were gone from her mind, and she was alone. She was free.

She stretched up towards the sun, feeling the warmth, the deepening hunger in her gut, the anger at her imprisonment. If she could, she would have snatched the sun from the sky and flung it down burning on the ruins of the city. She wanted to tear the stone, rend the city apart, rip the world along its fault lines and burrow back into the warm rock where she had been birthed. She . . .

She had been human, once. She had had a name . . .

There had been the sea once, the salt brine taste on her lips. There had been horses, and a tower, and a little boy who clung to her and called her . . . something.

It was fading, slipping through her hands to shatter like glass around her clawed feet.

Once she had been less than she was now. Now she was a god.

Now there was only the rage, the fierce hunger, the pain in limbs cramped too long and eyes burning from unaccustomed sunlight. The human part of her was a fading spark, rapidly diminishing, twirling down into gathering darkness.

Asta! Asta, come back!

Asta . . . The word was familiar. It echoed down to the tiny spark that was all that was left of her awareness. It carried memories, of riding and shouting and quarrelling and laughing, with someone who had always been there, for as long as she could remember.

Asta, it's me, Finn. Don't lose yourself in there. I can't follow where you're going.

Finn . . . She had someone once. A brother . . .

She looked down. Behind the whirling eyes of the Deity, she could see her own slender arm. There was a band of white at her wrist, making her skin look a shade darker than usual, and as she stared at it the band tightened and her arm was lifted like a marionette.

Asta, you have to want to come with me. You have to let go.
I don't think I can.

It was hot. Too hot, the sun was scalding skin that had been long in the darkness. Every inch of her body ached and she longed to lie down in cool darkness, to ease her hunger and raging thirst, to find a place of safety.

We all want that. The god was broken. It had killed hundreds, maybe thousands, but no more that the thousands Chesserai had sacrificed to keep its many mouths fed. It was exhausted, confused, wracked with pain, terrified by the city and everything in it. Its mouth was dry, its tongue lolled, its skin burned.

Let me take you. Asta didn't know if the god could understand her words, or even the meaning. She tried to project calm, security, and she was rewarded. She felt him retreat into his own head, leaving her in charge of the great, lumbering body. She swung around, her feet crunching glass to powder. She wanted to eat, to feel the crunch of blood and bone in her mouth, and she had to stop herself from reaching out and snatching a fleeing woman from the street. The dry ground cracked under her feet as she cajoled and pushed the Deity in the direction of the harbour.

The stout pontoon was no match for the weight of a god, and it gave way beneath her, plunging her knee-deep into cool water. Strands of fibrous seaweed embraced her legs, trying to hold her up, and her passage through the water sent up a crashing wave that swamped the smaller boats around her.

Something struck her shoulder and bounced off, like a pebble, falling back into the water with a soft splash. Asta swung her head round to see what had hit her, feeling the god's fury flare once more. There were men on the shore, tiny and insignificant in her eyes. They had horses, and weapons, and they wore bright livery and carried themselves proudly despite their thin coating of dust from the road. She could smell the fear on them, and it only angered her more.

Arrows and rocks rattled off her hardened skin, pattering into the water around her like raindrops. One struck her in the left eye, and one of the facets of her vision winked out, leaving her with three swirling panes on her left hand side. She swung her head, dizzy and disorientated for a moment while her vision adjusted. She lashed out, a clawed hand raking across the troops, tearing open those too slow to scatter and flinging their gushing corpses high into the air. The god raged, and Asta raged within him, trying to quench the heat, to bring him under her control, tightening the reins around him until he was calm, and moving to her will once more.

This has to end, Asta.

I know, she thought back. She took a long stride, deeper into the water that swirled around her hips, then her waist. She was free of the shore-hugging seaweed now, out of range of the arrows that the survivors still fired fitfully from the shore. The water quenched the fires that burned across her skin, and her huge feet sank into the soft sea bed, throwing up plumes of mud.

It would be easy, she thought, to lay back and let the water soothe her aches, massage her twisted limbs, fill her lungs. Peace, of a sort. Mercy . . .

Another step. Up to her chest now, her neck, and she could feel the power of the current dragging at her, enticing her onward. The sunlight gleamed off the shifting surface of the sea, dazzling her. She forced the god one step deeper, two, and as the waves closed oven her head she opened her mouth, letting the salt water rush in.

Her lungs were aflame. She could feel the god kicking against her, but feebly, as if he was too exhausted to fight, opening his arms to the sea as he sank down into the depths, carrying her with him, holding her tight to his mind. She was tired, too tired to struggle. She felt a tug at her wrist, but it was slight, too slight, and the force of the sea, the despair of the god, was too overwhelming. Asta let go, drifting into the darkness, letting the pull of the water overwhelm her.

TWENTY ~ NINE

THERE WAS LIGHT, sharp and piercing. It hurt her eyes, and she squinted away from it. Someone had a cool hand on the back of her neck, and she could smell the faint sweetness of breath. She was lying in a pool of cold water, and when she twitched, she felt sharpness under her arms and legs.

"You're awake. Don't try to get up yet." The chilly hand moved down to her stomach. "Your babies are safe. That was a dangerous thing you did, *sumri gudienne*."

"Erikah?" Asta croaked. Her throat was scraped raw; it felt like she had swallowed a blade. "What happened? How did you know—?"

"Your brother told me. At least," her brow furrowed. "I think he did. I had this urge to come up here, as fast as I could. The High Priestess was dead, and you were lying on the floor with water pouring out of your nose. I felt I had to rip the bottom from my dress and tie it round your wrist. All I did was hold it, and then, I don't know what happened, but you weren't in your own head, and then all at once you were."

Asta struggled to sit up. It felt like a horse was sitting on her chest. "And the Deity? What happened to him?"

"He walked out into the ocean, *gudienne*. He's gone." Erikah's eyes were wide, her voice wondering. "Truly you are a Goddess."

"No, he was a god, gods don't die . . ." Even as she said it, Asta realised she was mistaken. The creature whose mind she had ridden in had been mortal flesh, sharp intelligence twisted and broken, compressed into madness by years of abuse. Not a god, no more than she was, and he could die, had welcomed death. *Mercy* . . .

She gasped, and straightened. "Rhodan! Is he safe? Ilu, Red—?"

"I'm sure the kid's fine." Ilu's feet should have crunched over the broken glass as she approached, but they made no sound. "I lost Red in the chaos, but she strikes me as a survivor. As you are!" Her voice held a grudging note of admiration. "Can you walk?"

Asta looked up into Ilu's golden eyes, and thought of Som, crumpling on the rooftop. She didn't know, her sister didn't know, and she would find her as Asta had found Finn, that day in the cove. "We should—" she choked. "We should get back to the house. Som . . ."

Ilu crouched beside her. Her eyes were as hard and cold as metal. "I know," she said. "I felt it. It's always a risk, in our business. My mourning," her hand tightened on Asta's wrist, "is private. I'll mourn when we're all safe, not before. Say no more about it. I can't carry out my duty if I'm stricken with a mourning heart, and we still have work to do."

Asta nodded solemnly. She got to her feet, unsteady, gripping Erikah's arm for support. The Scattering woman had draped her shadow-cloak over Chesserai's body, but she couldn't hide all the blood that pooled around her. Asta stepped around it gingerly, trying not to shudder. "In that case," she said, "let's get out of here."

The Temple was quiet as they descended the spiral stair and crossed the charnel house of the hall towards the welcome daylight of the courtyard. Out of the shadows by the door, a fluffy black cat emerged and bounced ahead of them down the steps, his gait made lopsided by a pronounced limp. Asta hoped that meant Ranmiro was back in town. If he wasn't, at least he was keeping an eye on them.

There was more activity in the courtyard, a squad of worried looking young soldiers in uniform who seemed to have been given no orders beyond "keep an eye on the Temple." Their captain must have been five years younger than Asta, not much more than a boy, and from the way he flourished the rings that bedecked his hands she guessed he, or his father, had bought his position and he wasn't certain about hanging on to it. He bustled up to them, a conflict of self-importance and anxiety in his stance.

"Are you priests? We were told to detain any priests trying to leave."

"Do we look like priests?" Ilu snapped. She had her hood up, her face masked, but that didn't seem to be quelling the boy.

"You could be a priest in disguise." He glared at Erikah. "*She* looks like a priest. I can't let you pass."

"Are you in charge here?" Erikah asked. "Who's your commanding officer?"

"I think you should come with me." He reached out and put a hand on her arm, and squeaked as Ilu's dagger swept down to shear the thinnest slice of skin off the tips of his fingers.

"Do you have any idea," her voice was sweet, her eyes were granite, "who you're talking to?"

"What's going on?" The older voice came from the far end of the courtyard, and Asta looked around to see the man with thinning grey hair, his helmet under his arm, chest heaving as if he had been running. His eyes met hers and slid past, dismissing her as a foreigner, and coming to rest on Ilu. He sank at once to one knee. "Lady, forgive my junior. We had no idea any of you were here."

Ilu sheathed her dagger with a contemptuous snort. "Get up," she said. "It's not for you to know where I am or what I do. Nor to dictate my movements. Is the Emperor with the army?"

"No, lady." He seemed to have some trouble getting back to his feet, with a great popping of joints. "He remains in Kishtawar."

"Has he sent any word?"

"Not for you, lady. I'm sorry."

Ilu sighed. "Your pet idiot here is trying to detain us from carrying out our imperial duty. I don't want to end up obliged to kill him. We're leaving now."

"Certainly, lady." He scanned the three women again. "I need to just make a note of who you are . . ."

"You don't need to make a note of who I am. I was never here."

"Of course not." The old soldier scratched his head, looking flustered. "But the copperhead . . ."

"The *ambassador* from the Scattering is under my protection," Ilu said firmly.

He brightened at this. It was as if Ilu had lifted all responsibility from him. He nodded at his junior, who was still sucking the tips of his fingers. "Make a note," he said. "The Scattering ambassador and her slave were here, and *no one* else." He fell back to let them pass, with a low bow for Ilu and a nod to Erikah. "Better get your slave home quick, lady," he said. "His Imperial Majesty wants to free the bloody lot of them. Don't know how we'll manage . . ."

"I expect you'll survive," Erikah said sweetly, dodging Asta's eye. "Come on, slave. We should do as the man bids."

She managed to hold in her laughter until they were outside the front of the Red Temple, before she let it go with a spluttering and infectious giggle. Asta couldn't help but join in, and even Ilu's eyes creased with strained amusement above her mask.

"Oh, my *gudienne,* I'm so sorry!"

Asta clapped her on the shoulder. "Don't worry about it! I've gone from goddess to slave and back again so many times it's making my head spin!"

"So what will you be next, *gudienne?* Now you've done what you were destined to do."

"What I was destined to do? What do you mean?" Asta asked.

"There will be no more slaves. The Emperor has said so. That means no more tribute from my people, no more decimation. You drove their god into the sea; you broke the power of the Inyestan church. You *are* our Summer Goddess." She pointed at the sky. "It's the last day of summer, Asta. You died and came back. I'm sorry I ever doubted you."

Asta shook out her shoulders. "I'm no goddess, Erikah. I've had enough of this game of gods. I just want to get Rhodan back where he belongs, find as many of my tribe as I can, and pick up my life. Can you help me?"

"Whatever you want. But you should know you'll always be a goddess in Mikligard."

"Well, maybe that will come in handy. Let me have a think about it."

The streets were beginning to come back to life as they walked slowly up the Hill, nursing bruises and cuts, each woman busy with her own thoughts and reluctant to talk. Ilu's step slowed and she fell behind them, and Asta sensed she was putting off the moment she would be forced to face her sister's death. As they made their way through the darkness of the carriage house Asta heard running feet, and she was almost knocked over by the force of Rhodan's embrace.

"Tante Asta! Did you see the monster? It was huge!"

She hugged him back tightly. "I saw it. It's gone now. How would you like a ride on a boat?"

"Where to?"

"Back to where Erikah lives, and then home."

His gaze dropped to his feet, and he frowned. "Da won't be there. Nor mamma."

"No, they won't." She dropped to one knee and lifted his chin so she could look into his dark eyes. "But I will be. You can stay with me. And I'll take you to see your grandmother. I think she'd like to see you."

He fidgeted. "Da said she was dangerous . . ."

"Are you frightened? I thought you were a warrior." Asta drew back. "I was going to let you grow your braids, but if you're not brave enough—"

"I *am* brave enough!" Rhodan insisted. "I fought the monster. And Tante Som," his face crumpled. "I tried to look after her, but I couldn't get her to wake up."

Asta held him close, feeling the warmth, breathing in the scent of him. "I'll take you home," she promised. "You won't have to see such things again."

He wriggled out of her embrace, and she saw his expression clouding, shutting down. "Can I go and play in the garden with Marcio now?"

"Just for a bit." She would have to address the deaths he had seen, the scars in his mind. But not today. It could wait, until they got home, for both of them. Until she had the support of the survivors of her tribe. It was something they would both have to learn to live with. For now the cat would keep an eye on him while she packed and said goodbye. If they were lucky, they could leave on the morning tide.

In the event, it was two days before the Scattering ship was cleared to leave by the Imperial Troops, and that was only because something more pressing than hunting for runaway priests had commanded their attention, as the slaves revolted and threw off their chains. When Asta and Rhodan arrived at the harbour at dawn, they found that although the wind was with them, the tide dictated that they wouldn't be able to leave until noon at the earliest, so at Rhodan's insistence they took a walk along the shore to look at Abonnae' latest sensation.

Asta could smell it before she saw it, and she pulled the top of her shift up to cover her nose. Rhodan stuck his tongue out, and made a gagging noise.

"Want to go back?" she asked him. He shook his head, but his feet dragged a little slower against the dust of the road.

"We can go back if you want. It's nothing I want to see . . ."

Rhodan tilted his chin. "We're warriors, Tante Asta. We cut the braids from our defeated enemies."

"That we do." She ruffled his hair. "Too short for braids yet!"

"Soon," he insisted, and pointed. "Is that him?"

The dead god sprawled face down on the wild shore, where beach gave way to salt marsh. He looked shrunken in death, but he was still huge, and his body had gathered a crowd of curious Inyestan onlookers. Some brave souls, and some children, had dared to climb up on the body and were walking up and down while their more cautious friends called warnings from the sand. It was not an abusive trample; in a way it was caring, almost gentle. Someone had taken the trouble to close the one eye that was visible, and a few men and women, refugee priests, maybe, gathered round the great head and stroked it wonderingly.

Rhodan tugged at Asta's hand. "Can I touch him?"

"You have to be respectful. He wasn't our enemy, not really."

Rhodan nodded, and scampered off down the beach, feet slipping and sliding as he scuffed over the low, grass-tufted dunes. Asta followed more slowly, wanting to keep an eye on him but reluctant to get too close. The memories of the darkness inside the god's head were still too raw.

Rhodan slowed to a walk, reaching out a tentative hand to brush one outstretched claw. He could have sat quite comfortably in the palm of that upturned hand, but he just stood, quietly, as if lost in thought.

"Hey! Asta!"

The voice was too loud, too close to her ear. Asta startled, felt her heart lift.

"Red! What are you doing here?"

Red draped a companionable arm around her shoulders. "Looking for you," she said, cheerfully. "I guessed you'd come down here. I wanted to let you know I wasn't lying in a gutter somewhere, before I left."

"Left?"

Red pointed seawards, to where a small, nondescript ship

bobbed at anchor. "Some of us slaves, we helped ourselves to a ship. Things are getting ugly in town. People don't want to lose their slaves, and some slaves want to make themselves remembered. You know what I mean?"

"I know." Asta hadn't seen any violence on the streets yet, but she had felt the undercurrent of tension building up over the last few days. Freedom was a complicated process. "Where will you go?"

Red chuckled. "No idea! But sure as seagulls shit I'm not staying here. There's a world out there. Maybe we'll set up our own colony of freed slaves. Maybe I'll go back south, though I don't belong there any more than I do here. But there'll be some place for an old deaf slave-woman, I'm sure. What about you?"

"Back to the Scattering, first, and then on to my tribe." Asta shook her head. "I don't know what I'll find there, but I promised I'd get Rhodan home."

For a moment they both watched Rhodan making his way back across the dunes, slower now, walking as if he was tired.

"That's a good kid you've got there, horse girl. You look after him."

"I have to. I'm all he's got."

Rhodan stopped to pour the sand from his shoe. "Tante Asta, can we *go* now?"

"Are you done looking at the god?"

Rhodan frowned. "Is he in the Spirit Realm now?"

Red nodded, and waved her hand in farewell. *Good luck,* she mouthed, as Asta took Rhodan by the shoulder and steered him back up the beach.

"He's gone wherever dead gods go, I suppose."

Rhodan stuck his fingers in his mouth. He was wobbling another loose tooth. His reply was indistinct. "Is that the same Spirit Realm we go to? Or do people go to different places after we die?"

"He wasn't people. He was . . . something else."

"A god?"

"Some people believe that, yes."

"But you don't."

Asta didn't know how to answer that question. She lengthened her stride, forcing Rhodan to trot to keep up, leaving him too breathless to do more than point and gasp out, "What's that?"

It was a small shrine, tucked between the rocks of the shore. A low candle burning, and a strand of seaweed wrapped around it. Someone had picked out a pattern of tiny shells at the base, and had written on the rocks above, in charcoal.

To our drowned god, may you rise again more powerful than before.

"It's nothing." She caught his hand and pulled him on. "Erikah will be waiting."

"What does the writing say?"

"I don't know," she lied. Religion was a pernicious weed, forcing its roots into every crack in Inyestan society. She would be glad to be free of it.

Later, staring over the rail of the Scattering ship, into the dusk that had turned the city into a darker mass against the shoreline, Asta saw the lights. Hundreds of them, tiny candles burning all along the Inyestan shore, an offering for a dead, insane god. She had no doubts he would rise again, if not in body, then in the mind of some deranged priest or political schemer. The Inyestans twisted their gods to their will, and she was glad to be free of them, glad to be returning to a land without gods. But first, she had to make a trip to another land, one that needed her hand to heal its wounds.

Mikligard was cold and windy, the autumn gales battering the rocks of the harbour, and it took three uncomfortable, nauseating days for them to be able to make port. The ship carried not only Asta and Rhodan, Erikah and the survivors from her crew, but an army of liberated Scattering slaves, as many as they could carry. On the last day before they came into port, Asta discovered to her delight that it also carried Cymion, exhausted and nursing a broken wrist, but free, and very much alive, and the two women embraced long on the deck, heedless of the stares of the people around them.

Erikah had promised to send ships back to Inyesta to pick up anyone else who wanted to come, regardless of how few resources the Scattering had. Asta didn't plan to be around to see how that policy panned out, but she feared the worst. Erikah may have been unable to prevent the deaths of Syven and Heylan, but Asta felt sure that in her heart she was a woman who meant well, however misguided her policies might turn out to be.

Still, her policies were none of Asta's affair. She waited until the tearful reunions on the shore were done with before she disembarked, under cover of darkness, to make her way to the manse where she had been imprisoned. Every lantern in the building was aflame, and the council had gathered in the hall, to stare, to touch her clothing and her skin in a way that made her flesh crawl. She recognised most of them from the day she and Finn had spied on their meeting, but a few old faces had gone, and a few new ones stood in their place.

They surrounded a small table with a meagre spread laid out on it, biscuit and fish paste and a few strands of edible seaweed, and no one was eating, though she caught hungry glances in that direction. Everyone seemed to be waiting for her to speak.

"Listen," she began, though every face was turned to her in silent, eager attentiveness. "I suppose you take me as your Summer Goddess. I don't know how much Erikah has told you, but I do want to help. I think you've had a shitty hand of cards dealt to you."

There was a hissing intake of breath as she cursed. Well, their goddess had a foul tongue. Let them reconcile that with their scripture.

"I come from a land full of wide empty spaces. There's game there, and good land for growing things. Atrath could swallow the Scattering a thousand times over and still have room. If you want to, you could live there, in peace with my people. On one condition."

There was a mutter of surprise at this. One of the younger councillors cleared his throat. "But we enslaved your people. Everyone hates us. Why would they welcome us?"

"There's room for everybody. There might be some resentment at first, but living is hard." She caught herself. "Easier than here, but still hard. Hard enough that it keeps people too busy to think of constantly fighting, anyway."

An older man spoke up. "*Gudienne*, you speak well, but this is my home. I don't want to leave it. And what is your condition?"

"That every slave on the Scattering goes free, as of tomorrow. Shut the slave markets down. Give me back my people, so I can take them home."

There was a rustle of consternation. Asta glanced at Erikah, willing her to back her up. The redhead would not meet her eye. "The merchants will have to be compensated," she said.

"They can be. With land. In Atrath." She injected new urgency into her voice, "My people can trade with your people; we can trade your corals, your skills with metal working, for horses, fresh soil, and seeds to plant new trees. We can grow new life on the Scattering, if we work together. Or," she hesitated, "I can go home, and you can carry on how you are. You might do better, without decimation. Or you might lose just as many of your people to starvation and sickness, now you've lost your trade with Inyesta. I'm suggesting a new trade. One that doesn't deal in human lives. And as many of you who like can join me. But I'm not waiting. I leave tomorrow, and I leave with any Atrathenes you have here who want to come with me. Have a think about it."

The talk continued long into the night, and when Asta slipped away to bed the moons were high over the manse. Whatever the people of the Scattering decided, at least she had put their destiny back in their own hands. She wasn't sure if that was what gods were meant to do, but if she was going to be their god, she was going to go about it in her own way.

It felt as if she had barely slept, but it was a few hours after dawn when Erikah herself came knocking on the door of the very apartments where Asta had spent so long imprisoned, where now she walked as a free woman, despite her clipped ear. She had brought breakfast; warm sweet rolls wrapped in a cloth, and she nibbled at one as Asta washed and dressed, watching her over the top of the pastry with eyes that glowed with suppressed excitement. As soon as Asta was ready, even before she had time to eat, Erikah had hold of her arm and was tugging her towards the door, child-like in her enthusiasm.

"Where are we going?" Asta protested. "I don't want to leave Rhodan; he's still asleep." He needed it, she knew. All her mental and physical exhaustion must be nothing compared to that of her six-year-old nephew, who had fought off a god.

Erikah locked the door to the suite behind them, and handed Asta the key. "He'll be safe in there," she said. "We won't be long."

She refused to be drawn on where they were going, but her eager footsteps led them towards the harbour, towards the slave market, and Asta recoiled before its walls. "I'm not going in there again," she said.

Erikah gestured to the guards who had discreetly accompanied them from the manse, and the small cohort fell back respectfully. "Please," she said. "It's not . . . what it once was. You'll see. Trust me?"

Swallowing her misgivings, Asta allowed Erika to lead her through the door, into the arena of the slave market. She was battered by memories; it was crowded again, with people of all nations, some squatting in the dirt, others milling about aimlessly. She felt their curious eyes on her, and she wondered if any of the people here knew what she had done, how she had changed life on the Scattering for everyone? And if they would care if they knew?

"We gathered them over here, as many of them as we could find," Erikah was saying. "This was really the only building big enough, one that everyone was familiar with. It might seem in poor taste . . ."

Asta lengthened her stride to keep up with her, their ever-present guards fanning out to either side. "Who? What's going on?" But her step faltered as Erikah swept aside the door that led to a back yard of the building, and revealed her secret at last.

Atrathenes. Dozens of them, standing or sitting around in bored poses that grew suddenly sharp as she was revealed to them. Her people, people of all the tribes, and all at once they surrounded her, wanting to touch her, asking why she was here, what was happening, would happen next, and then . . .

"Tante Asta! Asta! We knew you'd come!"

Her people. Her tribe. Diminished by time and distance, by the diaspora that had taken and scattered them, but still . . . Heedless of everyone else around her, of Erikah, of the guards, she pushed her way through the crowd to where the little knot was gathered. Six women and eight children, a meagre remnant of the dozens snatched from the beach, but they were her people, and she felt a hard knot of love for them dissolve in her chest as she fell at last into their eager embrace. They were free, and she could take them home now. She could take them all home at last.

Asta stood at the edge of the cliff, watching the white sails gleam as they caught the sun in their fabric. The sight of white sails didn't make her heart catch the way it used to, but it still gave her a moment to pause, and think. She may have passed on the leader's robes, too exhausted in her core to carry them any longer, but she still retained the instincts of a leader, and she kept a closer eye on the sea than she had done before. She had felt so secure in the future, once, but now it would always be uncertain. Perhaps they should move away from the coast, abandon her father's plan? But that was no longer for her to decide. She would do what was right, for her children first, and then for her tribe.

She was interrupted by the sound of trotting, thumping across the turf. Rhodan pulled up. His braids almost reached his shoulders now, and he had strung bells into them. They jingled pleasantly as he dismounted.

"You wanted to see me, Tante Asta?"

"Where are the twins?"

"In the tower. Vallira is looking after them."

"And how was your grandmother?"

He frowned. "She doesn't want us to do this."

"Did she cuff you?" Nasira could be too vigorous when she wasn't watched carefully.

"Not this time. Are you ready? Can we go?"

There was a hitching post near the cliff, and Asta led the way over to it. "Bring your rein," she instructed. "The Spirit Realm is a dangerous place, you know that."

She looped one end of the rein over the hitching post, and tied the other to her right wrist. Her left wrist she bound to Rhodan's. "Any trouble, and I pull you out. Don't fight me."

He fiddled with the strapping on his wrist. "Will he be there?"

"I don't know." She had to be honest with him. It was the only way. "My father would never take me into the Spirit Realm when I was your age. He said it was too dangerous. He had some bad times there. So just be careful. Now, lie back and think of your da. A happy memory, just like we practised."

She lay back on the springy turf and closed her own eyes, letting herself fall, through darkness and shadow, into the realm of the much-loved dead. Beside her, she heard Rhodan squeak in surprise, and when she looked they were on the beach. Her heart constricted. Last time she walked this flat land, she had seen her father, listened to his reassurance, taking comfort in his words. But she wasn't here for her father now. She was here for Rhodan. And for Finn.

She looked down the beach. A figure was there, walking slowly up the sand. His braids hung down to his elbows, and they were fair, fairer than anyone else in the tribe. He wasn't looking at them, but staring out to sea.

Rhodan gave a cry and lunged forward before she could grab him, and Finn looked around and saw his son in the same instant. He was running, feet making no sound on the sand. His mouth was open and she could see the tears streaming down his face as they collided, father and son becoming, for an instant, one spirit, one mind.

Asta took a step back. Her own face was wet, and she made no effort to wipe away the tears. Her hand fell on a flat stone, and without thinking she skimmed it, counting the one-two-three-four-five ripples, as she stared out over that flat sea where no ship would ever sail.

Acknowledgements

Well, that's another one done. I always wonder when I finish a book if I have it in me to write another one, but it seems the well hasn't run dry quite yet. As always, there are about a million people I need to thank for helping to steer *The Summer Goddess* from an idea in my head to the book you're holding in your hands right now.

Firstly thanks must go, as always, to my Grimbold Family, to Sammy and Zoë, all my fellow Grimbold / Kristell Ink authors, and especially to Roz, who is the best editor, co-editor and writing buddy a person could wish for. She sees things in my writing I would never think of, and she makes me a far better writer than I would be without her.

Thank you to Jason Deem for the beautiful cover art.

Thanks to Kate, and to Joshua, Jasmine and especially Aiden. A lot of Aiden crept into Rhodan while I was writing this book, and it's dedicated to him, even if he's not old enough to read it yet.

Thanks to all my Bristol friends, and all my online friends – too many to name individually but you know who you are and you know how profoundly grateful I am for every single one of you. Also thanks to everyone who has read, reviewed, visited *Making Things Up For A Living*, tweeted, or generally participated in this world I've created. This book would not exist without you.

All my books, always, are dedicated to the memory of Colin

Harvey and Nathalie Cassiers.

Thanks to my Mum, to Saira, Nicky and Mark and to Xander – the newest and smallest member of our Tribe. Also to Jack and Jenny, Molly, and Will and Jane.

And biggest thanks, as always, to Chris and Lyra, who have my heart.

About the Author

Joanne Hall lives in Bristol with her partner, and they are owned by the World's Laziest Dog ™ She is a full time writer, part time editor and occasional procrastinator and is happiest when she's making things up and writing them down. She enjoys movies and music, and owns too many books she hasn't got around to reading yet.

Her short stories have featured in a number of anthologies, and she is the co-editor (with Roz Clarke) of *Colinthology* and *Airship Shape and Bristol Fashion*. When she's not writing or editing, Joanne can be found chairing BristolCon, Bristol's annual SF and Fantasy convention, and hanging about on Twitter. Her blog can be found at www.hierath.co.uk and she always likes to hear from readers.

A Selection of Other Titles from Kristell Ink

The Heir to the North by Steven Poore

"Caenthell will stay buried, and the North will not rise again until I freely offer my sword to a true descendant of the High Kings—or until one takes it from my dying hands!"

With this curse, the Warlock Malessar destroyed Caenthell. The bloodline of the High Kings disappeared and the kingdom faded into dark legend until even stories of the deed lost their power. But now there is an Heir to the North.

Cassia hopes to make her reputation as a storyteller by witnessing a hardened soldier and a heroic princeling defeat Malessar and his foul curse. But neither of her companions are exactly as they appear, and the truth lies deep within stories that have been buried for centuries.

As Cassia learns secrets both soldier and warlock have kept hidden since the fall of Caenthell, she discovers she can no longer merely bear witness. Cassia must become part of the story; she must choose a side and join the battle.

The North will rise again.

In Search of Gods and Heroes by Sammy H.K Smith

Buried in the scriptures of Ibea lies a story of rivalry, betrayal, stolen love, and the bitter division of the gods into two factions. This rift forced the lesser deities to pledge their divine loyalty either to the shining Eternal Kingdom or the darkness of the Underworld.

When a demon sneaks into the mortal world and murders an innocent girl to get to her sister Chaeli, all pretence of peace between the gods is shattered. For Chaeli is no ordinary mortal, she is a demi-goddess, in hiding for centuries, even from herself. But there are two divine brothers who may have fathered her, and the fate of Ibea rests on the source of her blood.

Chaeli embarks on a journey that tests her heart, her courage, and her humanity. Her only guides are a man who died a thousand years ago in the Dragon Wars, a former assassin for the Underworld, and a changeling who prefers the form of a cat.

The lives of many others – the hideously scarred Anya and her gaoler; the enigmatic and cruel Captain Kerne; the dissolute Prince Dal; and gentle seer Hana – all become entwined. The gods will once more walk the mortal plane spreading love, luck, disease, and despair as they prepare for the final, inevitable battle.

In Search of Gods and Heroes, Book One of Children of Nalowyn, is a true epic of sweeping proportions which becomes progressively darker as the baser side of human nature is explored, the failings and ambitions of the gods is revealed, and lines between sensuality and sadism, love and lust are blurred.

Fear the Reaper by Tom Lloyd

All Shell has ever wanted was a home, a place to belong. But now an angel of the God has tracked her down, intent on using her to hunt the demon that once saved her. The journey will take her into the dead place beyond the borders of the world, there to face her past and witness the coming of a new age.

A stand-alone novella from the author of *The Twilight Reign* series and *Moon's Artifice*.

www.kristell-ink.com

9 781911 497011